Instinct

Book One of the Gallery Series

By Widdershins

EP

*To Virginia
Thanks & Enjoy
& for the loan
of the pen!
Widdershins*

Eternal Press
A division of Damnation Books, LLC.
P.O. Box 3931
Santa Rosa, CA 95402-9998
www.eternalpress.biz

Mortal Instinct
by Widdershins

Digital ISBN: 978-1-61572-457-4
Print ISBN: 978-1-61572-458-1

Cover art by: Dawné Dominique
Edited by: Ellen Tevault

Copyright 2011 Widdershins

Printed in the United States of America
Worldwide Electronic & Digital Rights
1st North American, Australian and UK Print Rights

All rights reserved. No part of this book may be reproduced, scanned or distributed in any form, including digital and electronic or mechanical, including photocopying, recording, or by any information storage and retrieval system, without the prior written consent of the Publisher, except for brief quotes for use in reviews.

This book is a work of fiction. Characters, names, places and incidents either are the product of the author's imagination or are used fictitiously, and any resemblance to any actual persons, living or dead, events, or locales is entirely coincidental.

*Dedicated to
My wife,
with whom, all things are possible.*

Prologue

Arahona depleted her life-force by spinning monstrous threads from the substance of her physical form. They hung limp and hollow from her midsection and stretched her beautiful silvery skin tight over what remained of her body. She, once plump and full of life, shriveled and shrank in on herself, preparing to expire.

She spoke into the primordial chaos of the Mortal Realm surrounding her, a word in her mother tongue, a Command.

"Gallery!" A single word to cause Time to lurch into its relentless forward march. A single word to begin the evolution of mortal worlds and give rise to mortal life. A single word to name her creation.

The strands of the Gallery writhed into life. They twisted, tore gaping wounds in her body and then fled her terrifying mortality. Her flesh split and her bones shattered. Physical agony pierced her for the very first time. Her scream ululated through the essence of the embryonic physical realm and created the first flaws in the potency of its virgin borders.

The strands flung themselves at the burgeoning worlds as though to suck the life from them. That was not their purpose for they were obligated to fulfill their destiny, to become the Gallery.

They wove between time, space, and the dimensions of the physical realm. Each strand a supple hollow corridor with one end anchored to a Portal on a newly born world and the other woven into the warp and weft of the Gallery.

Chapter One

Eons swept past Arahona and left her marooned in their turbulent wake. Her birth agonies eventually faded and she gathered the last shreds of her power to heal her hideous wounds. She failed. She was too weak to return to her former glory.

She thought she'd understood the risks but hadn't believed it deep down in her spirit. Not really. Not until this moment. Despair swept through her heart.

She lifted her head and sought solace in the countless galaxies flung throughout the Mortal Realm as though from a careless hand.

An unfamiliar welling of sorrow rose to her breast as their extravagant birthlight faded and only ordinary starlight remained. Here and there, stars already aged beyond recall winked out. As she watched, it occurred to her that the Gallery, too, was doomed to fade and eventually cease to exist.

The last remnants of her strength passed away and she hid her face among her many appendages. Tears welled from her enormous eyes, crystallized and fractured into millions of flecks of golden dust. They slipped between the fibers of the Gallery corridors and came to rest on the softly yielding floor.

Suddenly she felt too exposed, her emotions too raw to contain such inexorable misery. With a flex of her will, she relocated herself inside the Hub, the very center of the Gallery. It billowed around her like a giant balloon, fragile, yet strong enough to cocoon her aching spirit. She sank to the floor and contemplated her folly. Her limbs grew numb and her heart slowed. At the last she refused to willingly fail.

"I will not let this come to pass!" She reclaimed her breath one last time, but her words flowed no further than the hollow emptiness where her measureless authority once existed.

She paused, and then with barely a grumble at the irony summoned an old friend, occasional lover, and oft-times enemy, from beyond the frontier of mortal existence.

It was an affront to ask for help. This creature was her nemesis with an exceptionally irritating personality. However, only she possessed the skills to accomplish what Arahona couldn't.

Why hadn't she realized her mistake in the beginning? Had hubris so blinded her that she failed to see the consequences of mortality, even though those same consequences were now claiming her life? After a moment of self-indulgence, she dismissed such thoughts as a waste of her limited time and energy.

The summoning continued and she waited for an answer to her call.

* * * *

In the Shadowlands, a place somewhere between the Mortal and Immortal Realms, the familiar command screeched imperiously, like fingernails down a chalkboard.

Sebenesh grimaced. Only Arahona would make it so tempting to ignore her. The call persisted. Disregarding it would only make it worse. Sebenesh hissed in acquiescence. To make sure she wasn't about to be ambushed or tricked into embarrassing herself, she shifted between realms with a very circumspect flick of her tail.

Galaxies whirled around her. Comets dipped their tails to the gravitational pull of a thousand suns. The Gallery, an intricate web, whirled with the movement of the planets and their stars throughout the entire Mortal Realm.

Sebenesh's jaw dropped and she straightened out to her full length to gaze around her. Arahona's audacity humbled her. This final act of their eternal competition belonged to Arahona, not that she would let her know that.

Sebenesh pulled her attention back from the Gallery. "You didn't call me all this way just to show off. What do you want?" Even before she reached immortality she had a notoriously short temper. "Arahona?"

Her voice echoed through the surrounding chaotic stellar spaces.

She received no answer. That would've been too easy. Distaining to even twitch her tail this time, she shifted inside the Gallery, into the Hub.

"Arahona?"

Dwarfed by the enormous space, Arahona lay curled up in a tiny ball of awkward limbs and tightly shut eyes. Sebenesh saw the raw wounds and the ill-mended bones and felt an Immortal's worst fear knot in the pit of her stomach. No further words were able to struggle past the sudden lump in her throat.

At the sound of Sebenesh's voice, Arahona roused from her stupor, and shook her ungainly limbs as though to drag one last effort from them. She struggled to her feet by the sheer force of her will. Taking Sebenesh's hand, she kissed it gently in recognition of all the unspoken words between them, which they knew would never be said. Through jaws clenched in agony, she grated out another desire.

"My task was to spin this web, and I have succeeded! Look. Is it not beautiful? It weakened me beyond recovering, but I was content." She paused as the rhythm of her thoughts stumbled. "Then this hideous mortality, not content with my life will take the Gallery's as well." She struggled for breath and then rallied the last of her passion. "I refuse to let this come to pass! Use whatever is left of my body, my powers, to protect my child from harm and save it from destruction." Her voice rattled in her throat, as much from her dying as from the force of her words.

She forestalled any protest Sebenesh might make. "We've always had this choice about how and when we leave immortality. This is my choice." Her voice grew faint and she collapsed into Sebenesh's arms. "Promise me," she whispered urgently as her spirit separated from her mortal body. "Make sure my Gallery will continue to be."

Arahona turned in Sebenesh's arms and addressed the Gallery itself, or perhaps the even greater entity that required this mortal deed of her.

"It's the best I can do."

* * * *

Arahona's words whispered around Sebenesh, caressing her body in a last farewell. They drifted along the corridors of the Gallery and faded away like a sigh.

Sebenesh struggled to comprehend how it was possible for Arahona to have gone so swiftly. A golden dust slowly spilled from her hands and spread out across the Gallery floor. Her heart cried in agony. Even the vast power of immortality couldn't undo what the Mortal Realm imposed on all who dared to tread there.

She wrapped her arms around her stomach as though she feared her grief would detonate inside her and scatter her remains like golden dust as well. She stood that way, rigid in the center of Arahona's creation until her tears came.

Never again would Arahona barge in on her unannounced. Nor

would they fight over silly little things, and make love while the cosmos reeled around them. She would never feel another heart beating as hers did, to the eternal pulse that gave life to them.

She cried her tears dry and passed beyond grief to contemplate the task Arahona had set upon her unwilling shoulders. Her sinuous coils curved into a decorous helix on the Gallery floor.

The heroic structure rocked gently to and fro around her, perhaps dancing on some cosmic wind with all of creation as its partner.

Sebenesh swayed with the movement, sinking deep into her consciousness, while her plan unfurled around her like the filaments of a delicate measure of silk.

She eyed the harlequin patches of smoothly woven cloth where events flowed as they should and the tangle of slip-knots and loops where they didn't. She shook her head wryly. Arahona would not be amused.

She flexed her will and shifted outside the Gallery. With another flex she slashed a ragged tear between the surrounding Mortal Realm and her homeland.

The Shadowlands quivered indignantly as a faint whiff of decay flowed through the opening but succumbed to her command and moved the essence of her Lair close. She drew a stream of unformed energy from its matrix and held it in her hands for a moment. It pulsed as though eager to bend to her will.

She smiled coldly. If only she could do the whole thing herself, there would be no need for such imprecise tools as those she was about to create. Although lingering in the Mortal Realm was forbidden, the desire to meddle remained overwhelming. Those who'd been commanded to enter paid a horrible price, as Arahona had so graphically demonstrated. Sebenesh had no wish to end her life the same way. Ill-fitting tools would have to do. True to her temper there would be little consideration for failure.

* * * *

Mortal Time sped by as she mulled over her plan. Beings evolved on countless worlds and eventually discovered the Portals. With great trepidation and excitement they became the Gallery's first great explorers. They evolved theories to explain their mysterious encounters in strange lands.

Sebenesh wondered if Arahona's passing and her appearance had been witnessed somehow. It amused her to see her deification materialize in many cultures on many worlds. She admirably restrained herself from destroying their illusions. It did no real harm and gave them a solid foundation to build their civilizations upon.

She hoped they would eventually outgrow their need for Goddesses, not that she would hesitate to use those beliefs to get what she wanted. Such scruples were for the foolish and weak.

However those mortal creatures fascinated her, she had a job to do and reluctantly turned her attention to it.

To begin with, she needed to maintain the Gallery, while she worked her plan to its ultimate conclusion.

She divided the unformed energy in her hands into three strands. With a single breath, she wove one of the strands into a race of translucent beings who named themselves the Skane.

To Sebenesh's surprise, they chose one of the smallest of the blossoming worlds for their home rather than remain star-borne wanderers.

Apart from great forests that covered its continents, the tiny world had remained devoid of intelligent life-forms. Some centuries before the arrival of the Skane, a nomadic tribe poured forth from the largest of the Portals and established their civilization there.

Fortuitous? Sebenesh knew better than to pursue her suspicions on that front.

* * * *

The Skane descended on the planet of Argol, as it had been named, and settled on Valder, the larger of the two continents, Dorial being the other more populated one to the east.

They delved deep into the stone bones of the earth and with nowhere else to stockpile the dross from their excavation, they flung it high into the sky, forming the planet's only moon. Raggedly shaped, and with an eccentric orbit, it looked ready to fall out of the sky at any given moment.

The sudden unintended appearance of this celestial body had significant impact on the geology of the young world, which cascaded into a shift in culture among the newly established societies from disparate science and exploration colonies to a more centralized and permanent system of governance.

The intended result of the Skane's excavation, a gigantic crater, filled with water from nearby underground reservoirs and became a lake vast enough to be called a sea. The surrounding forest, deprived of water, slowly died, and metamorphosed into a barely habitable desert.

It didn't take many generations for the Drowned City beyond the Seas of Sand to become legend, a story to be told in villages and towns across Argol to children eager to hear of mysterious adventures in faraway places.

The Skane established themselves within the depths of the lake, then turned their attention back to the Gallery, and took custody of their ward. They spun threads from their bodies, much as Arahona had, to manufacture swathes of fabric to repair the corridors that countless travelers wore out.

Throughout the ensuing millennia Sebenesh occasionally wondered how events would have turned out had she kept a closer watch over the Skane. Even she, immortal that she was, couldn't be everywhere at once.

* * * *

Her immediate concerns taken care of, Sebenesh contemplated her options for the two remaining threads of energy.

If she lingered in this realm of decay, she would suffer beyond imagining, so she needed to rely on mortals, with all their faults and failings.

Unfortunately, mortals of any species became quite unreasonable when being manipulated, even for their greater good. If they guessed what was really going on, events would shift out of alignment and she would be forced to take greater and more obvious action, risk additional exposure, and deviate even further from her plan. Therefore she must be subtle. Not something she excelled at.

She chose the home world of the Skane, merely because it was familiar.

Floating among the stars surrounding the tiny world, she milked a single perfectly round droplet of venom from one of her fangs. She infused one of the threads of energy with a basic consciousness to insure the droplets survival and bound the last of the threads firmly around them both. She smoothed the surface until it shimmered and gleamed in the starlight.

The venom Sphere contained enough energy to blast suns out of their paths and redesign the shape of the universe. It throbbed with a primal passion that aroused her killer instincts. She held it to her breast and savored its potency, tempted even now to release it and wallow in the devastation it caused.

She reluctantly shook herself out of her reverie. The Sphere had to be securely contained until needed, and Sebenesh trusted only one woman on the world below to accomplish that mighty deed.

While the woman slept, Sebenesh called to her through her dreams. She glimpsed the latest liaison in the woman's life and a roguish glint twinkled in her eye. Being a deity had a variety of fringe benefits and occasionally gave her license to indulge her voyeuristic urges.

A strange blurring sensation drew her attention back to the Sphere and obscured her vision of its ultimate destiny. She sighed in agreement and the strangeness passed.

The Sphere floated away from her and descended to the world below.

* * * *

Her Lair provided its dark energy one last time. She molded this subtle matter into a womanly shape, gave her a voice and a conscious will. Because names carry great responsibility with them, Sebenesh called her Truth Seeker.

Sebenesh paused before she sent Truth Seeker on her way. If the fate of the Sphere had been intentionally hidden from her, then perhaps she shouldn't tie Truth Seeker too closely to the fate of the Sphere.

With a casual wave of her hand that belied the tension she felt, she sent Truth Seeker on her way as well.

From Sebenesh's unique perspective, she'd acted almost instantaneously, but the relentless passage of mortal time subtly altered the weaving of her original design. If she lingered here with the enchantment of her immortal home wrapped around her, her plan would distort beyond redemption.

She passed back through the gap she'd ripped in mortality until only her head remained. If even one stray thread of energy from her manipulations escaped anything could happen. It wouldn't do to leave such powerful motes behind.

She looked around one last time and breathed softly to her lover's ghost.

"It's the best I can do."

Chapter Two

Vian walked up the side of the labrynthian knoll and unceremoniously dumped a bucket of dirt onto the heap already at the summit. Breathing deeply, she leaned over and rested her hands on her knees.

Many generations ago, the Gift of Earth had begun as a tradition to symbolize the intent to do sacred work. The symbol had grown into the very large, densely foliated hill whose crest Vian now stood on. Her heart took longer to settle each time she walked the ancient pathway. Thankfully she only had to do it at the solstices these days.

Twice a year was quite enough, she nodded emphatically. Except for times like tonight when she felt driven to do it. She hesitated to use such an emotionally charged word, but that was exactly what she felt, driven.

"Take that, you old Bitch," she said fondly and threw the empty bucket next to others lying limply on the ground.

"Do you know?" she inquired of no one in particular. "That over the years, I have personally raised you up by at least a meter." She was ignored, as usual, but with an acceptance born of a long and intimate relationship.

The near-full moon bathed the small plateau in its rose-amber glimmer. Vian tilted her head back and let its light wash away all the deep lines on her face. Her tall lush body looked as attractive now as it had when she ran up this same path as a young girl carrying a bucket overflowing with earth and tiny seedlings in each hand. Perhaps just a little bit different, honesty compelled her to acknowledge.

Vian's coloring was a variation of the golden translucency that came from the effects of traveling within the Gallery. Fourth or fifth generation ECHOs, called 'solid skins' by the disaffected, were unable to travel through the Gallery safely and reverted to the original genetic variety of the earliest colonists.

She looked toward the northern horizon where she clearly saw the brightly lit towers of Esparber, of which her village had valiantly resisted becoming a satellite. The darker shadows of tame woodlands surrounded both of the urban areas. Beyond the city and village, the brooding wildness of the forest shrouded its mysteries and allowed no light to be reflected.

Her village, Espinsal, spread out directly below her in a loose pattern of winding roads and pathways. The glow of lighted windows scattered softer yellow hues across the moonlit landscape. Summer smells of cooking and cut grass wafted up to her on a gentle breeze.

If she squinted hard enough, she could make out her little contribution to the lights off to one side of the village. Even though she had sophisticated power sources available, she clung to her eccentricities, of which her collection of antique oil lanterns was only one. These little quirks of hers sometimes had the effect of throwing an adversary off balance, which was the whole idea. She smiled wickedly.

The remainder of this night would pass before she could walk in her front door again. She hoped that a certain someone would think to extinguish the lights before she left in the morning.

Vian still felt piqued at having to leave her warm bed and Chalone's warmer body. However, only a fool would ignore such a strident summons as the one that had woken her out of a sound sleep. At least her summoner had the sensitivity to wait until she and Chalone fell asleep. It wasn't every day she felt the urge to make love until the younger woman fell into a deep blissful sleep.

Apart from feeling slightly put out, Vian enjoyed the walk up the 'Hill' to meditate. She liked the name. It had a healthy disregard for the pomposity usually attached to such sites of spiritual significance.

Her thoughts wandered back to Chalone. Their quite delightful and intensely physical interlude wouldn't last much longer. Chalone's heart had room for one great love, and Vian was wise enough to know it wasn't her. She shook her head to clear it of distracting thoughts that seduced her body into warm reminiscences and began her preparations.

She spread a gaily woven blanket over an old stump that had been lovingly cut and shaped into an armchair. Its ancient wood gleamed like rich dark toffee, and all who sat within its security reverently touched the long dead craftsperson's name carved into the wood as a gesture of thanks.

Vian sat down, arranged her skirts until she felt comfortable, and closed her eyes. Her thoughts flowed into the rhythm of her breathing and she relaxed completely.

She reached out with her senses into the rock beneath her feet and drew on its ancient solidity. The star-lit sky cleared away her mundane thoughts, and she focused her attention on the energies of water and air, fire and earth. The four elements thus called, created her sacred circle. From within its safety, she let loose the last remaining hold she had on her physical body and journeyed between the worlds.

Stars flared by her spirit vision as she surpassed the dreamscapes of the slumbering village. A single grain of sand on an alien world spoke to her in an ancient tongue taught to it when the universe was an infant. She passed unharmed through the heart of a dying sun and beyond the edge of all things to her sacred place of knowing.

The image of a lake high up in the mountains near where she'd grown up shimmered into being around her. Bulrushes and primitive ferns circled the lake as though to hide its secrets. Vian breathed deeply of the crisp clean alpine air.

An outgrowth of giant clear quartz crystals thrust into the air to one side of the lake. Their elegant simplicity and quiet strength drew Vian and she walked across the soft grass to admire them. One caught her attention, and as she reached out, a shard broke away and landed at her feet. She raised an eyebrow. That was a bit obvious. She sat on the grass by the lake's edge with the shard in her hand and waited.

Swifter than thought, the air around her wavered like a mirage and the crystal quickened, enclosing her inside its multi-faceted shape.

The ambient light within the crystal slowly faded until utter darkness surrounded her. A sound so pure it hurt her teeth vibrated into being, and the crystal resonated with the touch of an immortal mind.

Vian had experienced many strange and wonderful things when she journeyed but she felt so familiar with the landscape that she only had to reach out with her senses and receive the message, or better yet the messenger. This time her will was balked.

The darkness within the crystal grew thicker and heavier, slowing her thoughts. The crystal resonance turned to an ominous groan that creaked in sympathy with her bones. The dark weight pressed in on her limbs, crowding them against her body. She flexed her will to shift out of the crystal and back to the lake's edge, but the darkness surged closer. She exhaled and the dark solidness closed in until she had no room for her lungs to expand.

She struggled futilely until she remembered how to accept the darkness. She relaxed and it entered her as it had been earnestly attempting to do from the beginning. She rolled her eyes at her obtuseness and released control of her conscious mind.

The darkness crept in through her pores, along her veins, and into her muscles. Her bones and flesh dissolved and her skin had no purpose. Her mind crawled to a halt and her emotions became meaningless, her breathing stopped, and her heart ceased to beat.

A flash of insight impaled her spirit. The knowledge of what she must do, and why, suddenly and completely revealed itself. It was too much, too complex for a mortal body to contain. As her life-force began to unravel, she felt as though she was being torn in a thousand different directions without moving a muscle.

Her mind burst open and her survival instinct awoke. A tidal wave of primal fear, blood, and adrenaline, surged through her body. The surrounding darkness ignored her futile struggles and held her rigid. She couldn't twitch an eyelid. Her terror driven instincts overwhelmed her rational self and she thought only of shattering her prison.

She focused on her psychic strength, centered it all in the core of her being, and prepared to detonate it. The darkness flexed one last time and crushed her into unconsciousness before she managed to kill herself. In a gesture of compassion, aspects of the knowledge she had been force-fed were removed from her memory, to return only when she needed them.

Misunderstanding the strengths and weaknesses of mortals wasn't the first mistake Sebenesh ever made, but would be one that she regretted the most.

* * * *

The solid darkness surrounding Vian vanished as though it had never been. She opened her eyes and saw a pair of ducks and their convoy of babies chugging across the lake. They left a v-shaped wavelet in their wake that disappeared into the edges of the reed beds. The ordinariness of the image shuddered through her like an ice-cold shower. Something tickled her top lip and she absently brushed it away. A smear of blood stained her fingers like tangible proof of her battle for survival.

A familiar voice echoed across the lake, gently calling her home. It scratched against her confusion and dragged her lambent will and bewildered spirit back into the physical world.

The solid old wooden stump held her steady and gratitude

rushed through her body as she realized she was safe. She drew her legs up under her and laid her face in her hands.

The marrow of her bones chilled as her mortal senses inexorably awoke. Her lungs felt coated in razor-sharp icicles and icy tears flowed down her cheeks unheeded.

She stared at her fingers, still covered in dried and flaking blood. Something had gone very wrong, something she couldn't quite grasp. She shook her long silver hair out and hid the world from view while she sorted through the confusion of her vision.

Dawn flickered on her eyelids and recalled her to the present place and time. She reluctantly opened her eyes and shuddered in the chill air. The comforting warmth of the blanket slipped through her ice-cold fingers and off her shoulders. She cursed her frailties and bent to pick it up. Other hands, warm and strong, stilled her futile efforts. Someone straddled the stump behind her, pulled another thick warm blanket around them and wrapped loving arms around her waist.

"How long have you been watching over me?" Vian asked through chattering teeth and snuggled back into Chalone's warmth.

"I was watching from over there." Chalone nodded to where a copse of hardy shrubs provided a welcome windbreak from the morning's sharp breezes. "Only for a little while." Her hands, square and usually efficient, shook as if to belie her words. She'd followed Vian and watched over her trance body. It was her call that Vian heard and followed home. "Liar," Vian said.

"Thought you could sneak out of bed and get away with it?"

"It seems not." Vian answered, and reached back to pull Chalone closer. She let a hint of something more than her need for body warmth flow through her hands. Chalone willingly slid her hips in closer.

Chalone thought of herself as average looking, average height, and of average wit, her russet hair and green eyes her only outstanding features, therefore she sometimes wondered what Vian saw in her as a lover. That didn't stop her from thoroughly enjoying their union, but she wasn't about to be completely sidetracked by Vian's attempt at redirection.

"What happened to you?" she asked, with her mouth so close to Vian that her breath warmed her skin.

"Not yet," Vian answered quickly as a shudder of apprehension crashed against her consciousness and sent any romantic notions fleeing from her mind with their tails between their legs.

Vian abruptly sat upright. Of all the details she ought to remember from her journey, only one thought remained. To build a Circle of women and conduct a ritual, with no information on what for or why. She squeezed her eyes shut and tried to recall more but barriers of otherworldly energy blocked her at every turn. She shifted irritably in Chalone's arms, and then as Chalone kissed the nape of her neck, she pulled herself back from her fruitless conjectures.

"I'm just going to sit here for a while and watch the sun rise," Vian said, temporarily putting her disgruntlement aside.

"Then?" Chalone prompted.

"We'll see," Vian said.

After a quiet while the earth began to steam as the warmth of the new day burned away the nighttime dew. Vian stirred when Chalone suggested that perhaps it was time to leave.

The ritual was something Vian could focus on and then perhaps the next piece of information would be revealed. Her enthusiasm lasted until she stood up and flexed her legs. Her spine seemed frozen into the shape of a question mark and she felt numb everywhere else.

Although Chalone acted suitably sympathetic, Vian couldn't help feeling a little sorry for herself and groaned, loudly. Chalone encouraged her to move faster than she would have liked, but with several more heartfelt groans they soon walked arm-in-arm down the winding path.

At the foot of the hill, the path widened out to become the main street through the village. Shop fronts elbowed each other for space between the open grassed spaces and brightly colored flowerboxes. Mostly women who worked at the Hall of Lights or in some way connected to it lived in Espinsal and the surrounding hills. The village was a favorite gathering place when the shifts changed at sunrise and sunset, midday and midnight.

Chalone and Vian ambled along the wide thoroughfare, dodged the growing crowd and early morning delivery land-trucks, and took refuge in their favorite outdoor café.

Vian felt infinitely better with a full stomach and she watched Chalone chatting with the server, an old friend. She preened as Chalone blushed under her gaze. After breakfast she allowed Chalone to skillfully steer them out of the café and through the narrower cobbled backstreets and cottage gardens. Seduction worked both ways, and she knew when to take advantage of its siren call.

As Vian followed in Chalone's wake, she contemplated her world. The population of their planet, never large, remained scattered throughout the Gallery worlds. People owned very little in the way of material possessions. Although some craved other forms of power, the mostly transitory population, generally conservative in nature, was far more interested in exploring the infinite possibilities to be found within the worlds of the Gallery, indeed they considered it an unassailable right. Vian wondered how many more generations it might be before their world was abandoned completely. Abandoned that was, except for the ECHO's. She frowned. There wasn't a lot she could do about them any more. She'd surrendered her authority there a long, long time ago. The tidy village reflected this transient aspect of their society. Buildings were usually compact, efficient, one or two stories high, with surprising motes of individuality in color and design and had an air of impermanence surrounding them. There were a few exceptions. Chalone, Jalemi, and Pirelle's home was one. Vian's was in another category entirely.

Vian and Chalone continued their dance of heated looks and deliberate caresses undaunted by casual conversations with others until they arrived at Vian's front door. Once inside her bedroom and under the covers, more blatant explorations began.

Vian's skin still felt chilled as Chalone moved her hands slowly and sensuously, generating waves of heat for Vian to absorb. It didn't take long, and Vian expressed her gratitude for quite some time before Chalone, breathless, informed her that she had to go to work.

"Not true. Last night in a moment of unguarded passion you told me you have the afternoon shift," Vian corrected and crushed any further rebellion by pushing Chalone back on the bed.

Chapter Three

Chalone walked along the woodland path, and her feet barely touched the ground. Making love with Vian left her exhausted and energized at the same time, and she felt much too good to be bothered about being late for her shift at the Hall of Lights. She smiled and whistled jauntily as she approached the hedge surrounding the Hall.

As part of her work, she assisted travelers, those inexperienced and the most jaded of old-timers, in choosing the best Portal into the Gallery to satisfy their requirements. Some had firm destinations in mind, others wanted to meander along exploring whatever came their way, and still others desired something more exotic. She also advised those new to her world through the Gallery on how to make the most of their stay on Argol

She considered her guide duties a sideline to her more significant work, and wandered down distant branches of the Gallery corridors at every opportunity. In her time she had overthrown several theories about the Gallery and gained a certain notoriety doing so. It had been a trial for so private a person to endure the excesses of emotion directed her way as a result. She didn't really believe that she would quickly become old news and the gossips would find someone, or something else to fixate upon. With a few notable exceptions, it turned out to be true, but those early experiences left her with a visceral desire to bolt for the nearest exit whenever large groups of people focused their attention on her, which sometimes complicated her guide work more than she liked.

The path led her through one of the many openings in the hedge and she gazed up at the buttressed portico of the Hall entrance.

Rising three broad steps above a simple platform of white stone, the oval shaped Hall of Lights soared high in the air as though to reach beyond the edge of the sky. Thousands of sparkling crystal blocks made the walls, and sitting atop the walls, peaked like a forest of pyramids, a glazed roof gleamed in the sunlight.

Only the Gallery knew why all fifty Portals gathered in this one place radiating their unique patterns of light and color. Although they were anchored side by side in an oval-ish circle, they exited into the Gallery vast distances apart from each other.

Chalone greeted Pirelle, one of her home-mates in the staging area for travelers that officially marked the beginning of the Hall.

Pirelle stood tall with a shock of short dark blonde hair forever spiked by her habit of running her fingers through it. She had an air of innocence that occasionally bordered on the naïve, and preferred simple solutions to simple problems, which accounted for the state of her coif when she stumbled upon anything more complex. For all her height and bulk, none of which ran to fat, Pirelle carried herself with an unconscious grace that explained her many brief affairs. She wore a forest green tunic, bright crimson pants, and had tied her hair back with a blue and white bandana in a hopeless attempt to give it some sophistication.

"I'm sorry I'm late. Any problems I should know about?" Chalone asked.

"Not really," Pirelle answered in her deep husky voice and smiled down at Chalone with her deep gray eyes. She inclined her head toward parents and caregivers in the staging area dropping off a flock of youngsters. "One of Jalemi's groups is about to go through for the first time and you get to shepherd them with her." She looked meaningfully at Chalone. "I've covered for you and now you owe me a favor. As of this moment I'm off duty and," She paused theatrically. "I've got a date." Pirelle's avoidance of 'first timers', as she called those who had never before ventured through the Portals into the Gallery, no matter what their age, was as legendary as her lack of modesty about her social life.

"Don't wear yourself out then," Chalone said. "Because you'll need to get home in time to prepare dinner. Jalemi said she could use a good feed and she didn't mean it in a nice way."

"We all could," Pirelle countered. "You're useless in the kitchen."

"Am not! Make enough for Vian. She said she'd drop by."

"Are too! I shall outdo myself then," Pirelle said with a smile and a wave goodbye.

Chalone huffed indignantly at Pirelle's receding back. It wasn't that she couldn't cook. She had, in common with all those who had no interest in just exactly how a meal is put together, a complete disregard for the finer points of the culinary art. If it tasted good that was the end of her inquiries into the matter. Pirelle's opinion and expertise in the kitchen notwithstanding.

Jalemi finally gathered her flock together in a loose approximation of an orderly group, and Chalone judged it was time to join them. She walked over to her home-mate's group with a confident air. This was a big occasion for the children and seeing their shepherds at ease helped settle them. Somewhat.

Jalemi caught her eye and spoke loud enough to be heard over the noise of fifteen children looking for mischief. "I suppose Pirelle traded you dinner for shepherding, again."

"I got the best of the bargain, and so will your stomach." Chalone changed the subject. "I see that you're well prepared as usual. I only have to sit back and watch."

Jalemi's character wasn't compatible with the requirements of dealing with young children, which was why she perversely chose this aspect of her service to the Hall. It was a stubbornness that showed in every aspect of her compact body, long raven-black hair, saffron skin, and piercing gypsy eyes. She chose to wear tight fitting black leather or silk outfits that left no doubt that she had a classically shaped figure and knew how to flaunt it. "I always expect an appreciative audience," Jalemi said, nodding around her.

"I think you'll get it from the looks of this lot," Chalone said, deliberately ignoring Jalemi's double entendre and waited for the last of the children to precede her into the Hall.

"Any idea what my dear sister is going to feed us?"

"I didn't think to ask," Chalone admitted cheerfully.

"Why am I not surprised," Jalemi said, and picked up an unwieldy looking carrycase as she strode to the head of the line of children. Chalone stolidly refused to acknowledge the case and brought up the rear.

By the time they approached the first Portal, Jalemi drew her aside. "You have to stop doing that," she said.

"What?" Chalone said, then noticed that the air around her wavered like a carnelian mirage. "Oh." She gestured angrily to the metal case Jalemi carried. "It won't work. Their technology never works. As soon as we turn it on, the Gallery'll dissolve it, just like every other time!"

"I know," Jalemi said, waiting impatiently for Chalone to subdue her energy. "Right now you have to control yourself. It's not fair to them." She nodded toward the hovering children who'd become unusually silent.

Chalone turned away for a moment and willed her anger back inside her body. Jalemi was right, but when they returned, she'd have something to say to the ECHO representative who'd authorized yet another futile experiment.

The meal that evening turned out to be a hilarious affair with an abundant supply of delicious cuisine provided by Pirelle's gastronomic prowess, and wine from Vian's bottomless and most excellent cellar. Great chortling, impassioned storytelling, and gales of laughter rang throughout the house until dessert became a memory, and coffee and tea were in the offing.

The home Chalone, Pirelle, and Jalemi shared reflected their differing personalities. Total chaos followed Pirelle wherever she went; a room or two aesthetically arranged was obviously Jalemi's work; and the constant movement of certain furnishings pointed to Chalone's elusive pursuit of the marriage of comfort and functionality.

Oiled timber windows, rumored to have been installed by the same carpenter who created the chair recently graced by Vian's behind, frequently pierced the walls.

The house achieved a certain dignity for a few hours after the weekly chores had been completed. It was sufficient to satisfy any residual guilt the three women carried over from their childhood about a tidy household being evidence of good character.

The main culprits for the post-cleaning clutter were overflowing bookcases stashed in unlikely corners and nooks. All three women read avidly and preferred the tactile experience of paper and the smell of antiquity to the slightly plastic experience of electronic or visceral in-crystal media.

The women retired to the family room to relax and cast avaricious eyes at the box of chocolates Pirelle had brought home. Jalemi succumbed first, casually opening the box and saying that she had room for just one or perhaps two more.

Chalone caught Vian studying the three of them quite speculatively. She set her wineglass down and looked directly at Vian until her intensity silenced the three-way conversation going on around her.

"Out with it, Vian."

Jalemi and Pirelle turned and looked at her in surprise. She felt tempted to laugh as the very dissimilar looking sisters acted as the twins they surprisingly were. "Oh come on you two," she said. "I'll admit that the combined charms of Pirelle's cooking and my company could induce Vian to pay us a visit but it's highly unlikely." She looked back at Vian. "Don't you agree?"

Pirelle and Jalemi turned as one to look at Vian. Chalone smiled. The two of them could be so endearing, at times.

Vian swirled her wine around in her glass and gazed into its rosewood depths. It was one of the better pressings from the vines she'd planted long ago.

Her nonchalant silence generated a tension that stole the brightness from the room until she was the only source of light. "Of course you're right, Chalone," she said at last, and chuckled inwardly as she heard three explosively exhaled breaths. "Although the charms you mentioned are not without their merit." She smiled her special smile at the two women and the room brightened again. "I wanted to spend time here tonight because I need to make a decision about the three of you."

The gulf of silence that opened up compelled Pirelle to fill it before anyone fell in. "We'll need fortification then," she said and headed for the wine rack. Soon she'd refilled their glasses and with barely a sigh, sat back down and waited.

"Some women here have an idea of what I do," Vian said as though musing to herself, but really, she did nothing without due consideration. "A few have some well-founded suspicions, and fewer still that I trust with almost all I do." She paused and glanced at her glass again. "I digress. What I'm trying to say is that when I work, I select who I need, whenever I need, and use them as necessary, quite ruthlessly at times," she said, deliberately. "I'm telling you this now and I won't speak of it again. If you agree to what I am about to offer, it must be clearly understood that you'll do all that is required of you. To do otherwise may result in failure, and that I won't abide."

The distant night sounds of the village seeped into the silence Vian had again cast in front of them.

Finally Pirelle stirred and smiled at Vian. "Has anyone ever told you about this gift you have for completely killing the mood of a party?"

"Does that mean that you agree?" Vian asked, aware yet unmoved by Pirelle's attempt to diminish the impact of her words.

"Of course," Pirelle answered immediately and without much thought. "I've always trusted you. I don't see any need to alter that now."

Vian inwardly winced. Pirelle's absolute trust had set her on a pedestal that she tried in vain to escape. All the unknown factors surrounding the ritual, what the women might be asked to do, left her with an uneasy feeling that Pirelle's blindness might be too brittle to withstand the test. If so, it would be a hard lesson for her to learn. Vian needed Pirelle's strength as a Practitioner. She nodded and turned to the others.

Chalone avoided her eyes, so she looked to Jalemi.

"Yes!" Jalemi almost shouted, but before she could say anything else, Vian held up a quelling finger.

"That's all I need to know for now," she said warmly to take the sting out of her words.

Chalone rose from her armchair and walked across the room onto the balcony. The full-length memory-glass doors had been opened to the sultry summer night. She turned in the doorway to look back at her friends.

Jalemi started to speak, but again Vian gestured her to silence.

Chalone sighed deeply. "I know that this has something to do with your time on the Hill last night. I like the orderliness and simplicity of my life." She needlessly explained to them. Some wounds took a lifetime to heal and they all knew what Chalone's were.

"I like the energy we create when we do manifestation work in the Sacred Circles, or working in the Hall of Lights, or exploring the Gallery. All of these patterns are familiar to me and very precious."

She stepped further out onto the balcony and looked out into the night. Familiar landmarks, tangible proofs of the ordinariness of her life failed to soothe her spirit. Near and far, dwellings set into the hillsides glimmered under the waxing moon. The Hall of Lights shone like a beacon.

As she looked, that iridescent light dimmed for an instant and then returned to its usual radiance. She stared at it intently until she began to see spots before her eyes, but it looked as it always had. Dismissing it from her mind, she faced the welcoming light of her home.

Furniture creaked as Pirelle and Vian joined her in the night shadows. The three of them leaned back on the balcony railing.

"If I accept what you offer, Vian," Chalone said at last. "All these things will change. I don't know how, but they will." She understood that Vian wanted her sense of 'knowing'.

From the darkness at the other end of the balcony, Jalemi spoke in an impatient but kind voice. "Things are always changing, Chalone," she said. "You've been responsible for quite a few of those changes. We always have choices though. Ride the crest or get pulled along in the undertow. Speaking personally, I'm all for riding the crest." Vian wanted Jalemi exactly for this reason for the Ritual.

Chalone shivered slightly, and Pirelle hastily moved closer to her in an unconscious gesture of support and warmth. "Me too," she said.

The women waited and drank in the beauty of the night until Chalone was ready to speak.

"As much as I'm tempted to turn you down, you know I won't. Jalemi is right. Not that I'd tell her that."

"Yes!" Jalemi hissed in suppressed excitement and joined the others at the railing. "So tell us all about it, Vian. Why so secretive?"

"For now, I ask only that you prepare to join a Circle of mine tomorrow night," Vian said as she ushered them back inside.

"That's it?" Jalemi made a sound like a deflating balloon.

"No, that's not it," Vian said firmly. "That's all for now. I have to go. It's late and I have a great many things to take care of."

"Stay, for a while longer." Chalone said and laid her hand on Vian's arm.

Chapter Four

Vian dreamed she left the warmth of Chalone's bed and stood at the edge of the lake she'd visited in her trance journey. The shadows of eventide surrounded her and the family of ducks were snug in their nest concealed among the reeds on the far side of the lake. A faint silvery light threw the steep hillsides and valley depths into soft silhouettes.

Vian looked around and saw another aspect of herself standing nearby. Tears fell from the other self's eyes as she looked down at a shard of quartz crystal, cracked and flawed, in her hands. She grasped the shard so tightly that Vian felt her knuckles crack in sympathy. After staring at the shard for an eternity, the other self suddenly drew back her arm and cast the crystal far out into the water. The shard disappeared without a splash. The other self looked directly at Vian. "I hope you know what you are doing," she said, and disappeared into the mists at the edge of Vian's dreamscape.

"So do I," Vian whispered, as a great sadness welled up from deep within her spirit, strong enough to wake her with tears glistening through her eyelids. She brushed them aside, as if denying their cause. Chalone remained sound asleep and she lovingly touched her cheek. Her hand rested gently on Chalone's warm skin and this time she let her tears flow. "Well," she said after a while. "That answers that question."

Without disturbing Chalone, who could sleep through an earthquake, Vian rose from their bed and padded into the kitchen to make a pot of tea. While she waited for the kettle to boil, she reflected on how she found herself in this situation.

Unlike most of her decisions that wound a tortuous path through her personal and political motivations, it was rather straightforward. She wanted to be held in the arms of youth to celebrate her rite of passage through menopause. Or at least someone younger, she amended. Why she chose Chalone who she'd known all her life was still a mystery. Perhaps Chalone understood her reasons for wanting an affair at this time in her life and was happy to keep it, like Vian, simply an affair. Or perhaps it was something as primal as pheromones. She'd never asked Chalone and now the time for such questions had passed.

The soughing kettle drew her back from her thoughts. She busied her hands with the tea tray, carried it to the lounge room, and gratefully sank into her favorite armchair. She sat without focusing on anything in particular until the tea steeped and she poured herself a strong cup with a dash of milk. She contemplated it fondly. No matter what, there really was nothing like a good cup of tea.

Mulling over her dream, she half-heartedly tried to convince herself that it was the next piece of information she needed for the ritual. It didn't spring from the same place as the compulsion to call the Circle, and she knew it.

"Damn," she muttered into the bottom of her teacup and poured herself another. She alone made this decision.

Suddenly a gust of wind blew among the papers on the side bureau and rattled the portraits hung above the fireplace. It disappeared just as fast, leaving the rustling papers to shuffle down to the carpet and twitch like autumn leaves on a blustery afternoon.

A different realm of awareness exploded into being around Vian. As her consciousness leaped sideways to grasp it, a blistering globe of swirling colors enveloped her and took her breath away.

She gasped and fell back in her chair as though she'd been struck. Her tea spilled over the arm of her chair onto the floor. Flashes of possible consequences of the Circle reeled through her mind like images inside a kaleidoscope. She received nothing about the ritual itself, only a chilling understanding of the awesome power she would have to wield. Raging flames and shuddering earth teased the periphery of her vision.

The room twitched and returned to its usual staid self.

She thumped the arm of her chair in frustration, raising a little cloud of dust to stick to the wet patch. Now she understood why she had been compelled to say what she had earlier. She would use Chalone and the other women just as ruthlessly as she warned them she would.

Why couldn't she see the ritual itself? Why wasn't she allowed to know what was going on? Who was responsible for thwarting her ability to act with foreknowledge? How was she supposed to keep her women safe if she didn't know what was going to happen to them?

"This state of affairs is not acceptable," she said with quiet steel in her voice. The scattered papers angered her, but she neatly restacked them on the bureau anyway. Then she noticed the spill of tea and angrily cleaned it up too.

By the time she returned from the kitchen, she'd accepted that she wasn't supposed to keep anyone safe. The nature of any ritual required free will and the ability to make choices, safe or unsafe. That was fine and good, which really meant it wasn't, and she stalked over to the teapot. She disliked being used in this fashion, but as she ruefully reminded herself, she'd given her trust long ago and wasn't about to start second guessing the information she received on her trance journeys at this late date.

Only now, she'd involved Chalone.

As loving and engaging as Chalone was, Vian found herself missing intimate time with another woman who had seen as many sunsets and sunrises as she had, or as close to it as womanly possible.

She walked out onto the balcony with the final cup of tea from the bottom of the pot, and mourned into the quiet night.

Her tea cooled in her hands as she watched waves of mist billow through the vale below. A small nocturnal creature scurried out from the bushes and disappeared into the eerie moist shroud without a sound. Her thoughts flowed with these ordinary events of the night seeking a balm for her aching heart. Hours passed unnoticed and when the morning came her grieving was done, her resolve firm once more.

* * * *

When the summer sunlight surged through Chalone's open window early the next morning, awakening her with a start, she immediately wished she hadn't opened her eyes quite so wide. Hiding under the blankets, she groaned as the first stirrings of a hangover pounded at her temples, and resolved not to move any more than she absolutely had to. However, if she had to suffer this disgustingly bright light, then it was only fair that Vian did as well. She reached across the bed. Her fingers found only crumpled sheets and deserted pillows. She delicately raised her head and squinted around the room.

Across from her four-poster bed, a large dresser filled one wall and looked tidy enough, even though her clothes threatened to spill out onto the floor. Her writing desk held piles of books and a communication center, tidier still. Wide casement windows and bevel-edged glass doors that refracted the blistering sunlight throughout her room pierced another wall.

Nothing looked out of place so she supposed Vian had left early. She breathed in the skin-sweet scent of lovemaking. Her breath caught in her throat and her incipient hangover miraculously disappeared. She smiled and stretched sensuously.

Just out of reach on the pillow next to her lay a single perfect red rose. She stared at it for the longest time, one hand caught between the act of reaching for it and the whirl of her thoughts.

* * * *

Pirelle knocked on Chalone's door. "Hey, you two," she said loud enough to be heard throughout the house. "This wonderful day is passing and your favorite breakfast is melting!" After being unacceptably ignored, she opened the door half-expecting to interrupt something interesting.

Chalone leaned back against the headboard and gestured her in, signaling for her to close the drapes on the offending sunlight.

"What's wrong?" Pirelle asked as she complied and then sat on the edge of the bed. She studiously ignored the upper parts of Chalone's body revealed in all their naked glory. It wasn't as though she hadn't seen Chalone naked before, but this time it created an intimacy that she felt in the pit of her stomach. She finally noticed Chalone's chalky white expression. "You look like somebody died."

Chalone, unaware of Pirelle's initial reaction, leaned across the bed and picked up the rose as though it was so fragile it might break. She tilted it toward Pirelle.

"I think this means goodbye," she said with a catch in her voice.

"What is it?" Pirelle asked, confused.

"A rose," Chalone said. "Vian left it. Who else would think to use such a dramatic gesture to end this?"

Pirelle frowned. "Which 'this' are we talking about?"

"I always knew things would change between us someday. That it was destined to be nothing more than an affair, but I didn't expect it to change quite this fast." Chalone swallowed to keep her tears at bay.

"Oh," Pirelle said. "Why now? Why like this? I thought everything was fine. Did something happen between the two of you last night?"

"I don't know. It was. I didn't think so," Chalone said, baffling Pirelle further. She shrugged as she looked down at the rose.

"Perhaps I'll find out one day, but Vian's not big on revealing anything more than she has to."

Suddenly she grasped the rose and crushed it inside her fist. Thorns pierced her skin and a few drops of blood fell to the bed covers. She stared at them. A scream rose in her throat, but she couldn't find enough air to breathe it into life.

Pirelle quickly forced her fingers open. She took the rose and laid it on the bedside table, sensing it might be wanted later. She wrapped Chalone in her strong arms and held her firmly.

"I'm alright," Chalone said distantly and held onto Pirelle as though she was drowning. "Don't fuss."

"I'm not fussing. Of course you're alright," Pirelle agreed, gently rubbing Chalone's back in soft soothing circles.

"I just feel a little numb," Chalone whispered.

"Of course you do." Pirelle pulled the covers around them. Chalone started shaking and Pirelle was unsure whether it was from grief or rage or a combination of both. She held Chalone until she stopped shaking and her tears began. She listened as Chalone tried to find an explanation for Vian's inexplicable departure. When she stuttered to a halt and cried, Pirelle held her until she ran out of tears and broken words and fell into an exhausted doze.

Only then, she eased away from Chalone and pulled the sheet back around her sleeping body. She caressed her face, unknowingly duplicating Vian's gesture hours before. Her emotions played across her face like crosscurrents churning up the silt of a flooded riverbed.

She wanted to climb back into bed and hold Chalone some more. She wanted to get as far away as she could, as quickly as she could. She breathed deep in an attempt to convince herself she only reacted to Chalone's grief.

Before her emotions raised darker and more disturbing self-realizations, she chose the option that resolved nothing and quietly left.

* * * *

The land in front of the house Chalone, Pirelle, and Jalemi shared sloped gently down to a creek barely wide enough to warrant its single stepping stone to walk across. Pockets of wildly growing plants checkered the cropped lawns whose uneven maintenance was provided by the gaggle of geese that called this part of the hillside their home. One of the thickets sheltered the spring the creek rose from. Over the years an assortment of mismatched garden furniture had migrated from various parts of the village to this oasis. The heat of the sun rarely made it through the overhanging trees and on hot summer days, it offered a balm for the soul as well as the skin.

Pirelle walked into the glade and threw herself down on one of the benches. A dramatic gesture designed to arouse sympathy from anyone else who might have already been there. Unfortunately she was alone which only increased her misery, but she could always rely on one person at times like this.

* * * *

Jalemi finished her shift at the Hall of Lights and contemplated spending the remainder of the day with a woman she'd recently acquainted herself with, when a familiar internal lurch tugged at her solar plexus. Her eyes narrowed, but she put her plans for the afternoon on hold. Long experience told her she wouldn't have any peace until she answered the call. She set out for the glade, always the first place she looked.

Pirelle was so deeply into her tears that she could only stammer incoherently about Chalone being deeply hurt, and Vian, and a rose. None of which made any sense to Jalemi, so she sat next to Pirelle and held her hand.

Pirelle finally wound down and Jalemi tried again. "Start from the beginning. What's happened to Chalone?"

"Vian ended their relationship before Chalone was ready, and I found her afterwards."

"Oh," Jalemi said and nodded, understanding more than she let on. Pirelle's emotional outbursts made her uneasy, so she'd evolved a useful deflective mechanism. "That's why you're down here crying your eyes out. It all makes sense to me now."

Pirelle smiled half-heartedly and endeavored to explain about Chalone and Vian.

Jalemi tried to listen patiently, but she had few doubts about the true source of the passion behind Pirelle's tears. "Tell me, sister of mine, are you interested in Chalone?"

"Interested? How do you mean?" Pirelle asked in genuine surprise, then laughed. "Why? Are you worried about the competition?" She wrapped Jalemi in a bear hug. Their mutual attraction for women had been a source of some not-so-friendly rivalry over the years.

"Me? Absolutely not," Jalemi said in mock horror, throwing her hands up in front of her to ward off the very idea. Now that she had shifted Pirelle's emotional energy she relaxed. "I'll admit she's my type, but I feel more sisterly toward her than anything else. Don't avoid my question." She finished with a not-so-sisterly elbow to Pirelle's ribs.

In a voice that carried far less conviction than Jalemi's, Pirelle answered after some thought. "I feel like she's more of a sister too."

"Oh really," Jalemi said mischievously. "Well, let's go find our sister Chalone and ask her what she thinks on the matter."

"Don't you dare!" Pirelle squawked, wild-eyed and alarmed.

Jalemi took pity on her and relented. They walked back up to the house intent on finding Chalone and offering the kind of comfort only best friends could.

* * * *

Chalone sat in one of the scruffy old lounges kept on the balcony for conversation and contemplation. It was deep, well stuffed, and smelled of home. Her hair was still shower damp and her eyes more red than green and slightly puffy. She tucked her feet under a much-loved, oft-patched blanket, and cradled her injured hand in her lap.

"Pirelle told me what happened," Jalemi said, without adding what she really wanted to say.

"Feeling better?" Pirelle asked and sat next to her.

"Mm-m," Chalone answered. "Does the light from the Hall look any different to you?"

Jalemi and Pirelle looked at each other. That wasn't what they expected.

As directed, Pirelle squinted at the Hall calmly glowing just as it always had even under this summer sun until she was cross-eyed. "Not that I can tell. What are you looking for?"

"I'm not sure," Chalone said. "I thought I saw something last night."

"Why don't you speak to Vian?" Pirelle suggested and then paused. "Sorry."

"It's alright, Pirelle. Your mouth usually takes you where ordinary mortals fear to tread." Chalone shrugged. "I'm sure I'm in a state of denial. I keep trying to find ways to distract myself," she said, patting the abandoned book beside her. She held Pirelle's arm and leaned against her broad shoulder. Pirelle's heart missed a beat, but Chalone sat up again.

"I don't think this comes under that heading though. I'll contact Vian. Tomorrow," she added awkwardly and drummed her fingers on the cover of the neglected book. Pirelle and Jalemi watched her warily. "I need to do something about this right now. I'm going to see what it is that I'm not seeing." She gestured with her chin toward the Hall and abruptly left.

As she walked down the wooden stairs from the balcony Jalemi and Pirelle stared after her with their mouths slightly opened. They looked at each other and walked inside.

"Something's really bothering her," Jalemi said. "I wonder if I should go after her?"

"Leave it alone," Pirelle wisely advised. "She'll tell us when she's found something. She always does."

"I suppose so," Jalemi agreed reluctantly.

"I know so," Pirelle said and changed the subject. "I'm going to the baths for a good soak. Want to come?"

"No. I think I'll take advantage of both of you being out of the house. Go," Jalemi said, shooing Pirelle out of the door. Pirelle hugged her one last time for good measure and left as well.

* * * *

Jalemi's curiosity plagued her like an itch she couldn't scratch. She paced the length of her study seething with frustration as events inexorably began to move beyond her ability to influence. Her sister acted like her usual self again, Chalone ran off on a probably futile adventure in the Gallery, and Vian's behavior had gone beyond mysterious.

All her life she'd been the tag-along behind Pirelle and Chalone. Not that they saw it like that, they willingly included her in all their adventures. Asking permission to travel further and further into the Gallery wasn't the kind of adventure she sought.

She learned at an early age to fade into the background at will and silently observe her surroundings. It wasn't the proper use of her Practitioner skills, but she discovered the most useful information that way and therefore considered it justified.

She admired the way Vian played politics with the sub-council that managed the Hall of Lights and the greater council that governed their society. However, Vian risked everything in bold gambles, as much for the notoriety, as for the issue at stake.

Jalemi preferred subterfuge, usually without exposing herself, holding her triumphs to herself, savoring and hoarding them until needed.

The possibilities of what her participation in the Circle might mean surrounded her like a flock of dark and hungry raptors. The air grew thick and cold. Her breath came out in a chill cloud and shivers of apprehension and excitement slid down her spine like icicles.

She could do nothing about Chalone, whatever she'd seen was probably her imagination. Chalone didn't have that much imagination to begin with, she uncharitably and incorrectly concluded. Pirelle could be easily manipulated to do whatever she wanted, almost everyone thought Pirelle was the dominant twin because of her size. That left Vian. Vian was another matter entirely. A Circle was no place to play politics, no matter how tempting. Perhaps she wouldn't have to go to those lengths though. She'd get to the gathering place early, and if she uncovered more information before the ritual began, then so be it.

The door shut behind her and her room grew light and warm again.

Chapter Five

Chalone stalked around the Hall of Lights, glaring at it, daring it to look any different. Her thoughts marched around the venerable building faster than she did. Of course it wouldn't look any different. She didn't know what she was thinking, imagining something wrong with the Hall. She should be getting ready for Vian's Circle.

Vian. Her heart thumped in her throat and she deliberately turned her thoughts away from a flood of memories. *She. Would. Not. Cry.*

The Hall wasn't a small building though its appearance could be deceiving. In a thunderstorm it looked massive and ominous, at other times it looked ridiculously small. It could easily embrace thousands or seem crowded when it was almost empty. Even though it was ancient beyond reckoning, it looked unscathed by the passage of time or weather.

The translucent walls gleamed with swathes of light reflected from the Portals inside, just as they always had, so Chalone wrapped her fortitude around her and walked through the open archway into the Hall. She ducked around a small group of travelers just returning from somewhere deep within the Gallery. They chattered excitedly until one of them spotted her. They sensed they might have a captive even famous audience to tell their story to and veered toward her. Even on her best days she wasn't good at spontaneous conversations with groups and fortunately, before she embarrassed herself, Dajah the woman on duty, skillfully intersected their trajectory and herded them toward the exit. Chalone flashed a quick smile and turned back to her investigation.

The Hall's familiar ordinariness continued to set her teeth on edge with a dissonance she could almost taste. She looked at the ceiling high above. It was the same vaulted dome it had always been. She walked around the Hall toward the far end. The walls between the irregularly spaced Portals looked the same soft shade of white they always had. Nothing spoke to her of any wrongness. At a loss as to what to do next, she walked around and around the

Hall, resolving nothing.

Dajah pithily suggested she stop pacing because she was making her dizzy and would eventually wear a hole in the floor.

Chalone heeded the unspoken threat and sat on the circular bench in the center of the Hall. She leaned back on the huge granite outcrop that served as a backrest and stared absently at the Portals. She groaned in exasperation, but quietly, in case Dajah heard.

Muttering to herself, she shuffled a few meters along the bench to her right. Nothing. She shuffled around until she reached the far side of the bench, still looking at Portals and seeing nothing.

She stood up and slowly walked toward them, glancing out of the corner of her eye, letting her instincts find what her mind refused to.

On either side of each of the Portals, two crystal columns were positioned to stabilize the opening and keep them firmly anchored to the same physical place on the planet, in direct contradiction to the physics involved. Swirling between the columns, the Portals shone in a kaleidoscope of muted colors.

The explanation of why these two blatantly incompatible forces, the mystery of the Gallery and celestial physics, were able to co-exist without ripping reality apart was one of Chalone's early academic triumphs. Her meticulously documented investigation caused a sensation among researchers who'd tried to account for the phenomenon previously. She delivered her findings at the university in Esparber, and thereafter, a certain fringe of academia pointedly boycotted her infrequent lectures out of spite. Sadly this would have had a more dramatic effect had she been aware of, or cared about their opinions.

The light from one Portal shone on her face, as though challenging her to enter. When a hand lightly touch her sleeve, she nearly jumped out of her skin.

"What are you looking for?" Dajah asked.

Chalone recovered quickly, looked into Dajah's soft oval eyes for a moment, and then back at the Portal. "It's here," she said and frowned at the innocent object of her discontent.

"What is?" Dajah asked and stepped closer to the Portal, peering into it as though she expected to see something immediately appear through it. Its emanations etched the generous curves of her body in a shimmer of light and turned her amber skin a luminous bronze color.

Chalone laughed as she imagined Dajah's reaction if someone

did suddenly step out of the Portal. "I have no idea," she said, shrugging and sighing at the same time.

"Well then," Dajah said. "What are you going to do about it?"

"There's nothing I can do about it from this side, so I have to go through to the other side and find out what's happening," Chalone said disgruntled.

"Through to where?" Dajah asked. "This doesn't exactly take you to the World of Eternal Peace."

"It doesn't exactly take you anywhere."

Dajah wisely refrained from digging too deeply into Chalone's emotional state. She dealt with the issue at hand. "That's not exactly how the Destination Roll puts it."

"You know exactly how I feel about the Destination Roll," Chalone said, unable to suppress a snort of derision.

"Exactly," Dajah said wickedly, claiming the word game prize. "I was there when you shared your opinions with the Council. I quote, 'The Destination Roll is an outmoded and inefficient method of teaching new travelers how to use the Gallery that was written by a gaggle of ill-informed, ill-equipped, over-indulged scholars who relied on second-hand information gathered from questionable sources to compile their findings, rather than having the intestinal fortitude to do their explorations themselves.' You said it all in one breath."

"I was so nervous I don't think I breathed at all, but I'm flattered that you remembered." Chalone smiled nostalgically. "I didn't think anyone listened to me. I was very young and felt very passionately about the Roll then."

"You made a lot of those 'over-indulged' scholars take note when your expeditions rewrote most of it."

"They didn't like me very much though." Chalone said and dismissed them from her mind. "Thank you for reminding me."

"Of what?"

"That it's time to move on," Chalone said. "I want to ask you something on a completely different subject. Has Vian talked to you about joining her Circle tonight?"

"She has. Why?"

"I feel like I'm standing on the very edge of something," Chalone said slowly. "The Circle is part of it." She gestured toward the Portal. "Whatever's through there is another."

"You're not making much sense," Dajah said in her most practical voice. "If you want to look at it that way, every step we take puts us over that edge in some way or another. You participate in the Circle or not. You go through the Portal or you don't. Either way it's your destiny, your choice. You've discovered things about the Gallery that others never considered possible, let alone act on them."

"You sound like Jalemi."

Dajah wasn't enamored of Jalemi so she ignored the comment. "So, what's the problem with this Portal?" she asked and circled an arm around Chalone's waist.

"I have no idea," Chalone whispered and briefly hugged Dajah. She took a deep breath. "Wait for me?" When Dajah nodded, she stepped through the Portal.

Dajah stared at its shining surface half expecting Chalone to reappear at any moment. Eventually she returned to her office at the front of the Hall. After a respectable amount of time had passed, she found a perfectly valid reason to return to the Portal, then another and another. Finally she gave up pretending to work and sat nearby to wait.

* * * *

As Chalone crossed through the Portal her spine twitched at the temporal dislocation and her hind-brain informed her that she was about to be torn limb from limb. It never happened, but she always reacted and this time stumbled over the threshold. Her heart leaped into her mouth. Each corridor had a shallow depression that countless feet stepping out of a Portal made. All the thresholds were the same, even seldom used ones like this. A fact among the distractions of the last few hours she'd forgotten.

After a brief but severe talking to herself, she peered uneasily along the corridor disappearing into the infinite horizon. A silvery light emanated from the walls and illuminated its entire length. This particular corridor was wide enough for quite a few people to walk abreast and except for her presence lending it scale she could have been in any one of an endless number of corridors.

Ordinariness again.

As she did every time she ventured into the Gallery, she reached out and touched the rough corridor wall for luck. A flash of memory unraveled the present, and she was five years old again, before her mother left, and her world was still secure.

Vian guided one of her first class excursions into the Gallery, and it turned out to be a scary marvelous adventure.

Once they were all deep into the corridor, Vian asked the

children to think about what might be on the other side of the walls. Chalone answered immediately with the dismissive hauteur young children muster at the obtuseness of adults that there was no other side to the wall; that's why it was the wall.

Once the giggles died down, Vian asked the class to pretend they could burrow through the densely packed fibers the corridors were made of until they reached the other side. Before Chalone could open her mouth Vian quickly added that they could also pretend there really was another side. A long silence ensued as the children struggled with the concept. Many frowns appeared as childish logic came up with all sorts of answers. Suddenly Chalone screamed as her imagination sent her falling through the endless void she saw in her mind's eye.

The argument that exploded between her mother and Vian that evening was one of their more memorable ones. Her mother forbade her to see Vian, and although she couldn't follow the logic, Chalone was still scared enough to obey her. Her compliance ended when a pair of mismatched double agents rescued her from her bedroom. The three of them decided to sneak into the Gallery and test Vian's hypothesis.

Jalemi and Pirelle backed out at the last moment, but Chalone bravely stepped through the Portal. She stood right at the threshold, just in case there really were nasty monsters that stole naughty children out of the Gallery and ate them. For a bloodcurdling moment she thought she heard a distant crunching of bones, but it was only her teeth chattering.

Composing herself, she pushed her hand through the wall, which was an even braver thing for her do. She was truly surprised when the firm surface easily yielded. She buried the whole of her forearm in the strange woven substance, until some sort of barrier bumped against her fingertips. She nearly cried with relief. She couldn't burrow in and fall through the wall. Vian was wrong.

Suddenly she felt something take hold of her arm and push it completely out of the wall. She fell to the floor in fright, huddled in a tiny ball, and hid her face in her hands. *The monsters were real and they were coming to eat her up*!

An eternity passed.

Nothing happened.

Finally she sat up and stared around her. The corridor was empty and the place where she had pushed her hand in was as smooth as though she'd never touched it at all. She lay her head on her shaking knees, knowing no one would believe her, especially when she wasn't supposed to be in the Gallery in the first place, and considered her options. By the time she leaped back through the Portal and found Jalemi and Pirelle hiding in the woods beyond the Hall, she'd made her decision.

The following morning she informed her mother that she was going to study very hard with Vian, become a Practitioner, earn an apprenticeship in the Hall of Lights when she was grown up, and there was nothing her mother could do or say to change her mind. Her mother was self-aware enough to recognize her stubbornness and dedication as a positive trait. It was a turning point for both of them.

Unraveling the mysteries of the Gallery became Chalone's life's work, a much bigger job than she'd anticipated when she was five. Not once did she come across another story like her childhood adventure, but every now and then, she succumbed to the temptation. With no more than half her hand buried in the wall, she would always stop and turn away, call herself silly for chasing after ghosts, and pretend she'd never do it again.

* * * *

Chalone reluctantly left her childhood memories behind and put her hands firmly in her pockets.

"Damn," she said just to hear her voice, but the Gallery swallowed sound as easily as it did ECHO technology. "I'll just have to keep going."

As she walked along, the floor of the corridor gave a little with each step but felt as substantial as always. She eventually outpaced a perception shift that felt like a giant hiccup and wondered where or when she might be. Each corridor usually had thousands of junctions, but not this one, it just swept inexorably on. She leaned against the wall to consider turning back when something in the shadows just ahead caught her eye.

"Shadows? The Gallery doesn't have shadows."

She cautiously walked a few steps to where the light had failed and turned to look back at where she'd been. The light glowed evenly. She leaned against the wall again and tried to make sense of what she was seeing, or not seeing. The wall felt scratchy and warm and she slid her fingers between the warp and weft of the material seeking comfort or inspiration.

Suddenly a shudder rippled through the wall behind her. Something stabbed her fingertips. She leaped away as though she'd been stung. A jagged wedge of fear shot up her spine. She frantically scanned the empty corridor as if to find her assailant. She was alone. Nothing looked out of place.

Her chest ached, reminding her to breathe through the haze of white terror around her. Fingertips tingling with anticipation she gingerly extended her hand toward the wall and made contact with it. She felt only the ponderous sway every corridor had.

"I hate this! I don't understand. Nothing makes any sense!" she shouted.

Although she felt marginally better for her outburst, common sense told her to run as fast as she could back through the Portal, back to her house, into bed, and hide under the covers until she convinced herself she was having a really bad dream. Then something caught her attention that sent her back to the Portal deep in troubled thought.

* * * *

As she hurried away, tiny beings, who had squirmed and squiggled through the spaces between the compacted fiber walls since not long after Time began, had hope at last. From the moment they achieved consciousness, they knew their fragile efforts to preserve the Gallery were doomed unless they were able to obtain the help they so desperately needed.

They attended to the crack they'd used to create the ripple effect in the corridor wall and repaired it before any further damage could be done. Like weavers at a loom, they busily shuttled threads back and forth between the ragged edges of the tiny tear they'd hidden from Chalone with their bodies. Soon nothing remained of their intervention beyond a snippet of thread thriftily saved for another patch.

The wisp of air that caressed Chalone's cheek and sent her back to the Portal, they could do nothing about. It was already beyond them.

* * * *

A stream flowed underneath a bridge near Vian's house, into the pocket-sized lake in the center of Espinsal, then through the valley until it finally found its way to the sea. Just beyond the lake it diverted into a quiet backwater where a thermal vent sent plumes of steam through the water. The surrounding rocks made ample resting places, and trees and shrubs filled the air with their aromatic fragrance.

Pirelle spent her afternoon in and out of the pools and still basked on the sun-warmed rocks like a goldenrod lizard when Chalone arrived, shed her clothes, and slid into the waist-deep water. She sat down so that it lapped just under her chin and sighed long and blissfully. Pirelle left her rock and splashed into the water with her.

Chalone opened one eye. "I thought I'd find you here," she said.

"How'd it go?" Pirelle asked, still a little wary of Chalone's recent reaction to such questions.

"I found what I was looking for," Chalone said. The water took the weight of her body and she idly sloshed her toes back and forth. "I went through one of the Portals."

"Just because it was there, right?" Pirelle asked, splashing her.

"No." Chalone said and splashed back. "I was following my intuition."

Pirelle appeared to think deeply on that for a moment. "Well, my intuition is telling me to get into deeper water," she said, knowing Chalone would smile and all would be well. "Coming?" She held out her hand and towed an unresisting Chalone deeper into the soothing waters. "Now tell me," she said after Chalone had relaxed some more. "What your senses told you."

"That something is wrong."

"What?" Pirelle asked, looking around in mock concern. "Where?"

"In the Gallery, you mad woman!" Chalone touched her feet lightly on the bottom of the pool and bobbed around until she faced Pirelle. "Something happened while I was in there, that I don't have an answer for. It scared me right down to my toes." She looked at her terrorized appendages in sympathy. "I only wanted to get out of there. I took a flying leap out through the Portal and almost landed in Dajah's lap." She paused and laughed at the expression her re-emergence put on Dajah's face.

"Dajah was with you?"

"No. I asked her to wait for me in the Hall, just in case."

"Hmm," Pirelle said. "What are you going to do now?"

Chalone shrugged. "Talk to Vian? Go back into the Gallery? I don't know. It depends on what happens tonight, doesn't it?"

Pirelle drifted into the steam rising from the water and headed for the edge of the pool. "Ah, yes. Vian's magical and mysterious Circle. To which, we are going to be late if we don't hurry."

Chalone watched her climb out of the pool and unfold one of the soft robes stacked neatly near the edge of the water. She knew what Pirelle was thinking.

"Actually, I might be a bit late," Pirelle said with feigned casualness as she draped the robe around her gleaming wet body. "What's so funny?"

"Nothing," Chalone said deadpan. "Say hello to Dajah for me."

"How did...?" Pirelle began. "Don't answer. I'm not that predictable! I'll see you at the ritual." She gathered up her dignity along with her clothes and left.

Pirelle couldn't hide her feelings if she tried, especially when it involved a woman she was attracted to, but more often than not found reasons to end her affairs before anything got too serious.

Chalone occasionally wondered why Pirelle acted like that. She was certainly a magnificent woman, and if they hadn't been such good friends, she might have been interested in Pirelle herself.

The pleasant physical sensations following on the heels of that thought she firmly put down to the effect of the hot water on the blood supply to her brain.

Chapter Six

For lack of either divine inspiration or intervention, Vian chose the regular stone circle used for most of the Sabbats as the site for hers. As she approached it from underneath the woodland canopy, she came across an unfamiliar track. It looked as a pathway should, with leaves and twigs and gravel marking its twists and turns through the trees, but she could've sworn she'd never seen it before.

She smiled to herself. *Divine inspiration?*

The path led her to a small perfectly round clearing set in the heart of the woods. Leaves covered the ground and an old tree stood at its center. The tree was a familiar friend, but if Vian remembered correctly, it had been in the forest on the other side of the village and surrounded by a growth of adolescent aspens.

She paused at the edge of the clearing and reached out with her senses to make sure it was firmly connected to the same physical reality she inhabited. Satisfied, she walked into the center and touched the tree. A frisson of energy purled along its gnarled branches and caressed her hand. It sang to her heart in notes of pure energy. She knew where her ritual would be.

Divine intervention indeed. Sometimes the most profound magic slipped by unnoticed. Of course there were trees here yesterday, but that didn't mean there had to be trees today.

With a handful of women helpers, she raked the deep drifts of leaves scattered across the clearing into a perfect ring at edge of the trees. After the ritual concluded the leaves would be replaced to continue their decomposition unmolested.

Vian took a break from her toil and rested her arms on her rake. She reached for her water flask and wished for more time and more helpful bodies. It might have saved her some blisters.

Violet shades of awe radiated from the women working alongside her as though she'd been personally responsible for the clearing's mysterious appearance.

It wasn't as if they hadn't seen a manifestation appear in front of them, Vian argued to herself. This was the same thing, albeit on a much larger scale. The ritual hadn't officially begun yet, which did alter things slightly. Upon further consideration she concluded that their awe might be justified. She felt a bit awed herself.

Twilight draped its soft coolness across the glade as Vian and her helpers finished. Lanterns were hooked into tripods to be engaged when darkness truly fell. Small creatures of the day retired to their burrows and nests, and the night dwellers began to stir.

The raked earth completely surrounded the ancient tree. Each spring a few leaves valiantly sprouted, and turned golden each autumn. Now, in the middle of summer it was suspiciously bare of any foliage. Anyone other than Vian might've mistaken it for dead, but she felt the tiny thread of sap, its heart-blood, begin to beat faster.

She remained in the glade, standing companionably with the old tree until she saw someone step out of the forest shadows.

"She could've helped out," Vian muttered to her blisters, but rightly surmised that Jalemi wanted to talk, not work. "Why wait in the shadows?" She asked louder and startled the younger woman. "Come with me." Vian tucked her arm in Jalemi's. "Walk me home and you can tell me what's bothering you," she said, confounding Jalemi's purpose completely.

As they walked through the evening, Vian noticed a familiar shimmering in the air nearby.

* * * *

A very long time ago, on a day when she had a difficult decision to make, Vian went out for an early morning constitutional and came across an extraordinary sight. Four pillars, about a meter round and as tall as she, blocked her path. They called themselves Elementals, one each for Earth, Fire, Water, and Air. Although they shifted from one element to another at will, they each seemed to prefer their own when they wanted to get her attention.

She made four friends that day, but suspected they'd taken her on as a research project. Where they originated and why they chose to reveal themselves to her they wouldn't say but every so often they discovered something they felt she needed to know.

* * * *

Once Earth sensed it had her attention, it was unwilling to reveal itself in front of Jalemi and remained mute beyond her line of sight.

Vian and an uncharacteristically silent Jalemi ambled along until they reached the stone bridge that crossed the stream leading to her house.

It would've been better if Jalemi spoke first, but Vian needed to talk with her elemental friend and was in no mood to exercise further patience.

"Speak," she commanded, not unkindly.

Jalemi took a deep breath "Why won't you tell me ..." She realized that wasn't the approach she'd intended. "... All of us, that is, what's going to happen at the ritual tonight?"

"Why are you taking my decision so personally?" Vian countered, deliberately keeping Jalemi off-balance.

Realizing her ploy had failed, Jalemi opted for honesty. "It is personal. This is the first Circle of yours that you specifically asked me to join and I want to know what happens next."

"I understand that part, but you still haven't answered my question."

Jalemi muttered something under her breath that Vian didn't quite catch.

"I don't want to make a fool of myself," Jalemi repeated. "I might miss something important and not be taken seriously by... by everyone," she finished lamely.

"Is that truly what this is all about? I thought you were long past this stage," Vian said, immediately kicking herself for getting distracted, and grateful the darkness hid the abrupt appearance of a cinereous emanation surrounding her. It was something that only a handful of people had ever seen, and she was not about to give Jalemi that kind of access to her emotions.

"Forget I even asked," Jalemi muttered and turned to leave.

Vian caught her arm. "Don't you dare. You can not run away from the consequences of speaking your truth. Not around me." Vian released her arm and sat on a moss edged step at the foot of the bridge. After a rebellious moment, Jalemi accepted the unspoken invitation and sat next to her.

"If you don't want to make a fool out of yourself in a Circle, it's your responsibility to see that you don't," Vian said matter-of-factly. "You still have the ability to think for yourself whether you have all the facts or not."

Vian knew there were many aspects of Jalemi's shadow self that Jalemi was not ready to acknowledge. She debated whether to let her continue in the Circle. There were fewer Practitioners each year that had the skills and strength to stand the rigors of a

Circle. She still had high hopes for Jalemi, the most volatile of her generation.

In the end Vian chose to speak from her heart, hoping that Jalemi would hear with hers.

"You listen with your ambition, not your instincts and intuition. You thirst for the power that is here!" Vian slapped the weathered stonework of the bridge with the flat of her hand to emphasize her point.

The impact shimmied through the stone and up Jalemi's spine. She winced in sympathy and then realized that Vian could not possibly have physically created that kind of concussion. Her eyes flew to Vian's face but she saw no mystery there.

Elemental, Earth, still hovering out of sight, withdrew its touch from the stone after complying with Vian's silent request to enhance her blow. Mortals and their short incarnations fascinated all four Elementals and, for reasons known only to themselves, Vian in particular. So Earth didn't question Vian's request, it simply granted it and observed the result.

"Power, of itself, isn't necessarily a bad thing when it's harnessed with responsible actions and clear intent," Vian continued. "Unfortunately your desire is becoming an obsession and is clouding your perceptions. You act too fast, without thinking. You seek knowledge only for the power and status it brings. You may be able to go on as you have for a while longer yet, but sooner or later you will fall." A shiver pocked Vian's skin with goosebumps and the evening felt a little colder. "Harness your desire. Use it as a learning tool rather than let it play on your mind and become destructive. For tonight, don't try so hard. Sense the power that is available to you if you choose to wield it wisely." A long silence stretched between them, and Vian could only hope for the best.

"I'll answer your question," Vian said and smiled unexpectedly. Its warmth reached Jalemi's heart and partially healed the abrasions she'd created. "The reason I won't tell you what's going to happen, is because I can't. I wasn't told either!"

Jalemi looked at her in astonishment, but Vian stood up, ending the discussion.

"I will try," Jalemi said

Vian paused on the other side of the bridge and wondered if it would be enough.

* * * *

Vian lived in a haven of natural bushland between Espinsal

and the true wilderness that swept across the continent to the Eastern Ocean.

When she rounded the last corner in the path to her house, the Earth Elemental gusted ahead of her.

The air above her cottage flickered in an agitated pinwheel as all the Elementals combined their energies into a single intense blur of color. She ran the last few steps to her courtyard where they descended to meet her.

The Elementals existed almost exclusively in the present moment without any conscious connection to the past and only a vague desire to understand the future. Their communication flowed from that unique perspective. They intellectually understood the concept of memory and when they chose, could access the recollections of the elements they evolved from. However, what a lump of rock remembered as it was being spewed from a volcano a million years ago held little or no interest for them.

Vian, to whom information was the greatest resource, found this endlessly frustrating and the Elementals found her frustration endlessly amusing.

Earth developed the greatest ease in expressing itself in terms Vian had a frame of reference for, and it was often the voice with which they all spoke.

It separated from their combined energy mass and shifted into a body that looked like a cross between a polar bear and a pigmy elephant. It also had a unique sense of humor.

For a being constructed from the bones of the earth, it spoke in a surprisingly light and airy voice.

"We listen to the heart of this land," it said. "The heart becomes restless. It sends a stream of energy out from its core and directs it to this place." The bear-phant shook its ears back and forth to display its concern. "It is powerful enough to contain even us." The ears stopped swishing and remained very still as Earth contemplated the sort of force that could threaten its freedom. "This makes us uneasy. It is something we judge you would like to know."

"This place?" Vian repeated startled. "Do you mean where we are now?"

"Not here, but close by," Earth said.

Vian shook her head. Wrong question. The Elementals called the whole world their backyard and therefore had a very broad interpretation of 'close by'. She tried a different approach.

"Tell me about this energy stream? Why is it being sent here?"

"Elemental Air senses another energy flow in the skies above us. The land emissary rises to meet it," Earth explained matter-of-factly.

Vian blanched. Apprehension and suspicion swelled in her mind. Before she could draw any conclusions, Earth spoke again and her fears were realized.

"The land emissary is from the blood of the earth."

Vian turned even paler. She knew beyond a doubt what her Circle was for. *To master the Earthblood fire!*

Vian scowled at the momentary flash of light that eclipsed her vision and confirmed it. *How redundant.*

She hadn't heard mention of the Earthblood fire in a very, very long time. The ritual took many days of preparation and required a strong-willed highly-skilled Circle of experienced Practitioners to guide the forces necessary to manipulate the fire without being destroyed. As of this moment she had a scant hour to accomplish the same thing with a Circle that lacked among many things, experience.

Earth caught her in its paws as her knees buckled, and set her down gently on a nearby bench.

"Our news distresses you," it said. The other Elementals gathered around, taking on more solid forms as an offering of support. Fire resembled an ambulatory lava flow, constantly creaking and grinding as its surface broke apart and reformed. Water looked like an iceberg full of cracks, and Air flapped like a pennant caught out on a windy afternoon.

They crowded close, leaning against the bench until it creaked alarmingly. Vian recovered her composure enough to wave them back a little before they inadvertently harmed her.

"I'm alright," she said. "Your news just gave me a shock."

"Is this a dangerous thing to your people?" Air gusted curiously.

"The Earthblood fire?" Vian asked bitterly. "No. Not if its contained properly." Her anger bolstered her flagging energy and she surged upright.

The Elementals backed off even further. Experience taught them that when she radiated a particular color, it was a wise thing to retreat. Understanding emotions did not come easily to them, but Vian's persistence taught them to be aware and act accordingly. As she spoke to Earth, it sensed with some relief that her anger was not directed at them.

"Are you sure the Earthblood is already moving?" she asked

quickly.

"Oh yes. It comes." Earth nodded emphatically. A moment of silent consultation passed between the four Elementals and their solidity faded away as they left to pursue new adventures.

Vian sat back on the bench, her thoughts whirling furiously.

If the Circle wasn't strong enough, the Earthblood fire would shatter the land. Giant rifts would form in the crust of the earth and quakes would cause untold destruction on a global scale. She couldn't even begin to imagine what that destruction would look like.

If the Elementals were correct, and she had no cause to doubt them, the Earthblood was already moving, so postponing the ritual was out of the question. Not enough time remained to properly prepare herself or replace the women who were inexperienced. Most of those she needed were scattered throughout the Gallery.

It seemed that her Guide had underestimated the scope of Her command, and if Vian ever met Her in person, she would have a few succinct things to say to Her on the subject. In the meantime, she had precious few minutes to invent a way to cast layers of protection over the women in the Circle, then weave them into the flow of the Earthblood fire without searing them to a crisp.

She would have to improvise.

"That makes it simple then!" she shouted and threw her arms up in the air. "One of the most complex rituals this side of the Hub, and I have to improvise. Thank you so very much!"

She stomped into her home, paused only for a quick wash and a change of clothes, then stormed out her front door slamming it shut behind her.

A whirlwind of dust and fire and rain blew about in her wake. The Elementals decided to see how things turned out. After all they lived here too.

Chapter Seven

Against the dark of the night lanterns bobbed and wove through the woods heading for the glade where the old tree stood like a gnarl-fisted sentinel. People came from their homes, from the homes of their families, and from their private groves of contemplation, because for all its mystery this was a celebration of the potency of their lives. Their excited voices echoed through the trees and floated up to the stars.

Small animals retreated further into their nests and burrows. The instinctual knowledge of all wild creatures warned them that rare and unusual energies drew near, and it was not their place to be involved.

A crowd gathered at the edges of the glade and the sacred lanterns were lit. The scent of the sacred oils wafted up from the naked flames to rouse the senses. Only a handful of people intended to participate in the ritual itself, but friends and family came to support and observe. Word of this mysterious ritual had spread far and wide, Vian's reputation being what it was, and plenty felt curious to see what she was up to this time.

A single hand drum set a beat. Percussive instruments, easily carried, provided counter rhythms and staccato emphasis. The whole woodland pulsed with anticipation.

Everyone took advantage of the opportunity to catch up with old friends and make new ones, to flirt and to dance, faster and wilder until the energy reached its peak.

* * * *

Breathless, Chalone left the dancing and stepped into the Circle. She saw Vian standing next to the old tree, waiting for them all, and she faltered. Her smile faded and she wondered how they would both react. After Vian nodded an almost apologetic greeting, Chalone realized that Vian doubted she would come. She nodded slightly in return, sadly acknowledging that neither of them knew each other as well as they thought.

* * * *

Outside the Circle the drumming slowed, pulling the energy down to ground in the earth. The beat grew softer until silence and stillness filled the glade. The quiet drums and their drummers trembled with an energy beyond their ken. As they moved away from the Circle, they exchanged anxious glances. *What was coming?*

Their destination was a clearing not too far away, where trestle tables filled up with all manner of tasty foods and lanterns threw lively pools of light over the continuing celebrations. They willingly left their fears behind and welcomed the cheer.

* * * *

Before Chalone could decide what, if anything she might do about Vian, the rest of the women joined her in the Circle. Pirelle arrived breathlessly late, hand in hand with Dajah, which didn't surprise Chalone one bit. They stood next to her and Pirelle smiled smugly over the top of Dajah's head.

Dajah glanced up at her and smiled too. Chalone knew when someone was flirting with her. Probably innocently she decided, giving Dajah the benefit of the doubt. She turned away, more concerned about what she'd seen in Vian's eyes than her friends' romances.

Dajah misread her frown and leaned toward Pirelle feeling slightly offended but not really understanding why.

A rather subdued Jalemi approached their little group and stood on the other side of Dajah. She, too, saw Vian and nodded in her direction.

Twenty women joined hands, right over left, and closed the Circle around the old tree.

* * * *

The full moon rose. Its raw craters blazed with the radiance of the sun. The light struck the weathered branches of the old tree like a physical blow. The land quivered for a moment and then lay still, as though holding its breath.

At the edges of the circle a glow like burnished copper moved inexorably inward as the Earth responded to the moonlight's trigger. Lanterns that had been ignited with loving intent surrendered to this potency and winked out of their own accord. The glowing ground was more than enough to see by.

From the corners of their eyes the women glanced down at the glimmering. The ritual had begun. A fevered chill permeated the glade and sent shivers through them. They stood in hushed awe, hands still clasped in a ring around the old tree and waited for the past and present to collide.

* * * *

The Circle had long been promised, and the Lifeblood of the Earth, the throbbing heart of all the ancient mystical and magical power in the land, responded to its call. Asleep, the Earthblood remained content to vent itself through occasional volcanic explosions. Awake, it became a primal consciousness compelled by its nature to escape the confines of the planet's heart by any means necessary.

It rose through the molten rock, and pushed against the crust of the planet. Earthquakes shuddered across the continent as it crashed through tectonic plates, shouldering them aside without effort. It reached the softer layers of earth that held the essence of growing things and sought out the conduit that had been prepared eons before, a lifeline to freedom.

It reached for the sap of the old tree and flamed its brittleness into vapors. Roots juddered and writhed and loosened their hold in the ground. Cracks appeared around the foot of the tree and a snarling, grinding, tormented sound arose to the surface.

* * * *

A comet issued forth from beyond the distant stars and flew toward the tiny world. It eclipsed the moon with its shining tail and roared into the atmosphere. A trail of incandescent flames snaked from one edge of the horizon to the other.

A sonic shockwave rippled through the woodlands. Saplings crashed to the ground. Branches and leaves stripped from the branches of mighty oaks. The woodland animals retreated deeper into their burrows, families huddled together for comfort.

The women were thrown about, breaking the chain of linked hands. Their connection with each other, forged as soon as they stepped into the Circle, shredded as though it had never been a possibility.

Vian staggered away from the tree, fell to her knees, and sensed the raging Earthblood so near to breaking free of the earth. Springing to her feet and to her place in the Circle, she commanded the shaken but as yet unhurt women to return to their places. Her presence recalled them to their task, and although they reclaimed the circle of energy, they no longer needed to be in physical contact with each other for the ritual to continue.

* * * *

The Earthblood fire rose. It reduced the roots of the old tree to ash and boiled up through the surface of the earth. A searing flare of fire and thunder devoured each splinter, branch, twig, and leaf that had sustained the tree for all its long life. In its place a living writhing pillar of flame burned white hot.

The burning roared like all the wildfires of the world exploding at once, louder and louder, flames leaping higher, fed by the blood of the land. The air boomed and snapped at the women, jerking their hair and clothes in all directions. They held their hands over their ears in a futile attempt to shield themselves from the relentless noise.

All at once the roaring died.

Silence smacked against their tortured eardrums.

They looked to each other and then to the center of the Circle.

An almost motionless colossus of fire split the night sky like a bludgeon. It quivered with a barely suppressed intensity that spoke of the raging passions within.

The Earthblood fire waited. To be shaped by mortal will for an immortal purpose.

* * * *

Nothing, no one, moved within the glade. Distant thunder-like rumblings faded as the earth settled uneasily.

Vian broke the spell and walked toward the frozen flames. She glanced upward as the comet came from across the horizon to slow down as it approached them.

Now she knew what the Earthblood was for. *Stupid Guide*, she hissed imprudently, withholding this piece of information until now.

Quicker than she'd ever seen anything move, the column of fire writhed and spat out a tongue of the fiery energy at her. It entered her body, seared through her synapses, and focused its awesome power in her hands. The trail of fire writhed among her tendons and tethered her to her fate. She marveled that she remained unscathed.

She turned to the rest of the women and spoke to them, her voice wreathed in fire. "You will draw the Earthblood fire from me," she commanded. "Look up and see why!"

The comet hovered high above them, but they felt no fear, the ritual had already taken them beyond such an inconsequential emotion.

With the strand of energy linking her to the Earthblood fire shining inside her hands, Vian returned to the Circle. She approached the one woman she knew she could trust with the burden she was about to place upon her shoulders.

* * * *

Chalone cautiously took Vian's radiant hands in hers, knowing there was nothing corrupt in the Earthblood energy flowing between them. Dangerous, yes, as all power was, but safe when handled with due respect.

The tendril of flame surged throughout her body. It took control of her mind, and sifted through her memories. Every thought, every emotion, every act, every piece of information, every decision, reviewed by the harrowing presence in her mind. Dissected right down to her origins of instinct and intuition.

Her eyes almost bulged out of their sockets with the pressure in her head. She doubled over in agony, desperate to hold her skull together. Then, just as swiftly, her ordeal ended. She swallowed hard to keep her stomach where it was supposed to be.

Chalone had been tested and not found wanting in strength or commitment to the task ahead. But the Earthblood was not done with her. From an infinite distance away she heard Vian shouting. "Move the energy through you. You'll die if you don't ground it."

She stood upright, suddenly aware of the Earthblood fire still pounding throughout her body, desperately trying to fulfill the second aspect of its purpose. Her fright immediately cleared the fog of pain in her head. She flexed her will and connected her awareness to the earth, melding its endurance and impeccable strength with her will and the Earthblood's purpose. The oppressive pressure abruptly changed to an internal rushing vibration, sensual and passionate. So erotic it almost brought her to her knees. She sobbed the dregs of her terror out and pulled the ragged edges of her sense of Self inwards, forging a tool for whatever the Circle required of her.

Vian watched her struggle and knew the rest of the women would follow Chalone's example. She moved around the Circle, from woman to woman, and offered each one the same choice.

* * * *

Dajah quailed as Vian approached her with hands aflame. Fire terrified her. She couldn't believe Vian wanted her to take it, but Pirelle, always eager to soothe others, squeezed her hand with her comforting strength.

"Trust Vian. Trust me," Pirelle said. The contact warmed Dajah's heart and with one hand firmly in Pirelle's, she reached out for the fire.

* * * *

Pirelle, too, accepted the energy one-handed, and gasped as the same testing Chalone endured, raised the incipient sexual tension between her and Dajah to an almost post-orgasmic fever. Like a moth seduced by a flame, the Earthblood energy focused on the sensuality that danced between them. By the time they belatedly remembered to do the grounding only part of it acquiesced. The remainder separated from its source and cycled between them in an escalating feedback loop.

* * * *

Jalemi eagerly grasped Vian's hands and pulled the energy into her body almost before Vian released it, their conversation earlier in the evening completely forgotten. She surrendered to the siren call of the Earthblood energy without a second thought.

* * * *

Lila, Vian's oldest friend, stood like a statue, afraid that if she moved to take the fire, even breathe, she would shatter. Their eyes met and it seemed to Lila that only now did Vian truly see her. They smiled together and the moment passed. Lila took the fiery offering from Vian's hands and reveled in its passionate glory.

* * * *

Vian connected all the women to the Earthblood, and the ribbons of energy radiated out like the spokes of a giant wheel, bathing them all in its ecstatic embrace. The Circle was truly closed at last.

As Chalone watched Vian approach her once more, her heart lurched. Tears welled up in her eyes at the ravages she saw.

"I'm alright. Don't be afraid for me," Vian said, doggedly forestalling her, fully aware that she had aged. Years in a few minutes.

"Liar," Chalone whispered, then opened her Self for whatever was to come.

Vian suddenly leaned forward and plunged both hands into Chalone's chest. She drew the Earthblood fire, now grounded and malleable, from the very core of her being.

Chalone staggered back, stunned, clutched her hands to her breast and looked down in amazement. She saw no wound, no mark. A shimmering ribbon of energy shone through her fingers and flowed from her solar plexus into Vian's hands.

Vian smiled at the look on Chalone's face and turned back to the frozen pyre in the center of the Circle. She sent the leading edge of the ribbon rippling through the air. As it grew closer to the Earthblood fire, the rigid column throbbed and grew stronger and more restless. It absorbed the grounded energy and began to change. A crackling sound reverberated off its surface as the ribbon melded into its heart.

Vian walked the Circle once more, pulling a ribbon of energy from every woman and connecting it to the column. Each ribbon added to the Earthblood fire's transformation and it grew from a primal and uncontrollable force into a valuable tool. Tiny cracks appeared in its solid exterior. Waves of heat burst through, widening and melting their edges.

Vian flung the last ribbon into it, and finally like a volcanic eruption, an incandescent plume of fire, alive with potency and purpose, seared the night sky. It drew the eyes of the Circle of women up until they beheld the comet.

* * * *

Seduced by the dazzling potency of the Earthblood and as like calls to like, the comet descended into the dazzling tongue of fire in a wild hypnotic dance. It leaped sideways, then jerked around, swept low, and flung itself back into the heavens. Every pass through the column of Earthblood fire burned away more of its surface debris, exposing a perfect sphere of gleaming silver.

The Sphere paused for an instant and then repeated its dance anew, glorying in the radiance of the fire, completely innocent and unaware of its fate.

The women also watched the Sphere's frenzied dance and drew closer to the Earthblood trap. No mortal alone had the will to resist its potency thus aroused without divine assistance.

It wasn't until Vian felt the searing heat that she recalled herself enough to realize they were all in danger of being burned alive. With strength of will enhanced by the power of the Circle, she staggered back from the fire and directed a wall of energy at the women, strong enough to push them backward, well away from the edge of death.

* * * *

While the Sphere danced and the Earthblood fire raged higher and higher, the earth surrounding it pulsed with the urgency of a colossal heartbeat. Louder and faster until the beating rose from the earth around the Earthblood fire like a booming wave of solid air. The tortured ground, heated and battered beyond endurance, exploded. Molten rock rose high into the air to fall down in a rain of fire across the glade and surrounding woodland.

There was no time to think of running away, no time to escape. The women cringed beneath the lethal salvo, their doom upon them.

The sky cracked like a thunderbolt, the Earthblood rose up to enclose the Sphere, and a blinding flash of light strobed through the Circle. A strange blur of mist swept across the glade, taking the deadly missiles with it, though not the deafening sound.

When their vision returned, the women saw a single beam of energy where the wild Earthblood fire had been. It shone up into the heavens and held the Sphere captive within its purposeful embrace.

Chapter Eight

Throughout her adult life Jalemi cultivated a deep interest in all sources of power, personal, spiritual, political, no matter how obscure. As soon the earth erupted and the Earthblood fire spewed forth, she knew it for what it was.

When Vian approached her with the most formidable source of power she'd ever heard of, she surrendered her will in a single moment of ecstatic zeal. Out of the corner of her minds eye she recalled seeing Vian's hand slapping the stone bridge. The staccato memory peered over her shoulder like an unwelcome visitor until she scorned its counsel and it brushed aside without another thought.

The crushing presence of the Earthblood fire rifled through her memories and she quivered in exaltation, closing her ears to everything but the call of her obsession, deliberately ignoring Vian's adamant reminder to let the energy flow through her. She closed her mind and sealed it within her body, refusing to ground it in the earth and then flexed her will to create a mirror image of the ribbon to place in Vian's hands instead.

By denying the energy its freedom, she deliberately created a menace as dangerous as the accidental one threatening Dajah and Pirelle.

The rain of molten rock mysteriously disappeared and the Sphere hung motionless inside its prison. The Earthblood fire roared on and Jalemi fell to her knees with the lust of an irredeemable addict. Groaning, enraptured, she failed to see how swiftly it overwhelmed her frail abilities to constrain it. She leaned back and threw her arms wide as the fire detonated in her bones without harming her. She exalted and was the most powerful of them all.

"This...is...my...destiny!" she screamed into the booming sky.

Jalemi's psychic barriers abruptly collapsed and the energy flowed into every cell of her mortal body, instinctively attempting to return to the earth by any means available. She desperately tried to keep it within her physical body. It was not a prize she'd willingly surrender at the first challenge.

Between the indomitable energy and the resolute woman there

could be no quarter. The energy came from a source greater than she could ever be. It forced her body down into the earth, and buried her up to her elbows and thighs in the cold, cold ground.

At first, Jalemi's small triumph was too unimportant, too mortal, for the Earthblood fire to notice until the energy she'd imprisoned finally slipped the leash she'd tied around it.

Faster than thought, the energy surged past the barrier of her skin like water through sand and fled back to its source. The column of Earthblood fire wavered slightly as the impact stressed the integrity of its surface and tainted its impeccable containment of the Sphere.

Frantic, Jalemi flexed her will to grasp at the threads of energy abandoning her but the Earthblood fire was stronger than she could ever imagine. Her anguish was irrelevant to it. She screamed, convulsed, writhed uncontrollably, as a dreadful trap of her making sprang shut, leaving her wounded in spirit and body.

The earth, displaced by her unseemly insertion, sought to reoccupy the same space as her arms and legs by crushing the life out of them.

Excruciating pain shot through her body and crashed against her consciousness. She wailed for help, for surcease, but no one could hear her agony above the noise of the Earthblood fire.

She tossed her head back and jerked her body around, terrified, trying to escape the grasp of the earth. *How was this possible? How had it happened?* She hurt so much. She felt sure she was dying.

Through her maddened vision, she saw Vian and Chalone standing together as they witnessed the Earthblood fire's transformation. The sight wrenched her attention away from her agonizing danger.

Of course they would be together, congratulating themselves.

Anger revived her. Although quickly dismissed, the moment of jealousy remained tucked away deep in the recesses of her mind.

She twisted back to the Earthblood fire convinced her anger was strong enough to draw it to her, as she'd assumed Vian had done. She would wield it to numb her pain and free her from the earth.

In her heightened state of awareness from her pain and the ritual itself, she might've succeeded but for one thing. Right in her line of sight was the Sphere, wreathed in a pillar of the purest radiant light.

Her mouth dropped open and she forgot all about the Earthblood fire and how it rejected her. Her pain fled as swiftly as it appeared. The Sphere was an unsurpassed source of power beyond all mortal reckoning and she yearned with all her being, reached out with all her skill as a Practitioner, to posses it.

Energy, like water, flowed along pathways already established, and her attempt to reach the Sphere honed in on the tiny stress fracture in the Earthblood's containment shield.

* * * *

Sebenesh initially created the Sphere as an object of pure force, without consciousness, unable to exert free will. However, she realized that the Mortal Realm, and the fickle creatures it spawned, would sooner or later threaten the Sphere and force it to defend itself, therefore she imbued it with a tenacious survival instinct to be activated once the Earthblood fire contained it.

Jalemi's clumsy attempt to reach the Sphere through the flaw she'd unwittingly created in the Earthblood fire was enough to awaken this instinct. The Sphere began to create a burgeoning consciousness using the concepts Sebenesh had endowed it with; concepts based on her unique point of view. It was no surprise that it recognized the Earthblood fire as a trap, an enemy, and it struck at the flaw with a deadly shaft of psychic force.

The Earthblood fire shuddered and bled incarnadine flames from its virgin wound. The energy shaft flowed back to Jalemi, found the touch of the Earthblood fire inside her, and pierced her mind.

* * * *

By chance, or not, at that very moment, Chalone saw Jalemi half-buried in the ground. She shouted to Vian over the noise of the Earthblood fire.

Already exhausted by wielding the raw Earthblood fire into a malleable substance, Vian turned her tired attention to meet this new demand, just as the chaos escalated elsewhere in the Circle.

* * * *

After capturing the Sphere, the Earthblood fire no longer needed its connection to the women of the Circle. The energy that bound them together gently detached from their psychic bodies and returned to its source.

Pirelle and Dajah still clasped hands, unaware of the tiny thread of Earthblood energy locked inside them, flowing in an endless loop, seduced by their passion for each other.

The trapped energy swiftly reached critical mass and abruptly transformed into a solid physical form, became brittle, snapped, cracked, and shattered into tiny pieces. The almost invisible razor-edged shards writhed through their flesh and bones, frantically seeking the Earthblood fire, so near yet so unattainable.

* * * *

Pirelle screamed as the shards sliced through her skin. Fragments hissed and buzzed around her like a cloud of angry bees. They drew together like iron filings to a magnet, coalescing into a single ungainly lump of crystal that floated in front of her. It spun and spat tiny pinpoints of light in all directions until it drew the last remaining pieces from Pirelle's body like splinters. Her blood spattered onto its surface, seared into charcoal blisters. The smell burned into her brain as she gasped in horror at the bloody...thing, which twisted this way and that in front of her as though tethered by an unseen leash. For a moment her heart felt as though it would burst. Dajah's hand slipped from hers, as blood oozed from hundreds of tiny punctures all over her body.

Suddenly the repulsively beautiful thing rushed toward her and she flinched further away from Dajah.

* * * *

Unable to achieve the size and strength it needed in order to return to the Earthblood fire unaided, the crystal had no other way to survive except to reattach itself to the closest source of power, Pirelle. She threw up her hands in front of her face to no avail. It penetrated her body and transformed back into pure force.

The physical link between Pirelle and Dajah now severed, allowed it to flee down into the earth where it rejoined the Earthblood fire none-the-worse for its accidental incarceration.

* * * *

Bloody and battered, Pirelle remained on her feet. Numb with horror she watched the incisions on her body close over, until only the blood she'd already shed remained on her smooth skin. She gazed at her arms and hands in stunned amazement, touched her face to make sure the healing was real. Her fingers left bloody trails through the tears on her cheeks.

* * * *

When the contact between Pirelle and Dajah broke, a lesser amount of the cycling energy remained with Dajah.

She staggered one, two steps away from Pirelle. The tiny crystals in her body, severed from the Earthblood fire and too weak to return to the earth on their own, decayed and fractured into smaller and smaller pieces, shredding through her organs, muscles, and bone tissue indiscriminately.

Disoriented and half mad with the pain of her wounds, she stumbled toward Jalemi. Although she reached back for Pirelle to save herself from falling, neither of them moved quick enough. Her fingertips missed the end of Pirelle's outstretched hand by a hairsbreadth.

Everything moved around her in slow motion. Her terrible wounds corrupted her tears and stained them with her blood. What little strength she could muster leeched into her pain. Her knees gave way and she smiled vaguely at her clumsiness.

She blinked away her bloodstained tears and saw Jalemi, still enslaved to the Sphere, half-buried in the ground. She couldn't think of a way to avoid falling on her and feared Jalemi would be so angry at her. *Why should she care about that? What was Jalemi's opinion to her?* She felt confused and tired, so tired.

Her eyelids closed of their own accord and falling was the last thing she remembered.

* * * *

Dajah's hand brushed Jalemi's shoulder. The Earthblood energy still trapped within her body and the Sphere's tendril of consciousness within Jalemi's mind responded to each other like fuel and tinder, too separate in creation and purpose to remain inert.

A spark flashed between them, spiking a brutal explosion that heaved Dajah through the air to the edge of the Circle and onto the ground in a bloody heap. Bone-snapping muscle spasms wracked her body over and again until the volatile charge spent itself.

Her limbs lay broken and bent into impossible angles and her heart's blood slowly pooled on the ground beneath her.

* * * *

Jalemi's arms and legs were twisted out of their sockets when the concussion tore her from the earth and flung her away from Dajah like a used rag. She lay still, dazed and disoriented, and wondered what happened, but more concerned with her adoration of the Sphere.

The pain in her joints slowly penetrated the fog in her mind and seared like wildfire through her nerve endings. She screamed and thrashed about on the ground in torment. The more she moved, the more she hurt. The more she hurt, the deeper the Sphere penetrated into her mind.

Another force both familiar and terrifying rose up in front of her like a hurricane. The Sphere's thrall dissipated like fog before a tempest. Her pain escalated beyond endurance and a twilight state somewhere between the savage assault on her senses and the blessed relief of unconsciousness swept through her like a cool wave. She heard screams and angry voices that sounded like Pirelle arguing with Vian, as unlikely as that seemed. Something must have gone really wrong with the ritual for that to happen, although she couldn't think what. She wondered if sometime soon, anyone would come and see if she was alright.

The fiery pain in her arms and legs faded, her solar plexus collapsed, and her mind ceased to function.

Chapter Nine

The Circle of women, although freed from the puissance of Earthblood fire, still remained ensorcelled by the ritual. They focused on the majestic drama above them, the seduction and capture of the eldritch Sphere by the primordial Earthblood fire. Almost all of them were oblivious to the smaller, far more dangerous catastrophe evolving at their feet.

* * * *

This ritual drained Vian like no other she could remember, and she remembered a great many of them. It was the nature of participating in a Circle as primal as this one turned out to be. However, she retained enough energy to rehearse the slightly smug lecture she intended to have with her Guide.

The spurt of flame protruding from the pristine surface of the column of Earthblood fire interrupted her musings. It should not be there, she knew, but just at that moment Chalone called her attention to Dajah and Jalemi's plight. Her brain and eyes suddenly felt as though they needed to go in two different directions at once.

A wave of sorrow swept over Vian as Dajah's severed spirit reluctantly abandoned mortality. Even as she ached to grieve with it, she saw the virulent thread of energy lashing Jalemi's psyche to the Sphere. It contracted like a rubber band pulling her closer to the crack in the Earthblood fire.

"This is all wrong!" Chalone shouted, abbreviating a wealth of information into those few words. Vian had chosen her for this knowing.

Before she could rally her thoughts to deal with the two-fold disaster, Vian watched Pirelle, covered in blood but seemingly unhurt, start toward Dajah. The Circle shuddered as Pirelle abandoned her place within it. The flaw might still be healed, but the danger Pirelle presented by withdrawing from the Circle was immediate and dire.

Vian stepped in front of Pirelle and grabbed her by the arms.

Pirelle's face twisted in desperation. Somewhere in her heart she knew Jalemi and Dajah were beyond her help, but she struggled to escape Vian's grasp none-the-less.

"Stop, Pirelle! There's no time! This damage must be repaired," Vian shouted above the clamor of the fire.

"What are you talking about?" Pirelle shouted back. She shifted her weight as if to wrench herself from Vian's arms. "They need me! Jalemi needs me!" Her voice rose to a scream as she tried to break free of Vian's grip again. Vian thrust her face into Pirelle's until she was right under her nose.

"There's a crack in the Earthblood fire," Vian shouted. "The Sphere must not escape! It must not! Jalemi undermined the Earthblood fire's binding. If the Sphere gets free, everything will be destroyed!" Vian shook Pirelle hard enough to rattle her teeth. "The confinement field must be restored. Leave Jalemi. She'll live. Dajah is already dead! She's already dead!" Vian's voice thickened with an emotion she dared not give in to. "You must listen to me. If you don't we'll all be killed. All of us. The whole world! We have to reestablish the Circle. Do you understand?"

"No," Pirelle said, torn apart by two unbearable choices. She tried to shake Vian off one last time. "It's not true. You don't know what you're talking about. I have to take care of them." Her voice broke and she hung her head.

"There's no time, Pirelle," Vian said with brutal honesty and shook Pirelle, gently this time. "After we've finished we can take care of them. Come back. Now!"

Pirelle returned to her duty in the Circle as though her spirit were broken. She looked up and saw the pillar of Earthblood fire shudder as the Sphere careened from side to side seeking to take advantage of any further weakness. Giant sparks shot out of the flaw. In spite of her anguish she knew Vian was right.

She glared at Vian with her heart full of bitterness and shattered trust. Useless words of denial and rejection threatened to break past her clenched teeth, but she remained silent.

With a last wretched glance at her sister, Pirelle reached out with her senses and reconnected to the Circle, to the Earthblood ritual. She flexed her will and bridged the gap created by Jalemi and Dajah's absence. The integrity of the Circle flowed through her and around her and was renewed.

She watched as Vian pulled Chalone aside and pointed toward Jalemi. They nodded to each other and stepped to Jalemi's huddled body. Pirelle felt the Earthblood fire's shudder and quickly refocused to prevent the flaw from getting any larger.

* * * *

Chalone and Vian linked their minds, the joining made easier with the intimate resonance of having been lovers, and drew on the energy of the re-combined Circle. They wielded the essence of the Circle with an efficiency born of long years of practice. An indestructible barrier shimmered into existence between the Sphere and Jalemi and solidified to an adamantine hardness, surrounding her completely. The tendril the Sphere had so cunningly inserted into her blurred consciousness snapped against the barrier with an audible crack. It shrieked in thwarted frustration and retreated within the Earthblood fire, but not before it left a seed of desire behind in her mind.

* * * *

Now it was Pirelle's turn, and the task fitted her like a glove, direct and unequivocal. She wove Chalone and Vian back into the Circle and then called on the authority generated by the women of the Circle. Like a master crafter she focused it through her will, and gently compelled the edges of the fracture in the Earthblood fire together. She blended one ragged edge into the other until only a scar remained.

Pirelle withdrew the melding before the awesome magnificence of the Earthblood fire again ensorcelled the entire Circle. In that moment she understood Jalemi would never have chosen to resist the temptation. Tears of frustration and grief welled up in her eyes.

* * * *

Its containment of the Sphere complete, the Earthblood fire flared brightly as if rejoicing in a destiny fulfilled. A beam of solid light soared out into the heavens and down to the center of the earth.

The enchantment of the Earthblood fire faded away, returning to the center of the earth for renewal. It left the women in the Circle bereft of its strength and support.

Their minds and spirits had never been adequately prepared for the ritual and now that it ended, no one, not even Vian could recover unaided. The constant roar of the column of light assaulted their senses already battered by monstrous forces from beyond the stars and beneath the earth. They reeled around as though drunk and struggled not to fall to the ground. For one, it cost everything, for the rest the final cost was still to be paid.

* * * *

A soft wind preceded a mysterious wraith-like presence into the glade. Rather than stopping clods of earth in mid-air, Truth Seeker's mission was much more suited to her nature this time.

She drew tiny motes of dust and shards of leaves inwards and whipped them together in a gyre of magic and intent. A seemingly solid body with short dark hair and lustrous golden skin that glowed as though lit from within stepped on the anguished earth. She inhaled her first breath and laughed as it tickled her lungs.

Truth Seeker swirled among the depleted women and they gaped at her in wonder. She radiated calm, at odds with the bludgeoning noise around them and her perfect nakedness seemed lost on their overtaxed senses. She smiled and gently caressed each one with a warm and soft hand as though telling them they had done well and could rest now. A touch to the shoulder or cheek, and they crumpled to the ground.

She approached Chalone last and studied her for a moment. They shared the same tilt of their head. She leaned forward a little and acting on instinct alone, kissed her full on the lips. Chalone collapsed unconscious before any response to the sensual caress crossed her startled mind.

With the first part of her task complete, Truth Seeker turned to the column of light. She touched the uneven scar where Pirelle had sealed the breach. After her hand passed over it, nothing remained to mar its impeccable surface. Unaffected by the deafening roar she passed through the solid barrier. The Sphere shuddered at her otherworldly touch but could not refuse her. She embraced it and shared its brief memories. Although they came from the same creator, she was incomprehensible to it, and it couldn't gain entry into her newly formed consciousness. That was not, nor would ever be, the nature of their relationship.

Satisfied the Sphere was firmly bound within the Earthblood fire, and no harm had been done by Jalemi's interference, Truth Seeker passed out of the light and returned her attention to the women.

They remained forgetful within their dreamless sleep, and it was her third task to see that they remained forgetful. She reached into their minds and erased all knowledge of the Circle from the moment they stepped over the ring of leaves and walked toward the gnarled tree. She lingered over Vian, making sure her information gleaned from the Elementals was erased as well.

The wounded earth surrounding the Earthblood fire also drew her attention but she didn't have the power or the knowledge to return it to sleep or soothe its smoldering heart. She gently relocated the sleeping women away from its dangerous heat to the edge of the glade. With a satisfied nod at her handiwork, she decomposed her flimsy body and drifted up into the night sky.

Floating above the tiny world she pondered it for a moment, her mood pensive. Participating in the ritual had fashioned consequences far beyond that which bound her to the women or to the fate of the Sphere. She felt confused and euphoric from her first encounter with the consciousness of others. She knew so little and had so much to learn before she fulfilled her purpose.

Then in a startling shift of mood, she exalted. All sorts of emotions trilled through her like the pure sound of a bellsong. The Gallery was vast, and the worlds beyond even more so. She had Time enough to explore them all.

Before she followed her desires, one last compulsion from Sebenesh sent her back to the planet. She landed in the tiny glade, sought out Chalone among the still bodies, and hovered next to her. Chalone's deep even breathing fascinated her.

Another gentle caress, this time with her mind, tied a spark of her essence to Chalone's spirit and she was truly free of obligation. With a carefree flick of her will, she passed from mortal knowledge.

* * * *

High clouds blew across the sky and blotted out the moon. At the edge of the forest shadows, the unquiet earth heaved and buckled one last time. Sticks and leaves parted as the four Elementals slowly emerged from the forest floor. They entered the glade and passed by the unconscious bodies laid out on the ground. They approached the column of solid light without fear. It had no power to harm them now.

"This is worthy of remembering," Earth boomed emphatically over the constant noise, and leaned toward its heat as though to ease its ancient limbs.

Air lingered behind, fluttered above the unconscious women. "They do not remember," it said, curiosity whipping along the ends of its pennant tail.

"They do not need to. Their task is complete," Earth answered as surely as if Sebenesh had whispered in its ear. "The land remembers. It is still wounded."

"Is this what we are here to do?" Water pondered and then retreated from the Earthblood fire as tiny rivulets began to trickle down its frozen bulk. "Heal the land?"

Such questions involved the future, and therefore were enigmas to the Elementals until they were answered and became the present. They were here, now, and they resolved to try.

Fire moved as close to the column as it dared. "They are irrelevant," it said, dismissing the women. It circled the column of fire and returned to the others. "This is worth remembering."

All four Elementals contemplated the column and its containment of the Sphere, Water from a slightly more distant vantage point.

"Vian is valiant," Air said, still fascinated by the mortals at the edge of the glade.

They focused on Vian for a moment and agreed. "She is worth remembering too," they footnoted.

They combined their essences and remembered the Earthblood fire's deed, and Vian's courage, into the land. The earth responded and sighed in relief. It heaved one final tremor, settled, and grew still. The raging lava around the base of the column cooled and crusted over to become not-quite-ordinary stone.

"This noise is irritating. It does not need to be remembered," Earth said in a mildly aggrieved tone of voice. The sonic vibrations were shaking loose grains of sand from its bear-phant solidity.

"No, it does not," Air concurred and shredded the thunderous sound into tiny pieces that squeaked once or twice and fled into silence.

The Elementals left the column of light and as they passed over the boundary of raked leaves, Air spoke one last time.

"This Circle is unbroken but it has tried them grievously."

"Yes," the rest agreed. "We will do what we can."

A desert sirocco from a continent away answered them and blew languidly around the glade. It gathered up the raked leaves and warmed them in its currents, then broke apart into tiny whirlwinds and faded away.

As the moon slowly fell beneath the western horizon, warm

drifts of old leaves and a silent pearlescent column of light snugly blanketed the fallen bodies of twenty women.

* * * *

A tiny vole stuck its nose out of its burrow and twitched its whiskers. It had been quite a night and the creature had hours of work ahead to clean out the debris from its nest. A hunter's wings rustled somewhere in the trees and the vole scurried backwards. Perhaps the housecleaning could be left for another time.

* * * *

Slowly and painfully the women began to throw off Truth Seeker's healing mantle of unconsciousness. They sat up and plucked leaves off their garments in amazement. A few rose unsteadily to their feet, and helped others not so alert.

They saw, as if for the first time, the ominous stream of pure energy that punched up through the scudding clouds and down beneath their feet. They gathered together in bewilderment and awe.

"What is it?" a woman asked in shock as she distractedly tweaked another leaf from her windblown hair.

No one answered. What could they say?

"What happened?" someone else whispered into a long silence.

The more practically minded retrieved the overturned lanterns and re-lit them. The cheery swatches of yellow light illuminated two bodies lying still on the ground.

Pirelle snatched one of the lanterns and pushed through the women. She staggered toward Jalemi and Dajah and fell to her knees.

"They're both dead?" a voice above her asked, quivering in fright.

"No! No! No," Pirelle groaned and shook them. Dajah remained rigid and cold, but she cradled Jalemi in her strong arms, slowly rocking back and forth. Her broken words of comfort filled the dying night as the rest of the women gathered closer, confused and grieving.

Vian knelt and laid an arm across her shoulders. Pirelle violently shrugged her off and glared at her shocked expression.

Pirelle's face twisted into a mask of anguish. A sense of a betrayal she had no memory of roughened her voice. "What have you done?" she accused, as her voice broke into a thousand tears.

* * * *

Not long after the ritual began those waiting nearby saw the spear of fire erupt into the night sky. They were not unduly startled, strange things were wont to happen when a Circle as powerful as Vian's worked. Then the earth shuddered and great flashes of light lit up the trees brighter than sunlight. They abandoned their preparations for the feast, and some of them cautiously walked to the edge of the Circle to investigate.

The glamour of sleep and forgetfulness Truth Seeker used to mask her activities extended further than she'd intended and although changed in purpose, its potency remained. No one could move any further into the glade than the edge of the tree line. Incantations and technology both proved useless.

As Truth Seeker faded from the Mortal Realm and the Elementals returned from whence they came, the interdiction fell away. People rushed into the glade where the column of light shone balefully on their faces bringing their hasty feet to a voluntary halt.

Pirelle still knelt with Jalemi held tight against her breast. She half-crooned, half-mourned to her from deep in her throat. The rest of the women staggered about dazed, or collapsed into the arms of their rescuers.

Someone finally convinced Pirelle to let Jalemi go so that others could care for her. She followed blindly as they carried her away. No one else left the glade until they had all asked the same question there was no answer to.

By the time Vian had replied to that same question with the same three words over and over, her temper grew short. She told them she still didn't know, and it was time to leave. Time to attend their fallen.

Dajah's body was reverently taken up and borne away. Some women lay on stretchers and were carried from the field, others walked out on their own. Pools of light surrounded them all as they slowly moved toward the village and the solace of home.

Only Vian remained in the darkness to watch and ware. She glared at the strange column that had so inexplicably replaced the old tree. Up or down, there was no end to it.

Scalding tears spilled unnoticed from her eyes and burned down her ravaged face. She wanted to fall to her knees, beat the earth and scream. To release the torrent of anguish and rage that pounded against her ribcage. Only the force of her will held her body upright.

She turned from the fire, and looked around the glade. Nothing. Nothing to explain why death and injury came among them. Her shoulders sagged. Someone walked through the old dry leaves and stood near her. Without looking she knew who it was, as she'd known all along who it would be.

"Oh Sister of my Heart," Lila whispered. "What have we wrought?"

"We?" Vian asked, startled. She faced Lila and hastily scrubbed the tears from her eyes.

"Yes. We," Lila repeated firmly, and refrained from smiling at the look on Vian's face. She tucked her arm through Vian's and hugged it tightly to her. "Every one of us chose to participate. You weren't alone here."

"It feels like it at this moment," Vian said. She recalled her responsibilities and straightened up. "Is everyone taken care of?"

"Yes," Lila said and stepped back. Although the moment of physical closeness had passed, another kind of closeness had been acknowledged.

"You asked me what happened." Vian sighed deeply and shook her head. She looked at the column of light again. Within its confines bolts of pure white actinic light continuously dissipated and reformed into a scintillating display of energy. "I wish I knew."

On an impulse she moved closer to the column. Its potency throbbed against her ear bones, almost audible.

"What happened to Dajah?" she shouted. "What happened to Jalemi? What did You ask me to do that cost us such a price? I deserve an answer!" She drew a deep breath. "Dajah deserves an answer." She wrung her hands inside one another and looked forlornly around the glade. The wall she'd erected around her grief crumbled away. "I don't know what to do next."

She reached out to the column as though her hand retained a memory of what she'd accomplished. A lightning-fast spark of fire snapped at her outstretched fingers and burned her. The sacredness of the Circle longer protected her.

Defeat surrounded her spirit like a dark winged harbinger of wretchedness and despair. Burned and heartbroken, she collapsed. Lila caught her and gently cradled her blistered hand.

Lila's heart ached for the anguish in Vian's. Her love couldn't mend everything, but if any good did come out of this night, it was that Vian finally recognized that love as well.

"It's time to leave," Lila said. "There's nothing more you can do." She curved a supportive arm around Vian. "Come home."

* * * *

The Sphere knew fear.

Truth Seeker's systematic examination of its consciousness accomplished that. When the column attacked Vian and burned her, a tremor troubled the oasis of calm it had wrapped around itself. It stirred for a moment and reached out to taste the disturbance. Not sensing any threat, it subsided.

It was learning patience too.

Chapter Ten

It seemed to Pirelle, Chalone, and Jalemi, that the morning air hung warily across their valley. It throbbed with the grief of their unanswerable questions like a sour wound. Even the songs of the birds, usually so cheery, sounded hushed.

They sat out on their balcony, drawn together by mutual need. Each wanted to share the thoughts in her heart but not knowing exactly where to begin.

* * * *

Fear of what would haunt her dreams kept Pirelle awake and pacing through the broken ends of the night.

The accusation she'd flung at Vian echoed in her mind. Her instincts told her there was a kind of truth to it, but she couldn't remember what. Nor did she have a logical reason for the ominous anger that roiled in her stomach. She brooded at the far edge of the balcony with her back resolutely to the fiery beam of light emanating from the valley below and struggled to stay awake.

* * * *

Chalone rested in an easy chair trying to keep her exhaustion at bay. She'd slept fitfully and awoke feeling bereft in body and spirit.

She'd been right about the Circle, everything had changed. All the patterns she sensed so clearly had shifted out of their comfortable grooves. She felt cut off from the security of her certainties.

When she dared to reach out beyond the physical plane with her Practitioner senses, she found a perfect storm of confusing visions and unfamiliar emotions. Rather than face what that meant, she chose to remain veiled behind the truncated scope of her five bodily senses. At least until circumstances, or Vian, she amended wryly, shifted and she had no other choice but to act.

She watched Pirelle pace the length of the balcony, and knew it was useless to get up and keep her company.

* * * *

Jalemi lay on her side bundled in warm blankets, slowly recovering from her ordeal. Her joints had been placed back in their sockets and synthetic quickheals kept her from feeling them too much. There wasn't much more the Healers could do for her so they'd sent her home where she could recover quicker.

She doubted she'd ever recover. Even in the intense mid-morning heat she felt as though she could never be warm enough, as though the chill of the earth had permanently lodged in her bones.

She, too, had kept vigil with her thoughts throughout the remainder of the night but for different reasons than Chalone or Pirelle. A hunger for something she couldn't remember gnawed at her spirit like an addiction. Frustrated in her attempts to identify it, it none-the-less kept her mind off just how much she hurt, in spite of the Healers ministrations.

She looked from Pirelle to Chalone. They were immersed in their thoughts and wouldn't speak unless prompted to. She chose Pirelle because her sister's sullen behavior annoyed her more than Chalone's withdrawal. It went against her policy of not encouraging Pirelle's emotional outbursts, but many things changed with the dawn of this new day.

"Out with it, Pirelle. You've been brooding like a thundercloud all morning. If you don't start talking you'll become unbearable and I'll have to hit you." Not the most tactful way of starting a conversation but effective. Pirelle rounded on her and she recoiled at the deep lines of sorrow and shattered illusions that etched the usual softness of her sister's face.

* * * *

Pirelle had never fully confronted the intense darker side of her emotions before. Dajah's death tore at her so painfully that she pushed it to one side, denied that she too might have been responsible. She found it easier to blame Vian.

"Vian knew," she said. "I know she knew! Even before the Circle began. She knew what was going to happen!" A wild vehemence gleamed in her eyes.

The accusation roused Chalone. "Vian couldn't have known

Dajah was going to die. If she did, do you think she would've gone ahead with the Circle?"

"She told us as much when she asked us to join the Circle. That she'd use us all no matter what. You remember that conversation, don't you?" Pirelle said, forgetting that Chalone had a very good reason for recalling that night.

"Those weren't her exact words, but yes, I remember," Chalone said. Reminding Pirelle probably wouldn't have any effect on her present mood. "I also remember seeing Vian's face when we found Jalemi and Dajah. She was devastated."

"She must have known how dangerous it was," Pirelle said obstinately.

"Of course it was dangerous," Chalone said exasperated. "Working in a Circle is never risk-free. Unfortunately, unless one of us has a miraculous recovery, we'll never know, will we?"

"Vian didn't know," Jalemi said quietly, enabling Chalone and Pirelle to step back from the harsh words they were about to utter and later regret. The vicious red haze around them dissipated.

"She told me before the ritual she didn't know what was going to happen," Jalemi paused reflectively. "She wasn't worried, just focused. She has no more idea about what happened than any of us." Before Pirelle could think of anything to counter her words, she awkwardly raised herself on one elbow. "I think no one is supposed to remember. This amnesia is very selective. It doesn't make any sense unless it's supposed to be this way."

Pirelle snorted derisively, but Jalemi ignored her. Moving around to settle her aching joints into the least uncomfortable position, she gathered her newly formed thoughts together. "To begin with, some amazing things did happen." She nodded toward the column of light. Even in the heat of the day, it shimmered brighter than all the stone, steel, and glass of the city beyond. "What if we'd known about that beforehand and what it's for? I can feel its presence from here."

"We all can," Pirelle stated the obvious. "They can probably feel it on the other side of the world!" Even those not trained as Practitioners were aware of the impact the column had on the land.

"That's not what I mean," Jalemi amended. "I don't know why, but I can feel it calling to me from here. I can't imagine what it would feel like up close." Her voice faded, and she savored the thought as though it were the caress of a fine wine on her palate. "Anyway," she said, shaking her thoughts free of her inner musings.

"We were all there therefore we all had something to do with it. Not just Vian. I can only remember walking into the Circle and seeing that withered old tree. Then, it mysteriously transformed into the beam of sparkling light we see before us now." She looked directly at it. "There's something more, hidden inside. I can feel it."

Chalone thought she understood what bothered Jalemi. "So, if we'd known what we were dealing with, we might not have done anything, or even refused Vian's invitation?"

"I wasn't talking about that." Jalemi laughed briefly. "I was thinking more of interacting with the power that created it." She paused thoughtfully. "What if we had known beforehand?" she asked. "What might have happened? Maybe we'd've influenced the outcome, endangered it in some way," she spoke obtusely about her growing obsession as though that might trigger a memory, an awareness, but reluctant to name it openly in front of Chalone and Pirelle.

They were used to her circumlocutory way of talking about power, a personality quirk, they all had them, and thought nothing of it.

"You're talking hypothetically," Pirelle said, feeling the conversation had slipped away from the object of her scorn and refusing to accept that hypotheticals were all they had. "Dajah is dead, and something horrible happened to you. You can barely walk or move your arms. Until I hear anything that convinces me otherwise, I'm holding Vian responsible."

The balcony couldn't contain her vehement pacing any longer and she stormed down the stairs and through the garden, deliberately turning her back on the column of light again.

My dear sister," Jalemi said with some fondness. "She certainly knows how to make an exit." She shrugged, careful of her aching shoulders. "At least I got her to stop pacing. I'm not about to go after her and neither are you," she said as Chalone stirred in her chair. "She'll realize how unfair she's being and come back, eventually."

Chalone subsided. Jalemi was right, but she worried none-the-less. She worried about her relationship with Vian, what the strange column of light was for, where Pirelle was going, what could help Jalemi's aches and pains, where the wind in the Gallery came from. Her list went on and on until she had to stop herself from adding the fate of the universe to it.

It was enough that they had their days of mourning and a

funeral to prepare for. She sighed and gave Jalemi's hand a gentle squeeze before going inside.

* * * *

Angry at herself, the world, Chalone and Jalemi, and most especially Vian, Pirelle stalked through the woods toward the foothills of the southern mountains. The trail degenerated from well-tended to narrow and unkempt before she ran out of anger to propel her along.

A little rill of water ran along beside the trail for a while and she stopped to bathe her feet and hands in its welcomed coolness. She looked at the trees marching up the steep hillside above the trail and marveled at how ordinary everything looked. A part of her expected the outer world to match the shattered one she carried within. Before her thoughts carried her any further down that road, she hurried to her feet and strode along the track as though she had an urgent appointment somewhere else.

She focused on her surroundings, hoping to leave her troubles behind her. It had worked many times in the past and by the time she returned from her long walks enough time had passed for the trouble to have resolved itself. Usually. She was determined that this time would be no different. Eventually her sleepless night caught up with her and she chose a destination that would give her more than a few hours alone.

At the end of the trail stood a snug dry cabin she'd built when she was younger and claimed for hers. She'd conveniently forgotten that quite a few of her friends helped her, including Jalemi and Chalone. She wasn't overly fond of adventuring within the Gallery, an anomaly in her culture, and they all respected her need to call the place her own. As soon as she saw the cabin her energy field shifted from murky brown to an earthier lighter shade.

The cabin's solid safety eased her bruised spirit and inspired her to start a belated spring cleaning. Her sturdy oak larder had won the battle against an impertinent rodent, with only minor damage to a single corner. The creek that ran down the mountainside nearby tasted pure and clean. She felt pleased that the essentials of life remained intact.

Her housekeeping chores burned off her restless energy and she finally relaxed enough to sleep. She lay down and stared at the walls of her sanctuary. Although she hadn't found a resolution for her inner turmoil, the physical exercise distanced her from its immediacy. She thought about returning home and making up with Chalone and Jalemi in the morning, but they would probably want her to do the same with Vian. It had taken her this long to find a voice for her anger, and she wasn't about to let go of it or admit that she might be mistaken. Not just yet. She was even further from accepting that Vian had finally fallen from grace, that she was mortal. It was too hard and too soon for her to bear. She closed her eyes, and for a while sleep freed her from the vision of Dajah and Jalemi laying pale and still in the glade.

The cabin had a scattering of projects that needed her attention but the next day wore on. She grew bored and having done sufficient introspecting the night before took up a pick and shovel to keep from breaking something in sheer restless frustration. There was one more task she needed to do.

She chose a site on the gently sloping hillside at the hallowed ground where their dead were interred, cleared a large circle turf, and began to delve into the rich earth. With every shovelful she piled to one side, her anger penetrated deeper into her spirit, growing stronger and more defined, any lingering guilt and self-doubts extinguished under its weight.

In a few hours she excavated the circular pit that would be used to return Dajah's mortal remains to the earth. She leaned back on her shovel, satisfied on many levels. It was time to dress for the funeral.

* * * *

Eventide, the end of the day, the time for the dead to return home fell across the hillside where the funeral was to take place. A Returning Ceremony required that, as much as possible, all the people present at the moment of death be at the burial. Everyone came, except Pirelle.

Dajah's friends and family arrived and gathered around the pit that had mysteriously appeared in exactly the right place. Chalone, helping a crippled Jalemi, caught Vian's attention and gestured up the hill to where Pirelle stood like an otherworldly sentinel. Wisps of cloud blew in from the east heralding a storm.

Vian left Lila's side and met Pirelle slowly descending the ridge. She held out her hands in a gesture of conciliation but Pirelle pushed them away.

"I'm here for Dajah," she said. "She is a loss to us all and we are here to mourn that loss together, that's all."

It was no more than Vian expected. A lifetime of easy-going complacency had finally ended, and although Vian's feelings were hurt, she felt relieved that Pirelle was at last showing some spirit. Vian smiled to herself. She could outwait anyone and anything, Pirelle was no match for her.

* * * *

A damp breeze blew the misty clouds down the side of the hill. Whispered conversations died, and everyone drew closer in sorrowful expectation.

Dajah's shrouded body lay on a bier next to the pit. Vian gathered the women from the Circle closer. They were Dajah's companions at the moment of her death and custom required they speak first.

Others gathered behind them. Some were crying openly, while others mourned in their hearts. They all loved her and her death created an absence in their lives that would never fully ease.

Vian took a deep breath to speak the formal words that would begin the Ceremony. She willed away the tears that closed her throat.

"We who love this woman, return her to the Earth for transformation and change. We do this to honor her life among us, and ask that she be restored to us at the time and place of her Spirit's choosing."

The women of the Circle moved as one and took up the edge of the funeral cloth. With infinite tenderness they lowered Dajah into the ground. Her body looked so small and helpless surrounded by the cold earth. Although they knew her Spirit would return among them, they grieved deeply as they bore witness to this final stage of her passage through the Mortal Realm.

Each woman descended into the pit with her and spoke a few quiet words of farewell. They placed gifts beside the shroud to honor the connection they'd had with her. Some took longer than others but no one minded. All the rituals of their lives were sacred and none more so than those that revered Birth and Death and Rebirth.

An inconstant rain fell in ghostly swathes across the burial field. No one minded that either, it seemed appropriate. Evening gave way to night before all the goodbyes were said and only the original women of the Circle remained at the graveside. They replaced the earth over Dajah's body and tamped the last sod gently back into place. With the passage of a single season, no indication of Dajah's mortal remains would be visible and yet all would know where she rested. It was their way.

The rain began to fall in earnest as though to cleanse and seal the ritual. The newly turned earth smelled so clean and fresh that some of the women smiled through their tears. They joined hands, right over left.

The formal words to end the ritual begun such a few short days ago remained unsaid. Eyes met across the circle and smiles trembled. Dajah was with them, and they spoke as one. "Our Circle is open but unbroken. In Spirit we come together and with Peace in our hearts we part. It is accomplished."

Chapter Eleven

Jalemi dreaded going to sleep. Her dreams haunted her. She lay her head on her pillow and hoped in vain they would stay away. It was always the same dream. She reached for a shining prize she desired with all her heart, but a burning fire swept out of nowhere and destroyed everything. She retreated terrified but the fire always burned her to the bone. The pain would go on and on until it reached her lungs and she couldn't breathe anymore.

* * * *

One night Pirelle sat by her bedside when she struggled to wakefulness. She came back from the bathroom and Pirelle handed her a pungent tea, brewed bitter and thick. Jalemi added spoonfuls of honey to the mixture in hopes of making it a bit more palatable but the fumes alone made her eyes water. She set the cup down on her bedside table and flopped backward onto the covers.

"This doesn't seem to be helping," she said. "I don't think I'll ever feel safe going to sleep again."

They discussed her nightmares which obviously had something to do with the ritual. Like the Healers, they could only hope that time would eventually resolve whatever disturbed Jalemi's dreams.

"Let's talk about something else," Jalemi said. "What are you and Chalone doing at the Archives? The only time I get to see either of you is when you're babysitting me."

Pirelle settled herself comfortably on the end of the bed. "Well," she said. "We're doing research!" Jalemi's expression was priceless. Pirelle laughed out loud, glad she'd shocked Jalemi into showing interest in something other than the column of light and the content of her nightmares. "Chalone finally got around to telling Vian what happened to her in the Gallery, so Vian sent us off to find the Skane."

Jalemi gaped and sat up abruptly. "Wait a minute. Back up there. You're working with Vian? What happened? Chalone, I can understand, but why you?" She paused, but before Pirelle could draw a breath, she continued. "The Skane? Who are they?"

"That's what I said," Pirelle agreed. "Remember the stories they told us when we were children? I volunteered. Chalone needed another pair of hands and eyes, and I happen to have a set. I decided to put my feelings about Vian aside for the time being." Pirelle finished with a finality that terminated any further questioning on that topic.

Jalemi lay back down and smiled reminiscently. "I remember something Grandma Lila said about mysterious creatures being created to safeguard the Gallery." Lila wasn't their blood grandmother but she was Chalone's, and as they did so many of their childhood possessions, the three of them shared Lila.

"I was more interested in the adventures of Gorgoral the Sand-Swimmer," Jalemi said, remembering other tales from their childhood. Pirelle picked up a pillow and threw it at Jalemi. With Chalone, they'd argued many times over who would play Gorgoral, who would be Nolomi the Warrior woman, who almost always foiled Gorgoral's dastardly plots, and who would be Welf, Nolomi's faithful companion.

Jalemi ducked the pillow. "There's a point to all this?"

"It seems there's a grain of truth in all those stories."

"Gorgoral and Nolomi were lovers?" Jalemi asked, all wide-eyed and innocent.

Pirelle ignored her. "Apparently the Skane were a race of beings created to take care of the Gallery. There are so few references to them that even the Archive ECHO had trouble resurrecting anything, but Chalone got some leads from a few of the things the ECHO suggested. It's scary how those two think alike."

"Chalone is working with the Archive ECHO?" Jalemi asked, even more shocked than she had been about Pirelle working with Vian.

"Shocking, I know," Pirelle agreed. "It appears that the moon will rise tomorrow rather than the sun! Vian was at her convincing best, she twisted Chalone's arm, blackmailed her really, until she graciously agreed."

"I cannot imagine what Vian had on her," Jalemi said thoughtfully, wishing she had been present for that conversation. "So what happens when you find the Skane?"

"First we have to find out if they really exist." Pirelle held up her hand and folded her thumb down. "Then figure out how to contact them." She folded a finger down. "Then tell them that something is happening with the Gallery." Another finger fell. "And finally, convince them to look into it." Pirelle stared at her single raised finger in disgust.

"How are you supposed to do all that?" Jalemi asked, suitably impressed, although her mouth hinted at a smile.

"I don't know. All we have so far is a myth that says they chose to live on a world outside the Gallery rather than in the corridors."

"Where?"

"Here," Pirelle said and punched the bed in exasperation.

"Where here?" Jalemi looked directly at her straight faced.

"Again, we don't know," Pirelle said, so frustrated that she didn't notice Jalemi's teasing. "We don't even know what they look like, or if they still exist. But Chalone's convinced that something had to happen for the myth to be created in the first place."

"Well, that's a start I suppose," Jalemi said, scooping up the discarded pillow and throwing it back at Pirelle. "It sounds like it'll keep you and Chalone out of trouble. Temporarily at least!" She settled into the bed. "Good luck."

Pirelle noted that Jalemi had given up teasing her, which showed that she wasn't as oblivious as she'd pretended to be. Whatever shifted Jalemi's attention away from the terror in her dreams was alright by her.

"Chalone thrives on this, in spite of being at the Archives so much. I've never seen her like this before. She's almost, almost driven!"

Jalemi rolled over. "Our Chalone? Driven? She's spent way too much time with Vian. It's just as well they're not in a relationship anymore," she said irreverently. "Driven by what?"

"She's afraid of what she saw in the Gallery, of what it might mean. More so than she is about the ritual, and we both know how much that disturbed her. She can take a few seemingly random facts and make sense out of them. When we're in-crystal, she's making one intuitive leap after another. I can only follow along. I'm probably too practical to think like that."

"Huh!" Jalemi snorted. "Too impatient more likely. It's a family trait."

Pirelle absently nodded in agreement. The nightmare shadows had finally faded from Jalemi's eyes. "How are you feeling now?"

"Tired." Jalemi sighed. "Exhausted. I don't know how long I can keep this up."

"I know," Pirelle said sympathetically. "Something will change soon. It always does."

"You sound just like Chalone," Jalemi teased.

"None-the-less, true," Pirelle said mortally wounded. "And, I take umbrage at your earlier comment about being impatient!"

"Umbrage!" Jalemi snorted. "Isn't it time you were asleep? Don't you have to get up early and save the world or something?"

That, of course, was too much for Pirelle to take lying down. The two of them wrestled and threw pillows around the room like they used to do when they were children. Before long the air was full of feathers and muffled laughter. Trying not to wake Chalone was as much fun as not waking their parents had been long ago.

Jalemi didn't have any stamina so Pirelle won by default. The featherdown storm passed and they shook most of the debris onto the floor. Their heads lay together on the sole surviving pillow and soon the only sound emanating from the room was their slow deep breathing.

* * * *

Chalone stood outside the bedroom door a while longer then turned to go back to bed. Jalemi's screams woke her, and out of habit she got up to make sure that everything was alright. She arrived just before the pillow fight and then quite sensibly refrained from entering the battle-zone.

She was glad Jalemi felt well enough to tease Pirelle, but not so happy about what she overheard about herself, even if it was true. She wouldn't have used the word 'driven' though. *Dedicated perhaps?* Dedicated to using technology rather than her other skills, which she mistrusted because they would lead her to a place she had no desire to explore, fearful of what they might reveal.

She rerouted to the kitchen in search of comfort food for her sorely bruised feelings, and returned to bed with a tub of Pirelle's favorite ice cream.

* * * *

Even though Chalone and Vian severed the Sphere's initial link with Jalemi, the connection was so deeply embedded that they only managed to bar the Sphere from gaining direct control over her. That would not have been possible if she hadn't been, at least initially, a willing accomplice. That willingness allowed the Sphere to maintain a narrow tensile link into her mind.

It learned at an exponential rate, causing her nightmares. The thoughts, sensations, and images it seized from her mind, awake and sleeping, had no order to them, and not knowing what it needed to decipher, or judge, or edit, it accepted and integrated everything.

It used the twisted morass of information to create a deformed framework that connected all of it together. Thought patterns evolved that grew into a separate sophisticated consciousness. It extrapolated from the events of the Circle and understood how powerful it could become. It raged inside its Earthblood prison and vowed to be free to take revenge on all who had initiated its capture.

Now it could think for itself, it devised a plan to manipulate Jalemi into fulfilling its desire for freedom. It had the perfect lure to which she was already hooked, the Sphere itself.

* * * *

Jalemi's nightmares stopped once the Sphere evolved sufficiently, for which everyone, including Jalemi was thankful. Pirelle and Chalone ceased watching over her like a pair of broody hens, and spent more and more of their time at the Archives.

She felt a bit abandoned by them, but the voice of reason convinced her that it was for the best. There was great work to be done and she needed to be alone, alone to solve the riddle of the ritual that killed Dajah. Her success would be the first step on her path to power within their community. She never thought to question the internal voice that agreed with her so readily.

Eventually she walked to the Hall of Lights and resumed some of her duties, occasionally slipping out of character as the Sphere gained more and more control. Her friends and co-workers, Pirelle and Chalone among them, attributed it to the stress of her injuries. She agreed. It was as good a reason as any for the drastic change in her behavior and the patterns of her everyday life. All the while her unseen hitchhiker absorbed every detail voraciously.

A nameless craving ached inside her as she walked through the woods to stand for hours in front of the column of light. The more she focused on her obsession with the ritual, the calmer and happier she felt. The Sphere was content with her progress and allowed her that one obsession to occupy her personality.

It was about to learn that there was more to some mortals than it realized.

* * * *

Vian called on Jalemi one day to see how her healing progressed. Chalone and Pirelle's reports about the nightmares had her concerned.

As Jalemi ushered her into the living room, she felt surprised to note that Jalemi was unaccountably talkative and able to keep up her end of the conversation without any trouble. Not what she'd been led to expect at all.

The Elementals hovered politely just below the window near where Vian sat. They'd taken to spending a lot more time with her since the Circle. They gave her no explanation, it was not their nature to divulge their motivations. She was glad of their companionship as she organized her responses to the triple threat she sensed looming on the horizon.

Suddenly Jalemi blushed and shook in a violent spasm. Distracted by the unknown energy presence of the Elementals, the Sphere let her slip free of the coercive binding it had been building around her mind.

Jalemi saw what she had become and how easily the Sphere manipulated her. She forced the shame, and her sense of Self roused by it, into a tiny spark of consciousness and hid it away in the deepest darkest corner of her spirit.

The Sphere reestablished the shackles to her mind and the seizure passed in an instant. She resumed her usual mien and continued her conversation with Vian as though nothing had happened.

Vian saw the flush, and was about to say something, when the Elementals distracted her by suddenly disappearing from her awareness.

They'd become aware of the Sphere's link with Jalemi and immediately rushed to the glade to make sure it was still securely bound within the column of light. Once satisfying themselves that all was well, they dismissed Jalemi as too weak to be a threat to anyone else, except herself.

Vian shrugged off their erratic behavior and took up her end of the conversation. On the spur of the moment, she invited Jalemi to come to the special council meeting she'd convened.

Jalemi considered it, but attending what would surely turn out to be a pointless circus had no appeal for her. If the Sphere had been less distracted by the Elementals, it might have forced her to go.

Vian was surprised at Jalemi's refusal. She left soon thereafter, feeling vaguely unsatisfied with her visit.

* * * *

The Sphere realized that Jalemi was not as predictable, weak, or that its hold on her as firm as it had presumed. It would not risk another lapse in its concentration and let her escape again.

It manipulated her dreams one last time.

She dreamed that she rose from her bed, dressed, and walked through the village and the woods as though she were invisible. She walked across the leaf-strewn earth and stood closer to the mysterious column of light than she ever had in her waking moments.

She watched as her hand, almost of its own accord reached out to touch the column. A great commotion erupted behind her, almost waking her, but this time she knew if she stayed asleep, she would reach the prize unscathed. Then she heard Pirelle desperately calling her name, followed by a peculiar sound like cracking ice and ringing bells that came from all around her.

Such a strange dream.

Chapter Twelve

Built within the plateau at Glass Canyon to the east of the Hall of Lights, the Archive accommodated the collection of stories, myths, travelogues, histories, and other information from the worlds of the Gallery. Most were accessible to the general public, some were not.

Pirelle walked into the suite of rooms she and Chalone shared in the complex. The latest experimental in-crystal software had recently been installed, as well as a separate eating nook and private bathroom which were necessities rather than luxuries. Their schedule was such that they made far more use of the latter than the former.

Chalone lay in her bio-chair, already deeply meshed in with the latest batch of research crystals. Her snug fitting headset designed to her specific requirements linked her to the tiny crystal shard she was viewing.

Pirelle checked the overhead screen that monitored her mental and psychic states. Occasionally her eyelids fluttered and her breathing pattern subtly changed. Usually her screens went haywire when she was in-crystal, not any more, not since the Circle. Chalone defended the changes, calling them a result of pure research.

Pirelle thought otherwise but kept her opinion to herself. Chalone was right about one thing, everything was changing and those closest to Pirelle changing the most.

Pirelle settled her long frame into her own couch and instructed her terminal to link into whatever Chalone was viewing. It was a painless process and perfectly safe, but that didn't mean she had to like it.

The room around her disappeared.

* * * *

The sand left behind by a long gone river at the bottom of Glass Canyon produced glass renowned not only for its toughness but for its unusual beauty. It shimmered like a rainbow when held up to the light of the sun, and the most delicate of goblets would not shatter when dropped onto a bare stone floor.

Huge sheets of glass were electronically activated and then cut into smaller and smaller wafers to make memory crystals, used among many other things, as information storage units by much of the global ECHO infrastructure, including the Archive.

Most of the rooms in the Archive opened out onto the canyon wall, and flawed sheets of uncut memory glass were used as windows. Depending on the time of day and the angle of the sun, the startling colors from the hardy plants and animals and the canyon walls made for spectacular viewing.

A few of the rooms in the section where Pirelle and Chalone were housed had dedicated in-crystal research equipment and required specialized training to use. For most people, standardized head sets were provided in the public areas. The ECHO Archivists used their implants.

It was highly unlikely anyone using the Archives would actually meet one of the ECHOs whose duty shifts required interaction with the public for long enough to actually strike up a conversation. With few exceptions they remained as reclusive as all ECHOs the world over. One of those exceptions was Liesha, the current Head Archivist.

The ECHOs, an acronym for Enhanced Cybernetic Habitat Operators, ran the global communications and information infrastructure. The mysterious properties of the Gallery rendered the Hall of Lights the only organization beyond their reach. Although they were not a ruling class as such, they came close to it by default.

* * * *

Pirelle appeared in-crystal and immediately began to sweat in the humid air. She stumbled forward as her body adjusted to the lighter gravity, which may or may not have been her imagination, no one else ever mentioned the sensation. A sickly sweet scent of tropical flowers overwhelmed her, and rotted leaf mulch slid out from beneath her boots. Dense rainforest surrounded her. Sunlight probably shone on the jungle canopy above, but Pirelle couldn't see a single beam filtering through it.

Chalone knelt in front of an ancient weather-beaten stone tablet half-buried under eons of leaf litter. Concentration creased her forehead as if she could make the stone give up its secrets by the intensity of her gaze.

"Do you think you could turn the heat off?" Pirelle said, as she took her brightly colored bandana from around her neck and swiped it across her brow.

"Sorry," Chalone said without looking up. "Everything's preset." She ran her fingertip down a column of runes and consulted a small monitor next to her in frustration. Pirelle's boots caught her attention at last.

"Hello there," she said to the boots. "I didn't think you were going to make it in today."

"Having nothing better to do I decided you might need my invaluable assistance."

"How very generous of you," Chalone said, shoving some squished mulch against Pirelle's bright red boots, accidentally.

Pirelle grinned and looked at the stone tablet. "What have you found now? More dubious instructions on turning water into gold?"

Chalone slowly flexed her knees and stood up. She absently brushed her hair back off her damp forehead, a gesture that Pirelle found dangerously appealing. "Something that answers a lot of questions we didn't come here to ask," she said solemnly. "This tells how a 'Calling of the Earthblood Fire' ritual is done." She looked down at the ground for a moment as though delaying the news would deny its truth. "It describes what we were left with at the Circle."

Pirelle's face turned white, as did the energy around her. Chalone was unable to tell if it was with rage or fear. "It's supposed to be used in times of direst need," she said and took a metaphorical step back.

In the uncomfortable silence that followed, she could almost hear Pirelle's brain assimilating the information. After the longest of moments, Pirelle's color returned to normal and she resorted to her usual way of dealing with uncomfortable news.

"I didn't know that we had a direst need," she said, looking with unfocused eyes at the liana-strangled tree trunks among the forest undergrowth. "I wonder though, if Vian knew?"

"Leave Vian out of this." Chalone said abruptly. "She didn't know what happened, any more than any of us did, and you harping on it isn't going to change anything!" Chalone glared until Pirelle looked away and raised her hands in a conciliatory gesture. Chalone continued. "Perhaps we did have a direst need that no one knew about, and maybe Vian was told what she needed to know to begin the ritual and nothing more, just as Jalemi suggested."

"Well, if that's true, and I'm not saying it is," Pirelle said and held up her hand again as though expecting Chalone to interrupt. "I still want to know why the ritual was such a..."

Chalone did interrupt her. "I don't know," she exploded abruptly. "Why do you keep asking me? As though I have your answers for you? You think Vian confided in me? She never talked about her work, not to anyone, including me. Do you understand?" She shouted, more angry at herself for not being able to answer the questions Pirelle plagued her with, than at Pirelle herself. She walked a few paces away and deliberately relaxed her shoulders. She came back to Pirelle's side. "I don't have any answers for you. I wish I did. I'd like some myself."

"I know. I'm sorry," Pirelle said. She squeezed Chalone's hand briefly. It was the first time she'd initiated any physical contact with anyone except Jalemi since the ritual.

Chalone accepted the apology with a non-committal shrug and moved on. She looked down at the stone. "It's written in archaic Valderian. Here's what I've got so far. After the description of the Earthblood Fire ritual, it mentions some sort of 'key' within the Earthblood fire. Even with the help of the scanner I've only been able to decode about half of this gibberish." Chalone indicated the octagonal monitor at her feet, which abruptly disappeared having wrongly interpreted her gesture as a dismissal. The new in-crystal software wasn't perfect, as much as the ECHOS liked to promote it as being so.

Chalone made a pointed 'where is it?' gesture and the scanner reappeared with a single word apology tagged on top. "I'm fairly certain we called the Earthblood fire in our ritual." She glared at the note a moment longer. "It's basically a containment field to hold something very, very dangerous. Its not supposed to kill anyone, although it does warn against tampering with the energies without proper preparation and ritual controls."

"That's a big help to us now." Pirelle muttered sullenly.

"I know," Chalone said, hoping to restore their easy banter. Unfortunately, if she was honest with herself, Pirelle and Jalemi had changed while she felt stuck in limbo. Their three-way communications had altered without anything new to replace it. "There's also a passage about 'Taking the Key to the Shadowlands to Undo what was Cast Down'. Whatever that means."

Pirelle gazed absently at the stone for a moment. "Jalemi remembers what happened in her dream. I'm sure of it."

"I think so too. Maybe she's supposed to remember but can't."

"No," Pirelle said and sighed. "Something happened to her that wasn't in the plan." A silence fell between them. They'd both nursed Jalemi through too many nightmares to deny that truth.

"Well," Chalone finally said. "There's nothing we can do about it here. I suggest we leave the scanner to do its job and take a walk. See what else this crystal has to offer."

They left their uncomfortable conversation behind and squelched along a sodden path until they arrived at the in-crystal boundary where the tropical greenery ended abruptly and a gray nothingness took its place. Anyone stepping through it would wink out of the in-crystal environment and reappear at the Archives with a killer hangover.

"Remember when I dared you?" Chalone recalled.

Pirelle winced. It had taken her a week to recover. "I haven't forgiven you, and my vengeance will be sweet!"

"Ah Pirelle, what would I do without you?" Chalone asked only half-teasing.

"Let's not find out," Pirelle said, peering into the nothingness.

When they returned, the scanner had translated the remainder of the text. Chalone read it through and shook her head.

"I don't like this," she said ominously.

"What?" Pirelle asked from over her shoulder.

"It's about that direst need." Chalone frowned and shrugged Pirelle back a little bit. "It says, 'The Earthblood fire is powerful enough to shatter planets. It must be filtered through the life-force of the Circle participants in order to shape its purpose.' This reads like the Earthblood fire is conscious, a living entity."

"We were the filters," Pirelle said quietly.

"So much for free will," Chalone said, fully aware of the irony of the contradiction to their Practitioner teaching. "But I do understand why we couldn't know beforehand." She nodded obliquely at the tablet. "Would you have agreed if you'd known? If one of us had failed to hold the energy, we could have destroyed everything. Every living thing!"

"We obviously succeeded. So why did Dajah die? What happened to Jalemi?"

Pirelle spoke as though she meant to be heard far beyond the Mortal Realm.

"I will have an accounting one day! Whoever it is," she said, preempting any amendment Chalone might be tempted to make. "I will hold them to account."

Chalone acknowledged Pirelle's words with another shrug and

a nod of her head. At least Pirelle hadn't named Vian specifically. "Let's get out of here," she said.

* * * *

Tiny lights glowed brighter as the silent room reanimated their inert bodies. The ambient temperature rose high enough to warm blood and relax muscles. As always nutritious drinks were electronically delivered to the side tables beside each of the couches. As further protection against any obsessed clients trying to overextend themselves, the Archivists programmed the in-crystal links to hibernate until the drink had been consumed.

As though they had just woken up from a long sleep, Chalone and Pirelle slowly stirred in a duet of movements. They flexed their fingers and hands, ankles and backs. They removed the tight fitting headsets and opened their eyes, struggled up on one elbow, and reached for their revitalizing potions. They sat up slowly, gingerly stretching aching muscles and holding their heads in their hands.

"I can hear your bones creaking," Pirelle commented weakly.

Chalone silenced her with a look, and creaked across the sparsely furnished room to the huge picture window. She rubbed her neck and rotated her shoulders. A scrubby tree attached to the cliff-face on the opposite side of the canyon came into focus. Its tenacity, it's perfect balance of life and purpose amazed her. She turned away from the window and groaned as her muscles continued to protest. "I'm getting too old for this."

"Which 'this' are we talking about?" Pirelle asked as she looked out the window herself. The multi-hued stone striations running diagonally through the sandstone canyon walls had no power to move her.

"Being so tired," Chalone eventually answered.

"Maybe we could take the rest of the day off?" Pirelle headed to the kitchenette and refilled their glasses.

"We could do that." Chalone picked up one of the crystals set up for them to view and gestured toward Pirelle's couch.

"Humph." Pirelle addressed the ceiling. "Great idea, Pirelle. I think we'll do that right now, Pirelle." She took the crystal and looked at the notation on the protective covering.

"Interactive Only," she said and then frowned. "That's unusual for general research material."

"In most cases yes, but not the old tales," Chalone answered.

"This is the entire collection of 'Legends from the Seas of Sand'. I've sorted through hundreds of these old anthologies, and most of them are I.O. Some bright young thing probably thought they'd be easier to understand if you had to actually engage with the characters."

"I suppose so," Pirelle said dubiously. "Aren't you getting a little tired of viscerally experiencing every single earthquake, firestorm, and freezing mountain stream that's ever been recorded?" With a melodramatic sigh, Pirelle restored the crystal to Chalone's waiting hand and sank into her couch.

Chalone shook the crystal out of its protective sleeve and carefully inserted it into the I.O. slot. They put their headsets back on and made sure all the contacts were placed correctly. With a single blink an interminable grayness surrounded them. An arid wind instantly sucked the moisture out of their skins.

"Oh, no." Pirelle groaned and glared around her. "An Introduction? This could take hours."

"You're groaning an awful lot. Show some respect," Chalone said, smiling.

A disembodied voice begin to speak. "This crystal provides the total sum of knowledge about the legends of the Seas of Sand." Pirelle and Chalone looked at each other in surprise.

"Bright young thing, eh?" Pirelle chuckled. "You be respectful. I didn't know Vian was ever an archivist," she added thoughtfully.

"There's a whole lot we, me included, don't know about Vian. Now shush. I want to hear this."

The commentary continued on regardless. An Introduction didn't interact, it lectured. They sat down on the ethereal grayness and prepared for a long stay.

"The legends have been translated from oral histories. It is said that if the tales are ever written down, the Seas of Sand will be devoured. We have taken extraordinary measures to prevent any form of viewing that may be interpreted as readable because, as you know there is a grain of truth in all legends." Pirelle and Chalone could almost see Vian smiling as she spoke. They'd heard her say that very thing many times in the past.

Pirelle made a rude noise. "This reminds me of when we were back in school, and Vian lectured us on Ancient Protocols and Diplomatic Idioms." Chalone dug her elbow in Pirelle's ribs effectively shushing her again.

"Each tribe from the Seas of Sand took the stories and made them their own. Here, all versions of the same story have been compiled into a single narrative. Additional storylines can be engaged if required. Be aware that it is as easy to get lost in these stories of the Seas of Sand, as it is to get lost in the real Seas. Please do not hesitate to call on an Archive ECHO if you get into difficulties."

"Not if I can help it," Chalone muttered under her breath.

Pirelle pretended she hadn't heard. "This must've been set up as a teaching tool," she said. "I haven't heard that warning since I was a child."

* * * *

They sifted through the information the Introduction contained and none-the-wiser, prepared themselves for the shift into the central theme of the crystal. They held hands to ensure they wouldn't be deposited in different locations as a booming voice spoke. "How do you wish to experience the one hundred and seventy five separate references that make up the Legends of the Seas of Sand?"

"Chronologically," Chalone answered, drowning out Pirelle's groan.

Instantly the desert landscape that belonged to the wind and heat unfolded in front of them. Sand dunes crested one after the other as far as the eye could see, the constant wind sculpting and reshaping them. Not a blade of grass or tree marred their long graceful lines.

Both women were clothed in warm, finely woven sand colored cloaks that swept around their ankles and buttoned up the front, with deep hoods that could be drawn completely over their faces to keep out the sand and wind. Underneath, they wore heavy padded trousers and quilted jackets. Soft boots with wide soles for walking over the sand completed their ensemble.

They turned their backs to the gritty wind and saw a small oasis, their obvious destination. Primordial trees laden with fruits and scrubby berry bushes grew around the perimeter of a deep well, all vying for the precious water supply.

Their arrival triggered the program and the landscape flowed into motion. Evening fell in shades of violet and deep blue. From the other side of the oasis hollow clunking stock bells that comforted rather than frightened could be heard. The heat of the day quickly evaporated, and cold shadows gave way to a starlit night.

A campfire glowed and crackled fiercely in the ever-present wind. A circle of hooded figures hunched around it and one of them beckoned Chalone and Pirelle to sit among them. Without any fuss the people shuffled around to make room.

They sat in silence. Someone tossed the stubby end of a gnarled branch onto the fire and created an explosion of sparks that swept across the sand. Another, bent with age and so wizened that it was impossible to determine gender, stood up.

"We will begin the telling of the ancient tales." Chalone and Pirelle exchanged glances and opted for female.

The woman was an inspired story-teller. She created images with her words and flicked them into the firelight to give them form. Her voice split into many different characters as she faithfully portrayed the events of so long ago.

Every so often a battered horn goblet made its way around the circle. Chalone and Pirelle took courteous sips, grimaced under their cowls at the poisonous taste, and hurriedly passed it on. They did not want to miss a single moment of the Telling of the Creation of the Seas of Sand.

* * * *

Her name, she said, was Broon, and as she spoke she drew the firelight to her and wrapped the sparks and smoke around her like a shield. She flung her arms wide and disappeared. In her place the world of Argol hung above the flames.

"Our ancestors came from the other side of the Gallery," her disembodied voice said. "To an empty world with an empty sky. The moon had not yet been born."

Chalone and Pirelle looked at each other. This was new. The moon had always been there, celestial mechanics demanded it.

"It was not always so," Broon said from behind them. They looked up over their shoulders and the old woman grinned as she nudged them aside to make room for her.

"It was not always so," she said again. "This world turned quite well without its moon when the first travelers emerged from the Gallery."

She took a sip of the mysterious brew from the goblet, immediately spat the mouthful on the fire and then handed it on to Pirelle. The flames burned hot and consumed the image of the world. Pirelle and Chalone didn't even pretend to drink any more.

"The Seas of Sand were a sea of grass, but then a strange cloud descended from the sky and pulled the moon up from the ground. It left a big hole of course, and all the water drained into it. The land dried out and all the growing things died."

"We were all nomads we travelers, but thought to make our home here, and so an elder was chosen to go to the cloud and negotiate for our water."

"She walked through the last of the grass onto the sand. She walked for many days until she came to the great hole in the ground where the moon had risen. Water was pouring in from all the rivers and streams and the hole slowly filled up. She could see the cloud under the water, and leaped in to confront it."

The fire popped and crackled, and sparks flew away in the wind. Broon sat silent for so long that Pirelle felt tempted to lift up her cowl and make sure she was still alive. Broon patted her knee before she committed such a serious breach of etiquette.

"When she returned, she was changed. Her children did not know her, nor she them. She told the people that the cloud was a great race of beings who called themselves the Skane. They were sorry that the grass was dying, but they could not stop what they had created. Their need was greater than ours. Then she walked away from the people and was not seen alive again."

Another long silence ensued. Chalone knew how things worked in-crystal. She had to ask the right questions to move the story along.

"In what way had she changed?" she asked Broon.

"Not on the outside," Broon said. "The Skane had changed her on the inside. She was no longer one of the people."

Wrong question. Chalone thought for a minute and then tried again.

"What did she discover about the Skane?"

Broon nodded as though this was the right question. She answered at great length and in vivid detail. When she'd finished Chalone thanked her and pulled Pirelle to her feet.

"What's the matter?" Pirelle asked. "Doesn't that answer your question?"

Chalone ignored her. "End in-crystal sequence," she said.

Chapter Thirteen

Eventually, Pirelle managed to stand up although her knees buckled and she shook as though fevered. She made a hasty grab for the side of her couch until she could stand on her own, and shuffled toward the bathroom.

In a moment of sleep deprived insanity, she sat there and added up how long she'd been in-crystal. *Eighteen hours.* She had to be out of her mind!

Back in the dining area, the automated dispenser deposited a meal right in front of her she couldn't remember ordering. She slumped down on one of the chairs and ate voraciously in spite of her exhaustion. Chalone finally joined her and they stared out the window. Vacant reflections stared back at them from the dark glass.

"Feels like a storm coming," Chalone said to no one in particular.

"Where do you suggest we go first?" Pirelle asked. "Vian? The council? The Hall of Lights? Or Valder and the Seas of Sand?"

Chalone lay her head on the table and savored the still darkness behind her eyelids. "Vian. She'll want to know what we've found."

"I know," Pirelle said. The old storyteller had been very eloquent. "Look on the bright side. At least we'll have the pleasure of waking her up!"

Showered, dressed, and about as organized as she could be, Pirelle hustled Chalone to the private elevator that deposited them on top of the plateau a short distance from the main entrance.

Pirelle took a moment to breathe deeply and looked around the usually windswept plain.

A few centuries previously, someone decided to provide the Archive with a new entrance suited to its importance, rather than the utilitarian box that had previously sufficed. The ungentle winds that blew across the top of the plateau dictated a low sculpted shape whose design was viciously argued over, and then built just as ferociously.

The new and imposing edifice looked like the hull of a watercar, turned upside down and clad in an ugly imported stone. Over the years attempts had been made to call for a redesign, but it never amounted to more than bluster. Opinion was, if something worked why change it. Only dignitaries and researchers on self-important business pursued the issue now. Pirelle's gaze swept by it without a thought. Other vistas caught her attention. She stared at the column of Earthblood fire's eerie glow as if the intensity of her gaze could force it reveal its secrets. Nearby, Chalone breathed deeply to pull the physical world into her body after so long in a virtual one.

"It's so quiet," Chalone said, appreciative of the rarely still air. The constant in-crystal wind still rang in her ears. "What a beautiful night." She looked up at the lights of the city reflected on the underside of the cloud cover.

Pirelle didn't reply.

They walked to the landing field in silence and hastily appropriated an empty aircar. Someone still working within the Archive must have reserved it for their exclusive use and would be less than pleased to find it gone.

Pirelle programmed their destination, and leaned against the plush upholstery for support as the car rose off the plateau in a flurry of dust. The canyon lip flew beneath them and they plummeted down into the valley. The force of the dive flattened them against their seats and pushed their tiredness even deeper into their bones.

Pirelle closed her eyes, but a thought occurred to her. She and Chalone still discussed it when the car quietly eased back down to the ground.

* * * *

Vian's house was tucked neatly underneath a stand of ancient oak trees that had been mere saplings when she planted them. Arbors of roses, hydrangeas, honeysuckle, and jasmine framed the more formal garden at the front.

An unassuming porch showed its face to the world, but inside the house opened out to encompass vaulted ceilings above delightful spaces that fulfilled all sorts of needs.

Vian didn't welcome them with open arms but acted fairly civil given the hour. She shooed them into the main gathering room and excused herself for a moment. As she left, Lila entered from the kitchen.

"Lila!" Pirelle exclaimed, blinking rapidly for a moment. She turned to Chalone, and spoke without thinking. "Vian certainly has taken a liking to your family, hasn't she?"

Chalone wasn't really surprised to see Lila, it was just a matter of timing.

At her best, Pirelle was apt to step over boundaries, and get herself into more trouble than she could handle. *Like now.* Chalone felt too tired to do anything, except shrug her shoulders.

Lila defused Pirelle rather than confront her. "It proves is that Vian has a discerning palate for all her pleasures." She raised a single admonishing eyebrow and then addressed Chalone. "You look like you've been awake for the last three days. Both of you." She deliberately included Pirelle. Suitably chastened, and by way of an apology, Pirelle hugged her fiercely.

Vian returned looking much more attentive than when she left. She sat next to Lila and composed herself to hear what couldn't wait for a more civilized hour.

"We found references to a Calling of the Earthblood ritual that tie in with what we have out there," Chalone said quietly from the depths of her chair.

"So, that's what happened," Vian said. She quickly assimilated the information and began calculating implications.

"We couldn't find anything to tell us how to restore our memories, unfortunately," Chalone said, always sad when referring even obliquely to the ritual and Dajah's death. "But there's a place where we might find some answers. Its called the Shadowlands, where supposedly, a key is hidden that can unlock 'what was cast down'."

"Which unlocks all sorts of questions, doesn't it now?" Vian mused, unaware of her pun. Her calculations began to fall into place.

"We found the Skane," Pirelle butted in and then amended it as Chalone raised the very eyebrow she'd inherited from her grandmother. "Sort of."

Vian looked at Chalone for confirmation, but Chalone gestured for Pirelle to continue. Pirelle focused her will to project images into the air around her similar to the technique the old woman used. It had come as no surprise to Chalone and Pirelle that Broon had been a Practitioner. They'd accompanied the first travelers from beyond the Gallery and bred true as the tribes spread out across the lands.

A wraith-like globe hung between Pirelle's outstretched hands with blue ocean depths dominating the two land masses. The continents of their world peeled off of the globe like an apple skin. First the familiar one of Dorial where they lived, and floating behind it, Valder. Pirelle beamed proudly at the images she'd created.

"Most of Valder, west of the mountains, is made up of an uninhabitable desert, called the Seas of Sand. There are a few places left in the south that support subsistence farming," she said. "That's where the tribes live that tell the stories we experienced." The image zoomed in on a specific location. "The edges of the Seas of Sand fall into a huge inland lake, big enough to be a sea in its own right, that's gradually silting up as more and more sand is driven into it by the wind. The leading edge of the sand is called the Dreaming Place of the Skane. It wasn't made clear why, but that's not the issue." She glanced at Chalone as though to stress a point she'd already made. "That makes their location very specific. They're still there, buried within the sea, waiting until they're needed. So, it stands to reason that there's no danger to the Gallery." Firmly convinced her logic had resolved any potential danger, she allowed the image to dissipate.

Chalone perked up at this last conclusion and continued the conversation begun in the aircar.

"You're wrong. I don't think they're waiting until they're needed. It's called the Guardian's Dreaming," she deliberately corrected to underscore her point. "For a reason, they're asleep. That's why there's something wrong with the Gallery. Why I felt that wind in there. The Skane are asleep on the job!"

"You could have misinterpreted the stories," Pirelle said reasonably. "Like Lila said, we're both really tired."

"Don't patronize me!" Chalone snapped.

"I'm not," Pirelle said, injured. "This doesn't have to be complicated. Only when you're asleep, do you dream, and if you're some mysterious entity supposed to protect the Gallery from danger, you don't sleep."

"Come on, you know better than that." Chalone started to argue further but stopped herself. Pirelle was only trying to ease the weight of concern she felt about the Gallery, but she was reaching the end of her patience to deal with Pirelle's need to wrap things up all nice and neat.

The first drowsy chirp of the morning filtered through the thoughtful silence. Its cheery greeting broke the mood and Vian spoke first.

"Before the two of you go any further into your," she paused significantly, "discussion, we need to find out the truth."

* * * *

Undercurrents of thoughts and emotions charged the air and swirled around Chalone and Pirelle like an indigo trap about to be sprung. Vian had made her plans.

Chalone forgot her frustration and exhaustion and wondered what Vian might bully her into next, and if it meant the end of her enforced proximity to Liesha.

Pirelle, although feeling annoyed that Vian had taken over the conversation, hoped it would mean an end to the interminable Archive visits. Pirelle finally stated the obvious, "How? There aren't any Portals on Valder. None of our air or sea cars have that kind of range. It'll take weeks by sail. Even when we get there, the fastest landcar can only go to the edge of the desert, the rest has to be done on foot, or by shada." She winced ruefully. The experience, albeit of the virtual variety, had been a painful one.

"There isn't enough time. I can feel it slipping past us," Chalone said, unable or unwilling to comment further.

"There are more ways to deliver a message than to send the messenger halfway around the world," Lila said, entering the conversation for the first time in such a matter-of-fact voice that Vian almost laughed out loud, but grew silent as Chalone's expression immediately darkened.

Chalone felt as though the ghosts of her childhood had dogged her footsteps ever since she succumbed to Vian's blackmail, however innocuous it appeared to be at the time, and started her research at the Archives.

"The ECHO network," Chalone said bitterly.

"Yes," Vian agreed firmly and braced herself for the storm to come. "The ECHOs."

"I will not interface with them, Vian! I won't have them sorting through my mind and trying to coerce me into joining them! Pirelle can do the report. Better yet, they have access to the same data we found and can send their people in to Valder," Chalone snapped, edging into hysteria.

Shocked silence bounced off the walls for a moment.

Vian settled herself deeper into the couch. It wasn't as bad a reaction as she feared, but she needed Chalone fully functional and had to quash this little rebellion before it got out of hand. "It's not for you to say who you will and won't report to in this matter," she said firmly. "Right now I wouldn't inflict your state of mind on anyone, least of all an ECHO. I'm going to call a special sitting of the council and you will present your report to them. Clearly and concisely, without your personal feelings interfering."

Out of the corner of her eye, Vian saw Pirelle start to speak. She felt far too tired to deal with another personality clash, but wouldn't let either pass unresolved. However, one personality at a time. She held up a hand to forestall Pirelle and continued. "There will be an ECHO representative at the council, as always," she said to Chalone. "You will not interface directly with any of them. I know what upsets you about the ECHOs." Vian softened her voice compassionately. "They never have, and never will, try to recruit you. Your past would be too much of a liability, even if you were able to survive the training. They are individuals just like you and me, with thoughts and feelings."

Chalone stood up and towered over Vian. Fury and fear, and for some perverse reason, righteous indignation that Vian would think she couldn't make it through the ECHO training or be a liability to them, made her voice shake. "Y-You're wrong! They never actively recruit. They're far too s-subtle. They're not like us. They used to be before they gave up their families, their bodies, and their free will, everything, to become c-cybernetic machines." She almost spat the words. "Without thinking or c-caring about what happened to those they left behind." Chalone felt her years of carefully constructed calm break apart. Fury and anguish came pouring out of her mouth. "I loved her and she never thought about what might happen to me, she didn't love me! I was only five years old!"

"Sit down!" Vian commanded coldly.

The energy around Chalone turned a nauseous green color and she backed away, appalled by the pain that swept through her. "Sit down, Chalone. Please," Vian added gently.

Chalone sat rigidly, as though she had turned to brittle glass.

"Your words do you no credit," Vian said. "They aren't true, and I'll put them down to exhaustion. That's not an acceptable reason for attacking a group of people that you know only superficially, or Liesha, who you refused to have contact with since you were five. I understand why." Vian held up her hand to silence Chalone's protest. "I expected better of you."

Pirelle observed the exchange and decided to step in and make a point. "You're being unfair, Vian. Chalone's bettered your expectations. She's worked day and night for you. She's the one who found all the information we have."

"Stop defending me," Chalone snapped at Pirelle. "I don't need you to take sides in this. I can speak for myself."

If the tension in the room hadn't been so fierce, someone might have laughed out loud at the look on Pirelle's face.

"I apologize, Vian," Chalone said as exhaustion and her sense of honor softened her brittleness. "You're right. I don't see myself changing how I feel anytime soon, but I will talk to the Council." Chalone stood up again, this time to leave.

"I wasn't defending you," Pirelle said, hurt and defensive.

"Perhaps you weren't," Chalone admitted. "But you've been looking for an opening to strike at Vian for days and I won't let you use me to do it!"

"Use you!" Pirelle exclaimed, angrily standing up in her turn. "Use you," she repeated, her face going white. "How could you accuse me of..." She stuttered to a halt.

"Shut up, Pirelle. I'm too tired to argue with you anymore." Chalone walked away.

"Don't slam the door, dear," Lila said, having experienced Chalone's exits before. They never happened very often, but when they did, a locksmith was usually required. Chalone shut the door very slowly and deliberately. The click of the latch sounded like a gunshot in the silent room.

Pirelle stared at the door, waiting for Chalone to walk back in and return her universe to normal.

"That was unexpected." Vian stared contemplatively at the door. "I don't think I've ever seen her do that." She sighed and the spell was broken. She glanced at Pirelle and decided it would probably be best to keep the two of them apart for a while longer. "I want you to go home and rest," she said. "Then go back to the Archives and find out all you can about these Shadowlands."

"But..." Pirelle began and gestured toward the door.

"I'll talk to Chalone. You know how to do the research just as well as she can. Until this is resolved, I suggest we declare a truce. There'll be time later to resolve any outstanding issues."

Pirelle studied the carpet in front of her for a minute, knowing she'd behaved badly. She nodded her acceptance of Vian's suggestion, smiled wanly at Lila, and walked quietly from the house.

Vian and Lila looked at each other.

"I wonder when those two will figure it out," Vian said.

Lila nudged her. "That could have been handled better."

"Or worse," Vian replied grumpily. "They're grown up women. They can take it! Whereas I," She gestured melodramatically. "I have to call a council meeting and coerce some very stubborn members to attend." She meant Zikelun. "So don't start lecturing me old woman!"

"Old woman!" Lila spluttered. "I'll give you 'old woman'!" She steered Vian into the bedroom and shut the door firmly behind them. "Old woman indeed!"

Vian's body was as familiar as hers, but Lila still reveled in the newness of their loving. She pulled the robe down from Vian's shoulders and kissed the hollow of her neck. "How soon do you want to start working?" She teased, breathing softly against Vian's neck.

"Any minute now."

"Plenty of time for this then," Lila said and kissed lower down Vian's body as she imprisoned her arms in the folds of her robe.

"You're taking unfair advantage." Vian's knees turned to jelly.

"Yes, I am," Lila said muffled, and pushed Vian onto the bed.

Their bodies fitted together imperfectly. New aches and old wounds meant rearranging pillows and cushions, but as they made love those imperfections fled before their passion. They wove the history of their lives into every touch they gave and received. Each caress came from a wellspring of desire that remained unshackled by the passage of time. They sought the curves of each other's bodies with an anticipation that felt like returning home.

Chapter Fourteen

Chalone closed Vian's front door quietly behind her as Lila had so wisely advised. She felt furious at Pirelle, and furious with herself for letting Pirelle's irrational antipathy toward Vian get under her skin. What did she care about Pirelle anyway? Although she didn't envy Pirelle when she and Vian finally confronted each other, a part of her felt that Pirelle deserved to be on the receiving end of Vian's ire, while another part winced in sympathy.

She stopped at the stone footbridge and stared down at the dark water burbling on its way, oblivious to her turmoil.

She leaned on the parapet and rested her chin on her hands. Although she was surrounded by women who cared for her, no one could ease the growing concerns and fears she harbored.

"Everything's spiraling out of control," she whispered to the water and watched her tears fall into it. "I wish I weren't so alone in all of this. Pirelle and Vian, Liesha, the Gallery, finding the Skane, all of it." As her list threatened to get longer, she interrupted herself. "I know it's not strictly true," she argued, as though the water had responded. "There are Practitioner Circles but I can't ... I just wish ..." She paused and felt her body's response to her wish. "You know what I wish right this minute?" The water didn't answer, but she'd made up her mind anyway. She left the bridge, and instead of turning toward home, she strolled along the path into Espinsal.

She walked to Tallem's house with a spring in her step that had nothing to do with the contents of her latest list.

* * * *

Pirelle also closed Vian's front door quietly. She knuckled the tiredness out of her eyes and settled her shoulders as though taking on the unaccustomed weight of Vian's orders.

Her eyes obligingly refocused and she peered into the cabin of the empty aircar. After checking all the compartments thoroughly, she decided that Chalone had chosen to walk home rather than wait for her. That'd be just like Chalone, walking off her feelings. Pirelle smiled indulgently. She was prepared to forgive all slights, real and imaginary, and disengaged the navigator to search for her friend.

Expecting Chalone to be somewhere ahead of her striding briskly along, Pirelle guided the aircar by a slow circuitous route that covered most of the different pathways through Espinsal. The more time that passed without seeing Chalone, the swifter her indignation returned. Chalone had been unfair. She defended her, not using her to attack Vian. Honesty forced Pirelle to admit that there was some truth to the rest of Chalone's accusation. Guilt flushed her cheeks but she deliberately sidelined her thoughts by focusing on how tired she really felt. There was little more she could do without at least twelve hours sleep and a good meal.

She landed the aircar at her front door in early morning sun bright enough to make her wince and re-set the navigator to return from it whence it came. She tip-toed barefoot into her home ostensibly to keep from disturbing either Jalemi, or Chalone on the off-chance that she had already arrived home.

She checked on Jalemi who was sound asleep with her cheek pillowed in her hand as she used to do as a child. The short walk down the hallway to Chalone's room seemed to go on interminably. Although she couldn't hear any sounds of breathing through the solid wooden door, she decided to open it just to...to, she couldn't think of any reason to. With her shoes in one hand and feeling rather foolish, she turned the doorknob and prayed the old hinges wouldn't creak.

She backed out, closed the door just as quietly, and leaned against the wall, unsure if she felt disappointed or relieved.

* * * *

With a hot chocolate in one hand and her shoes still in the other, Pirelle took herself to her own unoccupied bed. Her pillows didn't feel as comfortable as the last time she slept on them, but she consoled herself with her hot chocolate and began to sort through her thoughts.

The quest for information on the Skane was important. She'd been so caught up in Chalone and Vian's project that she'd lost sight of her reasons for volunteering. To see if she could join the ranks of the very few people who had seen an ECHO up close and personal wasn't her first reason, but it certainly ranked up there. Her tired brain certainly wasn't going to acknowledge the obvious one.

Still, some time separate from Chalone might be a good idea. She sipped her hot chocolate and felt its soothing warmth spread throughout her body. Neither of them particularly enjoyed intense relationships of any sort, and simply by the nature of working closely together in-crystal, theirs had taken a very intense turn.

Not that she felt enthralled at the thought of going back to the Archives. Without Chalone's steady persistence, she'd probably ask the wrong questions and end up conversing with cloud riders from the Tarlus ziggurat. Pirelle snorted at the idea. She yawned hugely. It was time to go to sleep.

She turned out her light and punched her pillow, hoping to reform it into the shape she liked. She couldn't help thinking about where Chalone might have gone as sleep slowly came. She had her suspicions, not that she really cared, of course.

* * * *

Chalone eased from a deep dreaming sleep into a state of semi-conscious contentment that she hadn't felt in far too long. She stretched her legs and breathed in familiar aromas. Her knees turned to jelly as her hind-brain focused her attention on a sweet tenderness in certain regions of her body.

Her relationship with Tallem ended the previous year, although Chalone couldn't recall just exactly why. Yet, this was the only place she could conceive of being on this lovely morning. Selective memory loss, she smiled wryly, it's a very useful talent to foster on occasions.

She stretched again and sat up, reveling in an assortment of languid sensations. Her eyes rested on familiar objects as she looked around the room. Tallem was a creature of habit and nothing had changed since the last time she lay here. Such a contrast from her chaotic home. She blushed as memories of the dawn flooded back.

She'd rung Tallem's doorbell, out of breath, and unsure of her welcome, and Tallem showed great presence of mind pretending not to be surprised. They were in each other's arms before the door had properly closed. A passionate desire bereft of conscious thought propelled them toward the bedroom, shedding their clothes as they went.

Looking at the clock on the bedside table, Chalone calculated that she'd had about an hours sleep in the last two days and smiled self-indulgently. She didn't mind a bit. Her body had shed most of the tension that she'd carried since before the Earthblood ritual. Here in Tallem's house, in Tallem's arms, she set her responsibilities aside for a while. It was almost as intoxicating as contemplating how she might spend the rest of her day.

The summer air wafted through the gently billowing curtains daring her to dress in anything other than her skin. Clothing was always optional at Tallem's house. She critically examined her body in the mirror at the end of the bed, and noted that she'd been down in the Archives for too long. Her skin had faded to pale lavender. She brushed her fingers through her hair, which spiked her endorphin levels again. Times like these, she nodded to her reflection, every gesture no matter how innocent sparked a sensual electric charge.

Reveling in the feeling of her naked skin, Chalone made her way down the steep staircase to the ground floor where the smell of breakfast drew her like a siren's song. She walked through the house to the courtyard and lawn beyond.

Chalone immediately noticed that Tallem moved with a honey-melting-in-the-sun lilt to her step, not unlike herself, and her hair was cropped shorter than she'd ever seen it before. Chalone thought it framed her handsome square face perfectly and ignored the real reason why Tallem's hair was so short. It was too beautiful a morning for such intrusive thoughts.

She stood behind Tallem until she turned around. As her breasts and thighs came into contact with Tallem's, desire undulated through her body. The deliciously teasing moment lingered until they sat down at the breakfast table and smiled at each other.

The eggs were perfect, the garlic sautéed mushrooms plump and juicy, and the fresh baked bread rolls were crusty outside and steaming inside. Tallem asked no questions but Chalone knew she owed her an explanation. She took Tallem's hand in hers and marveled all over again at the feelings that rushed through her body.

"Last night I needed to be held," she began. "Everything just got too overwhelming. I know that's not very flattering, but I..." She stopped herself from regurgitating a list of her immediate past and returned to the present. Any explanation she offered would not really express why she returned, nor would it honor what had just passed between them.

Tallem squeezed her hand encouraging her to go on.

"Thank you for holding me," she finally said and leaned across the table to kiss her fully on the mouth. Tallem caught hold of Chalone's wrist with her strong woodcarver's fingers and pulled her closer. The remains of breakfast were forgotten.

There was no waiting to return to the whiteness of the bed upstairs when the neatly clipped soft grass was so close. Tallem tossed a hand knitted comforter onto the grass and pulled Chalone down, leaning across her body, pinning her to the ground.

Chalone's breath caught somewhere between her throat and her thighs. Tallem could take her so close to the edge, and then tease her unmercifully until she finally exploded. Without giving Tallem time to react, she twisted her body and rolled on top.

She kissed Tallem's eyelids, softly, tenderly, and then crushed her mouth, biting her lip, almost hard enough to draw blood. Tallem gasped and thrust her hips against the confining weight of Chalone's thighs. She moved her legs apart and enclosed Chalone with their solid firmness.

Heat radiated from both of them, demanding release.

Tallem threw her head back and Chalone alternated between kissing and lightly biting her neck and shoulders. She slid down until she reached Tallem's breasts. They looked firm and full, and nestled perfectly in her hands. She gently brought her finger and thumb together to capture a throbbing nipple.

"Harder," Tallem gasped, writhing her hips against Chalone's stomach.

"Not yet," Chalone teased. She reached up to the table and captured her abandoned teacup. The delicate hand-wrought pottery was half-full. She took a mouthful and made sure Tallem watched. She placed her lips over one of Tallem's breasts and without letting any of the liquid escape drew the nipple into her mouth. Tallem stared into Chalone's eyes as though she could tear them open with her gaze, and rewarded Chalone with a groan that came from the very core of her womb.

Chalone did it again.

She blew on the outraged nipple, puckering it, then took its tightness into her mouth, this time without the hot tea, and sucked the very breath out of Tallem's body.

She moved a little further down so that she could kiss around Tallem's ribs and along the side of her flanks.

Tallem groaned incoherently. She held her breath as Chalone's arms encircled her thighs.

Chalone reached into the softness between Tallem's thighs. Her mouth brushed apart soft lips and her tongue slid along folds of moist skin. Tallem stretched her thighs apart, but as her muscles quivered in anticipation, she clenched her legs tighter, not caring if she bruised Chalone. It would be what she deserved for torturing her this way.

Chalone was oblivious to Tallem's heels digging into her. A taste so precious, a sensation like satin, an ache that couldn't be assuaged any other way, swept through her. She held the precious flesh in her mouth for a long moment, poised to crush it between her teeth and tongue. Tallem lifted her hips and invited Chalone further in.

With only a subtle shift of her shoulders, Chalone began the touch that Tallem wept for. She slid inexorably in, not stopping until she buried her fingers deep inside Tallem, slowly building waves of pleasure. She matched the rhythm of her tongue and fingers to the thrusting of Tallem's hips, rocking back and forth, pushing harder and deeper.

Chalone surged upwards, half-kneeling, half-laying between Tallem's legs, and forced the wave of ecstasy about to explode through them to plateau to yet again.

Tallem spread her hands and grasped the edges of the rug. Her fingers dug deep and clenched into fists as she tensed every muscle in her lambent body. The rush grew from her womb, spreading outwards through her flesh, past the boundary of her skin, and out to the furthest edges of her awareness.

She exploded around Chalone's fingers, shuddered within her mouth, and bucked against the constraining weight of her body. Her eyes registered only pleasure, and her breath...she hadn't breathed for an eternity. She had no need of air.

She gasped as Chalone moved her fingers again. Not to take her back over the edge, but to ease the tightness around them. Gently sliding out, Chalone placed her hand covered in a delicious wetness gently over the quivering flesh her mouth had just finished ravaging.

Tallem let her legs fall away from Chalone's body and moaned softly as Chalone wove her way back up to her arms.

Tallem's eyes closed and she smiled.

Chalone watched her and smiled too.

* * * *

They finally rose from their grass-stained blanket and showered away the allure of their passion. Before her sense of responsibility returned sufficiently to ruin her day, Chalone checked her messages with the intent of acting on none of them. The extra hours in the sun had done her skin a world of good. She actually glowed.

A message from Vian blinked at her. When she opened it, it not only informed her of an extraordinary meeting of the Council that ordered the affairs of the region, but included an admonition that now she'd 'rested', Vian's quotations, she ought to have her emotions firmly under control and her thoughts in order by the time she gave her presentation.

Chalone was unwilling to delve into how Vian knew she was with Tallem. Her ways were not for the faint of heart, and Chalone knew she was lucky to have exited their affair as unscathed as she had.

She re-read the message and felt her blood pulse in her throat. Although this short time with Tallem had taken the edge off her anger and fears, it didn't smother her anxiety completely.

Tallem leaned into her back and looked over her shoulder at the console. She caressed Chalone's shoulders, but stopped when she read the message screen. "Council meeting th's afternoon," she said, pulling a face. Her slight western accent, usually unnoticeable, returned when she felt worried or upset. "Don't you 'void those things like the plague?"

"Usually. Not this time." Chalone shrugged and activated the delete key.

Tallem turned her around and frowned down at her. "I know that tone of voice. Have you got y'u self into more than you can handle, my love?"

Chalone had a perfect view of what she could handle, but that was beside the point. "I have indeed," she said, not completely joking, and relaxed into Tallem's arms, hoping she wouldn't pursue the conversation any further.

"You?" Tallem asked, straightening a little. "She, who is famous on all the known worlds with'n the Gallery? I don't think so." She looked intently at Chalone. "You're s'rious?"

Chalone nodded, close to tears.

"I'll walk with you to the chambers then. I have t' go in this afternoon anyway," Tallem said as she hugged Chalone and let her go, knowing that when Chalone felt upset, she accepted physical closeness for so long, then withdrew until the situation changed.

* * * *

Tallem also received a similar message from her workplace,

albeit without the admonition to behave.

She was one of the few non-ECHO's who had the authority to attend council meetings on their behalf whenever ECHO interests were on the agenda.

Frequently working with the ECHOs as a technical advisor, assisting in upgrading their global communication and command system, she'd been given the option to either become a fully integrated ECHO or have a simplified device implanted. It was a long and painful decision process, but her fascination with ECHO technology didn't extend to becoming permanently connected to the network. Not yet. At the time she'd had other considerations.

The implant she received was a simple contact point under her skin above and behind her left ear. From a technical point of view, there wasn't much difference between that, and the headsets used in the Archives. Tallem knew that for most people, it was a leap they were afraid to make.

She only ever mentioned her implant once to Chalone, who reluctantly accepted it but in the months after they parted, Tallem wondered if it had anything to do with their relationship ending. Like Chalone, she couldn't remember the details of why they parted.

With the implant she had all sorts of access to the inner workings of ECHO operations, but whatever they'd been processing since the Circle ritual was officially beyond her access codes. Lately her assigned activities had become infused with an urgency that she couldn't help noticing in spite of the calm face the ECHOs put on.

She scanned her private and highly illegal connection to the ECHO network, then activated her implant, and attached the pirate node to her console. She didn't doubt for a minute they knew what she was doing and allowed her to continue for their own reasons.

"Oh dear," she said a moment later. The ECHO scheduled for the meeting had unexpectedly cancelled and her replacement was listed on the attendance role. It didn't necessarily mean that she would actually be at the meeting, but was more likely to be present in the ECHO annex at the council building in case Tallem needed a back-up.

Tallem stared at the ceiling of her study for a moment, trying to find a way to explain the substitution to Chalone. Suddenly she smiled brightly, disconnected from the network, and walked out of the room.

She had acquired this information via an illegal access which meant that is wasn't common knowledge, and therefore telling Chalone would not be ethical. Sometimes leaving well enough alone was a very wise thing to do.

Chapter Fifteen

When Esparber was conceived, its founding citizens created a building code that prohibited any construction over six stories thereby forcing the bulk of the city underground. The buildings that did reach the maximum height were designed so that they complimented the surrounding hills and each other rather than battle each other for the eye's attention.

The grand underground hall where the council sat for its larger meetings was about a half an hour from Tallem's house. Judging by the number of people traveling in the same direction as Tallem and Chalone, it was going to be a very full session. They arrived with time to spare and sat together in a small courtyard off to one side of the council building. It had a fine view of the city and the various delegates walking toward the meeting. Most came from local interest groups but a few, identified by their appearance, accents or costume, had come from far away, even off-world.

Chalone tilted her head to one side. "I'd like to stay with you tonight," she said, startling Tallem who had been content to watch the passing parade. "Explore what we've started, re-started," she amended.

Tallem shifted in her seat to face Chalone squarely. "Any particular reason or just my womanly charms?" she asked, unwilling to expose her true feelings without further explanations.

Chalone sighed and looked past the neatly trimmed rose garden bordering the courtyard. She found no inspiration in the city skyline beyond, but held Tallem's hand in hers. "It's a complex answer," she acknowledged finally. "The most important thing is that I want to be with you again."

"The rest of the complexities?" Tallem asked, aware that her face showed her half-relieved and half-concerned feelings.

"Do you really want to know them right now?"

Tallem was not prone to abrupt decisions. She believed that complexities had a way of dissolving if there was enough compassionate listening. It was one of her most charming traits, evidenced by the women who hovered around her like honey bees attracted to the sweetest of nectar. "P'rhaps," she said after a long pause.

A soft chime wafted throughout the council forecourt.

"P'rhaps not," Tallem said. "It can wait." She nervously brushed her hands down her white shirt and neatly pressed pants. "That's m' cue. I have to go."

"What for?" Chalone asked, surprised and then eyed her suspiciously. "The first chime just calls the delegates to their seats. We don't have to go in until the second one rings." She narrowed her eyes still further. "What aren't you telling me?"

Tallem took a deep breath and spoke quickly, not giving Chalone a chance to interrupt. "I'm one of the ECHO's representatives at this meeting. I know that you know I'm not an ECHO, but because I've worked for them now for a while, on some of their most complex projects, I agreed to have an additional implant. It's more sophisticated than the last one, so I can interact directly with their systems. Although the council meetings are broadcast live, they ask me to attend in person for them sometimes, because the way something's said is as important as what's being said. I didn't tell you because I know how you feel about the ECHOs, and I didn't know you'd come back into my life like this. It is only part of my job with them, and..." Lack of breath caused her to run down like an unwound clock, and only then she realized she'd almost spoken with the precision of an ECHO.

Chalone stared at her for a moment and then laughed uproariously without any concern for the attention she attracted.

"What are you laughing at?" Tallem asked, as she looked around and responded with an uncomprehending shrug to the stares of bystanders attracted to the sound.

Chalone wiped tears from her eyes and shook her head, unable to stop another peal of laughter bubbling up. Eventually she took pity on Tallem and calmed down. "I have such a fearsome reputation, don't I?"

She took Tallem's confused face in her hands and kissed her soundly, throwing her equilibrium off even further.

"You have nothing to worry about. The ECHOs aren't as important in my life as I thought," Chalone said softly. "Go in. I'll be there when the second chime rings."

Tallem didn't even try to make sense of Chalone's about-face. She knew that Chalone wanted to stay with her and that was enough, at least for tonight. She would deal with tomorrow when it arrived.

* * * *

Chalone knew she couldn't do anything about Tallem's fears, except to remain constant, a gift she could give freely in spite of the doubts that seeped into her consciousness from her deepest feelings. Right now the lure of great sex and stability outweighed her reservations about the ECHOs getting their claws deeper into Tallem.

She leaned back on the bench, crossed her legs at the ankles, and wondered how her life became so complex in such a short time. Whether she meant the Circle and its aftermath, Tallem, the search for the Skane, or the council meeting, she wasn't quite sure.

She stood up abruptly, not willing to wait for the second chime to summon her, and followed in Tallem's footsteps to the Council chambers.

* * * *

A huge glass covered dome gently curved up above the courtyard in front of her. Impossibly thin and laminated to withstand changes in atmospheric pressure and occasional earth tremors, it was another useful application of memory glass. Sandwiched between the top two layers of glass, a liquid membrane reflected scenes from the community's history into the sky. If there was a low cloud cover, it was possible to lie on the grass in one of the city's many parks and watch the glorious light show above.

Chalone failed to identify the obscure piece of history screened above her and consoled herself by plucking a rampant burgundy rose as a buttonhole for her shirt. The aroma of the rose wafted along in her wake as she walked under the dome and reluctantly boarded a skeleton elevator just inside the main entrance.

She, who'd boldly travelled throughout the Gallery, fought down a wave of panic as the almost non-existent platform began its nerve-wracking descent to the chamber floor six levels down. At the bottom, she pried her fingers from the middle of the horizontal hoop, one of five that were the only things defining the passenger space, and walked out into the chamber floor.

A giant sunken circle with tiered seats rose up in concentric rings from a central dais, and breaking the uniformity of the tiers, discrete doorways led off into the unknowable depths of the city's bureaucracy. Council meetings comprised anything from twenty people to two thousand, although only on the rarest of occasions people filled the whole chamber. Fabrics of different shades and textures covered the seats and furnishings to reduce any noise to a background murmur.

A leather bound book of the Council Code of Ethics lay on a small raised pedestal in the middle of the dais. It could be consulted for clarification of the ancient laws that governed the planet, but was mostly for show. Few had read it from cover to cover. Vian was one of the few, and it turned out to be a very instructive seventeen hour marathon.

A holographic representation of the arena could be projected above the book so that when delegates voted or indicated a desire to speak, a light would flash on the display in the corresponding position. During heated debates, the image sparkled and flashed like fireworks.

From the bustle of activity around her, Chalone estimated that most of the delegates would be at this meeting. Such was Vian's prestige.

As a reward for some long-ago never-to-be-named service to the land, Vian had the power to convene a special meeting of the Council if she thought there was reason enough. Chalone couldn't remember her ever using this authority before. The last time had been long before Chalone or any of her contemporaries were born.

After some searching Chalone found the place reserved for her in one of the lowest tiers. Someone else's position of privilege she was unhappy to usurp. She hunkered down into her borrowed seat and watched the games begin.

As usual, the current Senior Speaker, whose office was designed to be nothing more than the person who spoke first, arrived late. Zikelun had been voted into the office the previous winter and had long-term plans for the reformation of her position. Although she was not able to completely ignore this meeting, she opted to be as unaccommodating as possible without being the instigator. Direct opposition to Vian was political suicide, Zikelun understood that quite clearly.

Looking around, Chalone found Vian seated in her usual place in the second tier. She seemed relaxed about the delay, casually swapping anecdotes with her neighbors and glowing with a predatory satisfaction. Clearly Zikelun had done herself no favors by alienating the most powerful woman on the planet.

* * * *

Finally the Senior Speaker and her small coterie of sycophants ambled in.

Although a tall woman Zikelun walked slightly hunched over. She had an unremarkable face, except for an odd-shaped scar that curved from her left ear across her cheek to below her chin. The delicate scar tissue was an excellent barometer for her temper. A fact no one ever told her, certainly not her companions. They were not the sort of people to relinquish such an advantage.

Without any apology or show of respect for the chamber, Zikelun addressed Vian directly. "You couldn't wait until the meeting scheduled for next week?" She took her seat directly opposite, rested her chin on her hand, and stared vacuously at the ceiling.

Vian took her words to mean that the meeting was now in session. She touched her console and her light came on in the overhead display. The room fell silent as she rose gracefully to her feet. Before Zikelun could splutter any sort of protest as this presumption of her role, Vian addressed the assembly directly.

"Two events have occurred recently that require this Council's attention. The first, I am sure you are all aware of, the grapevine being the efficient creature it is." She paused and smiled around her, a familiar expression that deceived only the uninitiated. "It was a ritual that called the Earthblood fire and created the beam of energy that shines from beneath the ground and into the skies above. The ECHOs tell us that the beam tapers to a fine point above our atmosphere, and to the center of the earth, then vanishes." She didn't mention that she had verified this with the Elementals, just to be sure.

She paused for a sip of water and was surprised to see the tiniest of tremors in her hand. She felt a sudden chill of foreboding in the pit of her stomach.

"We don't know if this energy represents a threat to us or not. We don't have enough information. Our oral histories tell us that in ancient times the Earthblood fire was summoned to the surface to protect us all. I need not remind you that when legends arise out of the ground, and bear such fiery fruit, it's time to pay attention."

Heads nodded in concern as Vian paused again to let the impact of her words sink in.

"I have instigated a search through the Archive." Vian nodded briefly toward Chalone. "And found a reference to a place called the Shadowlands. If anyone has any knowledge of this place, please inform me, and I will pass that information on to the head of the investigation."

Vian skillfully gave away very little. She had too many unanswered questions, and didn't have enough accurate information to open them up for a general debate. A frisson of tension shimmered throughout the room and the noise level rose again. Delegates looked to their neighbors and around the room, as though expecting someone to answer her request.

Although she received no immediate responses, Vian expected that by the evening's end she would be inundated with gossip and rumors. Her other reason for calling the council meeting had already been accomplished.

* * * *

Throughout Vian's commentary Zikelun overtly displayed various signs of boredom. Covertly, she continued to glance around the chamber like a sewer rat sensing a flash flood. Her dull brown eyes interrogated every nod and shake of head, every furrowed brow or indulgent smile. Control of the meeting had slipped away from her and she was unsure how Vian had managed it.

Vian interrupted the burgeoning discussions in the council chamber. "The second event," she said and waited a moment. "The second event," she repeated, louder. "The delegate from the Hall of Lights will explain." She gestured to the tiered seats across from her.

Chalone stood up and faced thousands of eyes suddenly turned her way. Contrary to her inner nervousness, she calmly related what happened to her in the Gallery. Shadows where none could possibly be, and strange winds that blew from nowhere.

She finished speaking and the overhead display immediately lit up like fireworks.

A few of the lights marked nuisance questions deliberately designed to focus attention on the speaker. They were all the same, and she gave them short shrift. The majority expressed a great deal of concern, asking her for further detail and opinions, which she was not prepared for, nor authorized, to give.

For some delegates her news sounded like she declared the world flat. It was an article of faith that the Gallery was immortal and indestructible. They would rather believe that Chalone was mistaken. Although she understood their position, being uncomfortably close to her first reactions, for their increasingly agitated questions she only repeated herself.

Before she reached her fourth repetition, Vian stood again and

Chalone sat down as seamlessly as though they'd rehearsed it.

"It is my belief," Vian said, stressing the last word. "That these two events bear some relation to each other and may present a great danger to us all."

At the word 'danger', Zikelun sat up and began to pay attention to Vian at last. She was too late. Her advisors, having the most to lose if she fell from grace, were much more attuned to the mood of the chamber. They sensed her reversal of fortune, and although they never left their seats and their expressions never wavered, Zikelun felt as though she sat entirely alone.

Vian's eyes narrowed momentarily. She had won. Whatever action she needed to take in the future, she would have the absolute support of the Council. Her heart quailed at the thought of wielding that power sooner rather than later. She showed none of her thoughts on her face as she finished her speech. "With the help of the ECHOs and my assistants, I will endeavor to clarify the situation as swiftly as possible."

Tallem stood as the ECHOs representative, breaking protocol and ignoring the flashing query lights as easily as Vian and Chalone had. She listened to Vian and Chalone's reports with growing uneasiness. "What assistance can the ECHOs give?"

"I need to send an ECHO with one of my assistants into the Gallery. I believe the ECHO will have the ability to report back immediately with any information they may uncover," Vian said, eager to hear that the ECHOs had managed to resolve their communication malfunction within the Gallery.

"We plan to have that issue resolved in the very near future," Tallem replied, dashing Vian's hopes. She glanced up at Chalone and suddenly her face paled. "You're going to send Chalone?"

"Yes," Vian answered compassionately. "She is the best we have."

Tallem paused to listen to her implant and then repeated the words expressionlessly. "We will consider who to send." She used a moment to get her feelings under control. "The choice is obvious, although there are...complications. How soon do you intend this expedition to begin?"

"As soon as it can be arranged."

"Very well. What about the Shadowlands search?"

"The Archive is assisting us. I have all the personnel I require at the moment, but I thank you for the offer," Vian said graciously, although she spared a wry smile for Pirelle who had made her feelings clear about being 'stuck at the Archives while Chalone went off and had all the fun'.

While Vian spoke, Chalone considered her new fate. She would have liked to continue her research at the Archives, but Pirelle, although protesting, was more than capable of finishing the task. The adventurous part of her, larger than she knew, felt eager to go out into the Gallery and explore. She was so engrossed in her inner musings that she didn't return her attention to the meeting until Zikelun huffed and puffed and stood up to speak.

"Have you any other business to bring before the Council, Vian?" Zikelun asked insolently, hiding her dread behind a wall of bluster.

"Not at this time," Vian said smoothly. "I will, of course, keep the Council informed of my findings."

"Very well," Zikelun said, pulling the dregs of her authority around her like a tattered and useless mantle. "I don't know why you felt it necessary to call this meeting and waste everyone's time, but it appears you have finished, so I suggest we adjourn and go about our business."

Loud voices discussing Vian's news drowned Zikelun's dismissal of the Council. She remained unaware that the delegates who had supported her, or at least, ignored her maneuverings in the past cast ominous glances at each other. Not a single word was exchanged but they reached an accord.

Chalone watched the flow of people as they moved from group to group. This was really where the council conducted its business. Her suspicions solidified, she made her way down to the chamber floor, moving through the room to eventually arrive at Vian's side.

"What are you up to?" Chalone asked softly, concealing her voice beneath the surrounding conversations. "There was no way this constituted an emergency meeting. We said nothing that they didn't already know."

"Your news surprised many of them. Don't underestimate the value of first hand information. What am I up to, my dear Chalone?" Vian asked, gleefully casting a swift glance at Zikelun being studiously ignored by those nearest to her. "Politics. I may need to order the council to act without due consideration for anyone's personal ambitions and the fewer people I have to trample, the quicker it will get done."

"Zikelun just lost the last of her supporters, who might have been taken seriously by the Council," Chalone said. "Very subtle."

"She'll be gone before the week is out." Vian said. "That's how long you and the ECHO have to find out what's going on in the

Gallery and for Pirelle to dig up some more information on the Shadowlands."

"Such insignificant tasks! They'll be completed in hours," Chalone said, rolling her eyes.

"Are you sure?" Vian asked, looking closely at her.

"About working with the ECHOs?" Chalone smiled ruefully. "Don't worry, Vian. I'll behave." She leaned closer and spoke for Vian's ears alone. "I can tell the difference between my feelings about individual ECHOs and the work they do as a whole. I just lose my perspective every once and a while."

"Well, don't lose it, while you're out there."

"I'll try not to disappoint you."

Chalone looked around the crowded room, gauging when they might be able to leave. They could have used Vian's prestige to commandeer one of the elevators, but Chalone felt wary of abusing such privileges. Vian knew there was no benefit in using that privilege to simply leave the room.

They waited patiently in the elevator queue, listening to the familiar complaints about the antiquated system.

Once in the elevator they found themselves squashed up against the rings as it rapidly filled to overflowing. Everyone held their collective breath as the overloaded machinery moaned and groaned to the surface.

Chapter Sixteen

The Shadowlands, where Sebenesh made her Lair had almost certainly existed forever. Arahona and Sebenesh discovered it not long after they came to consciousness. Its bleached harshness, stone arroyos, and staggering cliffs rejected their feeble efforts to recreate or destroy it. Although the challenge provided them with a small amount of amusement, the severe landscape soon lost its charm and they returned to their playground among other aspects of their Immortal Realm.

As she matured Sebenesh often felt drawn to the brutal simplicity of the realm and eventually made it her home. There she discovered something akin to a friend.

Whatever Sebenesh felt, the Shadowlands reflected. If she raged against some real or imagined slight, wave after wave of blistering storms scoured the bleak landscape allowing her a safety valve that otherwise might have destroyed all things in her way. The Shadowlands in turn gained a sense of itself in relation to other realms of awareness. As long as the Shadowlands did nothing overt to thwart her will, Sebenesh was content to let it be.

* * * *

Then Arahona called on her to save the Gallery.

When she returned to her Lair her plan became a timeline of all the events that needed to occur and took on a physical form. Sebenesh rolled it up and bundled it into a corner where it shone like a golden halo. The events it recorded flowed forward in a timely order and soon thereafter she forgot it was even there.

When Jalemi ventured forth as though sleepwalking to free the Sphere from the Earthblood fire, her actions shook the Timeline out of its glowing complacency and it did the only thing it could with the only power it had.

* * * *

Time stalled. All of creation, all the realms of existence paused.

* * * *

For a moment the Timeline seemed unchanged. Then something malignant writhed and struggled to rise out of the orderliness of its depths. Staccato sounds like gunshots shook it apart. Black streaks of dissonance obliterated its shining light and ripped the finely crafted fabric to shreds. A blood-curdling scream ricocheted around the empty Lair and vibrated throughout the realm.

The sound reached Sebenesh at the far edges of the Shadowlands where realms of existence overlapped and battled for territory. Physical matter collided. Coruscating bolts of energy shattered the remnants into oblivion. Nebulae shrunk to anti-matter and then exploded in galaxy shattering cataclysms.

Sebenesh stood at the edge of the primal spectacle. The struggle left her breathless and aching for something more to fill a void in her spirit she was unaware she had.

Suddenly everything stilled, then the scream from the Timeline hit her like a physical blow driving her forward into the leading edge of the maelstrom. Her instincts rose to save her from injury, but she recalled the impulse to destroy even before it became a thought.

Nothing moved. A star spanning lightning bolt froze within a handspan of her face. Waves of deafening sound halted in their maddened tracks.

Without taking her eyes from the spectacle in front of her, she retreated within the borders of the Shadowlands. No sound, no movement existed there either. Her heart thudded in her chest and she spun around to face her Lair. The Timeline finally had her attention.

* * * *

Time fractured. All possible futures ceased to have meaning.

* * * *

Sebenesh materialized in the heart of her Lair just as the huge tangled mass of writhing black streaks flew apart. The individual threads threatened to invade the walls of her Lair, break through and destroy all things in their path. They whipped past Sebenesh, avoiding her as though knowing she would be impervious to their effects. She whirled her arms over head and spun a net of pure force to gather them together before they moved beyond her ability to contain.

They reformed into the halo, but then turned in on themselves, disappearing into an endless maw until eventually the frenetic writhing slowed to a sluggish heaving and twisting. The ugly distorted thing hovered near Sebenesh as though chastising her for its downfall.

She hissed in consternation. *What happened?* How had it happened? She sent her attention through the boundaries between the realms and homed in on the Earthblood fire just as Jalemi was about to reduce her plan to shreds. Sebenesh couldn't get there in time, even with her immortal abilities.

Her temper, unpredictable at the best of times, boiled up like a towering thunderhead.

"Stupid, weak, greedy woman!"

She flung herself about her Lair, hissing and cursing, unable to contain her rage. Her immortal body protected her from the bruises and broken bones she might have otherwise incurred. Precious treasures from eons of selective acquisition shattered in her wake. The walls of her Lair shuddered and shrunk away from her passage. She finally ran out of swearwords and seethed to the end of her tantrum.

She stood still, her fists clenched. What could she do? Fang the whole Gallery to shreds? Release the Sphere to create whatever it could out of the debris, and be damned to her promise to Arahona? Anything that would deny Jalemi her prize.

"Yes!" She cast her eyes about her Lair, using the chaos she'd created to fuel her passion.

She gathered her will and compressed her sinuous coils to focus her intent. Saliva dripped from her fangs as she prepared to enact an Armageddon that would have no equal.

From beneath her, around her, the Shadowlands reached out and seized control of her body, soothed the tentacles of her thoughts, and allowed her a moment of respite. It gently suggested she take a deep calming breath, reconsider her impetuous decision, and allow herself to be guided to her loom.

Never would she admit that the Shadowlands saved her from herself, but from that moment on, it held a dearer place in her pitiless heart than before.

With her apocalyptical urges reigned in, she willed the tangled knot of her plan to her side for a closer inspection. The Timeline slumped and slithered across the room until she reached down for it with a shaking hand.

Shaking? Impossible! Unacceptable!

She extended to her full imperious height until she regained control of her traitorous limbs and refocused on the Timeline.

Faint lines of possibilities appeared in the midst of the dark seething mass. They gained strength from her attention and glistened for her consideration. Her mercurial nature switched again and she absently gazed out through her Lair's translucent walls and wondered how these possibilities could be of use.

* * * *

Time breathed, once.

* * * *

The growing numbers of possibilities did offer her an opportunity to resurrect something out into this disaster. Well fine, she'd try.

She cast her unique magic into the mass of threads and separated the brightly colored ones. With rock-steady hands she drew them out and carefully wound them onto shuttles.

This thread represented this mortal, and this thread another. They would follow these fragile weavings in her stead and thus repair her grand design.

Her loom rattled and rustled with the sounds of a new weaving. Her fingers flew from side to side, melding colors and patterns, working from instinct rather than intellect and tamping each new thread into its rightful place.

Halfway through she hissed again, unsatisfied with the chaotic fabric. She could see through the Time shattered distortions of her old plan to the new pathways beyond, but everything wavered. Options opened and closed even as she looked. Her tail slashed from side to side in frustration and ground the shards from her recent rampage into even smaller pieces.

The Shadowlands twitched, but she glared at it out of the corner of her minds eye until it wisely retreated.

With a careless gesture, she swept up the dusty remnants and relocated them outside for the Shadowlands to do with what it would.

Before she could return to her loom, tiny musical chimes

sounded throughout her Lair and her broken treasures reappeared as though new. She smiled in spite of herself and refocused on her work with something akin to enthusiasm.

Unfortunately, that vexing instability remained.

Mortals, she grumbled, could be tiresome once they made up their minds. There was no telling what they would do with her reweaving of the Timeline but the alternative, going back into the Mortal Realm and trying to repair the damage herself, demanded a price too terrible to contemplate.

Because of them she would have to constantly monitor this reweaving halfway to eternity and back. She muttered wrathfully of dire consequences if she ever, ever, had to repeat these last few moments.

The last shuttle emptied and she sliced the new Timeline from her loom. She growled a little under her breath, but knew it was the best she could do with what she had to work with. It didn't have the same perfection of form and function as her original plan, but she saw the beauty in it in spite of herself.

She returned her new weaving to the corner of her Lair where it hummed and pulsed with a life renewed. It bobbed around and eventually settled into a new dynamic shape. Threads of energy spun out from it and disappeared into the Gallery to complete their tasks in the new design. Others snaked toward the world of Argol.

* * * *

Time began again.

* * * *

Starting as a single point of motion, Time flowed effortlessly outward from Sebenesh's Lair. As it passed into the Mortal realms, it pushed the after-effects of the Reweaving of Time ahead of it. Like a tsunami, the further it travelled, the stronger the shockwave became.

* * * *

Reconciled to her vigil, Sebenesh wound her long sensuous body in her nest and settled down to recover her energies. She would not admit that even she, immortal, needed her sleep. Like all beings of her ilk, she slept with one eye half-open, just in case.

Being Sebenesh, she banked her wrath within the depths of her Lair, and swore that when she finally caught up with the author of this little disaster she would revive those ashes of rage and vent her spleen quite thoroughly.

It was the least she could do.

With her half open eye, she watched her new creation until she remembered to attach a thought to one of the threads and send it through the tangled layers of Time.

"Pirelle?" She hissed adamantly "Pay attention!"

* * * *

Pirelle was having one of the worst days of her life.

The morning after her confrontation with Chalone, she woke from a fitful dream-tossed sleep with a raging headache. Her temples pounded with every beat of her heart, but nothing would keep her from returning to the Archives. There she could distract herself from focusing on what she didn't want to think about.

On her way out of the shower, her communications console dinged. Vian's message about the Council meeting glowed ominously in the air near her head, complete with a suggestion, Vian's suggestions meant anything but a suggestion, that she not attend, it would do neither her nor Chalone any good under the present circumstances.

She batted the message away and thought furiously. Be damned to Vian and her commands, to Chalone and her accusations, even Jalemi and her weird behavior. She, Pirelle would do what she pleased. It pleased her to go to the Council chambers, sit in her rightful place as a Hall Shepherd, and not go to the Archives where she would inevitably get stung, burned, frozen, or otherwise abused. Miraculously her headache disappeared.

As she stood out on the balcony that overlooked the valley where so much of her life had recently turned upside down, she reflected that it was just as well Tallem lived on the other side of Espinsal. She really didn't want her suspicions about where Chalone spent the night confirmed.

* * * *

Pirelle refused to trust her well-being to a skeleton under any circumstances and opted for the wide stairs that rose from her side of the building to the main floor of the council chamber. She slid into her seat in time to witness Zikelun's futile battle with Vian for control of the floor.

When Chalone stood up to speak looking so vital, so alive, Pirelle thought her heart would break.

She closed her eyes in agony and slumped back in her lavishly upholstered chair.

"Oh no," she groaned out between clenched teeth.

Her immediate neighbors sought to offer their opinion that the Gallery wasn't about to collapse any time soon. It may take years, they said, perhaps not even in our lifetimes. They felt confident now that Vian gained control of the Council. Did Pirelle see how she outmaneuvered that useless Zikelun?

Praise for Vian cut Pirelle almost as deeply as realizing that she was, and always had been, in love with Chalone.

She endured their misguided solicitations until the meeting was adjourned, and excused herself on the pretext of meeting up with friends.

She desperately needed space around her that wasn't filled with people. Unfortunately people crowded her everywhere, milling in groups, blocking the exits. She turned and fled up through the tiers of seats until she found a relatively deserted area and collapsed onto the steps.

Blood rushed to her cheeks as she relived every incident, every touch, every conversation between her and Chalone that she could remember. It had always been there, the love, but somewhere along the way she'd fallen deeper and hadn't even known.

* * * *

By late afternoon gossip among their circle of friends made it clear where Chalone had spent the night. When Pirelle heard, confirming her suspicions, she almost drowned under the intensity of her jealousy. But it was too late to do anything about her newly discovered feelings, although she was momentarily tempted to rush to Tallem's house and drag Chalone away by sheer brute strength.

She hoped no one else noticed. Sympathetic glances and soft murmured words of condolence would be almost harder to bear than malicious ones. Pirelle had a boundary that the outside world never crossed in spite of her gregarious nature. She would not be seen to be made a fool of in love. Her heart felt as though it'd been battered and she knew it was her own folly that created the distance between her and Chalone. If she'd kept her mouth shut she might be the one in bed with Chalone, not Tallem.

Jalemi was worse than useless. Usually she could share her troubles with her sister, even if she did tease her unmercifully, but trying to talk to Jalemi these days was like communicating with a sleepwalker, and so Pirelle agonized in an isolation of her own making.

Chalone returned from the council meeting, distracted and avoiding her eyes. As if she sensed the change in Pirelle and recognized that it was too late to do anything as well.

When Tallem arrived it really was too much for Pirelle to bear. After a brief uncomfortable time, she excused herself and pretended to ignore their relieved expressions as she left for the Archives.

In spite of her good intentions, she spent the entire time sitting on the edge of her couch with her head in her hands, trying to think of how she could return everything to the way it was. Finally she slapped her helmet off her head and returned home surrounded by wisps of slate gray energy that carried the burden of her heart like sodden sea wrack.

* * * *

Trapped within her nightmare, Jalemi drifted out of the house that she no longer thought of as home. A wind blew up the valley and tossed her unbound hair all around her as she walked through the dark woods heavy with a gloom of pre-dawn fog, toward the Earthblood fire.

The wind, left to its devices, gusted back to the house and slammed the front door shut.

The sound boomed through the deserted house and woke Pirelle from a nightmare. She sat bolt upright. Maybe Chalone had returned. Her senses told her it was only Jalemi going out for one of her rambles. She lay back feeling defeated not only by her feelings for Chalone, but her inability to fix whatever had happened to Jalemi. Then, as if she had been stung, she leaped up and hurriedly dressed. Something was wrong. She could feel it.

Pirelle followed in Jalemi's wake to where the Earthblood fire glittered above the morning mist like a deadly bane.

From the edge of the trees, she saw Jalemi standing near the column of fire, as still as a statue with her head cocked to one side as if listening, then suddenly reach out with her hand.

Pirelle gasped in horror and broke into a run desperately screaming Jalemi's name. She was too far away, but at least she might catch her attention. She didn't have much hope. Her spirit knew Jalemi was destined to do this insane thing.

Before she'd taken a few paces, an invisible force from within the fire, filled with a malevolence so pure it was almost beautiful, refused to let her come any closer. The presence slithered against her mind and quickly withdrew leaving her with a very unpleasant taste in the back of her mouth.

Jalemi screamed in a mad voice that wrenched its way through her violated soul and twisted her face into a cruel mask of hatred. "You will not come any closer!" She turned back to the fire, intent on immolating herself.

Pirelle struggled to move forward just as the shockwave from the fracture in Time arrived and knocked her completely off her feet.

The earth shuddered. Jalemi wavered in front of her eyes and froze in place. For a moment she thought she heard other voices calling out to her from the edge of the clearing. Then a sharp crackling sound filled her ears and she heard someone calling her name.

"Pirelle! Pay attention!"

Chapter Seventeen

Chalone left the warmth of Tallem's bed before the sun rose and waited just inside the deserted entrance to the Hall of Lights for her ECHO counterpart. Even though the Hall occupied her attention for almost all of her life, she was afraid of what she might find if she walked any further in.

Against her better judgment she reached out to the energy surrounding her friends and family and saw that it shifted, swirling into new and dangerous patterns, caused unbeknownst to her, by the shockwave from the fracture in Time approaching. She abruptly shut down the connections, regretting she'd even peeked. Something was wrong on so many levels she refused to even categorize them.

Footsteps approached from behind her and she reluctantly turned, dreading who it might be. As the tall woman walked toward her across the muted floor of the Hall, the irony of how similar they looked wasn't lost on her, although Liesha's head was shaved, an affectation Chalone thought, because of her ECHO implants.

* * * *

All the mortal worlds felt the fracture in Time differently. For some it was earthquakes and devastation, others barely twitched as though shifting gears. Argol twitched.

A few tiles on the roof of the Hall of Lights slipped loose, and a single crack opened around one of the Portals. Atmosphere from within the Gallery corridor hissed out and instantly sucked back in.

Chalone, focused on seeing her mother, failed for the first time in a very long time to notice anything amiss.

* * * *

Liesha came reluctantly to this assignment knowing she was to travel with Chalone. It was only the importance of the mission that kept her from flinging it in the faces of the ECHO hierarchy who 'volunteered' her.

In order to travel safely within the Gallery, she'd disconnected her implants from the ECHO communication network. Inside the Gallery, ECHO technology functioned as usual, but the energy pulses from the other-worldly dimensions of time and distance gathered around the Gallery distorted transmission signals and made attempts to stay in contact with the network impossible. The thundering feedback induced insanity in the strongest minds, immediately followed by an unpleasant death.

The ECHOs hierarchy hoped Chalone would follow in Liesha's footsteps and use her deep affinity with the Gallery to resolve this mystery for them. Their ambitions were dashed when it became obvious that Chalone saw Liesha's departure as a personal betrayal, blaming not only her mother but all ECHOs.

Liesha was secretly glad her fiercely independent daughter had not succumbed to the blandishments of the heavy-handed ECHO representative who first approached her. The language her thirteen-year-old daughter used caused quite a scandal in ECHO circles.

She understood Chalone's feelings but had long ago made her peace with the consequences of becoming an ECHO. All that remained was for her and Chalone to create a peace between them. As soon as she saw Chalone's face, she knew it was not going to be easy.

* * * *

The tremor from the fracture passed. The Reweaving of Time enclosed both women like a deep breath. It held them for an eternal moment then released them unharmed. The new Timeline had no use for them. Yet.

* * * *

"I am sorry." Liesha said, her voice gentle and precise. The intimate communication of the ECHO network left her common speech a little rusty. "Their arguments were very persuasive. This is more important than any differences you and I have." Without thinking, she held out her hand.

"Differences," Chalone said severely, stepping back "That's a bit of an understatement, don't you think?" She used all of her willpower to keep her quaking emotions out of her voice, but as the lid she'd tamped down on her emotions since the Circle worked loose, her eyes betrayed her in spite of her best efforts. She looked away. Her shoulders heaved, and she quickly brushed the back of her hand across her face. After a moment she straightened up, squared her shoulders, and turned back. "Why you?"

Liesha, too, regained control of her undisciplined emotions. Like all ECHOs and Practitioners when they worked in their Circles, her energy field remained quite firmly inside her skin, so Chalone couldn't see how deeply her withdrawal hurt.

"I am the best qualified," Liesha said, rather proud of her matter-of-fact tone. "I have more experience separating from the network than most of my contemporaries." In her mind she dismissed the excruciating physical pain the disconnection caused her, but it hovered around her nerve endings like a toothache that wouldn't go away.

"They tend to be a rather conservative lot. Not given to retracing their steps, as they call it." Liesha smiled indulgently, and then caught herself. It would not do to reminisce about her colleagues foibles in front of Chalone.

"Like you, I have a great deal of experience exploring the Gallery. Did you know that some of the theories you broke into little pieces were mine?"

Chalone sought refuge from her feelings by keeping her responses simple. "Anything else?" she asked, telling herself that she and Liesha were nothing alike.

"Any other reasons are personal and have nothing to do with..." Liesha quickly looked to one side. "What is that?"

Chalone turned, glad of the distraction from a very painful conversation, to discover her fears manifesting in front of her.

* * * *

The lights surrounding the cracked Portal flickered and grew dim until finally only the solid bar of light along the base remained. A deep booming sound came through the Portal, something that should not be possible, and shook the stone floor almost jarring both women off their feet.

Liesha quickly waved back someone running toward them, who hurriedly retreated, calling for assistance.

As the shuddering continued, fine cracks invisible to the eye snapped open in the huge columns holding up the roof of the Hall.

The Portal surface bulged and retracted as it strove to remain intact.

"That is where we must go," Liesha said.

"I agree, but not quite yet. We'll probably die if we do"

"There or here, it does not matter."

Sometimes the ECHOs fatalistic view of the world really got up Chalone's nose, but she didn't say anything. She felt a little too scared to bother with such trivialities.

Their hearts beat faster as they staggered toward the damaged Portal holding each other's hand.

The floor stopped shaking. The surface of the Portal wobbled a few more times and then stilled. Its lights flickered back on, too drained by the assault from the unknown force lurking on the other side of the Portal to shine in their former glory.

Liesha withdrew her hand from Chalone's a heartbeat before Chalone thought to.

They somberly observed the Portal for a few minutes. Nothing jumped out at them. "I suppose we could go now," Chalone said unconvincingly.

"We have tried for a very long time to evolve a technology that will produce any measurements within, and of, the Gallery," Liesha said by way of an answer. "Nothing ever functioned beyond the first few moments of insertion. It is times like this I wish we had been more successful." She lightly touched the subdued crystal lights.

The dull globules glowed a little brighter, as though taking a measure of strength from her. Chalone blinked in surprise. She and Liesha definitely were not alike.

"That's why the ECHOs need people like me," Chalone said with brutal irony. "I don't think we should wait much longer," She continued. "Just in case whatever that was returns."

"That is a plan," Liesha said, matching ironies.

They hitched their packs onto their shoulders and passed through the Portal.

* * * *

They stepped into the shallow depression at the Portal threshold. Chalone laughed to herself as she almost tripped again.

Suddenly a gale force wind ripped toward them. It slammed them against the corridor wall and then reversed course, sucking them away from the relative safety of the Portal.

The corridor vibrated up and down and lurched back and forth as the wind swirled them around and banged them from side to side. Chalone reached out blindly and found Liesha nearby. Their fingers touched, hands clasped. They drew each other close and clung together. Liesha protected Chalone's head as the wind tumbled them along the buckling corridor.

It wasn't until they reached an intersection, an unknown distance from the Portal that the strength of the wind halved. It crushed them against the dividing wall, suspended between two equally deadly options.

The gale dissipated, the pressure dropped, and both women bounced onto the floor breaking their instinctive embrace. The corridor resumed its usual peaceful sway. Dust motes drifted out of the Gallery walls and coated them in a fine layer of shimmering glitter.

Chalone groaned. A mass of throbbing aches and stinging pains battered her body. Her face felt caved in, but she was only pressed up against the corridor wall. She opened her eyes, gingerly rolled over, and carefully sat up. The glittery dust obligingly floated up and she sneezed so hard her ribs creaked.

She wiggled her jaw to make sure it still worked. "Well. That answers that question."

She blew her nose on her handkerchief and looked around for her mother.

Liesha lay on the other side of the corridor. Chalone crawled over, wincing as she moved, and made sure Liesha still breathed.

Liesha's sturdy clothing had protected most of her body, but her face was another matter. The fine layer of skin that covered her implants had been abraded off. Silver and blue flickerings of energy glowed eerily within a lattice structure where her right ear and the soft tissue covering her jaw and cheekbone used to be.

Chalone dropped Liesha and recoiled in horror. She scrabbled to her feet in a panic drawn from her childhood nightmares, and ran a few tottering steps before she heard a faint sound. She stopped but didn't dare turn around.

Liesha's head bounced off the yielding but not actually soft corridor floor. It was enough to rouse her from her healing trance, a useful side-benefit of her ECHO enhancements.

"Chalone? Wait," she called weakly.

Chalone slowly turned her head, and by sheer force of will made her body turn with it. She glanced quickly at Liesha and then looked away.

"Does it hurt?" she asked in a small voice that struggled to sound grown-up.

"I'm fine," Liesha said raggedly. "Just a few scrapes and lots of bruises."

"Good. That's good," Chalone said. She couldn't move, even breathe. Her heart pounded in her temples so loud she thought it would break through her skull.

"Chalone," Liesha said again and stood up awkwardly. "Look at me. Look at my face." She took Chalone's hands in hers. "We have to do this," she said with infinite sadness and love in her voice.

Chalone had been waiting to hear that inflection in her mother's voice since she was a little girl and was helpless before it. Her throat contracted. Tears scalded her closed eyelids. "No. I can't," she cried. "Please don't make me."

Liesha let go of Chalone's hands and touched each side of her face, holding her gently.

Chalone closed her eyes even tighter and surrendered her childhood wounds to the inevitability of growth. She reluctantly laid her hands over Liesha's and then slid them around her shoulders in an ungainly embrace that had them trembling.

The moment stretched out and surrounded them with its intimate longing. Chalone's fingers touched the sides of Liesha's face with feather-light caresses and then reached the wetness of blood and the ragged edges of torn skin.

"I can't," she whispered. Before she could pull her hands away, Liesha held her wrists fast.

"Look at me," Liesha repeated gently but implacably.

Chalone shook her head and her tears tumbled to the Gallery floor. "You don't understand," she finally whispered. "If I do, then I can't hate you anymore." Shame reddened her face.

"Is it so important to hate me then?" Liesha asked, feeling her heart crumple.

Chalone dragged her voice up from the pit of her wounded childhood. "It's all I've had ever since you left. I survived because I hated you."

Liesha pulled Chalone into her arms and let her cry out all her pain. She cried so hard that Liesha began to cry too. "I am so sorry," she said over and over again to her sobbing child and gently rocked her back and forth.

Chalone wrapped her arms around her mother and let her tears empty her heart. There was nothing to refill it yet, but she'd found a kind of peace to stand on for a while.

"I didn't hate you, really," she said as her tears trickled to a halt. "I was so hurt that you left me behind."

"I know, my dearest child. You felt nothing that I did not feel as well." Liesha smiled sadly, acknowledging the moment was ending. She moved back and turned her head to show Chalone the translucent film slowly firming up over her exposed implants. "It doesn't hurt," she said gently as Chalone gasped in surprise. "I will be fully healed in about an hour."

Chalone nodded and snuffled into her handkerchief. She offered it to Liesha, who delicately refused, and drew hers from her pocket.

"I never knew you could do that," Chalone referred to the healing, not the handkerchief. The scientist within fascinated in spite of herself.

"I know. We don't broadcast it too widely. Prejudice still exists, even in a society as perfect as ours!" She finished, the irony back in her voice.

They leaned against the corridor wall and shared a few moments of silence. Their old relationship had abruptly ended, and a new one had yet to be forged. Finally Chalone looked at her mother, who instinctively knew what was coming. Liesha hoped the question would be asked without sorrow or anger.

"Why?"

"Which 'why' would you have me answer first?" Liesha smiled. Her tension eased and she felt at peace with her daughter for the first time in decades.

"Why did you leave me? Why did you become an ECHO? Although, they're the same thing I suppose," Chalone mused. "Why were you really chosen to come with me today? What are Vian and the ECHO hierarchy plotting? I guess something that we should pay attention to sooner or later, is where did that wind come from, where did it go, and…where are we?" Her list of questions ran down as an uneasy feeling rose in the pit of her stomach.

* * * *

They agreed that perhaps they should find the answer to Chalone's last questions first, and leave the other thornier ones until later when they returned to their world. They stood at the corridor junction without a clue as to which way led where.

"What do you think?" Chalone asked, turning around and peering down one corridor and then another, then the third.

"Which way did we come?"

"I would say that we have equal knowledge of how to navigate within these corridors," Liesha said. "So, let us use the tried and true method of guessing."

Chalone shrugged in agreement.

After arbitrarily choosing a corridor, they set about repairing the damage to their clothes and bodies.

They soon patched up their hurts with the med-kits they carried. Using an annealing tool that looked very much like an old-fashioned awl, some shapes didn't change with the passage of time and different uses, they mended the tears and scrapes in their clothing with patches of a different sort. Chalone stuck her finger through a hole and grimaced. All things considered, they'd been quite lucky. In spite of herself she tried to see Liesha's face out of the corner of her eye

Liesha caught her as they returned their depleted supplies to their packs.

"Do you really want to see?" she asked. Chalone nodded dubiously. To her vast surprise an ear and a complete covering of skin had regrown. She gently touched Liesha's face. The skin felt soft and as alive as hers. She kissed her mother's newly grown cheek and returned to her packing with a lighter heart. Liesha brushed away unexpected moisture from her eyes.

All patched up and ready to face whatever happened next, they walked only a few meters along the chosen corridor before it began to sway and shudder. A blast of rapidly moving air blew their hair back from their faces and snatched at their clothes. The temperature dropped alarmingly, and their breath ghosted from their mouths.

"This isn't good," Chalone said, stating the obvious.

Liesha muttered as she looked behind her, then forward. "This wind must be coming from somewhere, going somewhere. It does not materialize, create a windstorm, and then dematerialize!" She glowered as she trudged into the increasingly strong headwind.

"I suggest we turn around and see where it's going then, because we can't go any further this way," Chalone shouted. The corridor shook underneath their feet as the wind suddenly increased speed and pelted them with tiny bits of debris.

The wind hustled and bustled them along the corridor taking little heed of their tiny stuttering steps and backwards lean to counter it. It howled into the third branch of the intersection and effortlessly swept them right along it.

The corridor narrowed slightly and the sudden increase in air pressure elevated the roar of the wind to a deafening scream and cuffed them to the floor. Every breath had to be desperately snatched from the rushing gale. To their great relief, its raw force soon eased to a blustery squall they could stand against.

"This is getting annoying," Chalone grumbled, making a show of dusting herself off. "Either blow or not!" she shouted after the disappearing wind.

Liesha reached out and snatched something from mid air.

"What's that?" Chalone asked as another gust propelled her a few meters along the corridor.

"It's a meial leaf," Liesha said, amazed and confused. She twirled the heart shaped leaf by its stem.

"That's impossible," Chalone said. "There aren't any meial trees in the Gallery. Where did it come from?"

As if to answer her, a storm of leaves and bits of branches swirled along the corridor. Again the wind mysteriously vanished, dumping the untidy pile around her.

Chalone frowned. "This is too much to have come through a Portal on its own. No one could do this deliberately. The Gallery wouldn't allow it," she said, as her frown accused the leaves and twigs of committing a dire transgression of Gallery etiquette.

"What is happening?" Liesha asked as she looked at the leaves at her feet, down the corridor, and then back at Chalone, who shrugged and kicked at the pile. Liesha crumpled the meial leaf and tossed it aside. Deep in thought, she strode along the corridor the wind had pushed them into. She only slowed down when she heard Chalone struggling to keep up with her. "The only explanation I can think of," she said while she waited. "Is that a Portal has failed somewhere."

"That's impossible," Chalone repeated, too shocked by the concept to pay attention to what she said.

"Will you stop that?" Liesha asked brusquely.

"Sorry. It's an annoying habit. I do it when I'm nervous."

Liesha hugged her reassuringly and released her. It was another step in rebuilding their relationship. "Me too," she said.

"You babble when you're nervous?" Chalone would never have used 'babbling' to describe Liesha.

"No. I am nervous as well."

"You should hear me when I'm terrified!"

Liesha smiled. "Let us hope for both our sakes, it never comes to that."

Shoulder to shoulder, they walked along the corridor into the distant upwardly curving horizon.

Chapter Eighteen

Chalone and Liesha continued down the changeless corridor for a very long time. They walked briskly enough for the air to cool their abraded skin so they could forget for a few moments at a time what danger they'd been in. No wind buffeted them, no debris tripped them up, and no more corridors branched off to break the monotony. The Gallery sustained them indefinitely and a long age passed before either of them became weary.

They stopped at a part of the corridor that looked like every other part they'd walked through and sat down together. They weren't really tired, just worn down, and stretched their legs out in front of them.

After musing on her list, Chalone finally asked one of the questions out loud, "Why did you choose to become an ECHO?" She mused some more. "No one ever told me. They didn't believe a child could understand such a grown-up concept. Lila wouldn't say anything other than you would always love me, which I didn't think was a very satisfactory answer. I gave her a very bad time about that."

Liesha chuckled. "I think mother understood. She always had a big heart, bigger than mine. I am glad Vian finally realized it." She smiled cheekily, daring Chalone to make any sort of comment. Chalone could respond in so many ways, but she refrained from saying anything.

"However, to answer your question." Liesha gathered her thoughts around her. "I have a gift that you have inherited from me. An affinity with the patterns of life. We intuit how events and places, people and their actions, fit together to form something that is greater, or different than anyone else sees.

"When you were five, the ECHOs approached me to do a search in the Archives. It does not matter now what it was, but they also offered implants so that I could work directly with the archival information, similar to how you interact with the helmets but without the external equipment."

"Like Tallem?" Chalone asked. "Is that how they recruit?" Her suspicions returned in full force. She'd never been comfortable with Tallem's implant.

"Tallem? No," Liesha said, noting that Chalone started to refer to the ECHOs as something different than herself. Not something she could afford to let go unchallenged.

"We..." If she wore glasses, Liesha would've peered sternly over the top of them. "Do not need to recruit. We are always turning away candidates, in spite of the risks, of which they are comprehensively informed," she said with some asperity. "If Tallem does become an ECHO, it will be her choice. Her implant only makes information easier and faster to access." It was not the complete truth about Tallem's implants or her motivations, but that story was not Liesha's to tell.

"However, I accepted the implant and completed the task." Liesha paused and thought deeply.

The moment she'd inadvertently uncovered a part of the ECHOs long term plans still sent a chill of anticipation along her nerve endings. They'd predicted that Argol would become deserted as the population continued to disperse among the Gallery. It meant a whole planet to do with as they pleased, and they had big plans.

Liesha believed Chalone would make a magnificent leader for their great adventure, but ECHO secrets were not hers to share without consultation. Not here. Now they were on friendlier terms, perhaps Chalone would listen to her long enough to consider the possibilities later.

Liesha returned from her ruminations and saw Chalone looking at her intently. She shrugged delicately to divert that piercing attention.

"We should keep moving," she said. As they resumed their journey, Liesha continued her explanation. "I found I was suited to the position of Archivist and there was a need, a great need for one because the previous Archivist retired and had not trained a successor." This was again, a partial truth.

"I talked it over with Lila and although she protested strongly on your behalf, she finally agreed to look after you. I left straight away because I could not bear the anguish and confusion I knew you would feel. It was cowardly I admit." Tears closed Liesha's throat for a moment. "It was the hardest thing I had ever done up until then. I knew you would hate me. You were a child of very strong convictions."

"Still am."

"I have noticed that. I wanted to communicate with you while I completed my training, but it was not possible. The reconstruction of my body, the insertion of the implants, the indoctrination process required complete immobilization. It took years to undo all my instinctual reactions to the world around me in order to rely on my ECHO senses." She smiled to herself at the shocked look on Chalone's face.

Liesha knew she'd revealed as much of her metamorphosis as Chalone was capable of hearing without reverting to her more familiar distrustful self.

"Once I was able to function as a fully integrated ECHO, I again thought about contacting you, but you were an adult and had built a new life for yourself. Lila told me of your feelings, and I thought it best to keep out of your way. I did not make the wisest of choices, but I will be honest with you, I do not regret a single one of them. Had I known how deeply you felt betrayed, I would have chosen to tell you what was happening whether I thought you could understand or not, but I still would have become an ECHO."

There were the words Chalone feared hearing more than any others, and they didn't sting as much as she thought they might. She put herself in her mother's place and thought it through. "I would've done the same thing," she said, finally admitting Liesha's right to make unpleasant choices that hurt others and still be able to live with herself.

* * * *

Their survival depended on being able to trust each other. For Chalone, that trust was a new experience and she wanted to understand Liesha as much as she could in the shortest possible time.

Liesha wanted to know more about her daughter than she ever could hope to glean through third hand sources and the ECHO network.

Conversations passed to and fro without time ever being measured in loss of sleep or hunger. It could have been months or just the blink of an eye. In the end they talked themselves out and continued on in companionable silence.

Occasionally they passed small windfalls of debris. A light dusting of the glittery substance that stirred in their wake covered leaves, twigs, and strange fruits neither of them recognized.

Every once in a while the corridor shuddered and shook from side to side. After the first few times, their dread gave way to boredom.

Then they would sit down with their backs to the corridor wall, just for something else to do. After one of these breaks, Chalone stood back up and offered her hand to Liesha.

"Come on. Let's walk for another eternity. We have to arrive somewhere, sooner or later."

"Your optimism borders on the maniacal. Have I mentioned this before?"

"Obsessive was the word you used last time, and it's better than being fatalistic."

"Commence walking impertinent child!"

"Yes, Liesha." After another while, Chalone looked around. "Tell me I'm not seeing things!"

Liesha joined her. "This is new," she said.

"It gives one a reason to go on, doesn't it?" Chalone asked merrily.

They walked down the long sloping floor until their thighs protested at the strain. The corridor expanded until it widened so the walls on either side disappeared into a misty haze. The ceiling rose beyond their sight.

Feeling rather lost and insignificant amongst the endless nothingness, they moved to one side of the corridor to be instantly reminded of how small they were against its looming majesty.

"I've never come across anything like this before," Chalone said quietly as they followed the walls' comforting presence.

"I cannot recall it ever being mentioned in the Archives," Liesha added and gave up trying to see across to the other side. It was giving her a headache even with her augmented vision.

"It'll make quite a story when we return," Chalone said.

"A joint release," Liesha suggested, knowing the trouble Chalone had encountered with her reports in the past.

"Oh yes, with your name first. In fact I'll be the silent partner."

"We should make notes."

"Observe everything around us with great care and attention to detail."

"All this detail?" Liesha asked, with a grand sweeping gesture at the lack of anything to note around them. Laughing at their nonsense, they walked along until they finally saw something to observe.

A dark shadow on the surface of the wall loomed up ahead, an opening to another corridor. They ran up to it and touched the junction just to make sure it was real.

Just beyond it another corridor joined into theirs, and further along they saw several other dark openings. They looked up the curving slope of the wall and saw more openings, more than they could count.

Liesha pulled Chalone back from the brink of the minefield of oubliettes that crowded the floor of the corridor as well. "Which way now I wonder?"

"Your guess is as good as mine," Chalone said, unconsciously shrugging off Liesha's hand. She turned abruptly. " You feel that?" The breeze had returned

"Where is it coming from?" Liesha asked.

Both tried to identify the direction by the feel of it on their exposed skin.

Another breeze came from the opposite direction and left just as rapidly. Soon they were buffeted from all sides.

"Keep walking," Liesha directed, her frown firmly in place again, and made to follow a path through the openings.

"Wait." Chalone caught her arm. "Let's see what happens."

"Why? Have I missed something?"

"Do you remember your Gallery legends? The axis of the Gallery, where all corridors converge, where time stands still and distance has no meaning?"

Liesha took a moment to understand. "The Hub?"

"Everything fits." Chalone pointed at the openings.

"Perhaps you are correct." Liesha looked around with new eyes. "It is so empty," she said at last, sounding disappointed.

"What did you expect?"

"A little more life, more color, mythical creatures guarding untold treasures, food and wine to excess." Liesha laughed.

"There's lots more of this glittery stuff here." Chalone said and held out her sleeve for Liesha to see. "It's everywhere." A fine dusting of it covered them.

Liesha rubbed some of it between her fingers and studied it intently. "It is like nothing I have ever seen before," she said. "Where does it come from?"

"Maybe it's what the corridors are made of," Chalone offered and then cocked her head. A roaring sound approached them like an oncoming freight-car. "'All corridors lead to the Hub'," she quoted. "Now we know it's not just a metaphor."

"Yes, but where is it coming *from*?" Frustrated Liesha looked around yet again, and saw nothing. Again

"That's not the point right now," Chalone said over the sound of the wind. "It's coming *to* here. We have to find shelter before it gets any worse."

"You are right," Liesha yelled, releasing her futile annoyance to focus on more pressing survival matters.

They turned about surveying the area and then looked at each other. They saw no shelter, nowhere to hide.

"You're going to see me terrified any minute now," Chalone shouted.

"Come with me," Liesha shouted back at her. "Get closer to the wall, between the openings. There should be less turbulence." She took hold of Chalone's arm, determined not to let her go now that she had found her again.

The wind spilled out from hundreds of different corridors, jostled around them, and surged into the huge open area.

Gasping with relief as the main front passed them by, they pressed their bodies up against the wall, and thrust their fingers through the tightly woven surface hoping to find something substantial to cling to.

The temperature dropped dramatically and the rushing sound increased to an ear-popping shriek. Streamers of tiny flecks of glitter and pieces of leaves whirled by to be shredded by the wind. Suddenly a new sound assaulted them. They looked over their shoulders as they witnessed the birth of a maelstrom that would endure for a thousand generations.

* * * *

A great creaking rumbled throughout the Hub. Engorged with air from the incoming winds it began to inflate like a giant balloon. The walls stretched and gaps appeared in the fabric as the fibers struggled to expand quickly enough to meet this new demand.

Clouds of glitter billowed out until Chalone and Liesha choked on it. It got in their eyes, hair, inside their clothes, coating them from head to toe.

At last the fibers began to unwind and expand to their true length, filling the ever increasing gaps. Although the nature of the Gallery maintained the corridors' integrity, the fibers themselves were no longer dense enough for Chalone and Liesha to keep holding on to them.

Chilled to the bone, their fingers slipped and they twisted around, trying desperately to keep themselves close to the wall. They dug deeper into the writhing surface, and managed to regain their handholds.

The pressure increased as the wind filled the cavern faster

than it could expand. Up and down ceased to have meaning as the angle where the base of the wall met the floor disappeared into a curve that took all their strength to balance on. Bigger particles of debris splattered against them and then darted on toward the center of the continually expanding cavern. The noise from the windstorm screamed at them, but even if they could unbend their frozen fingers, they dared not release their death grip to cover their ears.

The turbulent air spun around and around in the center of the Hub. It had nowhere else to go.

The Hub ballooned further and further until there was no distinction between its walls, floor or roof. The air grew so cold that droplets of moisture drawn in with the debris began to freeze together and form ice crystals. Wind driven remnants of plants and clods of earth emptied out from the corridor openings. Boulders and whole trees shattered against each other and were dragged in to the heart of the ponderous tornado to form a concentrated disc of matter that spun like a dervish.

* * * *

The Hub ceased expanding, but the force of the whirlwind continued to suck everything inward, even the air. Chalone and Liesha struggled to breathe. Then they were no longer being pushed against the wall but pulled back from it. For a heart stopping instant, they were weightless. Their legs drifted away from the wall until they hung above the storm of wind and wreckage by their hands alone. Far below them the disc grew as the debris compacted together in the heart of the gyre. They could only gauge its size by the wreckage that flew past them and descended for a very long time before impacting on its surface.

* * * *

Chalone ducked her head to avoid an onslaught of twigs and slivers of dirty ice and rock shattered from larger shards. Her fingers slipped. Frantic, she dug deeper to stop herself from being sucked down to a certain death, but she lost contact with the wall. The wind shoved her aside.

Liesha caught hold of her with one hand, her grip impossibly strong. Tendons stood out on her arms like cords of iron. Chalone's wrist bones ground against each other.

"I will not let you go," Liesha shouted ferociously. Her words snatched from her mouth by the force of the gale.

She looked at her other hand in desperation. The strain on fibers she held was too much and they gave way.

She lurched upward to dig deeper into the wall, but her enhanced strength was not enough to keep them anchored. She looked down at Chalone. Neither of them could do anything.

Suddenly a razor sharp pain roiled along her arm. Thin black ribbons flicked out from the wall, wrapped around her wrist, and cut deep into her skin. For an insane moment they held her up.

She would endure any amount of pain if it meant she and Chalone would somehow be pulled to safety, but that hope abruptly diminished. Whatever held her jerked and unraveled from her wrist, as though it, too, had slipped and needed to save itself. Blood streamed down her forearm and froze on her skin. As she began to fall, she told herself that the grip on her wrist had only been wishful thinking. She held on to Chalone as though it were the last act of her mortal substance.

"I am so sorry," she whispered, knowing full well Chalone couldn't hear her.

It seemed to Liesha that they fell toward the ravening tempest below with infinite slowness. It struck her as hysterically funny that the maniacal wind which had nipped at their heels since they entered the Gallery, let them gently drift down to their deaths like two orphaned snowflakes.

* * * *

They fell into the tornado winds that seized them and shook them like broken toys. It buckled their bodies, twisted their limbs, and swept them away to certain destruction.

* * * *

The shredded fibers where Liesha's last desperate lunge had failed, frantically rewove themselves before the force of the wind created more havoc.

The weavers had never encountered destruction on this scale. It bewildered their soft and imprecise imaginations. Their rescue had come too late, and perhaps was a forlorn hope to begin with. What could they have done even if they had been able to hold on?

The tiny creatures gathered sadly together and mourned the

loss of the two women they had such hopes for, but it was a well-learned harsh lesson. They could not risk themselves like this again. They had to find another way.

How shall we accomplish this, they asked themselves.

Survive, came the unlooked-for answer. *Endure.*

They spun around each other in consternation. Another entity lived within the Gallery walls? Such a thing could not happen, and yet undoubtedly it had. Even though they doubted its origin, they took the advice to heart. No time remained to ponder this mystery here and now.

They wove themselves between the inner and outer surfaces of the Gallery wall, and edged further away from the giant distortion and the tragedy they tried so desperately to avert.

Other intact corridors would still need their unique skills. All was not lost as long as they had hope. Even a very tiny piece of it sufficed.

Chapter Nineteen

In an Age before Time began, Sebenesh floated in the middle of a protective sphere as is the way of all creatures when they come into being. She emerged into the Immortal Realm, and grew, and learned. She frolicked with others of her kind as they explored their domain and established increasingly complex relationships. None were more important to her than Arahona. The two of them were true friends and the bitterest of enemies. She loved no one more.

Sebenesh created her Lair and concealed it in the endless cosmos beyond the boundaries of the Mortal Realm, the Shadowlands.

When Arahona called to her to save the Gallery, Sebenesh drew from the potent essence of her Lair and journeyed between the realms to create the tools she needed to honor her promise. She fashioned the Sphere, to fulfill a colossal purpose; the Skane, to ware the Gallery; and Truth Seeker, who existed as a separate entity long before Sebenesh ever called her to service, to guide the Sphere.

* * * *

The Shadowlands existed on many realms of existence where neither mortal nor immortal trod, a playground for beings of pure energy vapors.

In a constant state of flux, they shaped themselves as whim demanded and returned to formlessness when their attention shifted. Following their instinctual imperative to flow and dissolve with each other, over and over again.

For an eternity they followed this pattern until Sebenesh and her Lair appeared. The new energy source drew them like delicate butterflies to a strange new nectar. The Lair became an outcropping of solid substance they could not pass through. They found it to be an amusing toy. Using it to hide from each other, only to hurtle away, giddy with the sensations of their new game.

Then something unexpected happened. One of their number, small and newly formed, began to spin in ever decreasing circles.

She spun in on herself until she ceased to be. The others crowded around, thinking this a new and wonderful game. They made up a new spinning dance and went their merry way, oblivious to her fate.

Sebenesh shifted the being away from her fellow creatures and swiftly wove patterns of conscious intellect throughout the translucent wisp of movement. She now had prime survival imperatives that would enable her to expand her character through experience and observation and create a sense of her Self.

Truth Seeker became her name and she set out for the far-away glade in time to save the remnants of the Earthblood ritual. When Sebenesh released her to follow her destiny, she darted away, eager to discover more, about everything.

Unfettered by either mortal or immortal passions, Truth Seeker traveled throughout the Gallery and the worlds scattered along its multi-dimensional corridors. Following her whimsical curiosity, she observed all that was possible and impossible. She dabbled in the strange spaces that separated the realms, and explored the very edge of existence.

She often returned to one such strange in-between place. A place she called the Bøundary, a place that seemed to have no end. The lifelines of all things crisscrossed it. She found herself completely surrounded by endless threads of something akin to light that flexed and twisted, began and ended. So many that she never found an end to them.

On a whim she sought out the lifelines of each of the women of the Earthblood Circle and observed them closely.

She witnessed the effect their daily actions had on each lifeline, tangling it with their confusions and passions, and then straightened out as they moved through their mortal lives. She could tell where they had come from, back through past incarnations, and forward to the very end of their current physical one. Once they died the lifeline faded and only probabilities of future incarnations became visible to her inner eye.

Her fascination for the beings she encountered throughout her adventures remained full of wonder, and without judgment, uncorrupted by the darker sides of mortal consequence. Birth, life, and death, in all their mundane and magnificent variations held her awed, but she never felt tempted to act independently of the mandate Sebenesh imbued her with. She was to observe only, until the time came to fulfill her destiny.

* * * *

She observed that solid life-forms had trouble with the density of the Mortal Realm. They frequently terminated themselves and others by making strange choices regarding their actions. This intrigued her and she decided to explore the concept. After some experimentation, simply a matter of focusing her conscious will, she condensed herself into a variety of solid forms. After a series of solid-form incidents, she dismissed any permanent restructuring of her body as a waste of effort and energy. Her diaphanous form traveled easily and swiftly through any environment. Her forays into solidity were to amuse herself more than anything else.

Her merry rambling life through the Gallery worlds changed abruptly, when Jalemi triggered the fracture in Time and Sebenesh rewove it.

* * * *

On a world at the furthest edge of the Gallery's reach, Truth Seeker observed a tribe of long-lived inhabitants.

Earth tremors and volcanic eruptions often punctuated the harsh realities of these semi-nomadic people. The acrid and hard to breathe air forced them to retreat into a series of caves. The air was purer there, and the tremors that caused whole mountainsides elsewhere to collapse never affected the caverns.

* * * *

Malawatea was a spirit warrior, a dream shaman, and although well past her youth, a fine hunter. She stood tall and broad of shoulder, wiry of sinew, and wore her hair clipped short, except for her proud spirit warrior braid pulled forward between her breasts.

Malawatea ruefully acknowledged that younger and more agile hunters overtook her prowess in the field. However, her people did not measure worth by the vigor of youth, but by the wisdom of experience. As such a one she remained highly respected.

She had been hurt during a recent hunt, not seriously, but enough for her to graciously volunteer to watch over the children and teach their lessons for a week or two.

The unquiet oceans surrounding their homeland often produced awe-inspiring storms that swept across the coast, drenching everything in their path. The tribes people welcomed them because the troublesome air from the volcanoes blew away and rich silt fertilized the floodplains. Thus their Mother renewed Herself.

As Malawatea watched over her rowdy brood including two sprung forth from her womb, a monster storm grumbled and tumbled its way up from the south. It uprooted trees, caused great swathes of damage through the forests, and flattened parts of their newly planted crops.

The children soon grew tired of squealing at the lightning flares and decided they wanted an adventure. They approached Malawatea like a pack of young hounds and good-naturedly nipped at her heels until she promised to guide them on an expedition deep into the caves.

She tucked the ornate head of her beautiful walking stick firmly into her hand to support her injured leg, picked up a supply of resin torches in the other, and limped after her willful charges like a leaf caught in a whirlpool not of its making.

The chance for an adventure, however tame, excited her as much as the youngsters. Being invalided out of the hunting parties had thrown her in with the younger members of the tribe in awe of her dream weaving talents. Such adulation could be wearing at times. Although a natural teacher, she was at heart a solitary warrior and relished time away from their adolescent, although discreet, admiration.

After a boisterous conference about which tunnel to try first, the children headed off. Their carefree chatter and laughter echoed along the well-used tunnels. There was no real danger, but who knew what might be lurking around the next corner waiting to scoop them up.

Malawatea's torch sparked tiny reflections in the tunnel walls. She asked the children to name the minerals that caused the tiny lights and the uses the medicine folk put them to. Some of them protested at their adventure being used as a lesson, but Malawatea refused to go any further until everyone understood that learning went hand-in-hand with any great adventure.

She lit her fourth torch by the time she reached her destination, a tiny bolt hole that led to an underground cavern. Inside it there raged a giant waterfall and a pool warm enough to swim in. All manner of creatures lived in the giant cave, but the children didn't know that most of them were fairly harmless. *What was the point of an adventure if there was no risk?*

Unfortunately a small landslide inside the bolt hole blocked the entrance to the magical cave. It scraped part of the existing rock wall away and exposed something that glittered brightly in the torchlight.

The Portal had originally been located on the surface, but the age of volcanism slowly reshaping the planet had shuffled it down through the earth until it was inside the cave system.

This more than made up for not being able to visit the cave. The children immediately wanted to investigate this wondrous thing, but Malawatea would have none of it. She put the children behind her and walked up to the sparkling object. It reminded her of the giant maw of one of the deep-sea fish they occasionally caught in their winter camp. Instead of razor sharp teeth, rows of brightly shining crystal lights winked at her. In between the crystals, hung a frozen waterfall of light.

She slipped into her spirit warrior self to investigate the object. It remained indifferent to her presence and she sensed no menace about it. She handed the torch to the eldest child, and reached out to touch the bright crystals. The distance between the nearest twinkling light and her fingers slowly decreased. The children held their breaths, as she did herself. When her hand touched it sparks leaped from one crystal to another until they all glowed brighter. The children exhaled a collective gasp and surged forward.

Malawatea was not so effusive. She motioned them back and reached into the center of the object. Her hand met with no resistance and disappeared right through the shimmering surface.

Her reflexes kept her from falling through, but she peered down at her arm. It had been amputated above her elbow. She held still for a moment and then backed away from the strange thing.

Her hand reappeared. This mystery was not something to explore with the children beside her. To their immense disappointment, she hustled them back to the home caves and passed them along to other adults.

She shared the story of the discovery with her people and good-naturedly endured the long discussion afterwards. Eventually she was chosen, as she knew she would be, to lead the group who would investigate the object.

Her people last saw the flickering of the torch she carried as she walked into the bolt hole and approached the mysterious glow in the tunnel wall.

The shock-wave in front of the Reweaving of Time finally reached this distant world with devastating effect. A great tremor shattered the rock in front of the bolt hole, completely sealing it. The actual Reweaving however, arrived unnoticed and unannounced.

The expedition lost no more lives. Everyone escaped back to the main cavern, although bruised and bloody.

Only when they were certain the quake had passed, and there was no more danger of rockslides did they try valiantly to reach Malawatea. After a day and a night passed and no end to the rubble was in sight, the spirit warriors journeyed between the worlds in trance, and searched for her in their way.

They found no evidence of her physical body, alive or otherwise, nor her spirit resting in the Afterworlds. No one believed she died, but they knew she had moved beyond their help. She would be missed and they mourned for their loss.

When her children grew to adulthood and found mates, they named the firstborn girl-child of every generation after her.

Down through the passage of untold years, her name lived on.

* * * *

When Malawatea and the children walked deeper and deeper into the cave complex, Truth Seeker wafted along in their wake. She looked forward to savoring their reactions when they discovered the Portal and hid behind a knuckle of rock that jutted out from the wall to watch.

Malawatea's forbearance disappointed her a little, although she admired her restraint. She knew just how much the warrior woman wanted to cast all caution away and step through the Portal to see what was on the other side.

Truth Seeker was about to flit back to the main caves, when Malawatea and a few others returned to the Portal. As Malawatea walked toward her place of concealment, the entire mountain range suddenly shook with a fatal violence.

The shock-wave reverberated through the crust of the planet, releasing the enormous pressure between two opposing edges of a major fault that had been building for millennia. Even the Portal could not stand against such puissance. The earthquake crushed it out of existence.

Malawatea didn't even have time to look up, or draw a breath before the rock above her head cracked and collapsed.

Without thinking Truth Seeker flowed from her hiding place, transformed into solidity and covered Malawatea with her body.

Abandoning her never crossed her mind.

Rock cascaded down, boulders the size of houses came to a halt within a hairsbreadth of Truth Seeker's back, tons more hammered into those already wedged against her.

The shaking and the noise continued on forever, but eventually the last rock slipped down and the last rumble faded away. Truth Seeker felt Malawatea struggle underneath her, struggling to escape, struggling for breath. She reached out with her senses and encountered nothing except the unyielding presence of rock and dust. The rock settled, solid and unmoving, but the dust sifted down and filled the gaps between the rocks like a suffocating pall.

Malawatea shuddered and lay still.

That stillness frightened Truth Seeker. *What should she do? What did she know about mortals whose fragile bodies broke so easily?* A thin trickle of the suffocating dust drizzled onto her half formed substance.

Air!

Malawatea needed to breathe.

Truth Seeker stretched her body throughout the surrounding wreckage and captured enough air for the beautiful warrior woman to breathe. She twisted it inside a bubble of her substance and carefully retreated through the gaps between the rocks.

Malawatea didn't move. The hastily gathered air arrived too late.

Truth Seeker drew as far away from the still body as she could which only served to bring more dust down on them. Death caressed her spirit with its icy talons and she panicked, wanted to escape, return to her diaphanous form, and leave this calamity behind her.

Nothing happened. Her emotions immobilized and confounded her. They felt strange and difficult and clouded her spirit with their darkness. She remained in a semi-solid form draped over Malawatea's body until it grew as cold as the surrounding rock.

The rock fall groaned and settled again. Dust drifted over Malawatea's face like a death mask. Truth Seeker saw it and horror pierced her soul. No matter what, she knew she couldn't leave Malawatea buried under the rock with the dust seeping into her body.

A long time passed before she summoned the courage to move. Some distance from her the falling rocks had created an air pocket. She stretched her substance completely around Malawatea and shouldered a pathway through the gaps between the rocks, dragging her burden behind her.

The space was bigger than it seemed. There was more than enough room for the two of them. Truth Seeker unwound herself from Malawatea and gently laid her out on the rubble strewn rock. Of its own volition her body solidified, two arms, two legs, opposable thumbs. She had no other way of expressing the confusion and revulsion she felt.

She hunched away from the confrontational corpse, unable to be close to it and yet unable to leave it to the empty darkness. She paced the length of the open space, having legs distracted her momentarily, but then she turned and almost tripped over Malawatea. She stopped in bewilderment, as though she had only just come upon the body laying there in the stygian darkness.

She sank down beside her, close, but not touching because Malawatea shouldn't be left alone in the dark. She didn't know what else to do. Weariness blurred her senses and she fell into a daze.

* * * *

When she came to, the darkness remained unchanged and her companion was still dead. She reached out with a soft-formed limb to touch the cold flesh only to stop before she finished the gesture. Her actions made no sense to her. Her thoughts tumbled into morass she couldn't navigate. She was not a mortal, to grieve, to bleed, to weep and wail at death. She'd witnessed such things many times, but until now those images had never troubled her effortless passage through existence.

Then an idea occurred to her that suddenly lifted a great weight from her spirit.

She was not like mortals, not at all. The infinite differences between herself and Malawatea glared at her as if she saw them for the first time. She was unique and had unique abilities at her command, abilities beyond the limitations of mortality.

She floated up with a sense of triumph. A simple manipulation of the energy between the worlds and her conflict would be resolved. Death would cease to haunt her.

Chapter Twenty

In spite of Sebenesh's makeover, Truth Seeker retained her memories of her ancestral home, the in-between place, neither a mortal nor immortal realm, and could enter it at will. She'd never been tempted to return, perhaps afraid of what she would find now that she had different eyes to see with, but the energy that sustained it was a different matter.

She reached through and pulled a sliver of its substance to her. It manifested in the tiny cave like a ripple of pure white light that vibrated through the air until it reached Malawatea's face. It hovered over her as though measuring her worth.

The light suddenly exploded and filled the entire cave. Malawatea gagged and struggled for breath. She shuddered and drew in a single ragged gasp, then another, and another. She breathed deeply and her heart pumped her lifeblood throughout her body again.

With its task complete, the light broke apart and attached itself to the surrounding rocks. The sharp-edged chunks flowed into each other and smoothed out into walls. The light shone through Truth Seeker's transparent half-formed body and illuminated Malawatea's return to life, alive but different.

* * * *

Truth Seeker did a little dance of delight. *It worked*! The strange emotional dissonance that had fogged her thoughts disappeared.

Although quite astonished by the success of her plan, she waited impatiently for Malawatea to wake up.

The acoustics in the space grew thicker as something else entered.

"So," a slightly amused feminine voice from beyond the lustrous rock walls rumbled. "You venture into unknown territory, my little Observer. You have surpassed yourself, with a little help of course."

Taken aback, Truth Seeker spun around trying to find the source of the voice.

"I am not upset with you. In fact this might just turn out better than I planned. Well done!" The voice faded, taking the last of its gift of light back with it. Silence and darkness encased Truth Seeker again, leaving her pleased at the unlooked for praise and yet bewildered and anxious about how many of her choices drove her actions.

Through the stygian darkness she sensed Malawatea stirring so she focused on her rather than the score of unanswerable questions that welled through her consciousness.

Malawatea spoke as though she knew she had died and awoken in the Afterworlds, as her people called their after-life.

"I did not know that I would need to breathe after I died. It is quite uncomfortable," she added ruefully, as she tried to move and found her body full of strange aches and pains. "Where is 'She who is the Order of All Things' who just spoke?" she asked in a deeply formal voice because she was unsure of just who or what might be listening and didn't want to offend. "Perhaps I might have a light to see around me?" she respectfully added, which was not an unreasonable request to make of the Afterworlds.

Truth Seeker retreated to the far side of the cavern feeling overawed by Malawatea's apparent calmness. Events momentarily moved out of her control. However, she granted Malawatea's request for light and compacted herself a little more densely to glow in the darkness.

Malawatea gingerly sat up. Her ribcage gave her trouble as she looked around her for the first time. "I am still in a cave." She spoke in her normal tone although tinged with disappointment. "So then, I'm not dead."

Truth Seeker decided that vocal chords might be useful at this point. She willed the appropriate organs into being and the fluidity of her body complied. She couldn't lie though, even if she wanted to.

"Technically, yes, and no," she squeaked, and hastily adjusted her new larynx. She hoped her answer would gain her a moment to perfect the organ. Unfortunately for her, Malawatea was a warrior and a mother, and knew an evasive response when she heard one.

"Explain yourself," Malawatea said calmly, and rose to her feet, the injury to her leg absent. She carried herself like a true warrior, perfectly balanced and totally at ease within her magnificent body. She faced the direction the voice came from and saw an oddly-shaped being glowing against the rock wall. Not wishing to startle the apparition, she brushed the dust off her snug fitting vest and short kilt, more in order to give Truth Seeker an opportunity to gather her thoughts than any concern about the state of her attire.

Truth Seeker had a new set of problems to deal with. Her newly formed throat developed an intense tickling sensation. If she'd thought to create tear ducts at the same time she created her vocal cords, they would have been watering enough to drown her. She swallowed desperately, and tried to look confident and composed.

A coughing fit doubled her over as she breathed in too deeply and overfilled her lungs. Suddenly tear ducts seemed like a good idea.

Malawatea studied her closely. This strange being acted like nothing she'd ever encountered before. "Are you a ghost-being?" she asked after Truth Seeker finally got the hang of breathing without choking.

Truth Seeker didn't know what a ghost-being was, and opted for a different kind of truth. "I'm from a different reality than the one you know," she yodeled as her voice sailed up and down through three octaves and eventually settled into a lyric contralto.

"It exists on the other side of the shiny, er...window you and the children discovered."

Truth Seeker's words resonated against Malawatea mind and her memories of the rock fall returned with such force that it staggered her. "I don't understand," she gasped. "I should be dead!"

"I know! I know it's confusing, but I can explain." At that moment a disturbing thought occurred to Truth Seeker. "I will," she said and held up her hand, "in just a moment."

She ignored Malawatea's startled look and disappeared before her eyes, thoughtlessly taking the light her body generated with her.

* * * *

Truth Seeker slipped into the Boundary and searched among the masses of threads for a particular one. There it was, broken.

She held its jagged bleeding end in her hands. It had faded to a dark colorlessness, the clear reflection of an untimely and violent death. Malawatea's resurrection was not reflected in her lifeline. She wasn't supposed to exist beyond her recent death.

Truth Seeker paced back and forth in the Boundary trying to resolve this conundrum. She glanced into the Mortal Realm where Malawatea waited patiently for her return. Not that she could do a lot otherwise. Truth Seeker abandoned her with no other option.

Truth Seeker resumed her pacing more for the pleasure of movement rather than a source of inspiration. *What wonderful things, articulated joints.*

The voice in the rock-light praised her actions which meant she had done something right. So, because Malawatea was indeed alive, then she was supposed to be alive. Truth Seeker still had the dilemma of the severed lifeline to resolve.

Perhaps if Malawatea was alive and breathing here in the Boundary, then her lifeline must recognize her life-force and start up again. *The perfect solution!* After all, life originated in the Boundary and returned there after death to become life again. It made perfect sense.

Truth Seeker reached back in to the Mortal Realm and drew Malawatea into the Boundary.

* * * *

Chaos shrieked at Malawatea. It seared her body like acid, ravaged her muscles and bones. Her skin froze into a white shroud and her blood caught fire. She vomited gouts of black energy that scorched the air and stank like a slaughterhouse. Her jaw clenched and crushed her teeth. Her tendons snapped and shriveled to dust.

Unable to escape the consequences of Truth Seekers mistake, she became an empty shell laying in a bloody heap in front of Truth Seeker's stunned and appalled mist-like feet.

"You! Ignorant! Stupid! Blind! Idiot!" The voice punctuated its exclamations with blasts of icy air that so terrified Truth Seeker she nearly collapsed on top of Malawatea's twice dead corpse.

For an eternity, the silence of the Boundary reigned and Truth Seeker cowered into herself, unable to comprehend what had just happened.

"Perhaps I overestimated your abilities," the voice said in an even tone just as frightening as the rage had been a moment before. "Mortal flesh cannot exist here, nor is there any renewal of Life in the Boundary. Your knowledge is incomplete. Life comes from beyond here, passes through as spirit and is reborn into mortality. You'd already succeeded in continuing a Life after its time had finished, and yet you were not satisfied."

"Her timeline..." Truth Seeker tried to explain.

"You can see them," the voice interrupted. "You do not have to power to alter them."

"I didn't know," Truth Seeker tried to defend herself.

"You didn't bother to find out," the voice pointed out mercilessly.

Truth Seeker sensed the voice turn its attention away from her, for which she felt mightily thankful.

Malawatea's tortured body shimmered in a radiant glow that eased the last moments of mortality from its visage. Bones mended, fingers straightened, and flesh clothed the ravaged skeleton once more. There it lay, a mere husk, suspended between the worlds.

Truth hammered brutally at Truth Seeker. She was no longer an observer. She'd given life to Malawatea, and she had killed her as well. Her spirit wailed in agony no less terrible than Malawatea's for it being of the heart rather than of the body.

"What have I done?" she said brokenly, as the lesson of Malawatea's fate shattered her innocent arrogance and showed her the consequences of power.

"You've certainly done more than enough," the voice said as Truth Seeker slid down beside the perfect body. One of her ill-formed hands rested above the dead heart. Tears she did not know she could cry issued from her overflowing eyes and fell onto the dead lips. She laid her head on her hand and wept.

The sylvan threads of lifelines pulsed around her with the energy of the living and paid no heed to this one being, kneeling at her victim's side in the shimmering Boundary twilight.

Malawatea's lifeline lay nearby. Truth Seeker picked it up and reverently draped it across the body. The lifeline shone for a moment as if it, too, bade her farewell. Malawatea's life finally ended.

* * * *

A long brooding silence passed before the voice, Sebenesh spoke again.

"Done is done, and cannot be undone. What happens from this point forward is the issue you must address now."

Truth Seeker opened her eyes. "I thought I might...I... I have no idea what to do next."

"Fortunately, I have many ideas," Sebenesh said. "First, you are going to need a body that you won't be able to unravel whenever the mood takes you."

Truth Seeker's head rose up from its cold tear-stained resting place. "I do?"

"You will use the one you've created. Once you inhabit it, you will have all your usual abilities with the added bonus of solid flesh and bones."

Truth Seeker assumed this was merely a suggestion for her to consider. The thought of taking over Malawatea's body seemed disrespectful and unsavory. Malawatea had only just vacated it and...and...a resounding psychic blow lacerated Truth Seeker's thoughts.

"Not only have you picked up some nonsensical notions of your own omnipotence in order to have created this situation in the first place" Sebenesh said in a stinging accompaniment the slap. "You seem to think that you have a choice in this matter. My original plan was a fair beginning for your talents, but now the Timeline has been rewoven and there's a great deal more for you to do."

Sebenesh informed her that due to the actions of one bewilderingly incompetent mortal, everything that existed before the fracturing of Time had now broken apart. Sebenesh busily rewove it, using another far less cohesive timeline. For it to work, many things needed to happen at the same time, and Truth Seeker had to play a integral part. She described her plans for Truth Seeker's future in great detail.

It was not a fate for the fainthearted or squeamish and Truth Seeker's reticence at utilizing Malawatea's body disappeared in an instant.

"I understand everything now," she said in a strange new voice, and found herself laying flat on her back, with tears on her forehead.

"I doubt that," Sebenesh disputed. "You understand enough. Now get up, you look silly laying there like that, and shift yourself to the Hub. Some of your charges are in danger."

Truth Seeker sprang to her feet in a body that bustled with life and wild passions. She reached out and touched nearby lifelines with fingers perfectly formed, long and sensuous.

Two familiar ones thrummed with dire tautness. Chalone and Liesha should have lived to very old age, but now they were about to meet a horrible death. Truth Seeker's new body remembered death, and fear fueled adrenaline coursed through her veins.

The Hub was far away from the Boundary, but she had a way to reach them in time.

* * * *

Sebenesh gave her one last command. "Find yourself another name to go along with this fine new body. Truth Seeker is no longer yours."

The nameless woman responded immediately, "Mor!"

"Mor," Sebenesh repeated. "That will do nicely. Remember what happened here Mor. Learn from it. I shall be keeping an eye on you from now on."

"I have no doubt of that," Mor exclaimed, but the threat had already lost most of its potency in the face of her new adventure.

She flexed her will and shifted the silky smoothness of her new body into the dominion of the Shadowlands.

Chapter Twenty-One

The little cave in the middle of the rock fall remained quiet and empty. The smooth walls stood like sentinels in the darkness. Above them rocks groaned and settled into their new configurations. Dust motes filtered down through the rocks and an occasional errant breath of air sculpted them into little ripples across the floor of the cave.

* * * *

Stillness matured into days, months, years, then became timeless.

* * * *

A handful of tiny sparks ignited in the middle of the cave and fled outwards. They struck the walls and then winked out. More followed, and stayed alight.

The cave began to sparkle as more and more of the lights came into existence and exploded in all directions. They grew brighter and brighter until the rock beamed.

A ripple of energy warped the center of the space. Something with a purpose entered the cave. As though a charge of static electricity had been ignited, the dust began to migrate toward it. A distinctly female body began to take shape. Shapely arms, firm legs, and finally, skin the color of a deep dusky twilight sky. The head moved as though surveying the empty space. Not conscious, nor completely asleep, it was as alive as a mortal could be after dying in the Boundary.

"What shall we do with you?" Sebenesh asked from somewhere else.

The dust woman ignored the question and slowly flexed her body. She moved one foot after the other, and walked to the nearest rock wall. She touched the rock, only to have the dust particles that gave her substance slowly flit to the stone floor. She tilted her head as though admonishing the motes for abandoning her. They flew up and outlined the shape of her fingers once more.

The rock walls had merged seamlessly into each other. There was no way out. Yet some tiny spark of her spirit still brokenheartedly yearned to go back to family, children, and tribe.

"I can't really send you back to who and what you were," Sebenesh explained. "Once you transition into life you won't remember anything of your past. You don't belong there anymore. A great deal of time has passed. Not even the land would look the same to you."

The dust-woman nodded slowly. She stood in the middle of the space and held out her hands in a supplication that required a solution.

"Even still, you refuse to die," Sebenesh replied, as if she'd spoken out loud. "You do present me with a dilemma. I will think upon this," she said and faded away, taking the light with her.

The dust-woman twisted from side to side in great agitation until the cavern walls began to glow again.

"I apologize," Sebenesh said softly and returned the light. "I forget you are still emotionally attached to the Mortal Realm. Be at ease. I will not abandon you here."

The dust woman relaxed and composed herself. She had work to do. She gathered more dust from the rocks around her and added them to her substance.

With each passing moment, the woman grew more solid and came closer to consciousness until finally Malawatea returned.

Her eyes, jet black orbs sunk deep into the austere planes of her face, slowly opened. She gazed in awe at the streaks of energy flowing and rippling throughout the cavern. Threads of living light shone like spokes in hundreds of pinwheels all around her. They knotted and tangled up, smoothed out, flowed straight and bunched together again. She saw into the Boundary.

She touched one of the lines. It thrummed like a taught bowstring and sent a sensuous ripple up her forearm. A wave of exotic memories crashed over her. Alien scenes, unintelligible languages, impossible emotions assaulted her senses. She quickly drew her hand back and the memory flash ended. She delicately strummed another, and this time sensed a settling into rich dirt, putting out roots, growing leaves and bright flowers that swelled into Autumn's harvest.

The life of a tree. Malawatea smiled, pleased she'd unraveled the purpose of the shimmering lines.

She needed to know something before the voice returned. She moved among the life-lines and played a note or two on each one, until she found the one she sought.

She saw one end anchored in her very first ancestor's past and the other terminating just beyond her fingertips in the knotted pain of her death. A thready wisp of vapor issued from the knot, and wavered about, as though unable to find a reason for its existence.

She swallowed nervously, and clasped her elbows with both hands. She dreaded touching it. It would connect her to a home she no longer had, nor was she the woman who belonged there.

She studied the end slowly undulating in front of her eyes, and in spite of herself, gently caressed it with one finger, drawing the memories of her life from it. They flowed over her and through her, filled the empty spaces between her hollow bones. She smiled as she felt her first lover caress her skin, then listened to the birth of her children, and smelled freshly picked corn baking in a bed of coals.

Through her previous self's eyes she saw the Portal that drew her to her death, and felt the knotted end of the thread tug at her breast.

The wisp of vapor represented her existence in the Mortal Realm after she'd twice died.

Through the thread of her lifeline, she gained an insight into Truth Seeker's existence, who created her, and why. A ghostly image of Sebenesh in all her rampant glory, creating the Sphere and sending it to its mortal doom swam in front of Malawatea like a vision. She thought about the countless lives that would be affected by the Sphere's destiny and the anguish they would feel as those titanic events swept them along. A determined glint shone in her eye. She called to the voice she knew to be Sebenesh.

"I have a solution to the dilemma of my existence."

Sebenesh read her intention and laughed. "We're making this up as we go along, aren't we?"

"There has never been a need such as this before," Malawatea said and smiled for the first time. "I am not the first to die out of my time as a result of this grand reweaving of yours, and I certainly won't be the last. When the Gallery and the Sphere have achieved their destiny, we can be returned to the Mortal Realm and there will be no unnatural disruption to these."

She gestured toward the endlessly shining threads of lifelines. "This will give all of us a chance."

"Not much of a chance, and a very, very long wait," Sebenesh warned.

Malawatea shrugged. "For those who are strong enough, it will suffice."

The light in the cave winked out and left the uninhabited mound of dust in the center of the space in eternal darkness.

* * * *

In a distant valley shrouded in mist and snow, in another cavern under another mountain, a pulse vibrated through the air.

Granite shuddered and a stone column rose up from the cave floor. More followed until a forest of them stretched to infinity. They were of a simple design, round and smooth to the touch. Between each column a shimmer of energy waited until needed.

This Necropolis would gather all the beings caught up in the Gallery's destruction too strong of spirit to succumb to the finality of death. They would face one final battle and if they won through, they would materialize here, suspended within the energy.

Malawatea appeared in the center of the Necropolis and stepped between the first two columns, into the first cocoon. There she would wait to be renewed or die forever.

* * * *

Mor materialized in the Shadowlands, caught one heel behind the other, and immediately tripped over her own feet.

What an uncomfortable experience. These mortal bodies were supposed to stay upright, not tip over at the first uneven surface.

She pushed herself unsteadily to her feet, dusted off her kilt and tunic and looked around for the shapes and energy flows so familiar to her spirit. Her jaw dropped in surprise, and she wondered if she arrived in the right place.

Before Sebenesh kidnapped her to save the Mortal Realm, her semblance existed here on the whim of errant breezes, her senses gauged atmospheric disturbances, and the subtle aromas of different chemicals were her language.

Now, she stood on an immense plain in a corporeal body. The air tasted familiar, but would the breeze caressing her skin lift her over the highest of the rock formations or shred her diaphanous form into tatters? She had no way of telling anymore. She almost leaped up into it to see, but the burden of her physical body reminded her that she was more likely to fall flat on her face.

Not only was the air different but the landscape as well. Huge outbursts of boulders punctuated the land and grasses of an unknowable color swayed in the breeze. Small bushes struggled for existence in the lee of the boulders, and stinging insects scurried underneath the fallen leaves. There was life here but of the sort that was small and used to hiding from danger or stealing from smaller and more industrious creatures.

From horizon to horizon the sky looked like a giant golden bowl turned upside down. It radiated warmth, the abundant life was proof of that, but there was no sun, shadows, or day and night.

* * * *

The Shadowlands existed because it wished to, and that was its purpose. All other concerns passed through without impacting on it. A part of its consciousness, something deep and eternal, remained alert and knew everything that occurred within its borders.

It sensed Mor's arrival and although she wore a different body, it still recognized her as one if its own and left her to her own devices.

She shut her jaw and studied her surroundings from her new mortal perspective. Everything really was the same. She saw it through different eyes.

She was in no hurry to reach Chalone and Liesha now that she was in the Shadowlands. It would be easy to bypass the physical structure of the Gallery and reach them in time from here.

She breathed in and out, deeply.

Breath.

She had no previous experience to compare with the exquisite pleasure she found in the simple act of breathing. It almost took her breath away.

In between breathing and sightseeing, she focused on how to rescue Chalone and Liesha.

Sebenesh had impressed on her the need to keep her identity, and the truth about the Shadowlands securely hidden. *Why*, Mor had no idea, but *who was she to question her testy creator's ways?*

She sat down on a lumpish piece of ground and sorted through her options. It didn't take her long to figure out she didn't have any. That didn't matter. She felt far happier making things up as she went along. *How hard could this rescue be?*

Chapter Twenty-Two

Liesha and Chalone held on to each other as tight as only those who knew they were about to die could. The frigid air chilled them to the bone but where their bodies touched a trickle of warmth flowed between them.

Even as she tumbled along the rabid currents of air, Liesha marveled that they still lived. She dredged up the last of her ECHO enhanced strength and angled their bodies so they rode the wild currents until she found a relatively uncluttered stream. It was a temporary respite. Soon even her unique strength would fail them.

A titanic explosion flashed bright enough to illuminate the entire nightmare and then disappeared in an instant. Through eyes almost blinded by frozen tears and blasting sand, she witnessed atmospheres of many different worlds ignite into giant fireballs. Then they were snuffed out by the raging winds before they detonated the entire field. Deafening concussions of energy swirled throughout the maelstrom.

Giant trunks of trees, huge slabs of bedrock, tangled masses of plant-life, and unidentifiable alien structures, ground into each other and swept along within the cycling gale. The women missed colliding with these gigantic knots of wreckage by the narrowest of margins.

The swirling hurricane winds propelled them along an eccentric orbit within the Hub, sometimes adjacent to the walls that confined the maelstrom, and sometimes so close to the center they saw the compressed mass of shining debris spinning there. Boulders the size of mountains ricocheted off each other and shattered into pieces, and every piece eventually crashed into that steadily growing platform.

One such mountain of jagged rock hurtled at them from across the far side of the Hub. They saw it at the same time. Their eyes met for a moment. It was all they had time for.

The giant boulder bore down on them. So close the sound of its imminent approach roared through the background din. Suddenly it shuddered and slid beneath them, matching its velocity to theirs.

With no wind to sustain their flight, they dropped into a

roughly gouged out hollow on its surface hard enough to knock them unconscious.

* * * *

Mor clung to a nearby protrusion, grateful she'd caught them at all. The forces within the Hub exceeded her estimations. She had to extend her unique abilities to their fullest to capture the giant piece of rock and keep it intact, while she maneuvered it across the Hub. Slowing it down and keeping it under her two targets exhausted her, and she doubted she could avoid any sort of future collision. Her lump of rock was just too big. From what she saw of the looming masses bearing down on her, she had very little time to complete her rescue.

She flexed her will and connected to the Shadowlands.

Just because she took a fancy to call the Shadowlands, it didn't necessarily follow that the Shadowlands would respond. Mor was in essence one of its children and she counted on that relationship meaning something to it. She lay on the freezing rock and stretched her arms around Chalone and Liesha, expending the last of her strength to warm them.

The Shadowlands considered her call, and ponderously gave its permission. She groaned in relief. Their rock had ceased to orbit the Hub and started its final plunge into the central mass of debris. Mor drew an edge of the Shadowlands to her. It wasn't very big, and she wondered if she had underestimated the Hub again.

The Shadowlands seeped through the solid rock as though it didn't exist and enfolded all three women in its embrace.

As the sounds and sights of the maelstrom faded, Mor hoped Chalone and Liesha still lived.

* * * *

The Shadowlands glowed eerily. Even though it boasted neither sun, nor moon, its inhabitants had ample illumination to go about their business. Its outer limits where it shared borders with other realms were darker and more dangerous. Close to one of those edges, a hazy flickering of energy distorted a small circle of earth, and three unconscious bodies materialized in the middle of it.

The Shadowlands withdrew itself from Mor's grasp and flicked its awareness over the unconscious women.

Mor, it recognized immediately even in her new

incomprehensible body. Chalone, it lingered over, before acknowledging her right to be present within its borders. Liesha presented it with a dilemma. The harsh artificial substances entangled with her organic flesh tasted alien and it couldn't decide if they were harmful to its harmony or not.

Her life hung in the balance until Chalone, still locked in her arms, unconsciously snuggled closer as though for comfort or reassurance. The Shadowlands suspended any judgment about Liesha's fate until it had gained more familiarity with her essence.

It raised the three of them up from the earth on a gentle wave of energy that carried away from the frontier between the Shadowlands and the Boundary. The Boundary was unforgiving of any trespass and it wasn't safe for mortal life to linger anywhere near it.

Having done all it needed to, the Shadowlands withdrew its awareness from its unexpected guests.

* * * *

Liesha woke first. She savored that first moment of awakening before her mind or body recalled the events that preceded her fall into oblivion.

It didn't last long. All the indignities her body had been subjected to began competing for her attention. Every inch of skin, every muscle and tendon, every organ, biological and artificial, ached with pain and misery, even her eyelashes.

She struggled to open her eyes through a blindfold of blood, dust, and mud, not quite believing she was alive. Warm, she felt warm. Her fingers and toes tingled as they thawed. Her ears rang with the surrounding silence.

She lay on her side, with Chalone spooned in front of her. How they'd been rescued, she had no idea, but she needed to find out. She elbowed herself to a semi-sitting position, being careful not to disturb Chalone, when someone or something groaned behind her.

As she quickly turned her brain slammed into the side of her skull. Her battered nerve endings did not appreciate moving that fast. She stayed very still until the pain receded, uncrossed her eyes, and slowly looked behind her.

Liesha saw the most beautiful woman lying next to her. Her skin was the a color of a rich burgundy wine, her body beautifully proportioned, and judging by the sculpted muscles inadequately covered by her scanty clothing, very fit.

The woman groaned again.

"That hurts," Mor said and then laughed. "That hurts! This is what pain feels like!" She rolled onto her stomach and suddenly grasped her head in agony.

"Yes," Liesha agreed. "That is what pain feels like." She winced in sympathy but smiled at how funny someone else's eyes crossing and uncrossing looked. She gingerly rose to her feet and Mor made to follow her. "Do not try and stand up. Not until you are sure you are uninjured."

Mor thought about the warning. Although her new body had gained certain advantages because of her unique acquisition, it was still composed of a fragile mortality. Liesha probably knew quite a bit more about the workings of mortal anatomy than she did.

She slowly flexed her limbs and stood. When Liesha steadied her with a gentle touch, her knees turned weak in a rush of emotion that had nothing to do with getting knocked unconscious.

Liesha smiled knowingly, and quickly turned away to help Chalone as she struggled to wake from a nightmare of gnashing stones and ravening winds.

A fine sheen of the glitter from the Gallery covered them. She tried rubbing it off her skin.

By the time Chalone recovered sufficiently to stand, Liesha discovered that without regenerating her entire top layer of skin, something she could do given enough time, the glitter had become a permanent addition to her complexion.

* * * *

Chalone leaned heavily on Liesha and they looked pointedly at Mor, who sighed. She saw no way of respecting Sebenesh's wishes regarding the anonymity of the Shadowlands, so she decided to tell as little of the truth as she could. "This is the Shadowlands..."

"The Shadowlands?" Chalone interrupted. Her brain caught up with what Mor actually said and she looked around her as if to take it all in at one time. "Who are you?"

"My name is Mor. I'm..." Mor paused, searching for an adequate explanation. "Constructed. Yes, I was constructed from the essence of this place. Not in this form," she qualified, gesturing at her new body. "I liberated this from an unfortunate woman who had no further use for it, but my spirit comes from this realm.

This is my home." She said the word with a tinge of wonder in her voice. Up until that moment, home had been a borrowed concept.

Chalone's thoughts raced. *The Shadowlands*! She may be able to solve two mysteries at once. She spared a thought for Pirelle and wondered if she would be relieved or not. "How did we get here?" She nudged Mor, who remained entranced by the concept of 'home'.

"I called to the Shadowlands and it answered," Mor said. "It's a skill I have."

"How?" Chalone persisted. "I thought the Shadowlands was a place, not something you can direct. Can you show me how you did it? How you directed it?"

"So many questions," Mor said. "I have so few answers you would understand. It's like a Portal, but different," she began, and then floundered in the face of Chalone's confusion.

"That doesn't help." Chalone tried not to move her head too much in her eagerness for answers. "Can you show me how you called this energy, this Portal?"

"I suppose so. Its not that hard, once you know how. We have to return anyway. You'll see how it works."

"Return, to where?" Liesha asked. "Surely not back to that, whatever it was, in the Hub?"

"The Hub? No," Mor answered, glad to be able to respond to a somewhat simpler question. "Back to your world, back to the time you entered the Gallery."

"I have so many more questions. Who are you? What are you?" Liesha asked, talking over the top of Chalone

"Why?" Chalone asked at the same time. "What's happening?"

Mor began to feel overwhelmed by their mother-daughter tag team questioning. She glanced at Liesha and something tweaked her insides. It spoke of limitless possibilities even in the midst of strange adventures. "Perhaps someday I'll tell you all about me," she said. "Not now. We have to go."

* * * *

Mor was as good as her word, she didn't tell them, but if either woman saw exactly what she did, that wasn't her fault. She relocated the three of them in a Gallery corridor right next to a Portal threshold.

"How did you do that?" Chalone asked again.

The corridor twitched.

Mor ignored her. "I can't return you to the exact time you left or to the same Portal. The one you used is about to collapse and if you're in it you'll be destroyed."

That didn't really faze either Chalone or Liesha. They'd come so close to being destroyed recently that it'd lost its charm. Mor continued speaking rapidly, regardless of their reactions. "We have returned to a time moments after you entered the damaged one," she said distractedly, as she listened to her internal instructions.

The corridor trembled.

"What do you mean, the Portal will be destroyed? That's not possible," Chalone reiterated her mantra.

A look of consternation suddenly crossed Mor's face. "Hurry!" she exclaimed. "You have to stop Jalemi. She is about to release the Sphere. The Reweaving of Time will not hold them for long."

Among the three of them, only Liesha paid attention to the temblors running the length of the corridor

"This is not good. Stop who?" she asked as she caught up with the conversation. "What is all this hurrying about?"

"What Sphere? What Reweaving?" Chalone asked. Her questions collided with Liesha's again.

"I can't tell you. We have to go, now," Mor shouted and pushed them through the Portal.

* * * *

The three of them stumbled into the Hall of Lights. Mor recovered the quickest. She glanced around, took in every detail and then fled back into the Gallery.

Liesha and Chalone tried to catch her, but she disappeared before they barely turned around. They looked at each other and shrugged. Mor would never be found if she didn't want to be.

"What are you two still doing here," Vian bellowed, as she stormed across the Hall.

Chalone grinned. "Well, that answers that question."

"We have been and returned," Liesha said. "Time folds within the Gallery."

Vian walked around both women, and inspected them closely, including their ragged clothes and fresh wounds. "I want to know everything," she said.

"That'll have to wait for a while," Chalone answered. "We have to find Jalemi. Something awful's about to happen. Where is she?" She walked toward the exit.

"I don't know," Vian replied. "What's going on?"

Chalone felt something brush against her pants. She looked down at a bit of paper scudding across the floor and watched it fly straight into the Portal Mor warned them about.

"Oh no," she gasped. "Not again!" She dragged Vian to the exit as fast as she could. Liesha grabbed her other arm and they hustled her along.

The Portal cracked and began to collapse in on itself. The crystals bracing either side buckled and held. For a heartbeat, the air in the Hall shimmied toward the wounded opening and then something flickered inside the corridor. The rushing ceased before it could do any damage. The three women stopped, looked at each other, then back at the Portal.

"Mor was right," Chalone said.

"Yes, but what stopped the Portal from destroying us?" Liesha countered.

"What, exactly, is going on?" Vian shouted in fear and frustration.

Before either Chalone or Liesha could answer, the flagstones under their feet began to rock and twist as though forced up from below.

Vian's mouth opened and closed a few times but words failed her.

* * * *

The Elemental forces of Earth, Air, Fire, and Water were created when stray motes of energy from Sebenesh's design of the Skane, the Sphere, and Truth Seeker, were left behind. They fell to Argol and melded with the spirit of the land.

In the beginning they had no concept of morality other than theirs, no idea of justice other than theirs, but they did intimately understand the need for balance in the world that nurtured them.

Through their friendship with Vian, they slowly came to appreciate the people who inhabited the surface of their world, found a measure of compassion for them, and an understanding of their nature.

The calling of the Earthblood fire and the caging of the Sphere resonated within their consciousness as a balance, albeit a violent one, none-the-less they remained wary.

They sensed the Reweaving of Time, and knew that events taking place held the potential for a shattering of all they held dear.

The Sphere was too dangerous for them to approach unaided. It had the power to disassemble them with a single thought.

They trusted Vian to act for them and do what was necessary, but without their help she would not be able to reach Jalemi in time. Because she was with two others who had such fascinating energies lingering about them, the Elementals didn't mind giving them a ride as well.

* * * *

The Elemental Earth preferred direct action and used what was at hand. It elevated the flagstones Vian, Liesha, and Chalone stood on and moved them out of the Hall, through the woods toward the clearing where the Earthblood fire shone unaffected by any purpose other than its own.

As they traveled, Liesha looked at Vian and then down at the rickety clacking stones beneath her feet. "You know something about this?" Vian nodded and Liesha raised an enigmatic eyebrow. "Then you also have a story to tell," she said.

"That, too, can wait I think," Vian said, looking at the trees rushing by her. She hoped the Elementals would explain their actions when she got to wherever they took her.

At the edge of the woodland, the stone sled shuddered and collapsed. Elemental Earth billowed up from the pile of rubble like a burgundy wraith.

"Now begins the Reweaving of Time," it said in a deep resonant tone. "It unbinds my command of the stones just as any working of Sebenesh's does. I can take you no further. You must reach the Earthblood fire and stop her."

"Stop who?" Liesha almost shouted.

"Jalemi!" Vian and Chalone cried in desperate unison.

The women ran through the underbrush. Branches tore at their clothes and grasses tangled their feet. A force in front of them exerted its twisted will to slow them down, but they pressed on, impelled by an urgency that came from the depths of their spirits.

Even though Mor returned them so swiftly, in spite of their haste and the intervention of the Elementals, Liesha, Chalone, and Vian, were too late.

Chapter Twenty-Three

The Sphere sensed Pirelle at the edge of the glade where the Earthblood fire burned. In gleaning a lifetime of small misunderstandings and resentments from Jalemi's memories, it concluded, just as Jalemi had, that Pirelle was slow to act and vulnerable to coercion.

Pirelle was stronger than either of them knew. She easily deflected the Sphere's attempt to stop her. Unfortunately the shockwave ahead of the Reweaving of Time arrived like the thunderous crash of a tidal wave, and succeeded where the Sphere had not. Pirelle stumbled to the ground just as a strident voice thundered inside her head.

"Pirelle! Pay attention!"

* * * *

The Reweaving of Time slowed Jalemi down but only for a moment. The overwhelming presence of the Sphere muffled its potency and drowned out the voices from beyond the fire screaming for her to stop.

The Sphere controlled her every move, and almost every thought. Tucked away in a lonely corner of her consciousness, a tiny spark of shamed and fearful resistance huddled down, hidden from its influence, but still able to see and hear everything.

The Sphere forced her to touch the Earthblood column.

* * * *

"It's too late." The voice in Pirelle's mind howled in a rage. "You're all too late! After everything I've done!"

Its sheer intensity pressed Pirelle further into the dirt, but she managed to lift her head enough to avoid suffocating. She squinted through one eye and saw Vian, Liesha, and Chalone running into the clearing, calling for Jalemi to stop.

When Jalemi disappeared into the column of Earthblood fire, the voice screeched up several decibels to an agonized crescendo.

* * * *

The Sphere commandeered Jalemi's Practitioner skills and she passed unharmed through the firestorm's magnificent swirling ring of energy.

From the inside it looked to her as though the fire wasn't even there. Jalemi sighed and felt at peace. Her fingers tingled as they brushed against the Sphere's shiny surface and an almost physical heat radiated from it into her mind.

* * * *

Sebenesh had chosen no clear mandate as to what the Sphere's ultimate destiny might be, that was Truth Seeker's duty a thousand generations into the future. It took the basic survival commands Sebenesh had given it, melded them with Jalemi's secret ambitions, and created a twisted destiny of its own.

Once they made physical contact, the Sphere easily pierced the forgetfulness barrier Truth Seeker laid across Jalemi's mind the night of the Circle. Filtered through its warped perceptions, it experienced the moment of its captivity. It knew the names and faces of all the women in the Circle, and it exalted.

Through Jalemi's eyes it saw three women enter the clearing. Two it recognized but knew all three posed a threat to its plans. It snaked out a tendril of power laden thought and tried to strangle their minds.

Vian, it couldn't penetrate at all, Liesha's implants stung it, but Chalone, fresh from her ordeal in the Hub, wasn't as quick to repel the invasive presence. It tapped into her surface emotions and most recent memories. Chalone repelled it from her mind but not before the damage was done.

* * * *

The first memory it liberated was of Chalone and Jalemi's insipid sister in a place that didn't really exist, in the Archives. The Sphere shrugged aside that irrelevance and listened intently to what Chalone said.

"It mentions some sort of 'key' within the Earthblood fire. Even with the help of the scanner, I've only been able to decode about half of this gibberish."

The memory warped to a strange room filled with the stink of freedom. The women in the room were all from the Circle.

"There's a place where we might find some answers," Chalone said. "It's called the Shadowlands, where supposedly, a key is hidden that can unlock 'what was cast down'."

Lastly, it witnessed how Mor sent Chalone and Liesha from the Shadowlands back to the Gallery corridor.

* * * *

A trill of excitement shivered through the Sphere.

It was the 'key', obviously. Using Jalemi to physically carry it to the Shadowlands, which thanks to Chalone's memories it knew how to access, it would unlock its power, and fulfill its vengeful destiny. Not that it didn't have certain abilities already, but being imprisoned did put a damper on its creativity. It released its hold on its current physical form and prepared to migrate into Jalemi's mind and take complete control.

* * * *

Snuggled down in her Lair after Reweaving Time, Sebenesh had only just fallen asleep.

With a soft malevolent hiss, she slowly uncurled and swung her mighty head in the direction of the Reweaving. It whimpered and slunk back in its corner.

"Not your fault," she said calmly, as though each word was a firestorm about to ignite.

* * * *

She unleashed her rage toward Argol. It travelled through the most recent conduit, straight into Pirelle's mind. Unfortunate woman, but nearest to Jalemi for the purposes of venting her spleen.

"It's too late!"

Then, just for emphasis she made sure the others heard her as well. "You're all too late!"

It was all gone. The Reweaving was for naught. Her attempt to avoid direct interference in their stupid mortal lives had failed. Miserably.

"After everything I've done!" She screeched, and quivered, looking for another outlet for her tantrum.

The contents of her Lair had suffered enough so that avenue wasn't an option. The Shadowlands sent her a definitive "No" even before she thought of using it. So, with great restraint she snapped a leash on her budding paroxysm of fury and focused on the issue at hand.

While the Sphere remained momentarily distracted, she decided yet again to destroy it before it wrecked a millennia's worth of effort in the space of a heartbeat. Or worse yet, have the audacity to track her down and attempt to destroy her.

Reweaving Time was a wonderful idea. She hissed as she transferred between realms. It wasn't her fault the Sphere developed a superiority complex. However, the author of that complex would not go unrewarded.

Sebenesh materialized in the glade, making sure that none of the women saw her. That would've been an unnecessary distraction for all concerned.

* * * *

Piercing the Earthblood fire wasn't a problem for her immortal vision. She studied the Sphere for the first time since she'd created it. In spite of her wrathful determination to destroy it, what she saw unsettled her.

It remained a newborn in many ways. Surviving as best it could with what it had at hand. She admired that. A wave of responsibility for it softened her heart. An emotion she stoutly refused to categorize as maternal.

She decided to reach out to it, reason with it, and convince it that it was a victim of some colossal misinformation. The misinformee standing next to it, she had other plans for.

Given time, she would reeducate it, and return it to its original fate. She disregarded any possibility that the Sphere might have a contrary opinion about her plans, as was her way when she made up her mind.

She flinched at how close she'd come to destroying something of exquisite beauty and value because of her thwarted temper. She really ought to get those apocalyptic impulses a little more under control.

Be damned to all those nay-sayers in the Immortal Realm. What did they know? What in the Mortal Realm could possibly harm her? This wouldn't take more than a moment and then she'd return to her nap.

She knew various lesser ways to breach the Earthblood fire in order to reach the Sphere before it shifted into Jalemi but she ached to vent some of her anger. She contemplated the colossal force shimmering so brazenly and smirked in anticipation.

Sebenesh unbound her invisibility. There was no point in doing this half-heartedly. So much for keeping the mortals ignorant of her presence. She raised herself up on her majestic coils, unfurled her great black hood, and bared her meter-long fangs. She was magnificent and perilous.

She spat venom at the Earthblood fire. It sped through the air, beyond recall or second thoughts, morphing into a compound strong enough to breach the column of fire.

* * * *

In its moment of transformation and unaware of its impending fate, the Sphere released control over Jalemi. It dissolved its solidity, became pure energy, and buried itself deep within her consciousness. It flowed throughout her body and immediately tried to escape from its Earthblood prison.

Jalemi woke.

That instant of freedom ignited the tiny spark of resistance and she battled the Sphere for control of her physical body. She rejected the oily presence inside her mind and locked her muscles in place.

* * * *

The corrosive venom reached the apex of its flight with an unstoppable malevolence.

* * * *

Sebenesh cursed. All her choices were doomed to failure.

The venom would burn through the Earthblood fire, killing Jalemi, which she felt only slightly ambivalent about. The Sphere would survive and in its current state of mind, combined with the unimaginable power it could manifest, would annihilate the whole of existence.

Each time she acted, unforeseen complications forced her into a tighter and tighter corner. Now she had nowhere left to turn. If she ever had a chance to tell Arahona what she really thought of her precious Gallery...

Sebenesh struck, cobra-like, and plunged through the Earthblood fire ahead of the venom, whipped her bodily coils around Jalemi, and leaped out through the other side.

Sensing a greater danger to it than allowing the Sphere to escape, the Earthblood fire granted the venom clear passage right through it.

Sebenesh couldn't escape from the deadly peril of her poison, and if she flung Jalemi away from her harder than necessary, then, so be it.

She crumpled to the ground as her bane came home to roost.

The venom charred her skin to a crisp in seconds. Festering blisters grew hideously large and then burst, spattering their corrosion over the rest of her body. She twisted violently back and forth, desperate to escape the searing agony radiating from every nerve ending.

The acid virulence dissolved the soft tissue under what remained of her skin and then wormed its way inward, devouring her muscles and withering her long beautiful body.

There would be a few moments before she died where she would revert to her primal self. If she couldn't deactivate the venom before the pain destroyed her mind, she would become a creature of unimaginable power free from the constraints of intellect. The Sphere would have nothing on her. She just might get her Armageddon after all.

She drew the coils of her tortured body to her and struggled to breathe through her tattered lungs. She reached out to the Earthblood fire as it raged into the skies, free of its mortal compulsion.

They were akin, primal, and incarnate, and perhaps the Earthblood was more potent than her venom. It would save her or destroy her.

The majestic plume of Earthblood fire twisted toward her broken body as the venom burned her eyes until they oozed golden blood. The Earthblood licked at her flesh, caressed her like a lover, and consumed her venom infected body with a voracious passion. All the beauty and grace of her immortal spirit fled before the unequaled agony of its cleansing fire. Her bones burned clean and turned to ash. The Earthblood fire danced closer to her tortured vitals, but her magnificent mind remained clear.

Sebenesh shrugged the agony aside. *So, it worked. No Armageddon then. The silly mortals would live.* The Sphere was beyond her. She hoped that someone, something, might intervene and control it, but she doubted it. Truth be told she was done trying to save them from it. She was done trying.

She surrendered her sanity and screamed and screamed.

* * * *

A gash in the sky broke open and a monstrous cloud, coming from an unknowable beyond, billowed forth. It brushed the Earthblood fire aside and hovered above the remains of Sebenesh's body. A spray of raindrops fell to mourn her loss.

The cloud reached down to the earth and rose through the wounded sky, sealing it as it went. A swathe of scorched earth and burned blood remained.

* * * *

The Earthblood fire's purpose was at an end. Not as promised by the Sacred Circle certainly, but complete none-the-less. It reeled in its potency and left the little glade in the woods for its home deep in the heart of the earth until the next summons called it forth.

The Elementals of Air, Earth, Fire, and Water, accompanied it down through the layers of earth and stone, down to the very core of the world. They swam the rivers of energy that connected all the places of Power on Argol's surface and they came to a decision. Momentous possibilities were at hand and it was fitting that they evolve to respond to them.

* * * *

The Sphere had escaped the Earthblood fire. Quite differently than it planned, but freedom was freedom however it came about. Soon it would purge itself of this puny mortal and her feeble attempts to vanquish it. It gloated over its cleverness, not realizing that it had exchanged one sort of prison for another.

Chapter Twenty-Four

Ashes that stunk of burned meat and seared blood blew fitfully across the glade. A circle of fire-glazed dirt and stone stared up into the cerulean sky like a sightless eye. Silence, as complete and utter as the end of all existence settled over the clearing.

Chalone, Vian, and Liesha cautiously entered the glade.

Vian thought that she ought to recognize the magnificent creature that courageously gave its life to rescue Jalemi. *Oh, how she wished she had more time.* She released a huge breath.

"Do either of you know anything about what just happened?" she asked.

"No, Vian," Liesha said. "We found nothing like this in the Gallery."

On the other side of the charred circle, Pirelle struggled up from the dirt.

"Help me!" She called out as she held Jalemi's rigid body in her arms. She brushed the soot and grime off Jalemi's face.

Jalemi was alive, her eyes wide open, darting rapidly from side to side, as though trying to see in a thousand directions at once.

Vian held Chalone and Liesha back. "Don't get too close. We have no idea what this is all about. I'll help Pirelle and Jalemi. I need to understand what just happened here and I think Jalemi has a lot of answers whether she knows it or not. You two will return to the Hall, and find me some answers I can use."

They looked ready to argue, but Vian glared them down. "You think I can't handle this on my own? Go. Now!"

Energy swirled around the five women. Angry red, shades of frightened white, and a color that none of them had ever experienced before, hyper-violet of unknowable events just passing them by.

Chalone glanced at Pirelle and then looked away. There were no words and no time. She'd barely escaped death in the Hub, what just happened here in the glade was a chaotic mystery, and she felt certain another crisis was building back at the Hall.

As she and Liesha left the clearing, the roiling energy dissipated into separate colors as the tensions in the air shifted.

* * * *

Vian reached Pirelle's side and looked deeply into Jalemi's eyes. This was going to take time. Something she didn't have. She put her concern for the Hall to one side and focused on the problem in front of her. She sighed and settled one of Jalemi's arms over her shoulders. With Pirelle taking the other, they half-carried, half-dragged Jalemi across the glade to the shelter of the trees. They found an old log and sat her between them.

* * * *

Jalemi knew Pirelle and Vian were near but all her senses focused inward. She felt cold and clammy but inside she burned. Her muscles constantly convulsed in spite of four strong arms holding her steady.

With an abrupt twitch, she pushed the Sphere aside, looked directly at Vian, and spoke as though she had to tear her voice from her throat by the sheer force of her will.

"I can't hold it back for long. It wants to get to the Shadowlands, but I don't know what that is. It's hurting me."

"You're strong, Jalemi," Vian said with great authority. "Stronger than you think. You can defeat whatever is inside you. We will help all we can."

"Yes! Help me," a strange hissing voice emanated triumphantly from her lips. "The Shadowlands. Take me there. Now!"

Jalemi gulped a lungful of air as though she'd swallowed something rotten.

"It doesn't see me as a threat," she said hoarsely and clutched at Vian. "It thinks it will gain control. Help me."

* * * *

Pirelle sat close to Jalemi but shied away from touching her. She had a mortal fear of possession, and obviously Jalemi struggled with something otherworldly.

Nothing was as it was supposed to be. Chalone left without saying a word and appeared to be enjoying a close relationship with Liesha. How that happened Pirelle couldn't begin to fathom. Something incomprehensible destroyed the Earthblood fire and then giant thunderclouds consumed it. Jalemi turned to Vian for comfort and advice.

* * * *

"Pirelle?" Vian asked for the second time. "If you can't clear your emotions, you endanger all three of us."

Pirelle started to speak, but Jalemi shoved her off the log.

"I can't bear you so close."

Pirelle stalked to a nearby tree and set her back to it.

Vian ignored her glare and held Jalemi's head between the palms of her hands. She linked her will to Jalemi, and they confronted the monster that threatened Jalemi's spirit and sanity.

* * * *

The Sphere was not strong or cunning enough to defend itself against their concerted might. Vian was a force of nature all by herself. A wordless struggle began and ended in a heartbeat.

Together Jalemi and Vian compressed the Sphere's consciousness like a fist crushing a ball of paper, until nothing but a tiny kernel of it remained. They couldn't cast it out of her completely. It had burrowed so many tendrils into her psyche since the Circle that to disentangle them would kill her and free it. Instead, they used swathes of energy to muffle its influence to a mere irritation in the back of Jalemi's mind.

Jalemi grabbed Vian's wrists and pulled her hands away.

"Don't touch me anymore," she said. "You're too strong."

"You have no idea," Vian said cryptically. "That's beside the point isn't it?

Jalemi nodded. She'd never make the mistake of reaching beyond her limits again, but now her limits were beyond anything she ever dreamed of. She would get to the Shadowlands of her own volition, not the Sphere's.

Vian refrained from saying all of the things she wanted to. 'I told you so's' never worked, no matter how much satisfaction she might glean. She learned a great deal about the Sphere's origins and its ambitions from that short contact with it. The irony of it linking with Jalemi wasn't lost on her, and she wasn't about to trust its binding any further than she had to.

Vian sighed as she slowly walked with Jalemi and Pirelle through the forest toward the Hall of Lights. If the fear she'd carried in her heart from the moment Chalone told her of the wind in the Gallery ever became a reality, what they would find ahead of them would not be pleasant.

"I have to see what's happening at the Hall," she said distractedly, "but I don't want to leave you two alone either."

"I'm fine," Jalemi said. "You go ahead. Pirelle and I will follow."

Vian looked at her intently, as if to find the truth of her words in her eyes, then she nodded and strode briskly after Liesha and Chalone.

* * * *

Pirelle looked at her sister, who looked right back at her.

"I'm still me," Jalemi said, reassuring both of them. "I've beaten it," she said softly. "I got what I wanted. I guess." A sadness she hadn't expected welled up in her eyes, and her voice broke. Pirelle's resentment dissolved. She'd never been able to withstand a woman in tears, especially her sister.

"How does it feel?" Pirelle asked a little while later.

"Like I have a giant itch inside my skull," Jalemi answered ruefully. "That I can't scratch." The sisters laughed together and all was well between them.

"We're all going to have to sit down sometime soon and compare notes," Pirelle said.

Jalemi tugged on Pirelle's sleeve as they neared the Hall. "I don't think so."

* * * *

Chalone and Liesha ran through the woods toward the Hall of Lights, but Chalone fell further and further behind.

"Slow down, Liesha. I can't run as fast as you," she gasped. "We have to think this through. I know what's happened," she added, "what's about to happen."

Liesha looked at her in surprise, but forgot whatever she was about to say as they broke free of the trees and saw the Hall.

* * * *

Roof tiles lay shattered on the ground. Stone pillars had fallen outward as though a giant hand brushed them aside without effort.

The backwash of energy from the collapsing Portal expanded the fractures in the pillars the shockwave from the fracture in Time had begun. It only took a few minutes, enough for Sebenesh's immolation, but the ancient pillars fell like children's toys.

The Portals stood naked under the bright sky. Some of them cycled through strange and disturbing colors. Others dulled to a brooding gray mass of menacing shadows.

* * * *

Pirelle and Jalemi joined Chalone at the edge of the crowd gathered just outside the Hall and stared, unable to believe their eyes

Vian stood in the center of what was left of the Hall, gesticulating wildly, issuing directives, and sending women scurrying off in all directions. Near her, Liesha talked into a headset she'd found somewhere.

Suddenly another tremor took down the last remaining columns.

"Get back! Everyone," Vian shouted and suited her actions to her words.

A Portal glowed fiercely, then shattered. Wind rushed through the broken Hall.

Chalone's face turned white. She barged through the fleeing crowd to Liesha's side. "The corridors are being ripped apart!" she shouted above the roar of rushing air and an alarm that no one had thought to shut off.

"I can see that," Liesha said too loudly as the sound eased, and picked up the headset the gale had swept from her head. She'd had no time to reintegrate her implants and used it to communicate with the ECHO network. "I am going to stop this."

The alarm finally fell silent. "You can't stop it," Chalone said.

"What do you mean?" Liesha suddenly grabbed her arms hard enough to cause bruises. Chalone winced and she released her grip. "Sorry," she apologized. "Tell me."

"Mor brought us back in time to the moment just after we left," Chalone explained.

Liesha looked blank for a moment and then she turned as pale as Chalone. "We are witnessing the beginning of the maelstrom in the Hub!" She looked aghast at the dying Hall.

"Not all of it. Our Portals aren't enough to create that monstrosity, but if this is happening throughout the Gallery...?" Chalone swallowed hard.

Liesha focused inward, listening to a strident voice issuing from her headset. "I still have to stop it here," she said with jagged determination.

"You have that kind of power? Why didn't you use it when we were trapped in the Hub?" Chalone accused.

"I was not able to. It requires many ECHOs, and our communications do not work in the Gallery."

Vian finished giving orders for crowd control, organized the evacuation of the nearby houses, and initiated the clause in the council charter that gave her immediate and total control of all the resources she ever needed or wanted. She interrupted Chalone and Liesha.

"Hurry," she said to Liesha. "If you can't hold at least one of the Portals, then we're marooned here forever. Everything we've all worked for will be lost."

"I am aware of that fact," Liesha snapped back at her.

Chalone looked from one to the other. "You both knew this would happen."

"Not exactly," Vian said. "The ECHO hierarchy have suspected something similar for a while. Hence their frenzied attempts to get their communications working inside the Gallery," she said pointedly and pulled Chalone away from Liesha, gathering up Pirelle and Jalemi. "Let's leave Liesha to get on with it."

She purposefully raised her voice to address the panicked crowd regrouping beyond the broken columns.

"Everyone! Return to your tasks. The ECHOs will report to us when they have stabilized the Portals. We are only in the way here." Resuming a quieter tone, she spoke to the three younger women. "We'll take Jalemi to my house, and wait there for Liesha."

Chalone looked back at Liesha, but Vian took her arm and firmly led her away. "You have to trust me on this," she said.

Chalone watched as Tallem walked purposefully up to Liesha and began to work on her implants from a toolkit she'd carried under her arm. They were so engrossed in reintegrating Liesha with the ECHO network that neither of them noticed they stood alone in the middle of the broken Hall with the winds of broken Portals swirling around them.

Chalone allowed Vian to lead her away.

"What's Liesha going to do?"

"She will act as the central focal point for a gathering of ECHO minds," Vian replied. "Through their channeled energy, she'll stabilize the remaining Portals and strengthen their anchorage to the Hall. I don't know how, just in case you were going to ask." She smiled at Chalone, preempting her question. "The ECHO's assured me it will work."

"Why her?"

"Timing, I suspect," Vian said dryly. "She's the only fully trained, experienced ECHO here. I have confidence in her. You should too."

"If she fails?"

Vian though for a long moment and then looked deliberately at Jalemi walking slowly behind them with Pirelle at her side. The image of the giant serpent-like creature burned itself into her eyes again. "I don't know," she said quietly. "Something..." A scrap of memory flitted in one side of her mind and out the other. "Aagh," she said dismissively. "Recent events suggest that the Hall isn't the only way off our world."

"That's not what I meant. We've only just reconnected."

"I saw that," Vian said and would not be drawn into further discussion. She doubted they'd seen the last of the malignant entity within Jalemi, and she had no desire to give it any more information than it already had. She regretted the few words she'd already spoken.

* * * *

From where it had been banished deep within Jalemi, the Sphere attempted to listen to the conversation through Jalemi's ears. A fire burned in its spirit. It underestimated Jalemi's stubbornness and trapped itself, but it could still plan, could still scheme. Jalemi was no more immune to its charms now than before.

* * * *

The women trooped into Vian's house and took up stations at windows or on chairs as their natures dictated. Vian initiated a strategic withdrawal to her kitchen to make tea. She leaned against the sink as she waited for the kettle to fill and covered her eyes with her hands.

She would forever see the image of the Earthblood fire consuming the serpent. Its energy, essence, felt so familiar. It traipsed around the edges of her memory, teasing her, daring her to remember.

Time. With enough time, all the mysteries in her life would be solved. She heard the kitchen door softly open and close. Lila wrapped her arms around her and breathed warmth into her spirit again.

* * * *

Chalone stood by the window that looked toward the Hall of Lights, turning a tiny sculpture of Vian's over and over in her hands as she waited for Liesha to save them all.

* * * *

Pirelle sat down with Jalemi and held her cold hands in her large firm ones. Here she was, two days later back in Vian's house and Chalone still wasn't speaking to her. Well, she wasn't going to be the first one to say something.

* * * *

Vian and Lila returned with a laden tray. Cups were filled with tea that no one drank. Thoughts occurred, but no one spoke. It was as though they'd silently agreed nothing more could be said or done until they heard from Liesha.

Chalone leaned forward, suddenly tense. Clearly visible even in the bright light of day, an explosion mushroomed up from the Hall. It sparkled in the sunlight for a glorious moment and then died away. She turned back into the room.

"I think she's finished," she said.

"Who?" Pirelle asked, thinking Chalone referred to Vian and the tea tray.

"Liesha?" Vian asked. When Chalone nodded, she said, mostly to herself, "Well, we're all still here, so I suppose she succeeded."

"You mean we weren't safe here?" Pirelle asked. It hadn't occurred to her that they were in any danger, not in Vian's house.

"Nowhere would have been safe," Chalone answered her. They were the first words she had spoken directly to Pirelle in what felt like a very long time. They were not the words she would have chosen, but it was a start.

A boisterous knock at the front door startled them all. Tallem walked in with a grin from ear to ear. "She did it!"

"We thought as much," Vian said, smiling at her infectious energy.

"Where is she?" Chalone asked uneasily, as she looked through the open door behind Tallem.

"She's unconscious," Tallem said and held up her hand to forestall any rush out the door Chalone might've made. "She'll be alright. It was just too much of a strain on her implants."

Tallem thought Chalone might either hit her or hug her. It was difficult to tell from the array of emotions that chased each other across her features.

Lila rescued them. She motioned Tallem to a deep wide sofa and set a mug of tea, black and sweet, just the way she liked it, in her hands.

"Start from the beginning, dear," she said and nudged Chalone to sit next to her. Tallem blinked in surprise. No one had called her 'dear' in many years.

* * * *

The energy pulse streamed in from many hundreds of ECHOs and focused on Liesha. Wild power thrummed through her body and her implants like an electrical charge with no place to ground. It reached critical mass and she activated all of the links she and Tallem had jerry-rigged to each of the remaining Portals.

Although no gesture was necessary, she stood in the center of the devastated Hall and threw her arms wide. The energy arrowed forth from her fingertips and pierced the heart of each Portal.

* * * *

The birth of the maelstrom in the Hub eclipsed her mortal resources and despite her best efforts one after another of the Portals slipped away from her control. Even if every ECHO in the world contributed to the pulse, she couldn't save them all.

The ECHO hierarchy tersely advised her to save a single Portal of sufficient strength to evacuate the population of their world as quickly as possible. Liesha realized that in light of this catastrophe they would've updated their timetable, but she didn't need yet another reminder of her duty at this very moment.

She released all but one of the Portals to their fate, spending valuable time and energy plugging the gaps they left behind to keep them from sucking in the air and land.

She hoped the Portal she'd chosen had a stable corridor on the other side of it. She trusted her instincts, they'd almost never let her down.

Her body had never been designed to channel such torrents of energy, even with all her enhancements. She fell to her knees under the strain. The Portal shuddered and the lights surrounding it began to fade. She pushed harder and felt a shift. The Portal responded and momentarily stabilized.

Acting swiftly, she melded the base of the Portal with the stone floor of the Hall. She directed the pulse beneath the Hall and fused the stone floor to the bedrock it had been built upon.

She had to make sure of one more connection and her ECHO training would be useless. She reached beyond the physical with her Practitioner training, some skills she never forgot, and tapped into the spirit world.

With permission from the eternal source that had spawned the Earthblood fire among many other wonders, she reached through time and distance and anchored the Portal firmly to the spirit of the land.

The lights surrounding the last Portal regained some of their former glory, and it remained stable, although every so often tiny tremors vibrated throughout the Hall.

* * * *

Liesha's implants overloaded. She immediately shut them down, preventing the rest of her integrated systems from cascading into failure and killing her. Released from her control by default, the energy pulse surged upwards and detonated harmlessly into the sky.

She collapsed onto the rubble and lay unattended until a team of ECHO technicians reached her.

Other ECHOs surrounded the remains of the Hall and warded the lone Portal. They set a series of monitoring instruments around it, and guarded those as well.

A panic driven mob would not be far behind Liesha's prodigious rescue of the one remaining Portal on the planet.

Chapter Twenty-Five

Tallem finished her story and sank back in her chair, the exhaustion she'd been hiding quite obvious in her body language.

Vian thanked her, and sent her off for some much deserved rest.

Chalone walked her to the door. "You didn't get this tired just sitting back and watching. What else happened?" she asked quietly.

Tallem shook her head. It wouldn't do to confess that she'd stood too close to Liesha. Her newly acquired implants overloaded the minute the pulse was initiated and she passed out. After a quick re-set in the field, she was fine, but at some point in the near future she really had to make a decision about where her allegiances lay.

There was nothing more Chalone could do for her that rest wouldn't cure. They hugged briefly and she left.

Chalone joined the others and poured herself a cup of tea to go with a buttered a piece of toast. All was quiet except for the bucolic sounds of a belated breakfast.

"What do you want us to do now?" Pirelle asked and hastily swallowed her last mouthful of toast and marmalade, in case Vian told her.

Vian needed Jalemi's insights on the Sphere more than she feared it listening in. "We share all that has happened to us since we last met." She talked over the top of Pirelle's groan. "We need to find some answers."

Chalone told of her adventures within and beyond the Gallery with Liesha, and ended with the bizarre encounter at the Earthblood fire. Pirelle spoke of her futile searches at the Archives and following Jalemi to the Earthblood fire.

Finally Jalemi talked about her capitulation to the Sphere. She remembered only fragmented details, but her honest telling of them left her spirit a bit cleaner and stronger.

"You all know what I've been doing," Vian said. She lied, no one knew it all. She basked in her secrets and then returned to business. "The key to all this is the Shadowlands."

Jalemi sat bolt upright on the sofa where she'd been

resting inside Pirelle's protective arm. "I remember," she said incredulously. The Sphere had broken Truth Seeker's binding of her memories. "I remember what happened at the Ritual!"

Her expression turned from wonder to mortification, as her part in Dajah's death played out before her minds eye. "It's all my fault," she cried. "You tried to warn me, Vian. I was so stubborn, so convinced I knew what I was doing. I created this whole mess." She waited for their condemnation.

Chalone leaned forward in her chair, rested her elbows on her knees, and rubbed her face with both hands as though to brush away a great exhaustion. "We all know," she said. "Pirelle and I found out about the Earthblood fire and the Shadowlands at the Archives. We don't have all the details, but we remembered enough to piece together what happened."

Vian knew who was really responsible. Lila watched her closely and leaned across to take her hand. That comfort reached straight into Vian's heart and took her breath away.

Jalemi shrugged off Pirelle's hand, and the Sphere twitched. Here was an opportunity.

"You knew?" Jalemi accused.

"You were in no fit state to be invited to the conversation Jalemi." Vian reminded her. "This changes nothing." She waited until all eyes turned on her again.

The Sphere subsided, it knew how to provoke Jalemi's weak points. Vian continued.

"We know that this thing inside Jalemi wants to get to the Shadowlands. We know that a being of great power came from between the worlds and tried to destroy Jalemi and it, by association," she said. "It's the only link we have to what's going on here." Vian looked at Jalemi.

"It feels like its sleeping," Jalemi said, crossing her arms stubbornly. "I have no intention of waking it up to ask it a few pertinent questions," she said, still smarting at being excluded from the Shadowlands discussion.

"I wasn't about to ask you to," Vian said bluntly.

"Let's call it the Sleeper then," Pirelle said. "That'll keep it separate from Jalemi." That drew a shadow of a smile from Chalone. Her heart took flight but Chalone turned away.

"Chalone," Vian said. "I need you to find out just exactly how Mor got you and Liesha back from the Shadowlands. If the 'Sleeper' knows about it, then it can only have come from either yours or Liesha's memories."

"How could it have possibly done that?" Chalone asked.

"It had no trouble accessing Jalemi's thoughts, although she was a willing participant." Vian looked sympathetically at Jalemi who cringed a little. "We have to assume that it did the same to all of us when we were delayed at the edge of the glade."

Chalone ran her fingers through her hair. "Mor never told us how she did it. I felt disoriented when we arrived at the threshold, but not much else." She sighed. "I need about a week of sleep and then I'll chase down all the dragons you want me to."

Vian smiled. "You have until tomorrow."

Chalone rolled her eyes. "About what I expected! I'll try and talk with Liesha in the morning. We'll see what we can come up with."

"Speaking of Liesha," Pirelle interjected. "There's the little matter of the Portal, and being marooned here if it fails."

"When it fails," Vian corrected. "I suspect we have until around the Autumn equinox for everyone who wishes to leave to do so. Which probably means evacuating hundreds of thousands of people. That's what emergency Council meetings are for, Pirelle," Vian said. "And why I defanged Zikelun. This morning I was asked to take her place as Senior Speaker, and I," Vian paused dramatically, "graciously accepted!"

Vian always had an ace up her sleeve. This time it was her plenipotentiary ace. She wondered what she would do if she ever found herself without one. It would be an interesting experience, but one she wasn't keen on exploring just now. In the coming weeks, she would need every resource, every favor, every ounce of cunning and deviousness she had, and all aces up her sleeves she could muster.

She smiled smugly to herself. On an impulse she reached out and enfolded Lila in a firm embrace, much to everyone's surprise, except Lila.

* * * *

Chalone felt tempted to seek out Tallem's bed, but the potential of that gorgeous naked body next to hers might prove too tempting.

She opened her front door warily, not wanting to talk, discuss, argue, or otherwise communicate with anyone. The house echoed emptily and she opted to feel relieved as she swayed toward her bedroom, shedding clothes as she went.

She managed to fall asleep in spite of thousands of thoughts whirling through her brain. When she finally woke, she was sure she could've slept twice as long and still not feel fully rested.

Before seeking out her mother she wanted to visit the Hall, or what remained of it, to see for herself what Liesha had accomplished.

A summer breeze caressed her skin through her loose shirt and pants. She inhaled the hazy air and let go of her lists and cares for the short walk to the Hall of Lights.

The new reality of her world hit her when she saw the once venerable old structure.

The grass lawn had been reduced to blackened ash. The columns were smashed into rubble. She threaded her way through the flotsam and jetsam scattered across the stonework. Shards of terracotta tile and the intricately designed flagstones buckled underneath her feet.

The lone Portal rose out of the middle of the cracked stone floor, a dull gray oval shape. Distorted in order to remain functional, it towered above Chalone's head, and stretched many times its original width in order to sustain the imminent exodus. Its apex sagged as if unable or unwilling to bear its own weight.

The residual energy from Liesha's handiwork congealed into a metallic fluid that slid like quicksilver tears down each side. It pooled where the Portal had been bonded into the stone, and against gravity crept back up to the top to begin the cycle again. It looked gruesomely hypnotic, and although Chalone was thankful the Portal had been saved, she felt the unnaturalness of the anchorage through the soles of her boots.

She cautiously approached the edge of the Portal and gently touched it's unpleasantly flaccid liquid surface.

Even though Portals were inanimate objects, the manner of their creation gave them a unique affinity with the beings that passed through them.

This weeping one shuddered under her touch and she quickly retreated, sympathetic to its reaction. Any form of physical contact now caused the Portal a visceral discomfort. That was the trade-off Liesha made in order for it to work at all. Chalone's heart wept that the Portal's simple gift of communion had been warped out of its natural shape and purpose as well as its physical symmetry.

She stepped around two side-by-side depressions in front of the Portal where Liesha had knelt under the pressure of her struggle and crushed the stone beneath her. They would always remain a mute testimony to her victory.

Chalone reluctantly entered the weeping Portal. She had to see for herself what existed on the other side.

The threshold looked ordinary, the corridor like every other corridor, but there were no ordinary corridors anymore. A foreboding rose up through her spirit. *What would happen to her world after all the people had filed through this threshold and disappeared along the corridor?* The ECHOs had a plan. Perhaps she could ask... *No.* She would leave Argol with her friends and almost all of her family. The ECHO's could have it.

The threshold shuddered as she returned to the Hall.

* * * *

A taciturn ECHO who looked to be only a few weeks out of the 'tank', otherwise known as the stasis chamber where their ECHO implants were activated, escorted Chalone through the hospital's interminable sterile corridors. She wondered if the ECHOs deliberately avoid any softness, any art, when they needed to be healed.

Eventually they entered a clearly restricted section. The hermetically sealed environment reeked of ozone.

A receptionist, a 'high skin' as Gallery travelers were called among the more reactionary and usually younger ECHOs, looked askance when Chalone stated her intentions. It seemed that her parentage smoothed many a path within these walls, because without further looks of any sort, she was conducted into another room.

This room seemed light and cheery, with a wide window in one side that overlooked parklands and the surrounding city. Chalone knew she'd descended at least thirty floors underground.

She shook her head. If the ECHOs wanted to play their games, that was fine as long as they let her see Liesha.

She could have sworn the room was much bigger too. It looked functional, with softly lit walls in muted colors, an overstuffed chair, and a long wide couch-type bed. A warm comforter covered Liesha as she lay on the couch. Chalone pulled the chair close and studied her mother's battered body.

The bruises Liesha had gathered from their adventure in the Gallery still mottled her skin. Her final struggle to keep the Portal intact had incised a deeper hurt into her sunken flesh. Her face and shoulder implants lay exposed above the comforter. It took Chalone a while to view them as just another part of Liesha that needed to be healed.

There weren't any wires attached to Liesha, for which Chalone was thankful, nor were there any machines in the room ticking, humming, pulsing, or pumping. Liesha looked as though she had grown tired and laid down on her back for a nap. She slept peacefully as though dreams couldn't disturb her.

"Mother?" Chalone whispered close to Liesha's ear. "I know you can hear me." This wasn't just a spiritual tenet. Only an ECHO's body slept.

"I need to know how Mor brought us back from the Shadowlands. Your implants might've recorded something." Chalone hesitated a moment, then lay down beside Liesha, and gently wrapped her arms around her.

"So many things have happened. I don't know even where to begin to unravel their meaning, but something's gone very wrong." She sighed. "I'm so tired I can't think clearly. I hope you don't mind sharing the bed. I can't stay on my feet any more."

A buzzy voice came through a tiny speaker on the wall near the head of the bed. "I know. We attended your discussion at Vian's house."

"How is that possible?" Chalone raised herself up on one elbow and looked at Liesha. "Tallem," she said in a slightly aggrieved tone.

"No. Tallem left before the discussions took place. She only engaged an already existing listening device that Vian gave us permission to install long ago."

It was a time when the ECHO hierarchy believed it was in their best interests to have a similar device in every building and home, worldwide. Not that Vian ever thought the ECHO's would use it. After it was installed, she had too many distractions in her life to worry about the ECHO's listening in on her every word. Very few of them were ever used, but they were there all the same.

The slightly unsynchronized tones smoothed out into Liesha's voice. "Do not blame Tallem. It is probable she forgot to tell you. There has been no time for a great many things to be said between us all." She paused as though consulting some source beyond herself. "I have reviewed the information stored in my implants. The Shadowlands Portals exist as a reflection of the Gallery Portals. When you step through a Portal into the Gallery, all you have to do is step back through the reflection and you are in the Shadowlands."

"That doesn't make any sense." Chalone grumbled, still miffed about Tallem being utilized as an assistant spy. "If you step backwards, you'll end up where you started."

"You will if you do not look for the mirror," Liesha said reasonably.

Chalone rested her head on her arm for a moment. "I'm sure that'll make sense soon, and someday you'll tell me how you figured it out. I'm about to fall asleep on my feet, on this bed."

"Rest against me then," Liesha said.

Chalone's breathing fell into a regular pattern even before Liesha finished speaking.

* * * *

Chalone was right. The room where she and Liesha slept was an annex to a much larger space where the temperature remained at absolute zero, and no light ever shone. A sealed environment housed the multitudes of hardware nodes of the ECHOs mind-web, the network that instantaneously linked them to each other and to the planetary infrastructure.

Here Liesha's consciousness, one among many, looked for answers in the data received from Vian's house and various other resources scattered throughout Argol.

As swift as thought, a dialogue began among the most powerful ECHO's, although heard by all above a certain level of training.

"We need to talk with Vian."

"Through Tallem?"

"No. Vian will only use our technology when she chooses . She must talk with the Hierarchs face to face. She is the new leader of the council. She will persuade the people."

"She is..."

"She is an uncertainty."

"Vian is Vian. She will suffice."

"What of this other matter, the Shadowlands?"

"There is a threat to our plans hidden there. Our Practitioners can sense it."

"The Shadowlands are beyond our abilities. We are bound to this reality."

"For now."

"Yes, for now. There are no others better suited to explore the Shadowlands than those who have already been selected."

"Perhaps not. It is not as though they volunteered."

"Did they not? There are forces at work here beyond what we

are capable of comprehending."

"For now."

"For now. We will do what we have been given this unique opportunity to do."

"What if they bring this threat back with them before we are ready?"

"We are prepared for that eventuality."

"Call Vian."

With ruthless confidence, the ECHOs concluded their discussion.

Chapter Twenty-Six

When Vian heard that Zikelun, ever the opportunist, had vanished she suspected she'd been one of those who plunged desperately through the Portal immediately after Liesha anchored it.

She replaced the ECHO guards, who were quite willing to let anyone through so long as they didn't break anything, with far more disciplined ones of her choosing.

This would not be a panic driven exodus, she sternly informed everyone from her new and autocratic position as Senior Speaker. There would be time enough for all who wished to leave their world to do so.

* * * *

"Vian?" Tallem asked, gently shaking her.

Vian rolled off the couch in her office and found herself in Tallem's arms instead of on the floor.

After restoring her dignity, Tallem handed her a cup of tea. "Are you awake?"

"No," Vian said bitingly. "I always fall off chairs when I'm awake!"

"This is important. The Hierarchs want to see you."

Vian choked on her tea. "What for? They never see anyone who isn't an ECHO or a candidate like you."

"I know, Vian, but they want to see you, and I'm not a candidate."

Vian heard that one before, but she held her tongue. "Alright. Let me, at least, slip into something more appropriate to their dignity," she said, aware of how that bunch of cranky old women would view another cranky old woman in crumpled clothes.

Tallem walked into the kitchenette to pour a cup of tea for herself. Vian's 'more appropriate' often took quite a while.

They rode in Tallem's aircar to the hospital first. Assured that Liesha was indeed well on her way to recovering from her dreadful injuries, Vian allowed Tallem to whisk her through various tunnels, she lost count, and terminated somewhere beyond the edge of the city.

An elevator, far more elegant than the old skeletons, seamlessly dropped them down further than Vian ever remembered the Hierarchs burrowing. Tallem respectfully took her elbow, guided her into her final destination, and beat a hasty retreat. As intrigued as Tallem was with ECHO politics, so much power concentrated in one place left little room for lesser mortals such as herself to breathe.

* * * *

Five of the deadliest and most revered women on the planet rose to greet Vian as an equal. Then six of the deadliest and most revered women on the planet sat in comfortable armchairs and discussed the fate of their world.

* * * *

Once the Portal collapsed, which by latest ECHO estimates would be sometime near Winter Solstice, there would be no second chances. Only those who had chosen to stay would be left on the planet.

Would they become second class citizens, Vian wondered, *on a world populated by the cybernetically enhanced, who would no longer have any reason to hide their true potential from an uneasy population? Or worse yet, a genetic pool the ECHOs could dip into if they backed themselves into an evolutionary corner?* She would do her best to convince everyone to leave but inevitably some would stay and face whatever fate had in store for them.

When Oyali, assured her in her most dismissive tone, that sufficient infrastructure would be retained to keep them 'comfortable', Vian inwardly winced.

For a moment she imagined this event from an ECHO perspective and thought it might be worth staying for, almost. She had another destiny to follow.

Redail smiled as if she read Vian's thoughts. She was perhaps the only one of these women Vian could remotely call a friend.

As soon as Liesha stabilized the Portal, the ECHOs sent their swiftest investigators along the length of the corridor and discovered a single habitable world connected to it, a world much larger than their tiny one, further down the evolutionary scale but eminently suitable. No Portals had been found, but most ECHOs didn't really have any affinity for the otherworldly aspects of the Gallery. Their training tended to weed out the most talented Practitioners.

Vian supposed that she'd have to start referring to ECHOs as a species soon. Such a pragmatic bunch, but she'd keep an open mind about any Portals on the new world.

Toosl, whom Vian suspected of being a little envious of the exodus Vian was about to lead off-planet, neglectedf to tell her that they'd also mapped the location of the new world in relation to Argol spatially. The Hierarchs believed that it was always useful to know where one's friends and adversaries lived, inside the Gallery or out.

Haol, by far the eldest of the five, handed Vian a case of memory crystals that had been created in the bowels of the Archives. It felt oddly heavy for its slender contents.

"These contain the information you will need to begin your new society," Haol said in a firm voice that caressed Vian like an old memory. "We wish you well."

The six deadly women never saw each other again.

* * * *

Vian walked into her courtyard and sat on her favorite bench. Suddenly Earth Elemental appeared over her and almost shocked her off her seat, for the second time in one day. She wondered if it might be worthwhile having security straps attached to all the seats she used.

"We are accompanying you on your journey," Earth told her and smiled its bear-phant smile. "We will prepare ourselves, and wait on the Hill for you to collect us when the time comes to leave."

Flabbergasted, Vian stared after Earth as it departed as abruptly as it arrived. She leaned forward to see if the rest of them hid around a corner enjoying the trick they'd played. Not an Elemental in sight.

"That's about the oddest thing that's happened to me all day," she said to no one in particular.

* * * *

As the days flew by she slept even less than she did before meeting the Hierarchs. She reveled in the enormity of the task she had chosen to undertake, and dragooned the ever efficient staff of the Council bureaucracy into taking on most of the organizational details, leaving her free to manage the overall project.

She had no illusions that the Sleeper's current silence had anything to do with its confinement. She drafted Pirelle and Chalone to shadow Jalemi again in case the entity tried to subvert her or spew forth more information about its obsession with the Shadowlands.

The Shadowlands. What place did it hold in the whole scheme of things? Vian massaged her temples. Some questions were beyond her ability to answer. She had so many other issues that needed to be resolved immediately. The list was almost too long for even Chalone, that champion of list-makers, to imagine.

* * * *

Vian strode into the Council chamber for the very last time. Unfortunately, her list had not decreased. As soon as she crossed one item off the top, another mysteriously added itself to the bottom. One thing at a time though. She swept her long hair back and faced the chamber squarely.

Every seat in the room was filled even though the meeting was more of a formality than anything else. It would give those who were talkers rather than doers their moment when the entire planet focused on their every word. The planet usually ceased to listen after the first sixty or so words.

* * * *

All the important decisions were already made. Vian called meeting after meeting. With her dominant personality, she wooed, badgered, bullied, bribed, and downright blackmailed her people into adopting her plan, the plan inspired by the memory crystals the matriarchs gifted her with.

It was the unique nature of the people of her world that helped Vian's cause more than anything else. The forced migration through the Portal gave them an opportunity to leave without any guilt at abandoning their home world. There would most certainly be other Portals to be found on the new world that would lead them back into the heart of the Gallery. For as long as it lasted.

Vian frowned. For as long as the Gallery lasted. That was the phrase Oyali used. The most disturbing fact the Hierarchs shared with her was that the Gallery was dying, ripping itself apart. Not soon, not in the foreseeable future, but certainly within a measurable time span. She wasn't surprised, really. Not after Chalone's story of the maelstrom in the Hub.

Vian told no one, not even Lila. Apart from herself, only the Elementals might understand the time scale involved, and they were too capricious to be trusted.

The council chamber grew quiet. The moment arrived for her to deliver a stupendous oration before a colossal captive audience.

She grinned wickedly.

* * * *

Pirelle, Jalemi, Chalone, and Tallem battled through the crowds surrounding the council building to their reserved seats at the rear of the chamber. They all knew what Vian would say. They'd either heard it from her directly or through their network of friends and associates, who alternated between grumbling at her highhandedness and praising her to the skies. Vian never inspired half-measures.

Even still, today would mark the official beginning of the exodus, and the room bristled with tension and excitement. There had never been such a meeting as this.

Many had already made up their minds to go. Some remained undecided. Others felt torn between the decision their families made and what they wanted to do for themselves. During these uneasy times, Vian was the glue that held their purpose strong.

Lila entered from a doorway nearby and joined them.

Chalone shuffled over to make room. "What do you think of Vian's plan to take a walk into the Gallery and exchange home worlds?" she asked and gnawed her bottom lip.

Change and more change piled on Chalone and her unconscious mannerisms showed the strain. Vian had her running all over the place, Pirelle waged an undeclared war with Tallem, and on top of it all, she and Pirelle watched over Jalemi in case the Sleeper woke again. She felt like a jailer and the jail at the same time.

Lila recognized the signs and hugged her granddaughter comfortingly. She embraced the others and answered Chalone's question. "I think it will shatter our society, and we will be better for it!" Muffled gasps rose from the people nearby.

"Let's be honest, for centuries the Hall has been the only thing that held our culture together. Now that it's gone, we're free to move on as well. We are a resilient people," she said proudly, knowing that her voice carried to all those listening. "It'll take generations but we'll recover. If this new world is as beautiful as the ECHOs say, then it's a change and a challenge I welcome!"

Without appearing to try, Lila eased the subtle tensions in the air around her. Heads nodded, and she knew her efforts to motivate people were as efficacious as Vian's.

Lila's answer was more than Chalone bargained for. She took the words to heart in spite of their incendiary nature, and relaxed a little bit more.

Below them Vian took center stage and told the assembled crowd just exactly what they would do, and just exactly how much time they had to do it in. Then, she called in her army of bureaucrats to answer the technical and logistical questions raised.

Several exhausting hours later, her voice hoarse and reduced to a whisper, she asked who would go and who would stay. Everyone in the room felt as though they could make the only decision possible and come to it without coercion.

Eventually the assembly broke up into smaller groups and she left them to it. She had her agents scattered throughout the chamber. No topic of discussion would get by her. No anarchy proposed she couldn't defuse.

An hour later, her friends extricated her from the "just one more question" brigade and almost carried her from the chamber. They bundled her into a landcar that Tallem commandeered with the ease and confidence of an ECHO. As they inched through the crowd, Vian tried to hide behind Lila.

"Wave to them, my dear," Lila suggested. "You've turned their world upside down. The least you can do is let them see you've survived the process."

Vian growled at her and hung out of the side of the car, waving and shouting encouragements. Lila held onto her coattail, just in case.

Leaving Vian to her fun, Chalone looked at Tallem driving carefully through the crowd. She didn't feel like making small talk and the one question she wanted to ask, she feared the answer to. She knew Tallem worked closely with the ECHO network and was considered to be a candidate to join them. Her heart didn't sink as far as she thought it might at the prospect, and that saddened her the most.

Their landcar reached the edge of the crowd, and Lila hauled Vian back inside and closed the door. Vian looked at her with rosy cheeks and a mischievous grin. "That was fun!"

Lila whacked her. "You fraud!"

As the car picked up speed, Chalone leaned back and felt Pirelle's warm shoulder next to hers.

* * * *

After the momentous Council meeting, the effort to return the decimated hall to some semblance of working order resumed. A temporary roof covered the Portal and anyone who had even a modicum of experience returned to duty.

People were marshaled into small groups, organized their allotted quantity of possessions, and herded through the weeping Portal.

Jalemi felt she could function now that the disorienting influence of the Sphere was banished from the forefront of her awareness. When she arrived to do her share of the work, she realized from the reactions of those around her that her previous behavior must have been noticeably out of character.

The Sphere took note and decided it needed to practice discretion when it regained control.

Jalemi worked harder than she ever had before. Partly because she was needed, but also because it expiated some of her guilt about her actions at the Earthblood fire ritual. The Sphere noted this too, and nudged her conscience to keep the flames fanned.

However, every time she came too close to the Portal someone, usually Chalone or Pirelle, appeared to distract her. At first she dismissed it as coincidence, but it became obvious they were taking no chances. It hurt to think she wasn't completely trusted. The Sphere blurred her perceptions and her hurt twisted to resentment. She found herself drawing on her inner strength more and more.

When she and Vian banished the Sphere, Jalemi reclaimed the hollow place inside her spirit where she'd hidden. She built an image of herself that she could connect to at any time, clear-headed and strong-willed and in complete control of her actions. She filled the hollow place with the image and called it her inner strength.

Even in its reduced state, the Sphere managed to burrow into the hollow place and replace the image with one of its own. From there it easily manipulated her emotions so that she came to rely on it more and more.

Every time Jalemi focused on the image of herself and drew

strength from it, she perceived only what the Sphere allowed her to. A perfect duplicate of herself that saw through her eyes and recognized the shapes of her thoughts, but had the heart of corruption.

* * * *

As the weeks flew by in a flurry of activity, the Sphere experienced life through Jalemi's senses with a newly-born awareness. The taste of chocolate ice cream, the texture of silk, children laughing, and jasmine scented air. All fascinating, but it still burned with a passion that constantly threatened to break through its sorely tested patience.

The Portal held to the ECHO's estimates of its endurance. Many thousands departed the world. They were not a people who set a great store in physical property or belongings. Their technology could recreate almost anything they desired, and they carried their technology with them in the tiny memory crystals.

Eventually the world grew emptier. Even Valder, on the far side of the planet, seemed deserted. The ECHOs pulled away from the Portal as though to remove themselves from temptation. They'd only lost a few of the lesser trained who'd agreed to have the higher functions of their implants permanently disabled. ECHO secrets were not for the new world.

* * * *

As Jalemi prepared yet another group to pass through the Portal, she stepped closer and closer to it until a hand reached out and plucked at her jacket sleeve.

"Where are you off to?" Chalone asked and pulled her back.

The Sphere rifled through Jalemi's thoughts. Chalone could be counted on to respond to emotional persuasion. "Time is running out," Jalemi said, frightened. "The Portal is weakening. Soon we'll be cut off from the Gallery. Everyone can see it. It's our turn now. We have a right to leave too. I won't be left behind again, caged in a prison I don't deserve." Jalemi's voice rose as the Sphere failed to contain the edges of its rage.

No, it would not be thwarted again. With a single thought, it switched its tainted doppelganger with Jalemi's consciousness and condemned her to the hollow place in its stead, this time as a prisoner, not a refugee.

"I know you feel a compulsion to go to the Shadowlands, but we can't leave until our work here is done," Chalone said.

"Shepherding a bunch of people to their doom," the Sphere snapped. "They have no idea where you and Vian are sending them, what you are sending them to. They could be falling out the end of a shattered corridor and die horrible deaths for all you know. The ECHOs aren't omnipotent. The Shadowlands should have been our destination all along. That's where we'll find everything we need." The Sphere gathered its energy to attack Chalone and quivered in anticipation of the injuries it might inflict.

"You might perhaps," Chalone said, sure she addressed something other than Jalemi. "Without us along, Jalemi won't be going anywhere."

Chalone held onto Jalemi's quaking arm and steered her away from the Portal, just as the Sphere expected.

It focused all its rage. Jalemi's hands shoved Chalone away as hard as it could and then pushed aside the bodies clustered in front of the Portal. The Sphere had no experience coordinating limbs and gravity, and Jalemi stumbled over a cracked flagstone and smacked right into the side of the Portal.

Furious at Jalemi's clumsiness and with physical pain sticking needles into its thoughts for the first time in its existence, the Sphere lashed out again, this time with its mind. The bolt of energy struck the sides of the Portal and the beleaguered structure canted at a dangerous angle above the small crowd.

Jalemi staggered through before anyone realized she'd left.

* * * *

As she hit the ground, Chalone knew she couldn't stop Jalemi. She jumped to her feet as quickly as she could, grabbed the nearest woman, and yelled at her to find Pirelle and Vian. The woman sped off as the crowd shuffled closer to the Portal, uncertain of what had happened and what they should do, but not about to give up their place in the queue to find out.

Chalone tried to shrug off yet another clutch of bruises in the making. It took her too long to shoulder her way through the crowd, and she reached the Portal the same time as Vian and Pirelle.

"Jalemi's gone," she announced to their gasped questions. "She'll try for the Shadowlands. I'm going after her."

"Both of you will go," Vian corrected and pulled Pirelle forward.

"Find her and stop whatever that thing inside her is planning to do." She looked hard at the fear in their eyes. "I will wait here for you, and if you don't get back with Jalemi before the Portal collapses, I'll be severely displeased. I'd hate to think of the others setting up business on the new world without my infinite wisdom to guide their steps."

"You're a megalomaniac, Vian," Pirelle said.

"Only when I have to be," Vian answered in all seriousness.

* * * *

Pirelle stood next to Chalone and looked into the Portal's murky center. "I hope you know what we're doing," she said and took Chalone's hand in hers.

Chalone returned an appreciative squeeze. "Not exactly. Liesha outlined the process, but I haven't had time to experiment. I guess we'll make it up as we go along."

"Figures," Pirelle said as they stepped through the Portal.

Chapter Twenty-Seven

Vian wanted to hold the desperate crowd back and give Chalone and Pirelle time to move further into the Gallery but she took one look at the ailing Portal and knew she could do no more for them. The hasty departures resumed.

* * * *

Esparber and Espinsal fell silent. ECHO technology and culture had no use for their urban landscapes. The few remaining people could inhabit them as they wished. Those who chose to stay wouldn't begin their new lives until the last visible remnants of the old had departed. Goodbyes had been said long ago and very few wanted to witness the final leave-taking.

By mid-afternoon of the day of Winter Solstice, the mass departure ended. Forlorn boxes and forgotten bags lay in scattered piles. No one cared to move them, not just yet.

The Hall looked almost deserted, except for a handful of ECHOs and others who came to witness the event. The last few dozen women traveling with Vian set their luggage down near the Portal and waited for her.

* * * *

Vian took her time to say goodbye to her long life on this world that she'd lived as though there were no tomorrows. It amused her to think that she would embark on the ultimate tomorrow.

At last she came to the Hill to say farewell to the venerable pile of dirt and the off-chance she might receive some last minute divine instruction. Not that she had high hopes. Her spirit world had been silent of late.

Before she began the long uphill walk, she toyed with the idea of hauling one last bucket-full of earth with her, but her back creaked at the very thought. She didn't think the Hill would mind, just this once. Instead, she took a pocket full of summer seeds from her garden and scattered them generously along the way.

They would bloom here long after she left. Her eyes grew misty and she wiped a tear away with the back of her hand. "I'm not going to cry," she said sternly. "You can't make me." She laughed at herself and continued walking.

Vian caught her breath at the top and told herself she really should get more exercise. Someone waited for her. "Chalone will be heartbroken," she said.

"How did you know?" Liesha asked. She looked hale enough but with an edge of fragility that spoke of just how badly injured she'd been.

"It was only wishful thinking on Chalone's part that you'd consider coming with us. The ECHOs have great plans for our little world after we're gone. You're too much a part of it not to stay."

"Assumptions can be dangerous."

"I do that sometimes." Vian shrugged and looked out across the valley one last time. "What brings you to the top of this rather beautiful place?"

"Chalone has already left then?" Liesha asked and tried to keep her face blank.

"Which answer would upset you the most, yes or no?" Vian asked bluntly. "Jalemi escaped through the Portal to the Shadowlands. Chalone and Pirelle have gone after her."

Liesha's face paled. "That Portal is not going to last much longer. They could be stranded there. I may never see her again!"

"By my estimation, the Portal will collapse around midnight tonight. We'll all be very lucky indeed if they return in time," Vian said grumpily. She sat down in the old wooden chair and leaned heavily against the armrest.

Liesha eased down next to her. "I wanted to ask you to look after her. I used to think she was not as strong as she looked, but I know that is not true. Chalone is brave and resourceful, and quite capable of creating her own destiny. We have only just reestablished our relationship, and I am leaving her behind, again." Liesha couldn't hold her tears in check any longer. "I want you to look after her anyway."

"This time she's leaving you. Ironic, isn't it?"

Liesha cried in Vian's arms. Her ECHO training flowed too deep for her tears to last, but when she pulled away, her spirit felt lighter.

"I have already said goodbye to Lila, and I will miss you dreadfully, in spite of all our disagreements over the years,"

Liesha said solemnly. "You are a woman who can move mountains and rewrite the future of our people. Do not forget me, and look after my mother and my daughter."

"Lila is quite capable of looking after herself." Vian smiled. "We'll both look out for Chalone." Vian hugged her.

"If she returns in time."

"There is that," Vian acknowledged and then she brightened. "Her chances are good. She has Pirelle with her."

"Pirelle and Chalone!" Liesha spluttered and started to laugh.

Vian looked startled for a moment and then remembered.

A long time ago two little girls ran away to the far side of the forest because they'd been punished for sneaking cookies from Lila's pantry.

They almost drowned when they tried to catch a fish with their bare hands, avoided certain death from a stampeding herd of deer they set off by stalking them, and dined on stolen green apples that made them very sick for days. They were eventually discovered hiding underneath the stone footbridge covered in dirt and scratches and rather put out that their adventure had ended.

Oh yes, Pirelle and Chalone could look after themselves alright. Vian and Liesha wiped tears of laughter from their eyes.

"If...no, when she gets back, I will talk to her," Liesha said, starting to feel wretched all over again. "Although I have no idea what I am going to say."

Vian nodded. *What else could she do?*

Liesha looked at the broken Hall in the distance. "Will you wait for them?" she asked.

Vian thought long and hard before answering honestly. "I don't know." She closed her eyes, leaned back, and let the winter sunlight ease her frown.

Liesha kissed her on the forehead and left.

* * * *

Energy moved around Vian in eddies and swirls that came from beyond the physical world. She breathed slowly in and out, and let it guide her spirit where it wished.

* * * *

A scream surrounded her like a solid wall of sound. It fragmented into a thousand separate syllables and echoed inside her skull. She opened her eyes to see a jagged crevasse that plunged down into an endless nothingness, and stepped hastily back before vertigo claimed her.

Another scream rose out of the depths and impaled her mind again.

"I am immortal. I cannot die! Cannot die!"

The words throbbed with more puissance than Vian imagined existing in the entire universe. She sensed the presence in the abyss existed separate from life and death, time and space, abandoned to its fate and ruined beyond knowing, yet surviving with all the passion and rage it could muster.

"I am," the voice screamed again.

"Who are you?" Vian shouted back and quailed at her daring.

"I am not alone?"

"No, you're not alone. My name is Vian."

In sharing the gift of her name, Vian knew she offered access to all she had been, and all she could become, but *how could she refuse*? The need was too great.

The voice reconstructed her life, breath by breath, touch by touch, until it found what it sought.

"Arahona," it said in agony so profound that it broke Vian's heart. "Ah, my Love. I understand now."

"No, you do not," Vian said and recalled nothing more.

Who Vian had once been stood on the edge of the abyss and addressed the forlorn spirit in a voice also not Vian's. "She who you loved is gone. This one now stands in her place."

Silence as tormented as the screams had been flowed up from the abyss. It hesitated as it approached the cusp of the precipice.

"Is this my fate?" the voice asked, changed as Vian had changed.

"This destiny is mine alone," the ancient one replied. "Yours is beyond me."

"Then I choose to live as I always have lived."

"Stubborn to the last as well. So be it."

* * * *

Vian stirred as though awakening from a maze of dreams. "Not Arahona," she said. "My name's Vian."

"For now you will be me," the voice from the abyss said. One by one Vian's memories realigned themselves with someone else's life and death. She lost awareness of herself and became a part of the re-creation of an immortal being.

* * * *

Pain.
She would not succumb.
The Earthblood fire recalled her to life. It scorched her tortured bones and she screamed and screamed and screamed.
Her Lair swathed itself around her like a cocoon and carried her remains home.

* * * *

"I am immortal. I cannot die," Sebenesh said, and returned from the only death an immortal can experience, oblivion. The words forced her indomitable spirit back inside her crushed body, reanimated each organ, re-fleshed her bones, and polished her scales. She woke and took up the destiny she had chosen for herself.

* * * *

Vian lay on a warm firm surface, smooth as polished granite. She felt every ache of every minute of her very long life. A deep sibilance vibrated through the floor and soothed her as a cat's purr would. She drew strength from it.
Having explored as much of her environment as she could without opening her eyes, she opened them.
A mother-of-pearl color took up her whole field of vision. Although she blinked, it remained the same every time she opened her eyes.
She felt silly but she had to ask the question. "Is anyone there?"
"I thank you for sharing your Spirit so that I could restore my Self."
"You're welcome," Vian said and looked all around her. The voice seemed to come out of the translucent walls.
"This is real," she said, not quite making it a question. "Not just a trance journey."
"I thought you might enjoy the experience."
Vian stood up. Words finally failed her.
"There is no urgency," the voice said. "Stay if you wish."
Vian considered the offer for quite a while. "I do have to go.

However time flows here, it passes swiftly on Argol."

"And waste this opportunity to tell me your opinions?"

Vian decided not to argue. She had no frame of reference around her to base any argument on. She refocused her attention on the moment and a thousand questions prioritized themselves onto the tip of her tongue.

Laughter surrounded her. "Your questions can wait. Go now. There is much left for you to do."

"You're certainly right about that," Vian said as she thought about all that occurred while she lingered here, wherever here might be.

She blinked and found herself back on the Hill. A breeze ruffled her hair as the last sunset of the old year fell behind the Hill and a chill air rose up from the earth. Heavy clouds formed on the horizon behind her. It would be a harsh winter this year. Vian hoped for a milder climate on the new world, but knew she would miss the seasons of her childhood.

As she reclaimed her physical body, she felt a weight pinning her to the old wooden chair.

Four crystal wands, brown, blue, green, and clear, each the length of her forearm lay in an untidy heap in her lap. As she bundled up the chrysalides in the warmth of her jacket and walked back down the Hill she wondered what the Elementals would look like when they emerged from their metamorphosis.

* * * *

Pirelle and Chalone paused just beyond the bile-green glow of the threshold. Ahead of them the corridor shuddered and vibrated with the strain of Liesha's meld. Its arched roof sagged and drooped as though it was barely able to maintain its shape.

"Lets get on with this," Pirelle said nervously. "I don't trust this corridor to stay accessible for much longer. Where do we start?"

Chalone looked around and shook her head. "I don't really know. From what Liesha said, the entrance should be right about where we're standing."

Pirelle peered down at the woven solidity underneath her feet. The mysterious fabric didn't seem quite so indestructible any more. "I hope you're talking metaphorically."

Chalone turned back to the Portal, unaware of Pirelle's hand still in hers, and turned Pirelle around with her.

The agony radiating from the Portal tore at her heart. Turgid colors wept down this side as well, but from inside the Gallery, the distortion reeked of despair. She turned her feelings aside, she had greater concerns.

"I think the Shadowlands Portal occupies the same place as this one, just in a different dimension," she said.

"Of course," Pirelle said. "I should have guessed that myself. How do we get to there from here?"

"This is the Gallery and we are Practitioners."

"Yes, *we* are," Pirelle said pointedly.

"I know," Chalone conceded. "I knew I'd have to let the otherworld in at sooner or later. It was just that..."

"Yeah." Pirelle agreed.

In spite of the distance between them, Chalone felt grateful that she and Pirelle were together on yet another great adventure. "I have an idea. Hold my hand."

"I am."

"Mm-m," Chalone murmured. "Yes, you are." She looked directly into Pirelle's eyes and lost herself in them for a moment. Her breast trembled as she inhaled the clean warm aroma she always associated with Pirelle. Their bodies swayed dangerously close and she dared not breathe another breath.

"We better get going," Chalone whispered and pulled back from a precipice she wasn't prepared to acknowledge.

She stepped closer to the injured Portal. "We have to reach out and sense the different field of energy," she instructed Pirelle. "Close your eyes and visualize another Portal right in front of this one, then walk through. Are you ready?"

"Absolutely not," Pirelle said, still trying to quell the wave of hope and desire that flashed through her body.

Chalone closed her eyes, and focused on connecting with the Shadowlands Portal. She felt a misty rain caress her face, and shook Pirelle.

"Should I open my eyes now?" Pirelle asked, then stared around in horrified wonder after she did. "I guess it worked."

A wall of gray fog twisted and swirled around them. It billowed over low hummocks of greasy rubble and sank into turgid pools of dead moisture. No tree, shrub, or anything else vaguely resembling life could be seen.

The fog momentarily lifted, exposing the blasted terrain stretching from horizon to horizon, then blew back in, hiding the desolation.

Pirelle finally found her voice. "This isn't how you described it.

What happened? Its as though the land is dead."

"I don't know, and I'm fairly certain I don't want to know," Chalone whispered.

"I agree," Pirelle said too loud. The Shadowlands spooked her and her voice jarred in the eerie silence. "Lets find Jalemi and get out of here." She turned around expecting to see the Portal behind her but the bleak landscape continued unbroken. She nudged Chalone.

Chalone searched the area intently and then shrugged her shoulders. "Why does this not surprise me," she said.

"I'm certainly not surprised. Any suggestions?"

"Not a one," Chalone replied as the sullen fog drifted closer. She looked down and spotted a set of footprints. "This is where Jalemi entered though." She pointed to the tracks heading between a large pair of slag hummocks.

"Terrific. Let's go then," Pirelle grumbled and started following the tracks. "These don't look like Jalemi's footprints but there doesn't seem to be anything else here to follow."

"Pirelle. Stop," Chalone called. "Just because we can't see the Portal doesn't mean it's not here. We have to make sure we know where it is."

Pirelle turned around and held out her hands in frustration. "What should we use, bread crumbs?"

Chalone stalked right up to Pirelle and stopped just short of her nose. She looked up into her eyes. "Your humor is a little underwhelming at times. We draw arrows in the dirt pointing to it, and memorize landmarks to make sure we can find our way back. If you have any suggestions as to what else we can do, apart from breadcrumbs, tell me now, before I get really annoyed with you."

Pirelle stepped back from Chalone's ire. She hadn't talked to her since that unfortunate night at Vian's. Pirelle's reply was the same this time as it had been at the beginning of their ill-fated adventure as children.

"I'll do whatever you want, go wherever you want, but only so long as we're home in time for supper."

Chalone shook her head and relented. She hoped they survived this adventure too.

* * * *

They followed the oddly meandering tracks through gray

hills and fog shrouded dales and gathered a damp sheen on their shoulders from the ever-looming fog.

At last the ongoing bleakness changed, although not for the better. Large splats of rain pocked the moisture limned cinder shards with darker spots.

"Did you order this?" Pirelle quipped, but raised her hands in protest when Chalone glared at her. "Sorry," she said. "I forgot myself for a moment. It won't happen again."

"You're terrible, you know that?"

"I know. It seems that baby sister, or whatever we're following, came this way too." Pirelle pointed to the ground where the tracks they'd been following led into the gloom as though forever.

The rain began to fall in earnest, and without another wasted moment, they hurried along the trail of footprints before any hope they had of catching up with Jalemi disappeared.

The cloudburst turned out to be a fickle thing and disappeared as soon as it had rained hard enough to soak them thoroughly and obliterate the tracks.

By unanimous vote, Chalone wouldn't let Pirelle have a say, they decided to walk in a straight line from where they saw the last markings.

"It's not as though we have anywhere else to go," Chalone muttered when Pirelle grumbled about her boots leaking.

The fog closed in and reduced their visibility again. Thoroughly wet, chilled, and defeated, Chalone agreed to turn around and retrace their steps. She and Pirelle peered through the shadowless murk one last time and were so startled they bumped into each other.

An opening in the side of one of the hills gaped at them through the mists.

"I think we've arrived," Chalone whispered as they unconsciously clung to each other, then very consciously moved apart. "Do you suppose we're expected?"

"I hope not," Pirelle said. "Now what?"

Chalone procrastinated. Walking into a dark cave opening was not high on her list of options. "Let's see if we can find the tracks first." She was disappointed.

They returned to the entrance and cautiously walked in. The air became drier and a musty smell clung to their wet clothes. A polished substance lined the walls so as to appear depthless. They walked first one way and then abruptly reversed direction.

"We're traveling through a labyrinth," Pirelle said quietly, and looked around startled. Her voice echoed eerily along the tunnel. Chalone nodded, and neither of them spoke again. It wouldn't do to forewarn whatever made this warren that it had visitors. The light grew brighter the further they walked.

A very soft sound echoed up the passage. Repetitive although not mechanical, and unlike anything they'd heard before.

"Chalone?" Pirelle whispered.

"Yes?"

"Do you have any idea what we're going to do when we find Jalemi?" Pirelle asked, more to hear the sound of a friendly voice than anything else.

"Not really." Chalone admitted. "You?"

"No. I just wondered." Pirelle touched the sleeve of her jacket. "My clothes are dry," she whispered louder.

"Mine too. Now shush," Chalone cautioned.

Pirelle shushed. The switchbacks came closer together as they approached the center of the labyrinth. The light brightened until it cast soft silvery highlights on the shiny walls. The strange sound grew louder, as though something breathed slowly and profoundly not too far ahead.

They slowed their pace and cautiously peered around every curve in the passage before committing themselves to it. At last, they leaned forward and saw the tunnel open out into a large dome. They walked around and stared in awe.

In the center of the space, a colossal mound of pillows and cushions rose up from the floor: all sizes and hues, tasseled and brocaded, herringbone-stitched and piped, gaudy and tasteful.

Pirelle almost laughed out loud at the absurdity of finding an enormous nest at the end of a long burrow. She didn't need Chalone to remind her to be quiet though. The sort of creature that might inhabit such a nest probably wasn't expecting visitors.

Nothing immediately jumped out and attacked them, so they cautiously approached the assortment of stuffed fabrics.

Chalone pushed aside one giant cushion, Pirelle moved another, and they peered in.

Nestled among the pillows, the giant serpentine creature they'd last seen being burned alive at the Earthblood fire opened one eye and looked right back at them.

Chapter Twenty-Eight

Chalone and Pirelle turned and ran but the tunnel had closed behind them. They tripped over each other in their haste to find another exit. Once they sorted themselves out Pirelle touched the barrier to make sure it was real. It was. A thrumming subsonic sound juddered along her finger bones. Almost as though the wall purred. She dismissed the notion as a figment of her adrenaline.

The deep rhythmic sound changed tempo as the recumbent monster shifted from a doze to fully awake.

Chalone and Pirelle learned at Lila's knee that when faced with no other alternative, confronting monsters in their Lairs was the only acceptable option. They steeled themselves for whatever might come, and returned to the heap of pillows.

"Ah-h. The stench of mortality," a sepulchral voice commented dolefully. "Who are you? Why have you come to disturb me?" Sebenesh was having fun.

"It wasn't intentional," Pirelle apologized. "We are looking for someone. A friend." She glanced at Chalone. "My sister."

"Sister!" During a long pause, the source of the voice considered something.

"I see. Come closer," Sebenesh said in her more customary tone. "I won't eat you."

Chalone didn't feel all that reassured and she could tell Pirelle felt the same way. They braced themselves for a vision of bloated coils and tattered flesh, but the center of the nest of pillows had been transformed.

They walked into Vian's lounge room, perfectly replicated, down to the collection of absurd oil lamps. A dark haired woman reclined in the overstuffed chaise-lounge Vian usually occupied and smiled at their astonishment. Over her voluptuous curves she wore a loose fitting silvery gown that glinted in the light like fish scales, or snakeskin. Immense power radiated from her coal black eyes. Even in her weakened state, she inspired awe.

"I created this simulacrum from your minds," the woman said. "I hoped you would feel more at ease."

"An understandable mistake," Chalone said feeling uneasier, if possible. "Acceptable none-the-less. Thank you for your consideration," she added, anxious not to offend someone who could transform matter at will.

"You are Chalone, you are Pirelle, and you are looking for Jalemi. Do you have any idea how much trouble she has caused?" The woman sighed and gestured for them to join her. She moved restlessly in her chair and underneath her sheer costume, bandages swathed her body from neck to toe.

"She tends to do that," Pirelle said being as agreeable as she could, for the same reasons as Chalone. She sat on her usual choice at Vian's house, the armchair.

"It was you we saw just now," Chalone said and sat on the first chair she found.

Sebenesh beamed at the décor she'd manifested, and not just for the effect it had on her guests. Vian's taste was eccentric, but she liked it. She tore her attention away from her cleverness and answered Chalone. "It occurred to me that you might find this body less startling than my true form."

Pirelle squirmed uncomfortably. "I don't understand any of this," she muttered under her breath.

"I don't suppose you do," the woman replied, "but that's not the point, is it?"

"What do you mean?" Pirelle shot back, startled at being overheard.

"Your sister has something that doesn't belong to her. Something that has now taken complete possession of her body and mind, and brought her here to find me. Unfortunately for Jalemi, I can't help her. Fortunately for me, what's inside her, can't find me."

"That doesn't help." Pirelle decided that she might as well continue as she'd started. *What was the worst that could happen*?

Sebenesh resisted the urge to demonstrate. "No, it doesn't," she said. "However, if you find yourself back here some time in the future, look me up, and I'll explain a few things to you," she said, much to Pirelle's consternation.

Pirelle sat bolt upright. *The woman was flirting with her*! Although just exactly what she offered remained unclear, as Sebenesh intended.

"You know where Jalemi is, don't you?" Chalone asked.

"I'm not strong enough to locate her exactly. The realm surrounding my Lair has changed, as I have been changed," Sebenesh paused. The sacrifice the Shadowlands made to preserve her body was hard to bear. Her poise was on the verge of collapse, but she sensed Chalone's agitation at her prolonged silence.

"I will relocate you nearby," she said hastily. "I can release her mind from the maze the Sphere has imprisoned her in, but it's up to you to convince her to voluntarily sever it from her spirit. There is no other way. The Sphere will try to influence you as well. Be wary of its cunning," she warned.

"What's this Sphere?" Chalone asked.

"Something that should have stayed asleep for a very long time, a very, very long time," Sebenesh repeated for emphasis.

"Jalemi somehow woke it up," Pirelle said, rolling her eyes at her sister's presumption.

"She has annoyed me severely," Sebenesh almost hissed.

"She does that too." Pirelle smiled a little. She was starting to enjoy herself.

"What happens once Jalemi is free of the Sphere?" Chalone persisted in spite of Pirelle and the woman veering off into divergent conversations.

"For better or worse, her destiny and that of the Sphere have merged beyond sundering. She must choose to be its custodian. The Sphere has tasted the fruits of mortality, and has grown beyond my abilities to constrain it any other way." Which wasn't the complete truth, but Sebenesh wanted Jalemi to suffer, just a little bit, for a very long time.

Chalone knew it wasn't in Jalemi's nature to refuse such an momentous commission and doubted that she would be overly upset by it.

Pirelle, too, contemplated how her sister would react, and felt a shiver run down her spine. She wondered what role she might end up playing and then smiled to herself at her pretensions. She wasn't the sort to tempt fate. That was her sister or Chalone. *Maybe not Chalone*, she amended.

Sebenesh also smiled, knowingly. "It's time to leave." She gestured in front of her and the air shimmered and split apart showing the dreary world outside her Lair.

"Wait," Chalone said. "Who are you?"

The room pulsed quietly as the woman pondered Chalone's question. "My name is Sebenesh. I am again an immortal. If we are all very lucky, we'll never see each other again."

* * * *

"Step through the gate." Sebenesh gestured toward the gap

in reality that bisected Vian's favorite occasional table. "You will emerge close enough to Jalemi to stop her, if you can."

Chalone and Pirelle rose slowly to their feet, their muscles stiff, as though they had been sitting for hours.

"Don't be concerned," Sebenesh reassured them. "The sensations will pass, and the experience has done you no harm." When both women looked confused, she smiled in spite of her wounds and reminded them. "This is the Shadowlands. All is not what it seems."

"What experience?" Pirelle asked, intrigued in spite of her recent resolve not to get involved in the affairs of the powerful and dangerous.

Sebenesh remained silent until Pirelle squirmed under her gaze, thinking perhaps she had gone too far. "Call it a test of sorts," she finally said.

"Did we pass?" The words slipped out of Pirelle's mouth before she knew it. She almost bit her tongue and wondered why she couldn't keep her mouth shut.

Sebenesh had fun subtly torturing Pirelle, but Chalone's restless energy pulled her back from her games. "That remains to be seen," she said with a frown that turned Pirelle a few shades paler, *such an easy mark*, then released her victim, none-the-worse for wear.

Chalone studied the gate intently. She glanced at Sebenesh. "You can create a Portal at will?"

"It isn't a Portal as you define them, but it is sufficient for my purposes." She motioned them toward the gate again.

"I might come back for those answers." Pirelle said cautiously. Sebenesh intrigued her.

"Words have power, Pirelle. Beware how you use them," Sebenesh said, her ennui becoming evident. "Now go, both of you, before our conversation depletes what little strength I have recovered."

Torn between leaving Sebenesh's unsettling presence, and her desire to find her sister, Pirelle played it safe and hastily stepped through the gate.

* * * *

Chalone wanted to ask more questions but thought better of it. "I hope you heal from your injuries soon. I have a feeling we're going to need your help again."

"A prophecy, Chalone? From you?"

Chalone prudently ignored the challenge. "I'm not prone to uttering them, but times being what they are..." She shrugged delicately.

"I know what you want to ask," Sebenesh said. "I don't have the answers you seek, not being a prophet myself." She teased gently. "Your destiny is unknown. Given time I trust that you'll find the resolution you crave." She chose not to mention exactly how much time would be involved. Chalone wouldn't have believed her.

Sebenesh grimaced as an agonizing spasm wrenched her body to one side. Pain she'd thought to keep concealed from mortal eyes brought tears that she hastily blinked away.

Chalone saw them and wanted to say and do many things, but none would've sufficed. Instead she waited until after the spasm had passed and Sebenesh regained her composure. She leaned close and gently kissed her forehead, looked into her pain-wracked eyes, and touched her lips to them as well.

Before Sebenesh had a chance to react, she hurried to the gate and left the Lair behind her.

* * * *

The unexpected gesture overwhelmed Sebenesh. She raised a blistered hand to where the compassionate caresses had been delicately placed.

After the Earthblood fire burned away the venom and saved her sanity, she existed as an immortal exists after death, lost to all senses and sensation.

Great power had been imbued in her Lair. As she sojourned in the abyss between the worlds of the living and the dead, it protected her shattered spirit just as the Shadowlands cared for her physical form. Her Lair could only do so much, Immortals being beyond its capacity to comprehend at the best of times. It offered her the only thing it could, the possibility of ascension to the living world.

She would be forever grateful to Vian for bringing that possibility to life.

She had been so badly hurt, so focused on surviving and healing, that she failed to pay attention to Jalemi and the Sphere.

The Sphere entered the Shadowlands with revenge as its purpose, and she knew with horrid certainty that it would destroy her without a moment of remorse. She had no one to succor her,

Arahona being well beyond recall. She prepared to meet her destiny as graciously as possible, vowing she would not go quietly.

Then Chalone and Pirelle appeared on her doorstep.

* * * *

She contemplated her recent visitors. Pirelle amused her. She was trustworthy and had the courage of a lion, but so young. Chalone was far more complex, and the outcome of her spirit's long journey through Time remained unclear.

They were uncertain champions at best.

Sebenesh's heart filled with the twin emotions of fear and trust, both unfamiliar. Tears glistened in her serpentine eyes. *Damn that mortal and her kisses. This is all her fault.* With one touch Chalone melted the rigid despair that haunted her since she'd returned to her Lair.

Sebenesh snuffled as ancient memories stirred passions she'd long thought behind her. Not lust, she would always have opportunities to satisfy that desire, but something deeper, something... "I will not utter that word," Sebenesh argued. "I have made my choice and I am content." The word rose from the core of her being anyway and carried with it all her heart's longing. She didn't need to say it, but there it was.

...something, mortal.

She abandoned her iron control over her abused body and returned to her sinuous form. Her gown slid from her disappearing shoulders to become her scaly skin once more. The hard walls and angles of Vian's lounge room vanished. Pillows reappeared and oil lamps turned into cushions. The chaise-lounge underneath her dissolved back into the heart of her nest and lovingly embraced her aching bones.

She buried her head in the endless coils of her body and rested as best she could.

* * * *

Chalone stepped out of the gate Sebenesh had created and back into the bleak landscape. Before she could get her bearings, Pirelle wrapped her in a tight embrace.

"What happened to you?" Pirelle demanded in a voice rough with chaotic tears. "You were supposed to be right behind me. It's been hours. I couldn't find you or the gateway. What happened to you? Where have you been? I've been searching everywhere!"

Chalone stayed calm within the circle of Pirelle's arms, waiting until she wound down.

"I was so scared," Pirelle finally said. "I thought I'd lost you." She looked so forlorn that Chalone acted without thinking.

She slid her arms up and around Pirelle's shoulders, feeling their strength as though for the first time. She held Pirelle's face between her palms, and brushed tears away with her thumbs. Pirelle's skin felt warm and so, right beneath her fingertips.

"I'm fine," She articulated slowly, making sure the words reached Pirelle through her distress. She smiled. "I was right behind you. Time must get distorted here." She shook Pirelle, hard enough to make sure she got her attention. "I'm fine."

Pirelle pulled her close and laid her chin on top of her head. They stood together, their bodies electric with perilous desire, moving closer with each breath.

They hovered between one moment and the next, each unwilling to be the first to move and afraid the other wouldn't move at all. An endless space neither desired to end stretched between them.

"We can't do this," Chalone said weakly, as she tried to douse the passion that had her thighs aching. "We have to find Jalemi."

They pulled away at the same time.

"I know. I never meant for this... I don't know that ..." Pirelle stumbled for words.

"Stop," Chalone said and clenched her jaw tight to stop her voice from trembling. If Tallem's name were mentioned, anything after that would be irrevocable. Another endless moment passed, this one uncomfortable "It'll be alright," she said at last.

No, it won't," Pirelle said grimly. "We've already gone too far for it to be alright."

"Nothing's happened, Pirelle!" Chalone defended herself or both of them. She couldn't distinguish which.

"That's sophistry, and you know it." Pirelle struggled to contain her desires, but Chalone's denial frustrated her. She wanted their feelings to be open and clear. "There's something between us. It's always been there. We were just too close to see it."

"I can't believe we're having this conversation." Chalone threw up her arms. "Here, in the middle of nowhere, in the middle of a galactic crisis!"

"If you're looking for the perfect place and time, we'll never say anything to each other." Pirelle pulled Chalone to her again.

"Look at me." Chalone resisted halfheartedly, but she knew Pirelle wasn't offering passion this time. "Look at me. We're not going to deny our feelings for each other. No matter how uncomfortable that makes you feel."

"I don't have any feelings for you." It sounded so absurd that Pirelle laughed, and Chalone had to laugh with her. "At least none I'm going to discuss with you."

"That doesn't let you off the hook," Pirelle warned.

Chalone nodded and laid her head against Pirelle's breast, content to have reached an agreement of sorts. Their embrace ended by mutual consent, and their thoughts returned to Jalemi.

* * * *

"She's nowhere nearby," Pirelle said, picking up the conversation from where it had been interrupted by denials and honesty, weakness and valor. "Otherwise I would have seen her when I looked for you."

"Sebenesh said we'd be close to her," Chalone recapped. Then she stared behind Pirelle. "The gate's gone."

Pirelle sighed. "I guess I won't be going back there then!"

"I know you, Pirelle. You'll find a way. Right now, let's split up and find Jalemi."

"Oh no! I'm not letting you out of my sight again."

"That's sweet." Chalone smiled, then shook her head. "And impractical. You search through that canyon and I..."

The sound of cinders crunching under irregular footsteps reached them and Jalemi staggered out of the fog.

Chapter Twenty-Nine

Jalemi crouched in the prison in her mind.

Something precious had been stolen from her but exactly what it was, she couldn't be sure of anymore. She knew she must remain still and silent so the thief would forget her and not return and hurt her body and mind.

The thief could not forget. It was too much a creature formed from her personality to forget and strangely enough it had no desire to cause her any physical harm. Although vengeance and retribution were a part of Jalemi's, and therefore the Sphere's emotional makeup, there was a more prosaic explanation for the physical pain she felt. Their two minds could not inhabit Jalemi's body, and not experience the dissonance that duality caused. Her nerve endings constantly screamed as though red hot needles were being forced through them.

What the Sphere did to Jalemi's mind was deliberate however. She was strong in so many ways, that if its attention slipped as it had when it sensed the Elementals the day Vian came to call, that if she were able to focus her will and intent, she would challenge the Sphere's control and that could be disastrous to its plans.

It swaggered into her hidey-hole and taunted her with its memories of her self-betrayal.

It hadn't stolen her body. She'd willingly given over control. How gullible she'd been. From the very first it had been preparing her to be its carrier to freedom. Her every action, thought even, had been at its instigation.

It eroded her will until she could do nothing but agree, and hope that it would eventually leave her be.

* * * *

In between bouts of twisting Jalemi's mind, the Sphere reached through the Shadowlands, assessing this new environment.

Something was damaged here, something that also had great power and throbbed like an open wound. Like any predator, the Sphere closed in for the kill only to be thwarted by its borrowed mortality. Jalemi's body staggered and threatened to fall.

The Sphere flung its thoughts at Jalemi like a javelin through her spirit. Again her weaknesses betrayed them. *Why was she so weak?* She was nothing more than a worm beneath its feet.

It lashed the tendons of her muscles, goading them.

* * * *

Such an outpouring of wrath shone like a beacon in the Shadowlands and finally swept Sebenesh's attention from the agony of her rebirth to a new and deadly threat. As she raged at the futility of her injuries, a ripple of primal elation surged through Sphere. It smiled a hideous grimace that strained the muscles of Jalemi's face, and forced her into a slow shuffling stagger.

Suddenly the Sphere heard familiar voices, and a cunning hope flared in its spirit. *How stupid they were to follow.* It changed direction and hurried as fast as its stolen body could manage.

* * * *

Jalemi felt the whiplash of the Sphere's elation and slunk even further into her darkened corner. She didn't doubt the Sphere was strong enough to ensnare Pirelle and Chalone and subvert them. She had so little regard for their strength. Then a tiny thread of hope sprung into her mind. If she waited long enough, the Sphere would relocate to one of them, and leave her alone. She would, of course, defeat it completely and its powers would again be hers. She nurtured her hopeless plan and the Sphere let her keep her delusion as something else to take from her when the need arose.

* * * *

Shrouds of mist and dense fog rolled over the Shadowlands. One such wave circled around Chalone and Pirelle, Jalemi and her unwelcome guest. Wisps of darker shadows staggered in contorted and erratic patterns within the edges of the mist to form an unbreakable rampart.

* * * *

Not that far away in her Lair, Sebenesh made sure the barrier would release the combatants only when the outcome had been decided. She still felt so sorely wounded that she didn't much care which way the battle went, but that was a momentary weakness. She would honor the agreement she'd made to free Jalemi from the baleful manipulations of the Sphere. The rest was up to Pirelle and Chalone.

Her wounds began to itch horribly and she felt a molt coming on. Her melancholy had passed and she was in no mood to be generous to anyone.

She snarled as she flicked out her tongue and tasted the currents of future possibilities. She hissed her annoyance. These wretched mortals would need her help one more time. Not here in the Shadowlands, somewhere else. Somewhere she couldn't possible get to in her current physical state.

So much for being done with them, she ruefully acknowledged. If she were being really honest with herself, she found a few of them unexpectedly endearing at times, a bit like a pack of unruly snakelings.

* * * *

Since the Sphere freed itself from the Earthblood fire, the Reweaving of Time had languished in its corner of her Lair like a dejected ball of string.

She willed it to approach and peered at it with a critical eye. With enough potency for one last undertaking, she flexed her will and flicked a whorl of her Self into it.

The Reweaving cheerfully wobbled back to its corner happy once again to have a purpose and to wait the passage of Time.

With a tired and scornful hiss Sebenesh closed her eyes, turned her head to one side, and tucked it under the nearest of her coils. A good long hibernation was in order. She'd helped out those ingrates for the last time.

Her nest of pillows and cushions slowly unraveled and blended into a cocoon that nothing this side of eternity could penetrate.

Sebenesh began the arduous task of shedding her old skin and growing a new one that would be resilient enough to last a thousand generations.

* * * *

Jalemi huddled in her fetid corner. Her desire to posses the Sphere warring with self-loathing at her plan to achieve it.

A shining whisper drifted above the befouled floor and broke apart the polluted energy around her.

She slunk even further back and pushed the voice away with the force of her terror. It said her name, over and over, with such potency that it overwhelmed her muffled fears and unwilling spirit.

She realized ignoring it wouldn't make it go away. "Leave me alone," she whispered, and shut her eyes tight just in case something else heard her.

Suddenly a pair of horrifyingly strong hands hauled her to her feet and shook her like a terrier shakes a rat. Sebenesh had no plans to kill her, not yet, and perhaps not ever, but she took great pleasure in the thought. She stood Jalemi up on her feet as she manifested as her primal self. "Open your eyes. Look at me! Now," she thunderously commanded.

"Shhh! Quiet," Jalemi hissed in terror. "It will hear you and come back, and hurt me, and say awful things to me."

Sebenesh recognized the Sphere's manipulations behind Jalemi's panic. The severe part of her spirit that understood such things applauded it's survival instincts, but Jalemi's sanity, Sebenesh's safety, and the survival of the Gallery was at risk. She towered like a giant cobra ready to strike and flicked her tongue out and in, tasting the exact nature of Jalemi's fear.

At that moment, Jalemi opened her eyes as she had been implacably commanded to do. She squeaked and scuttled back into her loathsome corner. A slithering sound crept closer and something wrapped around her legs pulling her back into fresher air and brighter light.

Jalemi found a tiny piece of courage that allowed her to finally reopen her eyes, and slowly look up at the delicate triangular head just above hers.

"Hello, Jalemi," Sebenesh said quietly.

"I know you!" Jalemi gasped. "From the Earthblood fire!"

"Exactly," Sebenesh said as though addressing a particularly dense student who'd finally got the right answer. "We have something else to discuss right now." Her adamantine gaze pinned Jalemi to the spot. "How long are you going to quiver here in this silly cage you've built for yourself?" she asked, unable to contain her displeasure, in spite of her intention to be gentle.

"Eeep," Jalemi squeezed out.

Sebenesh relaxed and Jalemi's ribs stopped creaking almost immediately.

"My apologies." Sebenesh said politely. "I forgot myself for a moment." Jalemi drew in a ragged breath and blinked in surprise, which Sebenesh took to mean that Jalemi accepted her apology.

"The Sphere has taken your physical form away from you. This is not a natural state for your body to endure. The Sphere won't return it in time to save your life. When you're quite dead, it will use your sister or Chalone in the same way it used you. You will never be able to control it!" Sebenesh crushed Jalemi's secret and hoped the truth might awaken her will to fight.

"There's nothing else I can do. Don't think I haven't tried," Jalemi said with the first spark of fire in her voice, unfortunately short-lived. "It's not my fault," she finished defensively.

"This is *all* your fault," Sebenesh bellowed and sent Jalemi reeling back into her corner, her eyes screwed tightly shut again.

Sebenesh reared up and hauled her back. She lowered her head until her nose almost touched Jalemi's, forcing her eyes open.

"Everything that has gone wrong is a result of you trying to grasp a power that you had no idea what to do with. Not the faintest! Not a clue! Vian tried to warn you, but you chose not to listen." Sebenesh paused to calm herself down a little. She felt Jalemi squirm in her coils, which only angered her further. She wanted to be done with this intimate link to Jalemi's polluted mind, and return to her Lair.

"I don't know why I should, but I'm giving you a chance to put things right," Sebenesh said relentlessly. "I'm going to release you from this little box in your mind, and put you on an equal footing with the Sphere for control of your body. The rest is up to you. If you are strong enough, you will be able to cast it out and make sure that it can never do to anyone else what it's done to you. It's a power that's beyond any mortal ability to wield. I hope you've realized that by now."

Before Jalemi could muster an argument as to why she thought that was a really bad idea, her world shuddered and turned upside down. Her stomach churned. She hastily shut her eyes, but Sebenesh's final command reverberated implacably around her skull. "Open your eyes. There are things you must see for yourself."

Blurred gray shapes wavered in front of her eyes as though layers of images were slightly out of focus. She blinked and tears gathered at the corners of her eyes. The images liquefied into distinct shapes, gray hills, valleys, and rocks. She breathed deeply, and realized she was in control of her lungs again, in control of her body again. At the same time, she felt another presence with her, inside her.

The Sphere's only nightmare came true. Somehow Jalemi had slipped her leash. The stench of the power of this forbidding place surrounded her, but she was still only one puny mortal with all the hooks the Sphere had insinuated into her psyche still firmly embedded. It had to only...jerk them.

Jalemi felt the Sphere struggling to control her movements. She panicked and the edges of her control frayed.

* * * *

The Sphere saw an aspect of Jalemi's spirit it had never met before. It was brutal and raw, stripped of all softness, and a force that would never, ever stop once unleashed.

If the Sphere gained supremacy, she would die as the serpent woman predicted, an unacceptable fate that finally awoke the sleeping beast. Without hesitation or effort, Jalemi's will to survive ripped the Sphere's consciousness from her physical body and thrust it into the dark prison she had just left.

"Stay there, you bastard," she hissed. "See how you like it."

"It suits me rather well," a slick voice answered her.

Her survival was no longer at risk and she fell for the Sphere's blandishments one more time. Its voice inside her head startled her.

"You're surprised?" The Sphere chuckled, and tried to keep her off balance, while it raged at yet another unforeseen reversal of its fortunes. "I've always had a voice, you just couldn't hear me like this," it said, callously mixing lies and truth. "I'm happy here. It feels comfortable. I can see why you created it." The Sphere sensed Jalemi wavering at the unexpected praise. "You did well with what you had."

"What do you mean?" she asked.

"The resources you had to work with were minimal. I was not an easy taskmaster," the Sphere said with just the right measure of admiration in its voice. Too much and Jalemi would not be fooled, not enough and it would lose her attention.

Suddenly another voice intruded on the conversation.

"Jalemi! Answer me," Pirelle said as though she'd been repeating the same words for quite a while. "You have to let it go completely or it will destroy you."

Jalemi refocused her vision outward and saw Pirelle standing directly in front of her, Chalone close by her side.

"Would you look at that," the Sphere whispered slyly. "You

couldn't separate those two with a carving knife."

* * * *

"You have to let it go or it will destroy you," Pirelle said yet again, and despaired of ever getting through. "Jalemi? Can you hear me?" she asked, stepping forward, but Jalemi held up a hand as if to ward her off.

"I'm here. I can hear you." Jalemi said in a voice not quite hers. She cleared her throat and spoke again. "The Sphere and I have been having a little talk and we've come to an arrangement."

Chalone pulled Pirelle back. "What sort of agreement?" She asked suspiciously. Pirelle looked mystified, and tried to shrug off of her hand.

"We agreed," Jalemi said harshly. "That we can be here at the same time, sharing this flesh equally and both get what we want."

"What is it you both want?" Chalone asked, as Pirelle finally stopped pulling against her.

"Power, of course."

Chalone's throat thickened with sorrow. She knew that very little difference remained between Jalemi and the Sphere's desires anymore. "That's not possible," she said.

Jalemi snorted arrogantly. "Of course it's possible. The Sphere has unlimited power, but cannot move independently, and I have control over my physical body."

"You've been misinformed," Chalone said.

"About what?" Jalemi asked mystified.

Chalone saw Pirelle glance at her with the same confused look on her face. The twin effect again. She almost laughed in spite of the situation.

"Everything," she said. "The Sphere doesn't have unlimited power, just a lot of it, and I suspect its very limited in what it can do right now. You don't have control of your body, not entirely," she qualified. "Only some of the words I hear coming out of your mouth are yours." Chalone took a risk and continued to speak honestly. "You're ambitious, we all know that, but the Sphere has distorted your ambition into something it can manipulate without you even knowing. That's the only power I see it using here."

A sudden wave of agony twisted Jalemi's features until she looked like a different woman, harsh and bitter.

"Untrue," she growled as though the Sphere forced the words out of her throat.

Pirelle suddenly rushed toward Jalemi before Chalone could stop her.

"Stay away from me," Jalemi shrieked. She staggered back a few paces as her face regained some of its normal appearance. "Don't you know how much danger you're in?" she whispered, as though speaking softly would prevent the Sphere from knowing what she said. "If you touch me, it will leave me and take over your body."

Pirelle pulled back, shocked. She hadn't understood why Chalone held her back until that moment. She moved closer to Chalone in mute apology.

Jalemi struggled to regain her balance on her aching feet and then sneered at her sister. "That's where you belong, isn't it? With your precious Chalone. It's always been Chalone. Didn't you know that? Everybody else did, and they laughed at you. I laughed at you! Chalone's so good and dedicated and famous. She never saw how you looked at her. You're pathetic."

Pirelle withered inside. *Everybody knew? Everyone laughed?*

Pirelle, the great womanizer. Never had her heart broken. Fallen for her best friend. What a cliché. They all laughed at her. She was such a fool. She threw a guilty glance at Chalone and moved a few paces away to a heap of rocks nearby and stared at them as though they could hide her shame.

Chalone watched her, and her heart sank.

"See?" Jalemi spat. "Even now you can't keep your eyes off each other. You make me want to throw up! I'm leaving. I have a Key to find!

Chapter Thirty

Jalemi hobbled away from the shocked silence her undeniably true words created and toward the fog bank. She stopped as though she'd walked into an invisible barrier and spun around almost stumbling again. "What is this? What have you done?" She accused.

"Not us," Chalone said as she blanked the last of her emotions off her face. The burgeoning feelings between her and Pirelle must not be used in the battle being waged inside Jalemi. "Even you should be able to recognize the handiwork of your creator." She guessed it was Sebenesh, but didn't know for sure. "She meant for us to stay here until we can resolve this."

"There's nothing to resolve," Jalemi hissed angrily as her mood changed again. "I am going to destroy you both, and then I will find my creator." She flung the word back at Chalone like a spiteful curse. "I will destroy her too."

"I don't think that's how this will all turn out." Pirelle spoke for the first time since Jalemi had named her secret. She, too, had put her feelings to one side. "You're still my sister. The Sphere can't change that." She edged closer to Jalemi. "I know you love me, and in the end you'll protect me." She took a firm hold of Chalone's hand and reached out to claim Jalemi's as well.

Chalone gasped, but before she could react, Pirelle held her tighter. "Trust me," she said. Chalone stared at her and then nodded.

Jalemi understood what Pirelle had done and in spite of her power lust, which the Sphere fanned at every opportunity, she recognized Pirelle's integrity, and felt her strength flow like a wave of glowing heat. Through Pirelle's touch, she sensed Chalone's mind, still and deep, offering her a place of calmness in which to make her choice. They risked their lives on her decision.

She paused though, torn between conflicting desires. She wanted to be free of the Sphere, but she would have to relinquish all the possibilities the Sphere taunted her with.

She was never clear just what tipped the balance, perhaps it was the gift Chalone and Pirelle had given her. They didn't judge her, or convince her to give up the Sphere. They waited and trusted that she would choose with her heart. The moment passed and she willingly linked her mind to theirs.

The three of them focused their will and materialized in the place in Jalemi's mind that had been her prison and her solace. Their differences made them strong, and their love for each other, in all its confusing forms, gave them strength. They sought out the insidious threads the Sphere had woven throughout Jalemi's mind, body, and spirit.

They had no time for subtleties and the severing was brutal. As each thread of its intent snapped, the Sphere shuddered with pain. Each time a piece of its essence disconnected from Jalemi, it wailed in despair.

"You need me," it screeched into their minds, trying to shatter their connection. The sheer volume of sound threatened to engulf them. The Sphere decided to try greed. After all, it worked with Jalemi alone. "I can give you everything you ever dreamed of."

"That's enough," the three-woman entity said. "The only ability you have now is to corrupt minds. Even that will be nothing more than a memory for you from now on."

"No! I have other power. I was created to change the whole universe. Jalemi, please," it pleaded desperately. "Let me stay with you. I promise I won't hurt you anymore, or anyone else."

Jalemi saw through three-fold eyes and accepted the truth of what her actions had created. Shame burned her spirit and she felt tempted to run and hide again, but Chalone and Pirelle stayed with her and she would not betray them.

Jalemi grimaced. As long as she was in this mood of self-honesty, which, she admitted, probably wouldn't last all that long, she would try and undo the damage she caused.

She released the three-way melding and gently pushed Chalone and Pirelle from her mind. She added a mental hug for them, and an admonition to resolve their emotional situation. Their response was tinged with deprecating humor and anxiety. The situation was far from simple.

Jalemi shifted her consciousness inward, without fear of enthrallment this time. Her spirit would always carry an ache for what she gave up. However, she smiled, and this time it reached her heart. She had so many other pathways to power.

She focused her will on her inner companion.

The Sphere remained silent, assessing what had occurred. Jalemi's unaccompanied return to the fray caught it off guard. Even with its intimate acquaintance with Jalemi, it had no frame of reference for the paradox of mortality. It was a creature of finite horizons and could be nothing else.

Jalemi, like all mortals, had the ability to transcend her limitations and make the unimaginable, possible.

With great compassion, she gathered the tangled and severed threads of the Sphere's consciousness and looped them around each other until they formed a large ball. She threw it up into the air and loudly clapped her hands.

A concussion reverberated in the sunless skies of the Shadowlands. The air between the three women wavered and coalesced into a dark opening. A flash of light strobed and the Sphere flew out from its center. The opening crashed shut and the Sphere, now returned to its original physical form and size, accelerated toward the surrounding wall of fog.

With a gut-wrenching crack, it sped past the women and ricocheted around the barrier, seeking a way out. It struck the pile of rocks and ended its bid for freedom buried underneath them. The impact with the resilient stones splintered two shards off its surface.

The Sphere quickly smoothed out the blemishes where the shards sheared off. Here was a chance to salvage something from its humiliating defeat. The rock pile collapsed around it and it gently rolled forward to lay quiescent at Jalemi's feet.

Jalemi, Pirelle, and Chalone leaned on each other for a moment catching their breath. The confrontation, only a few moments long, exhausted them.

With a quick squeeze of Pirelle's hand, Jalemi pulled away first and picked up the perfectly round silvery Sphere. She held it cautiously and addressed Chalone's earlier comments. "I haven't given up. I still have ambitions you know."

"I don't doubt that for a minute," Chalone said dryly. "You wouldn't be the Jalemi we know and love if you didn't."

Suddenly the Sphere began to shrink. Forces beyond the women's understanding reduced its beautiful color and size down to a jet black marble that lay uneasily in the palm of Jalemi's hand. "What does this mean?" Jalemi asked, not really expecting an answer.

Pirelle looked at it. "I think it's the handiwork of a strange being Chalone and I encountered somewhere over yonder," she said, waving vaguely off to one side. Chalone elbowed her in the ribs and shook her head slightly.

Pirelle guessed that Chalone didn't want her to talk about

Sebenesh, although she had no idea why. Even still, the rebuke stung. She returned to the rock pile to inspect the damage the Sphere had caused.

Jalemi peered at the tiny author of so much anguish and thwarted desires in her hand until she almost threw it away, almost. "Maybe this makes it easier for me to carry," she mused.

"Maybe," Chalone said warily.

"Skeptic." Jalemi grinned. "Thank you for coming after me, both of you," she added, to include Pirelle who focused on the rocks she examined. "I didn't mean what I said about the two of you."

"Yes, you did," Chalone replied with a sad little smile, and stole a glance at Pirelle. She hadn't forgotten Pirelle's reaction to Jalemi's accusations.

Pirelle sat down on the largest rock in the pile without really thinking about what she was doing. "What do we do now?" she asked and reached down as though adjusting one of her boots. A tiny glint between the rocks snared her attention. Her fingers found the shard and she tied it in her bandana. It would make an interesting souvenir.

The other shard slid further down between the rocks. It was in no hurry. She would be back.

Pirelle's question had only one answer. To find a way back to their world before the weeping Portal collapsed and they were marooned forever.

Jalemi buttoned the black marble inside her pocket. Close enough for her to keep it secure, yet far enough away that it couldn't intrude on her thoughts.

As they looked around for their trail of footprints, the strange fog bank shivered and parted. A bell-like chime sounded and a laneway leading straight through the hillocks and dells opened up.

Casting uneasy glances at each other and at the walls of fog that barricaded them into the narrow defile, they followed the mysterious trail. The fog opened a few meters in front of them and closed in on their heels. They had no way to see where they had been or where they headed.

Not that they had many other choices, Pirelle quipped, as they started off. Her spirit was the swiftest to recover and she was ready to leap into the next adventure.

Chalone shook her head, glad that no matter how much some things changed, the essential Pirelle never would.

Jalemi moved slowly and deliberately. Each step sent the immediate horror of her ordeal further from her consciousness. Her limbs loosened up and she breathed easier.

They walked until they felt weary, rested, and walked again. Their fog-bound pathway took a detour around a high mound of cinders, ash, and rubble.

"Do we have any idea where we're going?" Jalemi asked her sister, only half teasing.

"Not really," Pirelle said, "but this does look familiar."

Chalone spoke before Pirelle inadvertently revealed exactly where they were. She didn't believe for a minute that the Sphere had truly abandoned its quest.

"I remember this too," she said quickly. "The Portal is this way." She practically dragged Pirelle and Jalemi off to one side of the pathway. The fog obligingly opened up a tangent.

They stumbled down a small precipice and found themselves beneath the fog.

"Do you remember the landmarks around the Portal?" Chalone asked Pirelle, trying to distract her from revealing anything further about their visit with Sebenesh.

"I think we've arrived," Pirelle said, turning slowly in a circle, trying to catch a glimpse of the Portal.

"How can you tell?" Jalemi asked.

"Stands to reason," Pirelle said. "This is no place in the middle of nowhere! Not one to change the subject, but there's something we have to discuss before we return." Chalone and Jalemi looked at her and waited. "What are we going to do with our friend there?"

Chalone started to answer but Jalemi interrupted. "It stays with me."

"I can understand that, but what are you going to do with it? We've all seen what it can do to you," Pirelle argued.

"It's different this time. I understand why I have to take care of it."

"Well! That's different then," Pirelle huffed. "Do you mind sharing with us lowly mortals this lofty purpose?"

"Stop that," Jalemi said and thumped Pirelle. "You're being ridiculous again."

"It helps break the tension," Pirelle said.

Chalone was used to their ways but sometimes it could be a bit wearing. "Will you two behave," she said tersely. "We need to decide what to do once we return. The Portal is collapsing and we don't have a lot of time left over for a discussion."

"There's no decision for us to make. I'll keep it with me until I find out what else to do with it," Jalemi said firmly. "I am kind of responsible for this mess we're in, so its up to me to fix it."

"Kind of?" Chalone asked, faking a shocked expression. "It does make sense. Don't think for a moment you're doing this on your own."

"Well," Pirelle said, not really satisfied with the lack of detail but unable to think of anything else to add. "Let's get going then." She looked at Chalone. "You seem to know about these things, so, where's the Portal?"

Chalone smiled and gestured with her chin. "Right behind you."

Jalemi and Pirelle turned, squinted, and blinked as hard as they could. Nothing.

"You're bluffing," Pirelle said.

"I never bluff," Chalone said, as her smile lost its glow.

"I see," Pirelle said with a tinge of anxiety in her voice.

"The Portal?" Jalemi reminded them.

"Remember how we got here?" Chalone asked. "Close your eyes. Find it with your other senses."

* * * *

They entered the Gallery with the remaining Portal to their world at their backs. A low groan billowed around them and although they couldn't be sure, the fabric of the corridor looked a bit thin and stretched. It shook underneath their feet, as though fevered.

"I think we've run out of time," Chalone said and faced the Portal.

"We should probably hurry then," Pirelle said.

The Portal brutally assaulted their senses. It was tearing itself apart and tried to do the same to them, but eventually, after the passage of too much time for such a short journey, they were through.

The darkness of their last night on their home world had been thrust back by giant portable generators. Monochromatic light and shadows painted the entire area around the devastated Hall.

They staggered into the ruins. Chaotic waves of sound grated in their ears as the Portals' death throes surrounded them.

Jalemi collapsed on the cold stone floor and tried to catch her breath. The tiny black marble spilled from her pocket and rolled down a slight slope. It bumped against the boot of an anonymous woman in the very last of the groups waiting to leave.

* * * *

The woman, Wylinor, stood tall and lean, a native of Valder. If Pirelle or Chalone had seen her, they might've recognized her as perhaps a descendant of Broon's, the old woman who told them the Tales of the Seas of Sand.

Wylinor decided to join the evacuation at the last minute. The prospect of never having a choice to leave the home world prompted her to act before the choice disappeared.

The sight of the Portal's collapse and the hideous grinding sound gave her reason to doubt her decision, but she looked at the innocent little black ball in the palm of her hand and decided it was a good omen. With the others of her group, she gathered up her few possessions and stepped closer to the Portal. She'd brought a suitcase of clothes, and a helmet from her seacar racing days. Everything else remained behind with memories of a life she was glad to leave.

* * * *

Jalemi felt the Sphere change focus as it abandoned her. She groaned grief-stricken. Chalone and Pirelle tried to help her to her feet. "The Sphere!" She gasped as her heart shattered. "It's gone."

Her words submerged under the grinding noise, and even though she shouted them again and again, no one heard her. Tears fell from her unbelieving eyes as she desperately scrabbled among the broken stones and debris.

Chapter Thirty-One

It was perhaps one of the most frustrating decisions Vian had ever made but she remained, along with Lila, Tallem, and Liesha, to wait for Chalone, Pirelle, and Jalemi, whether or not they returned before the Portal collapsed. She surprised herself at the relief she felt when they popped out of the Portal before it was too late for her to continue her destiny on the new world.

* * * *

The tremors generated from within the Portal ceased and the sky grew noticeably thicker as thunderclouds drawn by the disaster rolled across the ruins. Cold silence descended like a lead weight.

"What happened?" someone asked too loudly.

"It does not matter," Liesha answered from where she had sought out Chalone "Something is holding the Portal steady. We need to take advantage of this respite, now."

Jalemi struggled out of Pirelle's grasp and looked wildly around her.

"What's wrong with you?" Pirelle asked.

"Leave me alone. There's nothing wrong with me. The Sphere slipped out of my pocket when I fell. Someone's picked it up."

Vian came up to her. "Think Jalemi," she commanded. "We're out of time. Find it with that connection you've fought so hard to keep."

Pirelle glared at Vian and held Jalemi's arm in spite of Jalemi's struggles to get free of her. "Can you sense who it was?" Pirelle asked hopefully. Jalemi shook her head, too distraught to think clearly.

"Yet again, you have failed!" A monstrous voice boomed across the ruined Hall. The final loss of the Sphere activated the last sending from Sebenesh, and she was not in a good mood.

* * * *

Sebenesh's arrival convinced Wylinor it was definitely time

to leave. She chivvied her group through the temporarily stable Portal and sighed with relief as she arrived safely on the other side with her new lucky charm in her hand. She shouldered her few possessions and began the long journey to her new home.

She never felt the touch of a cranky Immortal who took the essence of the Sphere and buried it deep in her spirit, far away from mortal temptation, to sleep for a thousand generations.

* * * *

Jalemi suddenly spun around. "It's gone into the Gallery!" She rushed to the Portal, but an invisible force yanked her back.

"You will follow. Once I am done with you," Sebenesh hissed implacably.

The spotlights ringing the staging area that used to be the Hall dimmed as a giant hooded snake superimposed on an unearthly beautiful woman in a sparkling golden dress appeared.

Sebenesh looked at the few remaining women waiting to pass through the Portal.

"Vian," she said in a voice so pure it almost broke Vian's heart.

"I apologize for neglecting to adequately introduce myself last time we met," Sebenesh said, tilting her head to one side. "Then, neither of us were quite ourselves, were we?"

"Apology accepted," Vian said graciously, after she cycled through awe, embarrassed, and arrived at slightly smug. "You had other things on your mind."

"Indeed."

Sebenesh looked down from her great height and sought out Jalemi. All grace and compassion melted from her demeanor.

"I'd hoped never to meet you here at all!" She settled down to Jalemi's eye-level. "Do you have any idea what I've been through trying to repair the mess you've created?" she asked in a strangely pleasant voice that never reached her cold, cold eyes.

Jalemi shook her head the tiniest fraction. "Not exactly," she squeaked.

Sebenesh sighed. "Of course not. I don't have time to tell you. I'd probably fang you to death just to ease my irritation." Sebenesh smiled frostily and showed her serpent fangs.

Jalemi turned even paler and edged behind Pirelle.

"You'll have to go through me to do it," Pirelle said.

"Yes. I would," Sebenesh agreed. Pirelle wasn't sure if that was a threat or a promise.

"Don't worry," Sebenesh continued. "I have something planned for Jalemi other than using her as a midnight snack."

She rose to her full height and towered above the ruins to address the gathered crowd. "The Portal to this world will remain for a few more minutes. If you are leaving, go now."

Sebenesh eyed the Portal as it shivered and murmured its agony deep into the ground. The sightseers who remained shuffled about uncertainly. She glanced at them.

"It will not be safe to stay near here once the Portal has collapsed. Take whatever precautions you need. Your fate is yours," she said, and scrutinized them as they scuttled back beyond the trees. They wouldn't remember her. Only their fear of the Portal would remain to haunt their dreams.

Sebenesh returned her attention to Jalemi. "The woman who took the Sphere is long gone," she said. "The Sphere itself is deep within her and I have rendered it unconscious. When Pirelle called it the 'Sleeper', she gave me an idea."

Jalemi almost looked at her sister, but didn't dare take her eyes off those fangs.

"It will remain hidden within her family line," Sebenesh continued remorselessly. "Until the time comes for it to wake and transform into its destiny. Jalemi, you and your descendents will watch over hers. Never directly interfere, but remain close at hand." Sebenesh paused and reared up for emphasis. "If you fail at this, I won't just bite you, I will annihilate you from all existence, for all eternity."

The night sky turned darker as ominous clouds shot through with streaks of lightning gathered directly over the Hall.

Sebenesh looked up at the sky. "Time has run out. I cannot hold the Portal any longer."

Jalemi started to speak but Sebenesh silenced her with a look. "I will tell you what you need to know, when you need to know it. Do you think I should trust you any more than that?" Someone pushed a bundle into Jalemi's arms and Sebenesh nudged her toward the Portal.

"Now go, before you are too late!" With a last surprisingly gentle shove, she pushed Jalemi through the Portal.

Jalemi stepped off the waning threshold and smiled. *At last!* She'd gained access to the true power behind all that had occurred these last few months. The corridor quaked and she thought she saw the fabric fray. Fear and exaltation trailed after her as she ran as fast as she could.

* * * *

"No," Pirelle screamed as the Portal collapsed further. "She's my sister! You can't separate us. I won't let you. I'm right behind you, Jalemi," she shouted.

Her fingers almost touched the edge of the Portal before Sebenesh dragged her back. She thrashed against the scaled flesh, and in her despair almost broke free.

Sebenesh raised Pirelle up to her eye level. "Where she is going, you are not permitted to follow."

"What do you mean?" Pirelle shouted and struggled anew.

"You chose a different path. You meddled in this, above and beyond helping your sister."

Pirelle's thoughts turned instantly to the tiny shard. It burned through the leather of her wallet and singed her conscience. "I d-don't know what you mean," she stammered and blushed bright pink.

"I think you do," Shake said and shifted the conversation into the spirit world where only Pirelle could hear.

* * * *

Vian leaned close to Chalone's ear. "You have no idea what this is about either I suppose?" she asked, as Sebenesh put Pirelle gently back on the ground.

Chalone, intent on what was happening, absently shushed her. All things considered, Vian took being shushed rather well, but it wasn't something she was ever going to let Chalone forget.

Pirelle suddenly lifted her head and looked straight at Chalone. She looked so distressed Chalone couldn't remain where she was. "What is it? What's happening?"

Pirelle shook her head. "I have to go as well," she said tearfully. "I'm sorry, Chalone. Something happened in the Shadowlands." A sibilant hiss gusted over her head. "Something I did," she hastily amended. "I have to go back."

"To the Shadowlands? No! I don't understand why. What did you do?"

"Apparently, it's what I'm going to do," Pirelle said bewildered. "I have to go now."

Chalone stepped back from Pirelle as though she had been stung. Tears welled up in her eyes and her heart felt like it was about to shatter into a thousand pieces.

"I don't understand," she repeated. "Where's everybody going?" She looked around at the remains of her family and her homeland. "This doesn't make any sense." She turned to Sebenesh with a fierce look. "Why are you sending them away?"

"It isn't my doing, Chalone," Sebenesh said quietly. "They made their choices."

"You're punishing them?" Chalone accused, her fists clenched by her side.

"No. There are consequences, and they have to face them. That's all," Sebenesh said with an undeniable firmness.

"That's all," Chalone repeated numbly. "What about me?" She turned to Pirelle. "What about us?"

* * * *

Out of sight among the rubble, Tallem, shook her head and ran her thumb along the skin over her implant. That answered that question.

* * * *

Pirelle slowly gathered a small bundle of her belongings from Lila. She avoided looking at Chalone. "I have to go," she repeated as though that would make it acceptable.

"No you don't." Chalone denied

"I'll come back for you."

"I wont be here when you get back," Chalone said in a sudden surge of bitterness. "None of this will be here. You'll never find me again, and all your brave words will have been for nothing."

Any answer Pirelle made would only compound the mess she'd made of their friendship. She aborted any attempt to touch Chalone and walked to the Portal without looking back, bending over slightly to get through.

Large cracks snapped open around the Portal.

* * * *

Sebenesh saw no reason to linger in the Mortal Realm. With Pirelle on her way to the Shadowlands, Jalemi gone, the Sphere asleep, and the Portal beyond her help, she'd accomplished all she could. She returned to her Lair and finally slept.

* * * *

Vian sighed. She would probably never meet the likes of the serpent woman again, certainly not where she was going. Her women gathered around her, although Tallem held back a little.

Chalone noticed the small movement in spite of Vian blocking her view. "Not you too?" she asked with a growing numbness.

Tallem reluctantly stepped around Vian. "The ECHOs asked me to stay. I'd a'most made up my mind before you and I... Before you came back," she amended. "Now, wi' everything that's happened...I...I decided to 'cept their offer."

Beyond arguing or denial, Chalone hugged Tallem in surrender. "Is there anybody else?" She glared around her and turned on Vian. "What about you? Have you decided to stay too?"

"Don't be silly, dear. I was only waiting for you," Vian scolded her as she bustled about, making sure the last of her possessions were packed neatly in two large carrysacks.

Chalone almost laughed at the dismissive ordinariness of Vian's response. She calmed herself, with a great effort, and picked up her bags.

* * * *

Vian sought out four very unusual items in her packs yet again. She was going to pester the Elementals into telling her how and why they metamorphosed themselves into those crystals, no matter how long it took. She glanced at Chalone and saw Liesha move to embrace her. She winced in sympathy.

"I'm not saying another goodbye," Chalone said, her heart overwhelmed by a desperate loneliness almost more than she could bear. "I don't care what you've decided to do," she said helplessly and stepped back.

"You do not have to. I am coming with you," Liesha said, and ignored the surprised gasps of disbelief from Tallem and Vian.

* * * *

Liesha had thought very hard since she and Vian talked on the Hill earlier in the day. Her reconciliation with Chalone highlighted how much she missed her family and how restrictive her life as an ECHO had become. Perhaps she wasn't cut out for the life after all. Then there was the state of her implants to consider. They would never be completely operational without a total reconstruction, not something she was prepared to endure twice in one lifetime.

What she had would suffice on the new world.

Chalone stood in stunned silence. Liesha joining the exodus shocked her more than Jalemi's, Tallem's, or even Pirelle's defection.

Liesha hugged her. "I imagine our new home will have enough challenges to keep me from pining," she said with a small laugh.

Chalone paused before the decaying Portal. "Are you sure, Mother?"

"I do not think I have ever heard you call me that before."

"Only once, so don't get used to it. It's not going to happen all that often," Chalone joked, trying to find some emotional balance in her quickly disintegrating world. "Come on then, let's get this over with."

Vian and Lila ducked through the Portal and disappeared. Chalone stepped halfway through and waited for her mother.

Liesha studied the remains of the Hall of Lights for a moment. She looked down at the two hollow grooves forever ground into the flagstones that paid homage to the titanic struggle she'd waged to keep the Portal open, and bade her old life farewell.

* * * *

Another cracking sound issued from beneath the Portal. The anchor, patched together by the force of Liesha's will, then reinforced by Sebenesh's immortal power, broke apart. Nothing could hold it together anymore.

The Portal swayed and buckled in on itself. Its last crystal light shattered. The tortured columns on either side cracked and sank to the floor. With nothing left to keep it upright, the Portal trapped Chalone halfway through to the Gallery with neither form nor substance in either place.

Sudden blinding flashes of lightning, thunder bolts, and huge sheets of rain lashed the Hall. An enormous gust of wind roared past Liesha toward the shreds of the Portal opening.

She immediately activated her imperfectly repaired implants and linked with the ECHO network. The saw-like sensation ripped into her brain but there was nothing else she could do to save Chalone.

She drove the pulse of energy stored in the network through her body and restored a small piece of the Portal for a moment. Her weakened body and implants channeled more energy than it had done when she was fully healed. Chalone slipped through to the threshold.

Blood wept from the corners of Liesha's eyes. She brushed it away with a desperate sweep of her hand and called on yet more energy until she felt something break inside her. She crumpled to the stone floor and flexed her will through the Portal so that Chalone could hear her.

"I will hold it for you. Go! Now," she shouted. The feedback from within the Gallery short-circuited most of her implants and nearly killed her there and then.

Chalone reached back to Liesha. "Come with me. We can go through together. Please. Come with me," she pleaded.

Liesha heard but remained adamant. "Stop this," she said as she clawed her way to her feet and stood unsteadily against the rising wind. "It is too late, my love. I'm already dying. You cannot save me. We both know the damage this kind of wind can do. In a few moments everything will be destroyed."

Liesha staggered to one side of the Portal to avoid the worst of the rushing air and debris already sucked from the woods beyond the Hall.

Chalone saw the reopened wounds on Liesha's body and knew she had to honor the choice her mother made. Her chest heaved and she wailed in agony as her heart broke all over again. Liesha was the final irredeemable loss. Her world had truly disintegrated around her.

She surrendered to the inexorable force Liesha still pushed at her and let it impel her past the threshold.

Suddenly a wild thought occurred to her and she turned back.

* * * *

Cracks in the earth broke apart the flagstones underneath Liesha's feet. Foul smelling steam billowed up and was sucked into the raw wound where the Portal once bravely stood.

The storm raged around Liesha as she faced the Portal knowing that this was likely her last moment alive. Freezing rain pounded down on her exposed skin so hard it hurt. *What would it feel like to move on to the next stage of her existence?* Less damaged, she hoped.

Chalone suddenly turned around, again! Liesha gaped at her daughter. *The child was suicidal. What would it take to save her?*

Chalone projected her voice through the Portal. "I love you mother, for always. You have to get away. The Skane knows how to get into the Gallery without a Portal. Find them and you can join us."

Liesha took up the hope Chalone offered and made it hers. It was all she had left of her family.

She staggered and fell, stood up again, and ran from the Hall of Lights as fast as she could stumble. Her ribs hurt, her head pounded, her limbs were bloody and bruised, but she made it to the edge of the woodlands.

Under the trees the bludgeoning force of the storm eased. She began to believe she might actually survive until a gale rushed past her toward the ruins of the Hall.

The Gallery corridor chewed great gulps out of her world as it retreated from the shattered Portal that had held it fast since Time began.

* * * *

Liesha kept on running as long as her body remained upright. Her tears of grief and pain mingled unseen with the rain. She reeled past deep gashes in the earth where whole swathes of trees used to stand. The crash and crack of the woodlands destruction filled her ears like a solid force. Rain froze to hail and hammered down on her. She couldn't see to put one foot in front of the other, but she did it anyway.

Eventually the suction effect waned and she knew she'd escaped the devastation. The corridor had shut down and her world was safe. True to her word to Chalone, she'd survived. The storm still thundered around her and her body...*Oh how it hurt.*

She struggled to draw in a breath although her lungs were probably as full of blood as with air. She'd lost her shoes somewhere along the way and her bare feet hurt from scrapes and bruises just as much as the rest of her. She pushed away from the security of the trees and began to run again.

* * * *

Liesha never remembered how far away she ran. When she eventually stopped in the hills somewhere above the Hall of Lights, she fell to the ground not far from death.

Every so often she dreamed she woke and heard women around her making sympathetic noises. They would give her brightly colored drugs and return her to blissful unconsciousness.

She never dreamed anything else. All her memories had been blocked until she recovered, as was ECHO policy for long-term rehabilitation.

Her mind rested while her body slowly healed around her new implants. They were the latest and best. If her mind survived her deathly injuries, there would be no ECHO who could match her strength, endurance, or abilities. The Hierarchs had great plans for her.

Word of her intended defection had travelled no further than the women who'd disappeared into the Gallery.

* * * *

Liesha woke and knew she wasn't dreaming. Her tongue stuck to the roof of her mouth and her eyes refused to open. Her tear-ducts obligingly filled her eyes and dissolved the film over them. Someone helped her sit up.

A shaved head came into focus. The bruises on the woman's face from her first-stage implants had faded to yellow.

Liesha drank deeply from the glass of water the woman held for her before anything resembling speech came out of her mouth. "I am alive then," she croaked.

"Looks like you're going to stay that way too," Tallem replied softly. She still hadn't caught the knack of formalized speech although her western accent was long gone.

Liesha's memories returned from the storage unit where they'd remained, while she healed. She shivered as they reattached themselves to her mind.

"Did Chalone get away?" she asked with a quaver in her voice.

Tallem's face reflected her worst fear. "We don't know," she said. "The destruction around the Hall is widespread. Most of Espinsal is gone. We can't even guess what it's like in the Gallery."

Liesha eased back onto the raised pillows and closed her eyes. She knew exactly what it would've been like in the Gallery. Tears trickled down her face and she felt too broken in heart and body to wipe them away. Tallem gently dabbed her face with a soft cloth, then took her hand, and sat beside her.

They stared at the walls, each other, and occasionally cried.

Liesha snuffled and reached for a handkerchief. She blew her nose rather wearily and patted Tallem's hand.

"I need my clothes," she said at last. "We have to find the Skane."

Epilogue

Sebenesh lay cocooned in her Lair and healed from the wounds that almost killed her. Quite a scare for an Immortal.

Her plan to save the Gallery from its mortal decay was off to an uncertain start and its ultimate success a thousand generations in the future remained in doubt. Time flowed differently for her and she supposed that quite a few of those generations had already passed.

She refused to take all that into consideration. It had gone very well and she'd be damned if she'd give Arahona the satisfaction of acknowledging her mistakes even if the old spider had gone where she'd refused to follow.

In spite of her best efforts to protect the Sphere within the Earthblood fire, she'd failed spectacularly. Now it would pass down the incarnate line of women from mother to daughter, waiting as they all would, until the tides that eventually swept away all things mortal caught up with the Gallery as well. It was a barely acceptable alternative.

The Sphere was indeed secure in the Mortal Realm at last, no thanks to Jalemi. Sebenesh crossly muttered the name in her sleep and settled further down into her nest. Jalemi's impetuous and volatile nature hardly prepared her for the responsibility she so actively sought. Sebenesh had a few succinct lessons in mind for the most errant of her apprentices. She was still annoyed enough to enjoy the thought. Her tail slid against the curves of her body with a sensuous pleasure that soothed her ruffled scales.

Pirelle was also well on her way to becoming the tool Sebenesh needed her to be. The matter of her being so easily lured by the shard of the Sphere was bothersome, although her taking the initiative in the first place was a pleasant surprise. When Pirelle finally got around to finding her way back to her Lair, Sebenesh decided she would explain a few things about the consequences of meddling in the affairs of immortal beings.

Of all the mortals Sebenesh had exploited, Vian stood out like a beacon, although Sebenesh wasn't entirely sure about Vian's mortality. She'd accomplished all that Sebenesh asked and more.

Vian's strange companions turned out to be yet another surprise. Sebenesh couldn't fathom where they'd come from or what their purpose could be. Although she really hated to leave the matter unresolved she'd have to, until she'd finished healing.

She rejoiced that Liesha survived. With Tallem accompanying her they would be a thorn in the side of the ECHO's schemes. A useful application of their talents, Sebenesh decided. The ECHOs needed a few lessons in humility on the way to achieving their grand design.

Although Liesha and Tallem didn't feature highly in her ruminations, Sebenesh decided it would be prudent to cast a wary eye their way every now and then, just in case.

She segued and wondered when she'd become so concerned about the fate of these mortals, these women.

Malawatea and Mor linked in death and after-life, an interesting match-up not of her choosing. Sebenesh couldn't decide if she ought to feel vexed with them or not. It annoyed her when things shifted from her more-than-competent design, but those two intrigued her.

Sebenesh totaled up the unknowns that had crept into her planning and wondered if anything might actually turn out as it was supposed to.

Then there was Chalone, the only one so dangerously unfinished. Chalone unsettled her.

Sebenesh's stomach roiled uncomfortably at how she'd reacted to Chalone's compassionate caress. Which, she admitted with a susurrus of her coils, was entirely her fault. She'd been careless, or perhaps she'd grown tired of her exalted isolation and Chalone reminded her of possibilities she'd thought long gone. *What a delicious irony.* Sebenesh chuckled at the thought. Laughter bubbled up and threatened to wake her. *Dear Chalone, what an interesting journey you have ahead of you.*

Knowing that subtlety would be required, Sebenesh called on the one person she could rely on to undertake this new challenge for the next thousand generations.

* * * *

Vian lived many seasons on the new world before she felt the subtle summons.

Her new home looked vastly different from the hand hewn logs and vaulted ceilings of her house in Espinsal. She still missed it. She missed so much of her life that she sometimes regretted leading her people through the last remaining Portal on their old world and into this new one.

There was no doubt the exodus had produced the very best in them. She shone with pride at what they had accomplished so swiftly, thanks in part to the ECHO hierarchy's parting gift. Once the memory crystal's initial information files had been exhausted, Vian had placed them in one of the many caves dotted throughout the mountains near their new home where they multiplied beyond anyone's expectations.

No one had, as yet, fully explored their potential. It was one of the many things Vian planned to investigate, one day.

As time passed and the colony's struggles shifted from survival to consolidation, old rivalries and ambitions rose to the surface.

* * * *

When the familiar call seeped through her dreamscape, Vian woke immediately and felt a frisson of fear and excitement. For just a moment she considered ignoring it.

Well, she addressed her summoner irritably, *look what happened last time.*

A note from the Author:

A very long time ago I had to submit an essay on the Theory of Phlogiston. I did say it was a long time ago! I must have skipped school when the teacher decided to illuminate our young minds on that particular subject, because on the day of the exam my eyes glazed over and my brain went "Oops" as I stared at the blank piece of paper in front of me.

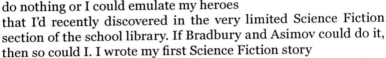

I had a choice. I could either sit in a very uncomfortable hardwood chair and do nothing or I could emulate my heroes that I'd recently discovered in the very limited Science Fiction section of the school library. If Bradbury and Asimov could do it, then so could I. I wrote my first Science Fiction story

Two hours later I handed in my essay to the teacher, and as I left I caught a glimpse of her face. She appeared to turn rather pale. From the hall I heard a bark of what I hoped was laughter but feared was an incipient heart attack. I thought I was done for, but with head held high I walked along with the other students, and we chatted nervously on how we thought we'd done.

I received my essay back the next day. The teacher had written across the top, "Don't ever do this again." Across the middle, "Well done." And in the bottom left-hand corner scrawled in red ink was the biggest "A" I've ever seen.

That was the moment my career as a writer of Science Fiction and Fantasy began, and the last time I ever had writers block.

I was born in England, grew up in Australia, moved to Canada in 2004 and married the love of my life. I'm a writer and shaman, a bicyclist and a feminist. I've been an architect, a seamstress, an athlete and a field hand.

Writing is my passion and my profession, novels specifically, and always with lesbian characters.

Blog: http://widdershinsfirst.wordpress.com
Blog: http://widdershinsfirst.com

Also from Eternal Press:

Beside the Darker Shore
by Patricia J. Esposito

eBook ISBN: 9781615724154
Print ISBN: 9781615724161

GBLT Vampire
Novel of 85,491 words

What might the ethical Governor David Gedden give up for one man's exquisite beauty? It's terrifying to consider when the man is a destructive blood prostitute and David is responsible for the state's peaceful vampire community. Blood sales in Boston are up, blood taxes support a thriving new nightlife, neighborhoods have been refurbished, and deaths by vampires have plummeted. David is assured reelection.

However, the blood addict Stephen Salando has returned from exile with one unalterable plan: to turn the good governor into a vampire. Stephen is an immortal dhampir, whose beauty obliterates reason, who rouses in David a fierce desire he's ignored his whole life. For David to have Stephen, he must ally with the community's archrival. To have him, he must become a potential killer himself.

Also from Eternal Press:

Another Way
by Nancy J. Gaffney

eBook ISBN: 9781615723737
Print ISBN: 9781615723744

Science Fiction Adventure
Plus-Novel of 126,065 words

A Planetary Guards Chronicle A thousand years ago, in the name of 'the greater good', a great betrayal occurred. In the name of righteous retribution and justifiable genocide, a peaceful planet is attacked. A civilization a thousand years in the re-building is razed. An idyllic society, steeped in music, literature, and civic duty, is forced to flee the only home they've ever known. In middle of the struggle for survival, Shannen 'Keeper' Everett, Jason 'Preacher' Carrack and Colonel Robert Preyar must find a way to stay alive and thwart enemies no one ever knew existed. The battle for life as they knew it is on.